ALSO BY CARL HIAASEN

Native Tongue

Skin Tight

Double Whammy

Tourist Season

STRIP TEASE

STRIP TEASE

A NOVEL BY

CARL HIAASEN

For Tom + Ginny —
Merry Christmas!

Carl Hiaasen

Alfred A. Knopf   New York   1993

THIS IS A BORZOI BOOK
PUBLISHED BY ALFRED A. KNOPF, INC.

Copyright© 1993 by Carl Hiaasen
All rights reserved under International and Pan-American Copyright
Conventions. Published in the United States by Alfred A. Knopf,
Inc., New York, and simultaneously in Canada by Random House
of Canada Limited, Toronto. Distributed by
Random House, Inc., New York.

Library of Congress Cataloging-in-Publication Data
Hiaasen, Carl.
Strip tease : a novel / Carl Hiaasen.—1st ed.
p.   cm.
ISBN 0-679-41981-0
I. Title.
PS3558.I217S77   1993
813'.54—dc20   93-12358
CIP

Manufactured in the United States of America
Published August 26, 1993
Second Printing Before Publication

For the amazing Esther Newberg

STRIP TEASE

1

On the night of September sixth, the eve of Paul Guber's wedding, his buddies took him to a strip joint near Fort Lauderdale for a bachelor party. The club was called the Eager Beaver, and it was famous county-wide for its gorgeous nude dancers and watered-down rum drinks. By midnight Paul Guber was very drunk and hopelessly infatuated with eight or nine of the strippers. For twenty dollars they would perch on Paul's lap and let him nuzzle their sweet-smelling cleavage; he was the happiest man on the face of the planet.

Paul's friends carried on with rowdy humor, baying witlessly and spritzing champagne at the stage. At first the dancers were annoyed about being sprayed, but eventually they fell into the spirit of the celebration. Slick with Korbel, they formed a laughing chorus line and high-kicked their way through an old Bob Seger tune. Bubbles sparkled innocently in their pubic hair. Paul Guber and his pals cheered themselves hoarse with lust.

At half-past two, a fearsome-looking bouncer announced the last call. While Paul's buddies pooled their cash to pay the exorbitant tab, Paul quietly crawled on stage and attached himself to one of the performers. Too drunk to stand, he balanced on his knees and threw a passionate hug around the woman's bare waist. She smiled good-naturedly and kept moving to the music. Paul hung on like a drowning sailor. He pressed his cheek to the woman's tan belly and closed his eyes. The dancer, whose name was Erin, stroked Paul's hair and told him to go home, sugar, get some rest before the big day.

A man yelled for Paul to get off the stage, and Paul's friends assumed it was the bouncer. The club had a strict rule against touching the dancers for free. Paul Guber himself heard no warning—he appeared comatose with bliss. His best friend Richard, with whom Paul shared a cubicle at the brokerage house, produced a camera and began taking photographs of Paul and the naked woman. Blackmail, he announced playfully. Pay up, or I mail these snapshots to your future mother-in-law! Everyone in the club seemed to be enjoying themselves. That's why Paul's friends were so shocked to see a stranger jump on stage and begin beating him with an empty champagne bottle.

Three, four, five hard blows to the head, and still Paul Guber would not release the dancer, who was trying her best to avoid being struck. The bottle-wielding man was tall and paunchy, and wore an expensive suit. His hair was silver, although his bushy mustache was black and crooked. No one in Paul Guber's bachelor party recognized him.

Raw sucking noises came from the man's throat as he pounded on the stockbroker's skull. The bouncer got there just as the champagne bottle shattered. He grabbed the silver-haired man under the arms and prepared to throw him off the stage in a manner that would have fractured large bones. But the bouncer alertly noticed that the silver-haired man had a companion, and the companion had a gun that might or might not be loaded. Having the utmost respect for Colt Industries, the bouncer carefully released the silver-haired man and allowed him to flee the club with his armed friend.

Amazingly, Paul Guber never fell down. The paramedics had to pry his fingers off the dancer's buttocks before hauling him to the hospital. In the emergency room, his worried buddies gulped coffee and cooked up a story to tell Paul's fiancée.

By the time the police arrived, the Eager Beaver lounge was empty. The bouncer, who was mopping blood off the stage, insisted he hadn't seen a thing. The cops clearly were disapppointed that the nude women had gone home, and showed little enthusiasm for investigating a drunken assault with no victim present. All that remained of the alleged weapon was a pile of sparkling green shards. The bouncer asked if it was okay to toss them in the dumpster, and the cops said sure.

Paul Guber's wedding was postponed indefinitely. His friends told Paul's bride-to-be that he had been mugged in the parking lot of a synagogue.

In the car, speeding south on Federal Highway, Congressman David Lane Dilbeck rubbed his temples and said: "Was it a bad one, Erb?"

And Erb Crandall, the congressman's loyal executive assistant and longtime bagman, said: "One of the worst."

"I don't know what came over me."

"You assaulted a man."

"Democrat or Republican?"

Crandall said, "I have no earthly idea."

Congressman Dilbeck gasped when he noticed the pistol on his friend's lap. "Jesus, Mary and Joseph! Don't tell me."

Without emotion, Crandall said, "I had no choice. You were about to be maimed."

Five minutes passed before the congressman spoke again. "Erb," he said, "I love naked women, I truly do."

Erb Crandall nodded neutrally. He wondered about the congressman's driver. Dilbeck had assured him that the man understood no English, only French and Creole. Still, Crandall studied the back of the driver's black head and wondered if the man was listening. These days, anyone could be a spy.

"All men have weaknesses," Dilbeck was saying. "Mine is of the fleshly nature." He peeled off the phony mustache. "Let's have it, Erb. What exactly did I do?"

"You jumped on stage and assaulted a young man."

Dilbeck winced. "In what manner?"

"A bottle over the head," Crandall said. "Repeatedly."

"And you didn't stop me! That's your goddamn job, Erb, to get me out of those situations. Keep my name out of the papers."

Crandall explained that he was in the john when it happened.

"Did I touch the girl?" asked the congressman.

"Not this time."

In French, Crandall asked the Haitian driver to stop the car and wait. Crandall motioned for Dilbeck to get out. They walked to an empty bus bench and sat down.

The congressman said, "What's all this nonsense? You can talk freely in front of Pierre."

"We've got a problem." Crandall steepled his hands. "I think we should call Moldy."

Dilbeck said no way, absolutely not.

"Somebody recognized you tonight," said Crandall. "Somebody in that strip joint."

"God." Dilbeck shut his eyes and pinched the bridge of his nose. "It's an election year, Erb."

"Some little twerp, I didn't get the name. He was standing by the back door when we ran out. Some skinny jerk-off with Coke-bottle glasses."

"What'd he say?"

" '*Attaboy, Davey.*' He was looking right at you."

"But the mustache—"

"Then he said, 'Chivalry ain't dead.' " Crandall looked very grim.

Congressman Dilbeck said, "Did he seem like the type to stir up trouble?"

It was all Crandall could do to keep from laughing. "Looks are deceiving, David. I'll be calling Moldy in the morning."

Back in the car, heading south again, Dilbeck asked about the condition of the man he'd attacked.

"I have no earthly idea," Crandall said. He would phone the hospital later.

"Did he seem dead?"

"Couldn't tell," replied Crandall. "Too much blood."

"Lord," said the congressman. "Lord, I've got to get a grip on this. Erb, let's you and me pray. Give me your hands." He reached across the seat for Crandall, who shook free of the congressman's clammy fervent paws.

"Knock it off," Crandall snapped.

"Please, Erb, let's join hands." Dilbeck flexed his fingers beseechingly. "Join together and pray with me now."

"No fucking way," said the bagman. "You pray for both of us, David. Pray like hell."

The next night, Erin was taking off her clothes, getting ready, when she told Shad that she'd checked with the hospital. "They said he's out of intensive care—the man who got hurt."

Shad's eyes never looked up from the card table. "Thank God," he said. "Now I can sleep nights."

"The gun frightened me." Erin was changing into her show bra. "He sure didn't look like a bodyguard, did he? The one with the gun?"

Shad was deeply absorbed. Using a surgical hemostat, he was trying to peel the aluminum safety seal from a four-ounce container of low-fat blueberry yogurt. The light was poor in the dressing room, and Shad's eyesight wasn't too sharp. He hunched over the yogurt like a watchmaker.

"I gotta concentrate," he said gruffly to Erin.

By now she'd seen the dead cockroach, a hefty one even by Florida standards. Legs in the air, the roach lay on the table near Shad's left elbow.

Erin said, "Let me guess. You've had another brainstorm."

Shad paused, rolling a cigarette from one side of his mouth to the other. He sucked hard, then blew the smoke in twin plumes from his nostrils.

"The hell does it look like?" he said.

"Fraud," said Erin. She stepped behind a door and slipped out of her skirt. "Fraud is what it looks like to me."

Triumphantly, Shad lifted the foil (intact!) from the yogurt container. Carefully he placed it on the table. Then, with the hemostat, he lifted the dead cockroach by one of its brittle brown legs.

"Isn't that your music?" he said to Erin. "Van Morrison. You better get your ass out there."

"In a minute," Erin said. She put on her G-string, the red one with seahorses. When Erin first bought it, she'd thought the design was paisley. One of the other dancers had noticed that the pattern was actually seahorses. Laughing seahorses.

Erin came out from behind the door. Shad didn't look up.

"Have the police been around?" she asked.

"Nope." Shad smiled to himself. Cops—they usually got about as far as the front bar and then forgot why they'd come. They'd wander through the Eager Beaver bug-eyed and silly, like little kids at Disney World. Cops were absolute saps when it came to bare titties.

Erin said she'd never seen a man get hit so hard with anything as the bachelor who got clobbered with the champagne bottle. "It's a miracle there wasn't brain damage," she said.

Shad took this as criticism of his response time. "I got up there as quick as I could." His tone was mildly defensive.

"Don't worry about it," Erin told him.

"He didn't look the type. Of all the ones to go batshit."

Erin agreed. The man wielding the Korbel bottle was not your typical strip-show creep. He wore a silk tie and passed out twenties like gumdrops.

Erin checked her stiletto pumps for bloodstains. "This is a lousy business," she remarked.

"No shit. Why'd you think I'm sitting here fucking with a dead roach? This little bugger is my ticket out."

As steady as a surgeon, Shad positioned the cockroach in the low-fat blueberry yogurt. With the beak of the hemostat, he pressed lightly. Slowly the insect sunk beneath the creamy surface, leaving no trace.

Erin said, "You big crazy dreamer."

Shad absorbed the sarcasm passively. "Do you get the *Wall Street Journal?*"

"No." She wondered where he was heading now.

"According to the *Journal*," Shad said, "the Delicato Dairy Company is worth one hundred eighty-two million dollars, on account of Delicato Fruity Low-Fat Yogurt being the fastest-selling brand in the country. The stock's at an all-time high."

Erin said, "Shad, they won't fall for this." She couldn't believe he was trying it again.

"You're late, babe." Shad jerked a thumb toward the stage. "Your fans are waiting."

"I've got time. It's a long number." Erin slipped into her teddy (which would come off after the first number) and her heels (which would stay on all night).

Shad said, "That song, how come you like it so much? You don't even got brown eyes."

"Nobody looks at my eyes," Erin said. "It's a good dancing song, don't you think?"

Shad was scrutinizing the yogurt. A hairy copper-colored leg had emerged from the creamy bog. Was it moving? Shad said to Erin: "You ever see *Deliverance?* The movie, not the book. That last scene, where the shriveled dead hand comes out from the water? Well, come here and look at this fucking roach."

"No thanks." Erin asked if Mr. Peepers was in the audience tonight. That was the nickname for one of her regulars, a bony bookish man with odd rectangular eyeglasses. He usually sat at table three.

Shad said, "What, all of a sudden I'm supposed to take roll?"

"He called and left a message," Erin said. "Said he had a big surprise for me, which is just what I need." She dabbed on some perfume—why, she had no idea. Nobody got close enough to smell it. Unlike the other strippers, Erin refused to do table dances. Ten bucks was ridiculous, she thought, to let some drunk breathe on your knees.

Shad said, "You want me to, I'll throw his ass out."

"No, if you could just hang close," said Erin, "especially after what happened last night."

"No sweat."

"It's probably nothing," Erin said. Next came the lipstick. The boss preferred candy-apple red but Erin went with a burgundy rose. She'd hear about it from the other dancers, but what the hell.

Shad sat back from the yogurt project and said, "Hey, come and see. It's just like new!"

"They could put you in jail. It's called product tampering."

"It's called genius," Shad said, "and for your information, I already got a lawyer can't wait to take the case. And a Palm Beach shrink who swears I'm totally fucking traumatized since I opened a yogurt and found this damn cockroach—"

Erin laughed. "Traumatized? You don't even know what that means."

"Grossed out is what it means. And look here—" Shad lifted the foil seal with the hemostat. "Perfect! Not even a rip. So the bastards can't say someone broke into the grocery and messed with the carton."

"Clever," Erin said. She checked her hair in the mirror. Most of the dancers wore wigs, but Erin felt that a wig slowed her down, limited her moves. Losing a wig was one of the worst things to happen on stage. That, and getting your period.

"How's my bottom?" she asked Shad. "Is my crack showing?"

"Naw, babe, you're covered."

"Thanks," Erin said. "Catch you later."

"Go on and laugh. I'm gonna be rich."

"Nothing would surprise me." She couldn't help but envy Shad's optimism.

"The way it goes," he said, "them really big companies don't go to trial on stuff like this, on account of the negative publicity. They just pay off the plaintiff is what the lawyer told me. Major bucks."

Erin said, "The customer's name is Killian. Table three. Let me know if he comes in." Then she was gone. He could hear the heels clicking on stage, the applause, the gin-fueled hoots.

Shad peered into the container. The roach leg had resubmerged; the surface of the yogurt looked smooth and undisturbed. A masterful job of sabotage! Shad placed the foil seal in a Ziploc bag and closed it by sliding his thumb and forefinger along the seam: evidence. Gingerly he carried the yogurt container to the dancers' refrigerator. He placed it on the second tray, between a six-pack of Diet Sprite and bowl of cottage cheese. Over the Delicato yogurt label he taped a hand-written warning:

"Do Not Eat or Else."

He reread the note two or three times, decided it wasn't stern enough. He wrote out another and taped it beneath the first: "Property of Shad."

Then he went out to the lounge to see if any asses needed kicking. Sure enough, at table eight a pie-eyed Volvo salesman was trying to suck the toes off a cocktail waitress. Effortlessly Shad heaved him out the back door. He dug a Pepsi out of the cooler and took a stool at the bar.

At midnight, the skinny guy with the square glasses came in and staked out his usual chair at table three. Shad strolled over and sat down beside him.

On stage, Erin was grinding her heart out.

She's wrong about one thing, Shad thought. *I* notice her eyes, every night I do. And they're definitely green.

2

Malcolm J. Moldowsky did not hesitate to address United States Congressman Dave Dilbeck as "a card-carrying shithead."

To which Dilbeck, mindful of Moldowsky's influence and stature, responded: "I'm sorry, Malcolm."

Pacing the congressman's office, Moldowsky cast a cold scornful eye on every plaque, every commemorative paperweight, every pitiable tin momento of Dilbeck's long and undistinguished political career.

"I see problems," said Malcolm Moldowsky. He was a fixer's fixer, although it was not the occupation listed on his income-tax forms.

There's no problem, Dilbeck insisted, none at all. "We were gone before the police showed up."

Moldowsky was a short man, distractingly short, but he made up for it by dressing like royalty and slathering himself with expensive cologne. It was easy to be so impressed by Moldy's fabulous wardrobe and exotic aroma that one might overlook his words, which invariably were important.

"Are you listening?" he asked Dave Dilbeck.

"You said there's a problem, I said I don't see any problem."

Moldowsky's upper lip curled, exposing the small and pointy dentition of a lesser primate. He stepped closer to Dilbeck and said, "Do de name Gary Hart ring a bell? Fuckups 101—you need a refresher course?"

"That was different," the congressman said.

"Indeed. Mr. Hart did not send anyone to the emergency room."

Dilbeck felt the heat of Moldowsky pressing closer—smelled the sharp minty breath and inhaled the imported Italian musk, which was strong enough to gas termites. Dilbeck quickly stood up. He was more at ease speaking to the crown of the man's head, instead of eye to eye. The congressman said, "It won't happen again, that's for sure."

"Really?"

The acid in Moldowsky's remark made the congressman nervous. "I've been doing some soul-searching."

Moldowsky stepped back so Dilbeck could see his face. "David, the problem is not in your soul. It's in your goddamn trousers."

The congressman shook his head solemnly. "Weakness is spiritual, Malcolm. Only the manifestation is physical—"

"You are so full of shit—"

"Hey, I can conquer this," Dilbeck said. "I can control these animal urges, you just watch."

Moldowsky raised his hands impatiently. "You and your damn urges. It's an election year, Davey. That's number one. Only a card-carrying shithead would show his face at a nudie joint in an election year. Number two, your man pulls a gun, which happens to be a felony."

"Malcolm, don't blame Erb."

"And number three," Moldowsky went on, "during the commission of the act, you are recognized by a patron of this fine establishment. Which raises all sorts of possibilities, none of them good."

"Whoa, whoa, whoa." Dilbeck wedged his hands to signal time-out, like a football coach. "Let's not jump to conclusions."

Malcolm Moldowsky laughed harshly. "That's my job, Congress-man." Once again he started to pace. "Why did you hit that man with the bottle? Don't tell me—you got something going with the stripper, right? She's carrying your love child, perhaps?"

Dilbeck said, "I don't even know her name."

"But still you felt this uncontrollable impulse to defend her honor, such as it is. I understand, David. I understand perfectly."

"It's a sickness, that's all. I should never be around naked women."

All the fight had gone out of the congressman. Moldowsky circled the desk and approached him. In a softer voice: "You don't need this shit right now. You got the campaign. You got the sugar vote coming up. You got a committee to run." Moldowsky tried to chuck the congress-man on the shoulder but wasn't quite tall enough. He wound up patting him on the elbow. "I'll take care of this," he said.

"Thanks, Mmm—Malcolm." Dilbeck almost slipped and called him Moldy, which is what everyone called Moldowsky behind his back. Fanatically hygienic, Moldowsky hated the nickname.

"One more request," he said. "Keep David Jr. in your pants until November. As a personal favor to me."

Dilbeck's cheeks flushed.

"Because," Moldowsky went on, "I'd hate to think how your constituents would look upon such behavior—all those senior citizens in those condos, those conservative Cubans down on Eighth Street, those idealist young yupsters on the beach. What would they think if Congressman Davey got busted with a bunch of go-go dancers. How'd you suppose that would play?"

"Poorly," admitted the congressman. He needed a drink.

"You still an elder in the church?"

"A deacon," Dilbeck said.

"Is that a fact?" Malcolm Moldowsky wore a savage grin. "You get the urge to chase pussy, call me. I'll set something up." He dropped his voice. "It's an election year, deacon, you gotta be careful. If it's a party you need, we'll bring it to you. That sound like a deal?"

"Deal," the congressman said. When Moldy had gone, he cranked open a window and gulped for fresh air.

Every few years, the Congress of the United States of America voted generous price supports for a handful of agricultural millionaires in the great state of Florida. The crop that made them millionaires was sugar, the price of which was grossly inflated and guaranteed by the U.S. government. This brazen act of plunder accomplished two things: it kept American growers very wealthy, and it undercut the struggling economies of poor Caribbean nations, which couldn't sell their own bounties of cane to the United States at even half the bogus rate.

For political reasons, the government's payout to the sugar industry was patriotically promoted as aid to the struggling family farmer. True, some of the big sugar companies were family-owned, but the family members themselves seldom touched the soil. The closest most of them got to the actual crop were the cubes that they dropped in their coffee at the Bankers' Club. The scions of sugar growers wouldn't be caught dead in a broiling cane field, where the muck crawled with snakes and insects. Instead the brutal harvest was left to Jamaican and Dominican migrant workers, who were paid shameful wages to swing machetes all day in the sweltering sun.

It had been this way for an eternity, and men like Malcolm Moldowsky lost no sleep over it. His task, one of many, was making sure that Big Sugar's price supports passed Congress with no snags. To make that happen, Moldowsky needed senators and representatives who were sympathetic to the growers. Fortunately, sympathy was still easy to buy in Washington; all it took was campaign contributions.

So Moldowsky could always round up the votes. That was no problem. But the votes didn't do any good unless the sugar bill made it out of committee, and this year the committee of the House was in bitter turmoil over issues having nothing to do with agriculture. No fewer than three formerly pliant congressmen had been stricken with mysterious attacks of conscience, and announced they would vote against the sugar price supports. Ostensibly they were protesting the plight of the migrants and the disastrous pollution of the Everglades, into which the growers regularly dumped billions of gallons of waste water.

Malcolm Moldowsky knew the dissenting congressmen couldn't care less about the wretched cane workers, nor would they mind if the Everglades caught fire and burned to cinders. In truth, the opposition to the sugar bill was retaliation against the chairman of the committee, one David Dilbeck, who had cast the deciding vote that killed a hefty twenty-two-percent pay raise for himself and his distinguished colleagues in the House.

Dilbeck had committed this unforgivable sin by pure accident; he had been drunk, and had simply pushed the wrong lever when the matter of the pay raise was called to the floor. In his pickled condition, it was miraculous that Dilbeck had found the way back to his own desk, let alone connected with the tote machine. The following noon, the bleary congressman turned on the television to see George Will praising him for his courage. Dilbeck had no idea why; he remembered nothing of the night before. When staff members explained what he'd done, he crawled to a wastebasket and spit up.

Rather than admit the truth—that full credit for the deed belonged to the distillers of Barbancourt rum—David Dilbeck went on "Nightline" and said he was proud of voting the way he did, said it was no time for Congress to go picking the public's pocket. Privately, Dilbeck was furious at himself; he'd needed the extra dough worse than anybody.

And now his fellow politicians were striking back. They knew Dilbeck depended on Big Sugar for his campaign contributions, and they knew Big Sugar relied upon Dave Dilbeck for the price supports. So the House members decided to screw with him in a major way; they aimed to teach him a lesson.

Malcolm J. Moldowsky saw the ugliness unfolding. It would require all his subterranean talents to save the sugar bill, and he couldn't do it if Dilbeck got caught in a sex scandal. After years of slithering through political gutters, Moldowsky was still amazed at how primevally stupid most politicians could be, on any given night. He hadn't a shred of pity for Congressman Dilbeck, but he would help him anyway.

Millions upon millions of dollars were at stake. Moldy would do whatever had to be done, at whatever the cost.

The other dancers knew something was bothering Erin. It showed in her performance.

"Darrell again," said Urbana Sprawl, by far the largest and most gorgeous of the dancers. Urbana was Erin's best friend at the Eager Beaver lounge.

"No, it's not Darrell," Erin said. "Well, it is and it isn't."

Darrell Grant was Erin's former husband. They were divorced after five rotten years of marriage and one wonderful child, a daughter. The court battle was protracted and very expensive, so Erin decided to try out as an exotic dancer, which paid better than clerical work. There was nothing exotic about the new job, but it wasn't as sleazy as she had feared. The money just about covered her legal fees.

Then Darrell got cute. He filed a petition charging that Erin was an unfit mother, and invited the divorce judge to come see for himself what the future ex-Mrs. Grant did for a living. The judge sat through seven dance numbers and, being a born-again Christian, concluded that Erin's impressionable young daughter was better off in the custody of her father. That Darrell Grant was a pillhead, a convict and a dealer in stolen wheelchairs didn't bother the judge as much as the fact that Erin took her undies off in public. The judge gave her a stern lecture on decency and morality, and told her she could see the child every third weekend, and on Christmas Eve. Her lawyer was appealing the custody ruling, and Erin needed dancing money now more than ever. In the meantime, the divorce judge had become a regular at the Eager Beaver lounge, sitting in a dim booth near the Foosball machines. Erin never said a word to the man, but Shad always made a point of secretly pissing in the Jack Daniels he served him.

Urbana Sprawl said to Erin: "Come on, don't make me beat it out of you." They were taking off their makeup, sharing the chipped mirror in the dressing room.

A customer, Erin admitted. "Mr. Peepers, I call him. His real name is Killian."

"Table three," said another dancer, who was known as Monique Jr. There were two Moniques dancing at the club, and neither would change her name. "I know the guy," Monique Jr. said. "Funny glasses, bad necktie, shitty tipper."

Urbana Sprawl said to Erin: "He giving you a problem?"

"He's missed a couple of nights is all."

"Wow," said Monique Jr. "Call the fucking FBI."

"You don't understand. It's about my case." Erin opened her purse and took out a cocktail napkin, which was folded into a tiny square. She handed it to Monique Jr. "He gave me this the other night. He wanted to talk, but Shad was sitting right there, so he wrote it down instead."

Monique Jr. read the note silently. Then she passed it to Urbana Sprawl. Mr. Killian had printed carefully, in small block letters, with an obvious effort to be neat:

I can help get your daughter back. I ask nothing in return but a kind smile. Also, could you add ZZ Top to your routine? Any song from the first album would be fine. Thank you.

"Men will try anything," Monique Jr. said, skeptically. "Anything for pussy."

Erin thought it was worth listening to Killian's pitch. "What if he's for real?"

Urbana Sprawl folded the note and gave it back. "Erin, how does he know about Angela?"

"He knows everything." It was her first experience with a customer who'd gone off the deep end. For three weeks straight Killian had been swooning at table three. "He says he loves me," Erin said. "I haven't encouraged him. I haven't told him anything personal."

"This happens," Urbana said. "Nothing to do but stay cool."

Erin said he seemed fairly harmless. "It can't hurt to listen. I'm at the point where I'll try anything."

Monique Jr. said, "Tell you one thing. The little prick needs to learn how to tip."

Shad poked his head in the doorway. "Staff meeting," he announced, coughing. "Five minutes, in the office."

"Beat it," snapped Urbana Sprawl, who was largely nude. Shad truly didn't notice. Eleven years of strip joints had made him numb to the sight of bare breasts. An occupational hazard, Shad figured. One more reason to get the hell out, before it was too late.

Erin said, "Tell Mr. Orly we're on the way."

Shad withdrew, shutting the door. To Erin, he resembled a snapping turtle—his vast knobby head was moist and hairless, and his nose beaked sharply to meet the thin severe line of his lips, forming a lethal-looking overbite. From what Erin could see, Shad also had no eyebrows and no eyelashes.

"Creep," Monique Jr. said.

"He's not so bad." Erin slipped into a blue terrycloth robe and a pair of sandals. She told the other dancers about Shad's plan for the dead roach.

"Yogurt!" Monique Jr. cried. "God, that's disgusting."

Urbana Sprawl said, "I hope it works. I hope he gets a million bucks and goes off to live in Tahiti."

Dream on, thought Erin. Shad wasn't going anywhere unless Mr. Orly told him to go.

Orly's office was done in imitation red velvet. He hated it as much as anyone. The vivid decor had been the choice of the club's previous owner, before he was shot and dumped in the diamond lane of Interstate 95. Orly said the crime had nothing to do with the man's taste for imitation velvet, but rather with his inability to account for gross profits in a timely fashion. Meaning he'd skimmed. The imitation velvet remained on Orly's walls to remind employees that, unless one is very good at it, one does not skim from professional skimmers.

As the dancers assembled before Orly's desk, he became overwhelmed by the commingling of fruity perfumes, and began to sneeze and cough spasmodically. Shad brought a box of tissues and a can of Dr. Pepper. Orly made quite a spectacle of blowing his nose and then examining the tissue, to see what had been expelled. Erin looked at Urbana Sprawl and rolled her eyes. The man was a pig.

"All right," Orly began. "Tonight let's talk about the dancing. I been hearing complaints."

None of the strippers said a word. Orly shrugged, and went on: "Basically, here's the problem: You girls gotta move more. By that, I mean your asses and also your boobs. I was watching tonight and some of you, I swear, it's like watchin' a corpse rot. Not even a twitch." Orly paused and popped open the Dr. Pepper, which foamed out of the can. When he licked the rim with his tongue, several of the dancers groaned.

Orly glanced up and said, "Has somebody got a problem? Because if they do, let's hear it."

Erin raised a hand. "Mr. Orly, the style of our dancing depends on the music."

Orly motioned with the can. "Go on."

Erin said, "If the songs are fast, we dance fast. If the songs are slow, we dance slow—"

"We been through this before," he cut in. "You wanted to pick your own songs, and I says fine on the condition that they're good hot dance songs. But some a this shit, I swear, it's elevator music."

Urbana Sprawl said, "Janet Jackson, Madonna—I don't call that elevator music. Paula Abdul? Come on."

This was the wrong approach with Orly, who didn't know Janet Jackson from Bo Jackson. He put down the soft drink and rubbed the moisture into his palms. "All I know is, tonight I see a guy sleeping like a baby at table four. *Sleeping!* His face is maybe twelve inches from Sabrina's fur pie, and the guy is fucking snoring. With my own eyes I gotta see this." Orly sat forward and raised his voice. "Tell me what kind of a stripper puts a customer to sleep!"

Sabrina, who was combing a chestnut wig on her lap, said nothing. The dancers preferred not to argue with Mr. Orly, who was boastful about his connections to organized crime. Besides, some of the women weren't very good on stage, and they knew it. Listless was a charitable way to describe their dancing. Erin tried to help with the routines, but generally the other dancers were not keen on rehearsals.

Orly said, "Fast, slow or in between—it doesn't matter. The point is to take what God gave you and move it around." He sneezed suddenly, reached for a tissue and plugged it into both nostrils. He continued speaking, the tissue fluttering with each word: "Think of it as humping. Humping to music. What counts is not the goddamn speed, it's the motion, for Christ's sake, it's the attitude. I don't pay you girls to bore my customers, understand? A man who's sleeping isn't buying any of my booze, and he sure as hell ain't stuffing any cash in your garters."

It was Erin who spoke up again. "Mr. Orly, you mentioned attitude. I agree we've got a morale problem here at the club, but I think I know why."

This got everybody's attention. Even Shad perked up.

"It's the name," Erin said. "Eager Beaver—it's a very crude name."

Orly yanked the tissue out of his nose. Normally he would've fired a woman for such a remark, but Erin brought in lots of business for the club. She was one of the few dancers who could actually dance.

"I like 'Eager Beaver,'" Orly said. "It's catchy and it's clever and it damn near rhymes."

Erin said it was crude and demeaning. "And it's bad for morale. It gives the impression we're a bunch of whores, which we're not."

Orly told her to lighten up. "It's a tease, darling. We're a strip joint, for Christ's sake, who's gonna pay a seven-dollar cover to watch *nice* girls?"

The man had a point, yet Erin persisted. "I'm aware of the nature of our business, but it doesn't mean we can't have some pride. When friends and relatives ask where we work, some of us lie about it. Some of us are embarrassed to say the name."

Orly seemed more amused than offended. He looked at the other dancers and asked, "This true?"

A few nodded. Orly turned to Shad. "How about you? You embarrassed to work here?"

"Oh no," Shad said. "It's my life's ambition." He winked at Erin, who tried not to laugh.

Orly rocked back in the chair and folded his hands behind his head. His white shirt was stained the color of varnish at both armpits. "The name stays," he announced.

"What about a contest?" Erin suggested. "To come up with a better one."

"No!"

Urbana Sprawl said, "I remember when it was the Pleasure Palace. And before that, the Booby Hatch."

Monique Jr. said, "And I remember when it was Gentleman's Choice, until the state shut it down for prostitution."

Orly cringed at the word. "Well, now it's the Eager Beaver, and it will stay the Eager Beaver as long as I say so." He still owed two grand on the new marquee.

"Fine," said Erin, "Eager Beaver it stays. Very classy."

He ignored her. "The bottom line is, work on your goddamn dancing." He opened a drawer and pulled out a stack of videotapes. "This is from a joint in Dallas. Take it home, study how good these girls move. Three, four hundred a night in tips is what they make, and I'm not surprised."

Shad handed a cassette to each of the dancers.

Urbana Sprawl said, "Mr. Orly, I don't have a VCR."

"I got one you can rent."

Erin said, "Four hundred a night, huh? Maybe it's worth a trip to Dallas. Maybe they've got some openings."

Again, Orly ignored her. "One more item," he said, "then you can all go home. It's about what happened the other night. The fight on stage."

Monique Jr. said it wasn't much of a fight, just some guy swinging a bottle.

"Whatever," said Orly. "You didn't see a damn thing, OK? Anybody asks about it, you go tell Shad."

Erin was surprised by these instructions. Fights broke out frequently at the Eager Beaver, but Mr. Orly seldom took an interest. "What's going on?" she asked. "Is it the police?"

"The bottom line is, you don't get paid to answer questions. You get paid to take off your clothes." He drained the Dr. Pepper, burped and tossed the can at Shad, who caught it effortlessly. Orly said, "Now. We all clear on this?"

The strippers muttered apathetically.

"Good," said Orly. He started a sneeze, but caught himself. The dancer named Sabrina shyly raised a hand. Orly told her to make it quick.

She said, "The guy who was sleeping at table four? That wasn't really my fault, Mr. Orly. He was on pills."

"Darling, I don't care if he was on a fucking respirator. In my club, I want their eyes open. Understand?"

The dancers rose and, in an arresting gust of perfume, bustled out of the office. Orly told Erin to hang around for a minute. When they were alone, he said, "That guy didn't hurt you the other night, did he?"

"Which guy—the one who grabbed me or the one with the champagne bottle?"

"Either," Orly said. "I mean, if you got hurt, let me know. Cuts, bruises, whatever, we'll get you to a doctor. It's on the house."

On the house? Erin was stunned. She told Orly she was fine.

"Good," he said, "but just so you know: it won't happen again. Shad's been spoken to."

"It wasn't his fault—"

He cut her off with the wave of a hand. "A bouncer's job is to bounce. I pay that asshole good money."

Erin stood up to leave.

Orly said, "One more thing. I wasn't talking about you in here tonight. When it comes to the dancing and all—you're the last girl needs to look at some frigging video. You're one a the best we ever had."

"Thank you, Mr. Orly."

"The music I don't get. It's awful damn soft but, hey, you make it work. They can't take their eyes off you."

"Thank you," she said again.

"Keep it up," Orly said. "You need anything, I mean *anything*, lemme know."

Erin walked out of the office absolutely certain that she was in the middle of trouble.

When she got to the car, the man she called Mr. Peepers was waiting.

3

When Paul Guber regained consciousness, the first thing he saw at the foot of the hospital bed was a lawyer. He knew without being told; it was a man who could've had no other purpose in a three-piece suit.

"My name is Mordecai," the lawyer said. Over a vast belly he clutched a thin burgundy valise, brushed leather. "I'm here to help in any way I can."

Paul Guber's brainpan sloshed with morphine. He tried to speak but it felt as if he were spitting ash. His field of vision was narrow and electrical around the edges, like a cheap television. A woman came into the picture, her lips moving.

"Darling, how do you feel?"

It was Joyce, his fiancée. Paul Guber saw her reach out and touch a lump in the blanket—his left foot. Paul Guber was pleased to discover that he wasn't paralyzed.

Mordecai said, "Your friends told me what happened. I was sickened, to be very honest. Such a world we live in."

Paul Guber blinked rapidly to improve his focus.

"You are lucky to be alive," confided Mordecai.

Paul wasn't so sure. He wondered what Richard and the others had said to Joyce about the bachelor party. The appearance of a lawyer in his hospital room caused him to suspect the worst.

He opened his mouth to launch a provisional defense, but Mordecai halted him with a flabby pink palm. "It would be better if you didn't," the lawyer said, smiling like a wolf.

By way of introduction, Joyce said, "Mordecai is my cousin. Uncle Dan's oldest son—you met Uncle Dan. I called him the minute I heard what happened."

She didn't seem the least bit homicidal. Paul Guber was relieved, but wary.

Mordecai said, "You probably don't remember much. That's to be expected."

But Paul remembered everything. Joyce patted his shins under the bedcovers. "Oh Paul," she said. "I can't believe such a thing could happen."

"In my game," said Mordecai, "it's known as gross negligence."

Paul coughed. It felt like someone had taken a cheese grater to his throat.

"Don't try to speak," the lawyer advised again. "You've been beaten severely, resulting in physical and emotional damage. *Permanent* damage, as a result of gross negligence."

The words came out of a tunnel, but Paul got the general idea. The lawyer was itching to sue somebody. Paul wanted to nip that scheme in the bud—prolonged litigation against a strip joint would please neither his employer nor his future in-laws.

"We're not interested in who did this," Mordecai was saying. "We're interested in how it was allowed to happen. Accountability, in other words. We're interested in compensation of a magnitude that no simple street thug could afford."

Joyce moved to the front of the bed and began stroking Paul's forehead. "Someone's got to pay for this," she said quietly.

Mordecai was quick with the follow-through. "You are not the only aggrieved party, Mr. Guber. The cancellation of a wedding is a heart-wrenching event for all concerned. I'm thinking of the bride-to-be."

"All those engraved invitations," Joyce elaborated. "The musicians, the florists, the deposit on the reception hall. The Hyatt's not exactly cheap."

Paul shut his eyes. Maybe it was all a dream. Maybe there was no naked lady dancing to Van Morrison.

The lawyer said, "I could scarcely believe it when your friend Richard described the circumstances. Getting mugged on the grounds of a synagogue!"

Paul groaned involuntarily.

"Don't worry, we intend to pursue an action," Mordecai said. "You can depend on it." He raised the briefcase as if it held some secret power.

"Unh—" said Paul, but Joyce pressed two fingers to his lips.

"Rest now," she whispered. "We'll come back later."

"And not a word to anyone," said Mordecai the lawyer. "In my game, the best client is a helpless client."

Paul Guber felt a stab in his arm, and he opened his eyes to see a beautiful nurse injecting him with drugs. He was so grateful he could've kissed her on the lips.

Erin's mother lived in California with her fifth husband. She wrote biweekly letters to Erin—richly detailed accounts of shopping sprees. Always the letters ended with a plea: "Quit that awful job! Leave that awful place! Come live with us!"

Erin's mother didn't approve of nude dancing as an occupation. Erin didn't approve of marrying men for their money. The two women seldom conversed without argument. Each of Erin's successive step-fathers had offered financial assistance, but Erin wouldn't take a dime. It infuriated her mother. Money was the name of the game, she would say. We girls ought to stick together!

Erin's real father, who was also rich, had died in an automobile accident when she was young. One night he got drunk and drove his Eldorado into a drainage canal. The three young women in the back seat managed to climb out and swim to shore. It was just as well for Erin's father that he did not.

On the way to the funeral, her mother said it was a shame the sonofabitch hadn't lived, so she could've divorced him in a manner consistent with his sins. Over the years, Erin's mother came to be an expert at divorce, and also at widowhood. It was no coincidence that each of Erin's stepfathers was wealthier and more elderly than his predecessor. As Erin grew older, she accepted the fact that her mother was a restless gold digger who would never be happy, never be satisfied. On the other hand, her husbands knew exactly what they were getting, and didn't seem to care. It taught Erin one of life's great lessons: an attractive woman could get whatever she wanted, because men were so laughably weak. They would do *anything* for even the distant promise of sex.

Erin had almost forgotten this precept until her marriage broke up, and she was left broke and fighting for her daughter. It hit her on the day her divorce lawyer explained what it might cost to gain permanent custody of Angela. Erin was dumbstruck at the figure, which was more money than an office secretary would earn in two or three years. It all depended, said the lawyer, on how big of a prick her ex-husband Darrell intended to be. The biggest, Erin replied.

She knew then that a regular nine-to-five job wouldn't do, that she'd have to find another way. That night she'd gone home and stood at the bedroom mirror and slowly removed her clothes, starting with the blouse. It looked ridiculous. She put on some music, Mitch Ryder and the Detroit Wheels, and tried again. Erin had always been a good dancer, but she'd never seen herself dancing in a full-length mirror, stark naked. Even though she had a good figure, she felt silly. She thought: Who in the world would pay to see this?

The next night Erin went to the Eager Beaver to get a sense of the atmosphere. The place was crowded and the music was very loud. It took about an hour before she relaxed enough to take inventory of both the talent and the clientele. Erin noticed that many of the women were extremely poor dancers who tried to compensate with stage gimmicks. A common move was to wheel around, bend over and show off one's buttocks. Another trick, when hopelessly out of rhythm, was to halt midstep and lick one's own index finger in a salacious way. It spurred the male audience from boredom to wild cheers. Erin watched in amusement as customers lurched toward the stage, whistling and waving beer-soaked currency. How easily amused they are! she thought. There was little difference between this and what her mother did; it was the same game of tease, the same basic equation. Use what you've got to get what you want.

The following morning, Erin drank two cups of black coffee and phoned her mother in San Diego. "Guess what?" Erin said, and delivered the news in a chirpy tone.

Erin's mother disapproved. She said it was a tawdry way to make a living, even for a few months. She said it was no place to meet high-class guys.

"The money's good," Erin said, "and I think I can do it."

"Not with those tits," said her mother.

The modest dimensions of Erin's breasts had been an issue for a long time. Erin's mother (who was on her third set of saline implants) believed that surgical enhancement would increase Erin's chances of attracting a good man. She pointed to Darrell Grant as an example of the lowlife trash that was drawn to small-bosomed women. She insisted there was a mathematical corollary between the size of one's boobs and the financial viability of one's suitors.

Erin said she was satisfied with the God-given size of her breasts, and confident that customers would find her sexy.

"Ha!" Erin's mother said. "You'll see, young lady. You'll see who gets the biggest tips—the girls with the knockers, that's who!"

Erin's mother was wrong. Her daughter was quite a dancer.

Erin was startled to meet Jerry Killian in the parking lot of the Eager Beaver lounge. He handed her a bouquet of yellow roses, and a small box containing a diamond lavaliere. Then he told her that he loved her more than life itself.

"Try to get a grip," Erin said.

"I am lost."

"Obviously."

"Lost in love!"

Erin said, "You don't know me. If you're in love with anything, it's my dancing. And possibly the fact that I was naked at the time."

Killian's face twisted in pain. "I would love you as much," he said, "if you were a bank teller."

"Fully clothed?"

"In a potato sack," he declared.

Erin accepted the roses but gave back the diamond necklace. She unlocked the car and laid the bouquet on the front seat. She felt around on the floorboard for the .32, just in case.

"Erin, I know all about you. Did you read my note?"

"Anybody can go down to the courthouse, Mr. Killian. It's all in the files."

Abruptly Killian dropped to one knee, on the pavement. "I'm a serious man."

"Don't do this," Erin said, wearily.

"I love you. I can fix the custody case." His voice was burning. "I can get your child back."

Stay cool, thought Erin. She was dying to ask him how it would work, how he would do it. "Mr. Killian, get up. You're ruining a perfectly good pair of pants."

Killian maintained his genuflection. He folded his hands at his breast, as if praying. "The judge has aspirations for higher office. He has an eye on the federal bench."

"And I suppose you've got connections."

Killian glowed. "One phone call, and he will see your case in a different light."

"I'll tell you about this judge," Erin said. "He comes to the club, sits in the back and doodles with himself while I'm dancing."

Killian said, "That's good information. We can use that."

"Forget it—"

"Please," he cut in, "don't underestimate me."

Erin was thinking, What if he can do this thing? What if he's really got some pull?

"Tell me about your connections. Why should a call from you make a difference?"

Killian said, "Not from me. From a certain United States congressman."

Erin took the car keys from her purse and jangled them impatiently.

Killian merrily went on: "Think about it, Erin. A U.S. congressman asks a favor. Would you dare say no? Not if you had hopes of getting a federal judgeship. Not if you needed some pull in Washington."

He touched her arm lightly, and she noticed that his fingers were shaking. He said, "Your little girl—her name is Angela. She belongs with you."

Erin felt a hitch in her breath. The sound of her daughter's name, coming from this stranger, filled her with sorrow.

"I'm single myself," Killian said.

"Don't get carried away."

"You're right, Erin. I'm very sorry." He stood up, brushed the dirt from his trousers. "I've been working on this plan, making progress. Give me another week and you'll have a new court date. And I think you'll find the judge to be much more open-minded about the case."

He was bowing to kiss her hand when Shad tackled him from the side. It hardly qualified as a scuffle, as there was no resistance from Killian. He seemed to go limp. When his eyeglasses flew off, a dreamy look came to his face.

Erin told Shad not to hurt him.

"Why not?"

Killian was stretched out on the damp asphalt. When he raised his head, pebbles stuck comically to one cheek. "I'm a man of my word," he said in a marbly voice.

Shad pointed at him. "Don't come back, you little dork."

"Do you speak for the management?" Killian inquired.

Shad placed a size-thirteen shoe on his windpipe.

"Be careful," Erin said again.

"It's so tempting."

"But I love her," Killian croaked. "I am lost in love."

Shad shook his head. "You're pathetic," he told Killian. "But you got good taste."

"Don't underestimate me. I am not without influence."

Shad looked at Erin, who shrugged.

"Be my wife," Killian cried.

Shad leaned over and seized him by the collar. "That's enough a that," he said.

Erin started the car. Shad didn't let Jerry Killian off the ground until she had gone.

The next night, in the dressing room, Monique Sr. announced that Carl Perkins was sitting at table seven.

Erin, who was repairing a heel, glanced up and said, "Carl Perkins the guitarist?"

Monique Sr. beamed. "Is there another?" She regularly spotted celebrities in the audience. Last Tuesday it was William Kunstler, the renowned attorney. A week before, Martin Balsam, the actor.

The sightings were imaginary, but none of the other dancers made an issue of it. Each had a private trick for self-motivation, some inner force that pushed her toward the stage when the music came on. For Monique Sr., the inspiration came from believing that someone famous was in the club, someone who might be impressed by her moves, someone who could whisk her away and change her life forever. Erin thought it clever of Monique Sr. to choose personalities whose names were well known, but whose faces were not exactly national emblems. Carl Perkins, for instance, was a stroke of genius. In the smoky blue shadows of the Eager Beaver, a dozen customers might resemble the legendary musician. It was a bulletproof fantasy, and Erin admired it.

"Old Carl tipped me forty bucks," Monique Sr. was saying. "Not that he can't afford it. He only wrote 'Blue Suede Shoes.' "

"Great song," said Erin, tapping the new heel in place. Monique Sr. was an encyclopedia when it came to rock 'n' roll.

Shad entered the dressing room without knocking. He handed Erin a wrinkled envelope, marked up with red postal ink: her most recent letter to Angela, returned as undeliverable.

Urbana Sprawl said, "Oh no."

Erin bitterly crumpled the letter in the palm of her hand. The bastard Darrell had done it again—moved away without telling her. And taken Angie.

"No forwarding address?" Monique Sr. asked.

Erin cursed acidly. The man was such a despicable asshole. How had she ever fallen for him?

Shad said, "Take the night off, babe."

"I can't." Erin whipped out her lipstick and hairbrush, and got busy in front of the mirror. "Dance, dance, dance," she said, softly to herself.

Monique Sr. had fictitious celebrities to motivate her; Erin had Darrell Grant. The divorce judge had ordered him not to go anywhere, but it was like talking to a tomcat. Every time her ex-husband went mobile, Erin saw her legal fees go up another five grand. Finding the bastard, then serving him with new papers, cost a fortune.

"Your lucky night," Shad told her. He held another envelope; it was crisp and lavender, with familiar block lettering. "I took the liberty," he said.

"You opened it?"

"After what happened, yeah. You're damn right."

Erin said, "I told you, he's harmless."

"If he's not," said Shad, "he will be."

Erin read the message twice:

The plan is in motion. Soon my devotion to you will be proven. Still awaiting the smile, and the ZZ Top.

The other dancers clamored to see the note, but Erin tucked it in her purse. "No, this one's private."

"One thing—he doesn't listen so good," Shad said. He'd warned Mr. Peepers that his attentions were unwelcome.

Erin was determined not to get her hopes up. Monique Jr. was probably right; Killian was probably trying to get in her pants, nothing more. Maybe the business with the congressman and the judge was hot air. Maybe it wasn't. The question was, How far would Killian go to impress her?

She began brushing her hair, with long even strokes, and listened for her song on the speakers. She was due up next on stage.

. . .

Malcolm J. Moldowsky had no qualms about dealing with the owner of a mob strip joint. It was better than dealing with congressmen and senators.

At first, Orly was cagey and snide. He asked why a bigshot congressman's office should give a rat's ass about who hangs out at a nudie joint. But as soon as Moldowsky raised the subject of liquor licenses and the renewal thereof, Orly became a model of friendliness and cooperation. He identified the customer at table three from credit card receipts and then, when the customer returned to the club, Orly phoned promptly with the news. By that time, of course, Moldowsky knew the man's identity. By that time the man had made contact with Congressman David Lane Dilbeck.

Still, Moldowsky was grateful for Orly's information. It was good to know Jerry Killian's movements.

"Nothing happened," Orly said. "My help got there first."

"The young lady wasn't hurt?"

"Not at all. But the bottom line is, I can't have some horny creepoid chasing my best dancer."

"I understand, Mr. Orly."

"See, I got prettier girls. Longer legs, bigger tits. This one, she ain't even a blonde. But she can dance like I don't know what, and she's built up a good clientele, which is what pays the freight in my business."

"It won't happen again," Moldowsky assured him.

"This girl, pass her on the street and you wouldn't look twice. But the moves she's got, I swear to Christ."

"Natural talent is rare," Moldowsky said, "in my line of work, as well."

"You understand, I can't have guys hanging in the parking lot, waiting for the girls. Some hardass cop shows up and it's loitering for the purpose of solicitation. I been through that before. Like you say, I got a license to think about."

"Mr. Killian's been having some personal problems."

"Who doesn't," Orly said. "It's a fucked-up world, no?"

"Yes, it is." Again Moldowsky praised Orly for his assistance and discretion. "If there's anything we can do to repay the favor, please let us know."

"Just put in a good word," Orly said.

A good word? For who—the Gambino family? Moldowsky smiled to himself. "Done," he said to Orly.

"Also, my brother's got a little trouble with the IRS. Maybe you know somebody over there."

Nothing's ever simple, Moldowsky thought. "I can't promise any miracles," he said. "But I'll make a few calls."

Orly thanked him, and added, "I'm not looking to give this Killian guy any trouble. I'm trying to save him some. My man Shad, he's in a mood to break the fucker in two."

Moldowsky said, "Mr. Killian won't be back."

"Whatever."

Orly didn't ask for details. And Moldowsky had no intention of telling him.

Darrell Grant had been living in a suburb called Lauderhill, which offered an exceptionally wide selection of rundown apartments. He'd rented a furnished duplex on a dead-end street where every front lawn, without exception, had an automobile on blocks. Erin wondered if it was a zoning requirement.

In front of Darrell Grant's apartment was a rusted Buick Riviera with a holly tree sprouting from its dashboard. The license plate revealed that the car had been there since 1982, long before Darrell Grant's arrival. Why he hadn't moved it was no great riddle: tow trucks cost money.

The other half of Darrell's grim duplex was occupied by two young Mormon missionaries, who greeted Erin politely as she came up the sidewalk. The missionaries were oiling their bicycles in preparation for another journey among South Florida's sinners. Erin admired their high spirits and fortitude; it was a tough neighborhood for proselytizing.

"Have you seen Mr. Grant today?" she asked.

The missionaries said no, Mr. Grant hadn't been around in a week or so. Erin went through the motion of knocking on the door. Darrell had taped aluminum foil over the inside windows, so nothing was visible from the front. As Erin headed toward the rear of the duplex, one of the young Mormons warned her to be careful because the yard was full of wheelchair parts.

Erin carefully stepped through an obstacle course of rusting rims, loose spokes, brakes, frames and footrests. She surmised that the wheelchair-stealing business must be doing pretty well for Darrell Grant to abandon so much valuable inventory—that, or the cops were on his back again, forcing a hasty departure.

Typically, Darrell had left the back door of the apartment unlocked.

When Erin opened it, she saw that her ex-husband truly was gone. As was his custom, he had stolen everything that wasn't nailed down, plus several items that were. Furniture, carpets, appliances, lamps, plumbing fixtures, ceiling fans, water heater, phone jacks, even the toilet tank was missing. Darrell Grant was nothing if not a master scavenger; he had painstakingly pried the tiles off the kitchen floor. Erin couldn't believe there was a big market for second-hand linoleum, but it was possible that Darrell was ahead of the curve. The commerce of stolen property wasn't immune to recessionary trends.

Darrell had cleaned out every room except one: Angie's bedroom. Erin gasped when she walked in.

The walls were bare except for a dozen old nails and a heart-shaped mirror. The floor was strewn with broken dolls: beheaded Barbies, dismembered Muppets, eviscerated Cabbage Patch Kids. The dolls had something in common: each had been a gift to Angela from Erin.

That was Darrell Grant's way. Weak in the verbal skills, he was inclined to express himself with displays of idiotic violence.

Erin's heart pounded in anger. She envisioned Darrell in their daughter's room, methodically separating the dolls from Angela's other toys, then attacking with a steak knife or pruning shears or God knows what . . . and leaving the mirror up so he could watch his own performance.

No! Erin thought. That wasn't the reason for the mirror. He'd left it for Erin, so she could see herself at the moment of discovery, could see the shock on her own face when she found what he'd done in Angie's bedroom. Could see herself crying.

But she didn't cry.

Touching nothing, she backed out of the room. Then she hurried outside and asked the friendly Mormons if she could borrow a camera.

Darrell Grant's sister lived in a trailer park thirty miles south of Miami. She shared a doublewide with a man who worked nights as a security guard at the Turkey Point nuclear power plant. The guard's name was Alberto Alonso. He greeted Erin warmly at the front door. The fact she was a professional stripper made him absolutely giddy.

"Come in, come in!" Alberto sang out. He opened his arms and attempted a hug; more of a lunge, actually. Erin deftly skirted his grasp.

"Where is Rita?" she asked.

"Out with the cubs," Alberto said. "Lupa's new litter—you want to come look? We got an albino."

"Maybe later," Erin said. Lupa was the family pet, a fifty-fifty cross between a German shepherd and a wild Mt. McKinley timber wolf. At regular intervals, Rita bred Lupa with other wolves. She was able to sell the cubs for three hundred dollars each, sometimes more. It was the newest rage in macho dogs, since pit bulls had gone out of fashion.

"Six babies," Alberto reported, "and the only male is albino. You should see the size of his balls!"

Erin said, "You must be very proud."

"I'm trying to get the power company interested."

"In what?"

"Wolf dogs, what else?" Alberto's grin revealed many crooked gaps. Erin didn't know how anyone could invest full confidence in a security guard with so many teeth missing.

"Think about it," Alberto was saying. "Packs of wolves patrolling the perimeter. There goes your terrorist threat. There goes your sabotage."

The screen door opened and Rita charged in. "Al, how many times I tole you—they ain't no guard dogs. They don't got the disposition for it."

She wore a housedress, thong slippers, a catcher's mask, and canvas logging gloves that went up to the elbows. The sight of her reminded Erin that none of Darrell's siblings had grown up to be remotely normal or well-adjusted. In the Grant family, procreation had become a game of genetic roulette.

"Hello, Rita," said Erin.

"Oh. Hi there." Rita took off the catcher's mask, revealing a nasty track of fresh stitches from the midpoint of her forehead to the bridge of her nose. "Lupa," she explained. "She damn jumpy around those cubs."

Alberto said, "Erin, honey, how about a drink?"

"Water would be fine."

"No, I mean a *drink*."

Rita said, "Make that two."

"Just water," Erin said. "I can't stay long."

Alberto was plainly disappointed. He shuffled to the refrigerator and began grappling with an ice tray. Rita tugged off the logging gloves and said, "Well, this is quite a surprise."

Erin said, "It's about Darrell. He's gone again."

"Now don't get all worked up."

"You know where he is?"

"No, ma'am, I do not." Rita lowered herself onto a black Naugahyde sofa, which hissed beneath her weight. She said, "You still workin' at that tittie place?"

Rita wasn't going to be easy; playing dumb was her life's work. Alberto was the weaker link.

"I hear the money is good," Rita remarked. "But it damn well ought to be."

Erin said, "When's the last time you talked to your brother?"

"Lord, I'm sure I don't remember."

Alberto reappeared with water for Erin and a bourbon for Rita, both served in Fred Flintstone jelly jars. Out of the blue, Alberto said, "What about private parties? Some of the boys at the plant were asking. They were talking about getting a banquet room at the Ramada."

"I don't do private parties," Erin told him. "I dance at the club. That's it."

"What about the other girls?"

"You'd have to ask them, Alberto."

Rita said, "He's been up to your place. What's the name again?"

"The Eager Beaver," said Alberto, helpfully.

Rita furrowed her brow. "I thought it was the Flesh Farm."

Alberto said, "No, that's another one."

"Well, anyhoo, he's seen you dance."

"Really?" Erin didn't like the idea of Alberto tiptoeing into the club, sneaking a peek. She could picture him giving a full report to the guys down at Turkey Point. It was pathetic, really. Erin was the closest thing to a celebrity that Alberto would ever know.

"I hope it was a good show," she said sweetly. "I hope you got your money's worth."

"Gawd." Rita lit a cigarette. "It's all he talked about for weeks after. You'd think he ain't never seen pubic hairs before."

Alberto Alonso reddened, finally. Erin said, "You should've told me you were coming. I would've sent some champagne to the table."

"Are you kidding? Pink champagne?"

A howling commotion erupted in the backyard. Rita grabbed the catcher's mask and hurried out the screen door.

"Careful now!" Alberto shouted after her.

Erin motioned him to sit down. "We don't get to visit much anymore," she said.

"Well, the divorce and all."

"Doesn't mean we can't still be friends," Erin said.

"I'd like that," said Alberto. He scooted the chair closer. "Friends it is. You and me!" His breathing had become audibly heavy, and his eyebrows looked moist.

Erin didn't often see men sweating from their eyebrows. "There's two sides to every story," she went on. "Darrell had his faults."

"Now that's a fact. He is no saint."

From outside, they heard Rita shouting curses at the wolf dog. Then came a chilling feral scream.

"Damn," Alberto said. "Another cat, I'll bet."

Erin lightly touched his knee. "I need to find Darrell. It's very important."

"He moved away, Erin."

"I know that."

"Don't worry, honey." Alberto flopped a fat moist hand upon hers. Clumsily he tried to intertwine fingers, but Erin pulled away.

"Where is he, Alberto?"

"Rita would kill me."

"It's my daughter we're talking about."

Alberto nervously glanced toward the screen door. "Look, he calls here a couple three times a week. Needing money, per the usual. But I'm not sure where he's at." Alberto attempted another hand-holding, but Erin shook him off.

"Anything would be a help," she said. "State, county, whatever. I'll settle for an area code."

Alberto said, "Rita's the one he talks to, not me. Darrell never told me anything about anything. He don't trust law enforcement, period."

It was a reach for Alberto Alonso to classify himself as law enforcement, but Erin let it slide. Alberto's job applications had been rejected by every municipal police department in the southeastern United States. Though he had the heart of a lawman, he did not have the acceptable psychological profile. "Squirrelly" was the term most commonly heard when Alberto's file came up for consideration.

He told Erin: "Don't worry, I'm sure Angie's fine."

"She's not fine, Alberto. She's with that fuckhead ex-husband of mine."

Alberto was shocked into silence. Outside, the chaos in the backyard abated suddenly. Rita poked her head in the screen door. "Where's the damn shovel?"

Alberto said, "I thought it was with the rakes."

"Well, it ain't!" The door slammed.

Erin asked Alberto for some aspirin.

"You got a headache?"

"A killer," she said.

"Poor thing." He stood up and cupped her face in his hands. "You feel hot, honey."

"Alberto, it's not a fever. It's a headache."

"I'll get you some Bayers. Be right back." He went to the bathroom and began searching the cabinet. "I got Advil!" he called out. "Tylenols. Anacins. Excedrin PMs. You prefer tablets or them new gel-caps?"

Alberto returned to the living room with an armful of pills, powders and capsules. Rita was there, settling into the Naugahyde, sucking fiercely on a cigarette. Erin was gone.

"Well, well." Rita's voice cut like a blade. "If it ain't Marcus Welby."

Erin was fully aware that the theft of U.S. mail was a federal offense, punishable by fines, imprisonment or both. She was also aware that in the Southern District of Florida, the United States Attorney spent exactly zero man-hours in pursuit of mail thieves, as the government's time was consumed by the prosecution of drug dealers, gunrunners, deposed foreign dictators, savings-and-loan executives, corrupt local politicians and crooked cops of all ranks.

The workings of the federal justice system were well-known to Erin because her previous job, before becoming a nude dancer, was typing and filing intelligence reports for the Federal Bureau of Investigation. Erin was efficient, precise and perceptive. In some ways she was sharper than the FBI agent to whom she reported. Although his filing system was flawless, his street instincts were shaky. Erin liked him and tried to help, but the agent was young, inexperienced and hopelessly Midwestern in his approach; South Florida ate him alive.

When Erin was dismissed from her job, the agent (whose name was Cleary) was more distraught than she was. He tried everything within bounds of the bureau's turgid hierarchy to reverse the decision, but it was no use. Erin had been reclassified as a security risk after her husband had been charged with the fourth felony of his life: the grand theft of eleven wheelchairs from the Sunshine Groves Retirement Village. It didn't matter that Erin was separated from Darrell Grant at the time—he'd phoned her from jail, and that was that. Phoned her at work, the moron! Told her to hurry and ditch the Camaro and for God's sake don't let the cops look in the trunk. Darrell Grant, yelling these instructions, forgetting that most phone calls out of the Broward County Jail (and all phone calls into the FBI building) were automatically recorded.

Erin herself was never suspected of complicity, for on both audio tapes her words to Darrell Grant were clear:

"You asshole. Where's my daughter?"

Although she didn't want to leave the job, Erin wasn't bitter. She understood the problem. Nobody should be married to a career criminal, but it was especially important for employees of the FBI. Agent Cleary was crestfallen, and wrote a glowing letter of reference, To Whom It May Concern, on official FBI stationery. For him that was quite a daring gesture. As it turned out, the letter was not needed when Erin applied for work at the Eager Beaver lounge. "Show me your boobs," Mr. Orly had said. "Fine. When can you start?" Erin didn't have the heart to tell Agent Cleary of her new occupation.

Ironically, the felony charge against Darrell Grant was dropped, as he'd agreed to become a secret informant for the sheriff's department. His first task was ratting out three of his scumdog thief friends; for this, Darrell was rewarded with a pristine new past, courtesy of the DELETE button on the sheriff's crime computer. The vaporizing of Darrell's prior record was egregiously illegal but not without precedent; if questioned, Darrell's handlers could always claim it was an accident. Crime computers were famous for spontaneous erasures.

In the subsequent battle for custody of Angela, Erin found herself fighting not just Darrell Grant, model citizen, but the detectives who so foolishly believed that he was working on their behalf. Whenever a new court date was set, the detectives conveniently arranged for Darrell Grant to be out of town on an undercover assignment. Affidavits attesting to the urgency of the mission were available by the handful. On the rare occasions when Darrell actually showed his face in court, not a soul came forward who would swear to his felonious exploits. The file room had been purged as neatly as the computer's memory. On the issue of Darrell Grant's criminal character, the judge was left only with Erin's word, which he coolly rejected.

Broke and discouraged, Erin refused to give up. She planned to pursue Darrell Grant through the legal system for as long and as far as necessary. Angela was in peril not because Darrell was abusive, but because he was unfailingly careless. It was only a matter of time before something bad happened to him, and then the real nightmare would begin. Then Erin's daughter would be delivered into the custody of the great state of Florida, which was not known for its attentiveness toward children.

Angie would never be a foster child. Erin wouldn't let it happen. To save the girl, she would do anything, including stealing Rita Grant's mail off the kitchen counter.

Erin put on a Jimmy Buffett tape, lay down on the bed and went through Rita's letters. She wore cutoff jeans and a baggy Hawaiian shirt and wraparound shades, electric blue. Her hair was in a ponytail, tucked under a pink cotton baseball cap. Her bare feet bounced to the music, and she was feeling better about her prospects.

Most of the stolen mail was worthless to Erin's private investigation—the electric bill, a Penthouse subscription reminder, a homesick letter from yet another wayward sibling (Darrell's youngest brother, feigning insanity at the state hospital in Chattahoochee), and a membership notice from the National Rifle Association, to which both Rita and Alberto had hopefully applied.

Only one item was of interest to Erin: the telephone bill. FBI training wasn't necessary to scan the long-distance entries and pinpoint Darrell Grant's location. He hadn't run far: Erin counted seven collect phone calls from a number in Deerfield Beach. It made perfect sense. Deerfield Beach was overwhelmingly populated by retirees. Where you had retirees, you had wheelchairs.

Erin turned down the stereo and picked up the phone. Her hand trembled as she dialed—not from nerves, but from anger. It rang six times before he answered. Erin used her old-lady voice. She said she was calling from the St. Vitus Society, collecting donations for the homeless.

Darrell Grant said: "Donations of what?"

"Anything you can spare. Food, clothing, medical equipment."

"Like wheelchairs?" Darrell Grant asked.

Erin listened for the sound of a child in the background. She heard only a television, tuned to a talk show.

Darrell Grant said: "Hello? You mean like wheelchairs?"

"Actually, we've got plenty of wheelchairs and gurneys. But any other medical equipment would be most appreciated."

"That's too bad," said Darrell Grant. "I got some used wheelchairs in pretty good shape."

Erin resisted the urge to scream something terrible into the phone.

Still using the old-lady voice, she said, "Well, we've just received a shipment of brand-new ones donated by the hospital district. But thank you anyway."

"Yeah? What kind?"

"I really couldn't say. Can I put you down for some canned goods or bedding?"

"Sure," Darrell Grant said. "Better yet, I'll haul the stuff over there myself. Gimme your address. And spell the name a that saint again, would you?"

Erin smiled. What a champ.

Moldowsky didn't know that Jerry Killian was crazy drooling mad with love. Not that it mattered; blackmail was blackmail.

"Where's Dilbeck?" Killian demanded.

"I'm here as the congressman's personal representative." Malcolm Moldowsky took out a monogrammed notebook. From an inside pocket came a gold fountain pen. "All right, let's have the terms."

"Not so quick."

They were seated on the top deck of the *Jungle Queen,* a gaudy ersatz paddlewheeler that motored up and down the Intracoastal Waterway in Fort Lauderdale. It was Killian's idea to meet there, safely surrounded by yammering tourists and conventioneers.

He said, "I specifically asked to meet the congressman."

Moldowsky sighed a patient sigh. "Mr. Dilbeck is very busy. This morning he's touring Little Haiti. This afternoon he will dedicate a domino park in Little Havana. This evening he'll be speaking to the Democratic Sons and Daughters of Nicaragua in Exile."

Killian whistled derisively. Malcolm Moldowsky said, "It's an election year, my friend."

"He has nothing to fear from me."

"He's a busy man is all I'm saying."

Killian folded his arms. "So he sends a guy who smells like a Bangkok bidet."

"You're referring to my cologne?"

"No offense. I'm a Brut man myself."

Moldowsky doodled placidly on the notepad. "No offense taken."

"He's an excitable boy, your congressman. Beat the living Jesus out of that schmo in the dance club." Killian awaited an explanation, but Moldowsky continued to draw, saying nothing.

"He's got a problem around the ladies," Killian went on. "I think he needs help, before word gets out."

Moldowsky said, "May we get down to business?"

"The only reason I mention it is I'm concerned. He could hurt somebody, or get hurt. They're tough places, those dance bars."

"I'll pass that along. Can we begin now?"

Point by point, Killian explained his demands. There were only two. Moldowsky listened impassively and took notes. When the blackmailer finished, Moldowsky looked up and said, "This is completely outrageous."

The *Jungle Queen* blew four long whistles. The captain was trying to get the attention of a bridgetender.

Killian said, "Which part is outrageous?"

"The money, of course. A million dollars!"

"Forget the money. What about the other part?"

Moldowsky eyed him. "Forget the money?"

"Sure. I was just busting your balls." Killian gave a hearty laugh. He signaled a waiter for two more beers.

Moldowsky said, "Just so I've got this clear: You don't want any money. Not a dime."

Killian removed his thick eyeglasses and held them to the sunlight, inspecting for smudges. He said, "For a guy who dresses so sharp, you're thick as a brick. No, Mr. Personal Representative, I don't want money. All I want him to do is fix a simple court case."

"Keep your voice down."

"*Grant* versus *Grant.*"

"Yes, I got it the first time," Moldowsky said. "A custody matter. What's your interest in the case?"

"None of your business," Killian replied. "And if you pursue that line of inquiry, I will go instantly to the police and report what I saw at the Eager Beaver. Headlines are certain to follow."

Finally the drawbridge opened to let the *Jungle Queen* pass, and the tourists broke into silly tourist applause. A waiter appeared with beers. Moldowsky and Killian drank in silence until the merriment subsided on deck.

"This is a great boat ride," Killian said brightly. "They've got one like this down in Miami, right?"

"In Biscayne Bay. A tour of celebrity homes." Moldowsky remained polite even though he'd decided that Jerry Killian was a flake. Flakes could still cause trouble.

"Like who? Which celebrities?" Killian asked.

"The Bee Gees."

"Which Bee Gees?"

"The whole damn bunch. They've all got mansions on the water."

"Is Madonna's house on the tour?"

"Undoubtedly," Moldowsky said, with a sigh. He steered the conversation back to blackmail. "What makes you think Congressman Dilbeck can influence a local divorce judge? I mean, even if he wanted to."

"Easy. The divorce judge is sick of being a divorce judge. He wants to move up in the world, namely a seat on the federal bench. For that he needs political connections."

Moldowsky frowned. "But it's the Senate that confirms—"

"I know that!" Killian angrily gripped the edge of the table. "I *know,* you pompous fuck. I know it's the Senate that confirms. But a letter from a congressman would be helpful, would it not? It might carry weight with certain senators on the Judiciary Committee, correct?"

"Sure," Moldowsky said. "You're right." His eyes were on Killian's ratty necktie, which was soaking in his beer mug. Killian noticed and removed it quickly. If he was embarrassed, he didn't let it show.

"The judge would be impressed to hear from a United States congressperson. That's the point, that's what we're talking about, Mr. Personal Representative—not influence so much as the appearance thereof. Who cares if this hayseed ever makes it to the federal bench? We want him to think he can. We want him to think Dilbeck has the clout to make or break. And I've got a feeling you're just the sneaky little maggot to deliver that message."

Sometimes Malcolm Moldowsky regretted his own coolness. After so many years as a political fixer, he'd lost the capacity to be personally insulted; virtually nothing provoked him. In his line of work, emotions were risky. They distorted the senses, led to grave miscalculations and foolhardy impulses. Naturally it would've been fun to punch Jerry Killian so hard that he puked up blood, but it also would've been counterproductive. The man was motivated by forces deeper and more urgent than greed, and that made him dangerous indeed.

So Moldowsky said: "I'll see what I can do."

"I thought you would."

"In the meantime, you can't go back to that strip club." Moldowsky closed his notebook and capped his pen. "If you show your face in the place, the deal's off. Got it?"

"Fair enough," Killian said. "I can handle that." But his heart ached at the thought.

Suing a synagogue was challenging under the best of circumstances. Mordecai was having difficulty finding guidance. His law books were barren of precedents. Enthusiasm was equally hard to come by. When he told his mother of the case, she slapped him across the face with an oven mitt. It was her way of reminding him that two of his uncles were Orthodox rabbis.

Mordecai's plan for the Paul Guber case was further hindered by the victim's own friends, who couldn't recall the name or location of the synagogue at which the savage attack had occurred. The young men blamed their confusion on darkness, the late hour and alcohol, but Mordecai knew better. Collective amnesia was a sure sign of conspiracy. He considered asking Paul Guber for the true details of the incident, but that would've required Paul to open his mouth and speak, thus ruining a key plank of Mordecai's legal strategy. He wanted the jury to behold a stockbroker rendered mute and helpless by violent trauma. A stockbroker who could still work the phones wasn't nearly so pitiable a plaintiff. Mordecai's plan called for poor Mr. Guber to remain silent.

The lawyer decided to try visual aids. He got a map of Broward County and attached it to a tall easel. With colored pins he marked the location of every synagogue from Tamarac to Hallandale. Mordecai's idea was to assemble Paul Guber and his buddies in front of the map; either it would jog their memories, or help them agree on a plausible story. Synagogues in the most affluent neighborhoods were denoted by shiny green pins—Mordecai's subtle way of suggesting a suitably prosperous defendant.

The map was brought to Paul Guber's hospital room, and his friends gathered on each side of the bed. Mordecai stood back and waited. The men squinted at the map. They mumbled. They pointed. They rubbed their chins in feigned concentration. It was a dreadful scene. After an hour, Mordecai ordered them all to go home and think about it.

Outside the hospital room, Paul's fiancée said, "What does it mean?"

"It means I'm losing interest," the lawyer replied.

Back at the office, Mordecai's secretary seemed relieved to see him, which was unusual. She took him to the conference room, where a new client was waiting. It took all of Mordecai's courage to shake the man's hand.

"I'm Shad," the man said. "We talked on the phone."

The man was broad, bumpy and hairless. He wore a tank top, parachute pants and black Western boots. He had the grip of a wrestler.

Mordecai's secretary vanished. The lawyer took a seat at the table and motioned for Shad to do the same.

"You got a fridge?" Shad said.

"Pardon?"

Shad opened a brown grocery sack and took out the Ziploc pouch containing the undamaged foil seal; this he held up, dramatically, for Mordecai to see. Then Shad reached in the sack and removed the container of Delicato Fruity Low-Fat Yogurt. "Blueberry," he announced, removing the Glad Wrap.

"Ah yes," said Mordecai. "You're the one with the insect."

"Roach," Shad said, firmly. He pushed the yogurt across the table. Mordecai examined it tentatively, finding nothing.

"It's in here?" He peered at the flawless creaminess.

"You bet," Shad said. "We're talking jumbo."

Mordecai lifted the wax carton up to the light. "I wish I could see it."

Shad offered him a spoon and said, "Happy hunting."

The lawyer hesitated. "First we should get some pictures." He buzzed the secretary and told her to bring the camera. Moments later, she buzzed back to report it was out of film.

Shad said, "Hope you got a fridge."

"Well, of course."

"And I'd like a receipt."

Mordecai was offended. "You don't trust me?"

"Not yet," said Shad.

"Don't worry. We'll have a contract."

"Still, I'd like a receipt. That's my future there." He pointed at the yogurt carton. "That's my retirement."

Mordecai explained the customary arrangement in such cases. When he got to the part about the contingency fee, he saw Shad stiffen.

"Forty percent? That's what you get?"

"It's standard, Mr. Shad. You can check around."

"Forty motherfucking percent!"

"Most attorneys quote similar rates."

"Is that so?" Shad lowered his head and leaned across the table. "I had a guy took a rat case for thirty-three, plus expenses."

"Well," said Mordecai, unsettled, "my forty includes all costs." He didn't want to hear about the other case, but he needed to know. "When you say rat . . ."

"Baby Norway." With his hands Shad indicated the size. "About yea long. It was up at the Beef N' Reef in Wilton Manors. I open the steak sauce and there she comes, bingo, a rat! Lying there on my Rib-eye Special. Talk about traumatized."

The image made Mordecai pause. "And you filed suit?"

"Yeah, but something happened. The other side . . . I really don't know. They sued me back, believe it or not, and my lawyer said I was better off to forget the whole thing." Shad spoke of the experience bitterly. "I never paid the bastard a nickel," he added pointedly. "That was the deal."

"It's the usual contingency contract." Mordecai felt better now, back in familiar territory. "Suing a big corporation isn't easy. It's hard work. Expensive, too."

"On the phone you said they'd settle."

"They probably will, Mr. Shad, but not without a fight. That's where I'll earn my forty percent—if we win."

Mordecai wasn't displaying the fiery optimism that Shad would have liked. He wondered if he'd made the right choice in attorneys. "How long does yogurt stay good?" he asked.

The lawyer said he didn't know.

"You better find out." Shad held up the carton. "When this shit starts to turn, watch out, Mother. The stink is so bad it peels wallpaper."

Mordecai said, "We'll freeze it if necessary."

"It ain't lunch," said Shad, "it's evidence. So don't go fucking up the chain of custody."

"Certainly not." Mordecai thought: Chain of custody? What's the story on this guy?

Shad said, "Tell me about your ace shrink."

"A good man. I've used him on other cases. You should start seeing him as soon as possible, and as often as possible."

"And who pays for that?"

Mordecai smiled paternally. "Don't you worry. Eventually the Delicato company will take care of all expenses. In the meantime, we need to build up a detailed medical record."

Shad said, "I never been to a shrink. I got a feeling I won't like it."

"It's important to document your pain and suffering. It will help determine the final damages."

"The money, you mean."

"Exactly. The court needs to know the ordeal you've been through. You might even consider quitting your job."

"Can't do that," Shad said flatly.

"Lost income would greatly enhance a jury award. How about taking a leave of absence?"

Shad said no, he couldn't quit work. Mordecai backed off. They could discuss it another time. "What kind of job do you have?" he asked.

"I'm in the entertainment business," Shad said.

"Really?" Mordecai couldn't imagine it. "Are you a . . . performer?" He was thinking: Circus.

Shad shook his head. "Security. I provide security."

"May I ask where?"

"At a bottomless joint."

Mordecai took a deep breath. He imagined jurors would do the same. He imagined how it would be in court, watching helplessly as the sympathy drained from their eyes. Mordecai felt very sorry for himself; it had been such a crummy day. First the Paul Guber debacle and now this. Why didn't he ever snare the choice plaintiffs—the adorable little kids, the winsome young widows, the sad but plucky pensioners?

Not me, thought Mordecai. I get a bouncer from a tittie bar. Not a normal-looking bouncer either; some hairless pop-eyed "Star Trek" reject.

The man named Shad said, "The hell's the matter? If your heart's not in it, just say so." He probed the yogurt with the spoon. "I want you to see this."

"Not necessary," the lawyer protested. "I believe you."

Mordecai kicked with both feet, rolling the chair back from the conference table. He got up just as Shad struck paydirt.

"Ha!"

"My God," said Mordecai.

"Did I tell you? Is that a fucking roach or what?"

The prehistoric pest filled the spoon. Shad raised it to the level of Mordecai's eyes. The lawyer gaped in revulsion. Wings askew, the dead cockroach knelt in a creamy blue puddle. Its yogurt-flecked antennae drooped lifelessly.

Shad was very proud. "Well?"

"Put it back," the lawyer rasped.

"Just think," Shad said, "sittin' down to breakfast and—"

"No!"

"Makes you want to gag, don't it?"

"Yes," Mordecai whispered. For balance he clutched the corner of the table. "Put it away now, please."

Shad carefully dropped the insect into the yogurt and stirred gently. Soon the crispy corpse disappeared from view. "There," he said. "Now, where's that fridge?"

"I'll get Beverly to show you." The lawyer mopped his jowls with a handkerchief.

"Does this mean we got a deal?"

"It does," said Mordecai.

Times were tough, and a roach was a roach.

Monique Sr. announced that Alan Greenspan was drinking a beer at table fourteen.

Orly clapped his fat hands together. "See! Another reason you gotta work." He didn't want Erin to take the night off. "Famous comedian in the audience, you shouldn't miss the chance."

"Alan Greenspan," Erin said pleasantly, "is an economist."

"That's the one." Monique Sr. stuck by her claim. "Check him out yourself. Corona from the bottle, no lime."

"Not to mention it's Tuesday," Orly carped. "Tuesday being oil wrestling. Only one of our busiest nights."

"I don't wrestle," Erin reminded him. "Not in oil, not in custard, not in mud. No wrestling for me."

Nude oil wrestling was a tradition at the Eager Beaver, but Erin declined to participate. In her view, professional dancers shouldn't roll around in a wet tub with shirtless, semi-tumescent drunks. As a second-ary issue, Erin didn't like the looks of the oil. Orly was vague about the brand; one day he'd say it was Wesson, another day he'd swear it was Mazola. Erin had a hunch it was neither. Once a health inspector showed up for an on-site bacterial census. Amazingly, not a single living microbe was found in the wrestling vat. The mystery was explained later the same evening, when the health inspector returned with four of his civil-service buddies. They shared a front-row table and all the Amaretto they could drink, courtesy of Mr. Orly.

"Tuesday is a big night," Orly was saying. "Bottom line is, we need all our best dancers."

"Please, Mr. Orly. It's personal."

"Tell me."

"I'm meeting my ex-husband," Erin said, "to discuss future custody arrangements for our daughter."

Here Urbana Sprawl interjected her opinion of Darrell Grant, describing him so vividly that Mr. Orly immediately offered to have him killed.

Erin said, "That's not necessary."

"Beat up? Crippled? You gives the word." Orly pantomimed dialing a telephone. "That's how easy it is when you know the right people."

"Thanks, but I can handle it myself." Erin played along with Mr. Orly's Mafia routine as a matter of politeness. He looked about as Sicilian as David Letterman.

Urbana Sprawl urged Orly to give Erin the night off for the sake of her lost little daughter. Orly wasn't the least bit moved. He said, "Promise me this is really a domestic-type deal. Promise you're not sneaking down the street for an audition."

"Oh right," said Erin. "My lifelong dream is to work for those freaks."

Mr. Orly was paranoid about losing his best strippers to the Flesh Farm, which recruited aggressively with signing bonuses. The owners recently introduced Friction Dancing Night to compete with Nude Oil Wrestling Night at the Eager Beaver. Friction dancing was not so much dancing as it was rubbing, vigorously, against the frontal surfaces of fully clothed customers. It was demonstrably more erotic than oil wrestling, and not nearly as messy. Orly was definitely feeling the pressure.

"Tell me the truth," he said to Erin.

"I told you the truth. I'm meeting my ex-husband." She picked up her purse to indicate the conversation was over. "If you don't believe me, ask Shad. He's coming along."

"My Shad?" Orly's eyebrows twitched with concern.

"As a favor to me," Erin explained. "There could be trouble."

"Then be damn careful."

"I will."

"Because good bouncers are hard to find," Orly said. "Harder than dancers, believe it or not."

Erin first met Darrell Grant at Broward General Hospital, where her mother was recuperating from an operation in which her navel had been cosmetically inverted. Erin's mother had paid a plastic surgeon $1,500 to transform her "outie" bellybutton to an "innie." Erin was unaware that such a procedure was available, but her mother assured her that all the big-name fashion models had it done.

Erin was standing at her mother's bed, admiring the surgeon's work, when Darrell Grant appeared with fresh linens and a clean bedpan. He worked as an orderly at the hospital and, as Erin later learned, it was there he acquired his taste for narcotics and his aptitude for boosting wheelchairs. In appearance, though, Darrell seemed anything but a criminal. Erin was still naïve enough to believe that all crooks had bad teeth, greasy hair and jailhouse tattoos. She assumed that cleancut, good-looking men possessed the same natural advantage as cleancut, good-looking women: the world treated you better, and consequently there was no reason for unwholesome behavior.

And Darrell Grant was uncommonly handsome, with a lean face and bright mischievous eyes. He took her to the hospital cafeteria and charmed her with a hastily fabricated story of his life. The centerpiece of the yarn was an authentic Bronze Star, which Darrell Grant kept in the breast pocket of his hospital garb. He told Erin he'd won it for killing a Cuban sniper during the invasion of Grenada. Erin chose not to question Darrell's tale, knowing the Pentagon had given out about a hundred thousand medals in appreciation for making the tiny spice island safe once again for Holiday Inns. Much later in their relationship Erin would learn that Darrell had actually acquired the Bronze Star, along with two cases of Michelob, in the burglary of an American Legion post.

They dated for six months, to the horror of Erin's mother. She had steered a long line of doctors, lawyers and accountants in her daughter's direction, and Erin had found them all too serious and self-absorbed. Some of them were old enough to be her father. Darrell Grant was impulsive, full of tricks, and he made her laugh. At the time, that seemed important. Erin's decision to marry him was sudden and cataclysmic, and it had the desired effect of freeing her from the clutches of her mother.

The sociopathic side of Darrell Grant didn't surface for about eighteen months, until he abandoned all pretense of honest labor and devoted himself full-time to larceny. To explain the odd hours and fluctuating income, he told Erin he was selling medical equipment. Darrell's boyish wit and warmth evaporated dramatically under the icy twin spells of amphetamines and methaqualone; he was either a dervish or a zombie, depending on the chemical cycle. Newly pregnant, Erin didn't want to bail out of the marriage without giving Darrell Grant a chance to reform. The thought of divorce was almost as daunting as the thought of her mother's shrill I-told-you-so.

When he learned that Erin was expecting a child, Darrell vowed to change his ways. He got off the pills, removed all stolen property from the garage and took a job selling rustproofing at a Chrysler dealership. He was a new man, for about a month. One Thursday, Erin returned home from work and found Darrell in the living room, chiseling the serial numbers off a pediatric wheelchair. Confronted, he broke into a rage and slapped Erin twice across the face. The amusement ended abruptly when Erin punched him in the larynx, pushed him to the floor and whacked him in the testicles with a mop handle. It was Darrell's first glimpse of his wife's temper, and it made an impression. From then on he never laid a finger on her; instead, he vented his feelings by destroying things that she valued—artworks, furniture, photo albums, her favorite clothes. By the time Angela was born, the marriage was irretrievably pulverized.

Erin didn't torment herself with remorse. She'd gotten conned, and learned a lesson. Now it was time to concentrate on getting Angela back.

Waiting in the car with Shad, Erin outlined the latest plan.

"So it's a trap," he said.

"Exactly."

"He won't be bringing no wheelchairs for the poor."

"No," said Erin, "he'll be looking to steal some."

Shad spit something out the window. "And you were married to this asswipe?"

"We all make mistakes."

"Don't you hate it," Shad said, "when love turns around and bites you like a damn rattlesnake? It happens, by God. Happens every day."

Erin showed him the photographs of the mangled dolls in Angie's bedroom. "Christ almighty," he said.

"My daughter is the one I'm concerned about. That's what this is all about."

Shad said nothing for several minutes. Then he asked Erin if she was satisfied with her lawyer. "I'm not so sure about mine," he added. "He needs some firing up."

Erin said, "My lawyer's all right. It's the system that's so frustrating."

"Tell me about it." Shad was glad to chat with Erin about these matters; he felt they were warriors on the same battlefield. "If there's such a thing as true justice," he said, "you'll get your little girl, and I'll get rich off my dead roach."

"That would be nice," Erin said quietly.

The car was in the farthest, darkest corner of a parking lot attached to a strip shopping mall in Oakland Park. The address Erin had given Darrell Grant belonged to a bankrupt video store, located at the other end of the plaza. A few movie posters remained in the window; from the car, Erin could make out the blown-up likeness of Arnold Schwarzenegger in sunglasses.

Shad said, "How do you know he's coming tonight?"

"Because I told him they ship the wheelchairs every Wednesday morning. He'll be looking to load up on inventory."

"Any particular model?"

"He favors Everest-and-Jennings," Erin said. "Rolls and Theradynes are good, too."

Shad was intrigued. He'd assumed all wheelchairs were pretty much the same. "Rolls as in Royce?"

Erin said no, it was a different company. Shad asked why her exhusband didn't steal cars like everybody else.

"Because he couldn't hotwire a goddamn toaster," said Erin. "Cars are too complicated for Darrell Grant."

Shad spit out the window again. He seemed to be aiming at a particular curbstone. "You want me to—do what exactly? When he gets here, I mean."

Erin said, "Let's play it by ear."

"I could break something. Maybe start with a finger." Shad wiggled one of his pinkies. "Depends how serious you are."

"I just want to talk with the man." Erin leaned against the headrest and closed her eyes. She thought about the young bachelor beaten senseless on stage at the Eager Beaver—was he still in the hospital? She remembered the rabid expression on the face of his attacker, the wheezy primal grunts as he swung the champagne bottle.

Erin thought: Is it me? Do I bring that out in men?

Then here's Orly, now Shad, offering to maim her ex-husband. A casual favor, like jumping the car battery or hooking up the stereo.

"The ulna is a good one," Shad was saying. He tapped Erin's forearm to show her the spot. "A crowbar right about there, we'll have his attention."

Erin sat up. "Can I ask you something? Do I seem the type of woman to be impressed by violence?"

He grunted noncommitally.

"I'm serious, Shad. Is that your opinion of me?"

He cocked his huge head and stared at her curiously. In the darkness he resembled a shaved bear. "It's what I know best, that's all—kicking ass. On account of my job."

"Then it's not me?"

"Ha! No, it ain't you."

"Because I am *not* impressed by that sort of thing."

"Is that why there's a gun under the seat?"

Erin couldn't think of a sharp retort.

Shad grinned. "It's all right, babe. You're entitled."

"I've never used it," she told him.

"But you might." Shad folded his arms. "All I'm saying is, violence can be helpful. Sometimes it's the best way to make your point."

"Not with Darrell." Erin's ex-husband would cherish an injury. What better proof that she was hanging out with a rotten crowd, and was unfit to care for Angela! Darrell, the conniving bastard, would milk a broken limb for all it was worth. He'd wear the cast until the plaster rotted off his arm.

"Your call," Shad said.

"I just want to talk with the man."

"Fine."

But deep inside, Erin briefly savored a vision of Shad pounding Darrell Grant into dogmeat. She probably should've been ashamed by the feeling, but she wasn't.

Especially when she thought of what he'd done to Angie's dolls.

At midnight Shad went looking for a Coke machine. Erin put on a Buffett tape and turned the volume low. She liked the Caribbean songs the best. Her imagination set sail, and before long she was dreaming of pearly beaches and secluded harbors. She was barefoot in the surf, wiggling her toes into the sand.

When she opened her eyes, her shoes were gone. Both doors on the old Fairlane had been opened. When she got out of the car, she stepped on something plastic, which cracked into sharp pieces. The Buffett cassette on the pavement.

Erin froze. "Shad?"

A hand grabbed her by the hair, twisting hard, jerked her head back so that all she saw was sky. She felt something sharp against her throat.

"You still snore like a pig." It was Darrell Grant.

Erin shook uncontrollably. It was embarrassing to let him see her so afraid.

He said, "I can't believe you tried to set me up. I can't fucking believe it."

"What?" Erin didn't recognize the pitch of her own voice.

Darrell Grant slapped a hand across her mouth, told her to shut the hell up. They both heard the footsteps. "Your boyfriend," Darrell whispered. "This'll be choice."

Shad came out of the shadows with a Diet Coke in one hand and an unopened can of Canada Dry in the other. He put both cans down as soon as he saw the long knife at Erin's neck. Darrell Grant told him not to try anything stupid. Shad's expression remained invisible in the darkness.

"I got an idea," Darrell said. He told Shad to lie on his belly or else get a bucket to catch Erin's blood. Shad nodded and got down on the ground. Darrell Grant released Erin and immediately pounced on the bouncer, digging his knees into the other man's enormous shoulder blades. Laughing, Darrell managed to cinch Shad's thick wrists with a pair of flexible plastic handcuffs.

"Knock it off," Erin said, still shaky.

With both hands Darrell Grant poised the dagger at the crest of Shad's bare skull; the smooth flesh dimpled under the pressure of the blade.

Again Erin told him to stop, and again her ex-husband cackled. He rolled the knife handle back and forth in his palms, so that the point twirled against Shad's skin. Erin saw the first drop of blood, blackish in the dim light.

"That hurt?" Darrell Grant asked.

"Nope," Shad replied, truthfully. He felt little in the way of physical pain. The doctors didn't seem to know why.

Erin said, "Since when do you carry a knife?"

"Since when do you hang out with ugly bald-headed Amazons?" Darrell Grant got up and whipped the dagger like a sword through the air. He was batty on speed. "I suppose it's just a coincidence that you're here in this very parking lot tonight? *En garde!*" He slashed a Z in the air. "What, you think I'm blind? I saw your car from three blocks away, Erin. Jesus, you'd make a great spy. Maybe next time you can set off fireworks."

She said, "You're such an asshole."

Darrell Grant grinned crookedly. "Is that how they speak at the St. Vitus Society? That *was* you on the phone, right? Talking about all those brand-new wheelchairs."

"You've lost your mind."

"Then explain this!" Accusingly, he pointed the dagger at the Fairlane. "And this!" He poked Shad with the toe of a tan cowboy boot. "You fucking set me up!"

Erin said: "Darrell, I'm keeping a list: assault with a deadly weapon, false imprisonment, burglary, possession of narcotics—"

"Shut up," he snapped. "What'm I supposed to believe, that you and Igor stopped here to make out? I know you're lonely, Erin, but this is ridiculous. I seen handsomer iguanas."

She thought of the gun in the car, gauged the steps back to the driver's side. Then she pushed the idea from her mind. Shooting Darrell would mean she'd never see Angie again. The judge would make sure of it.

"Junior?" It was Shad, speaking from the side of his mouth. He had no choice, being face-down on the asphalt. "Junior, listen up. The lady and I work together. She was giving me a lift home when this piece a shit excuse for a Ford overheated. We pulled in to let the radiator cool, and that's it. That's the whole story."

Darrell Grant dropped to his haunches and tweaked Shad's nose. "Well, I'll be damned. It talks."

Wonder drugs, thought Erin. "What's with your hair?" she asked. Darrell flared at her caustic tone. For a man whose profession was stealing from invalids, he was surprisingly vain about his appearance.

He said, "I lightened it a touch. So?"

"And the stubble," Erin said. "Come here, let's see."

"No way." He stood up, sullenly.

"Is this your Don Johnson period?"

"Shut up, Erin."

She was trying to take his mind off Shad and further mischief with the knife. "I'll bet you got yourself a white linen Armani to go with the hair."

Darrell Grant said, "Fuck you." When he put the dagger in his belt, Erin felt slightly better about the situation. She hoped he was down-gearing for a simple argument.

Then he stood on Shad's head with the heels of his cowboy boots.

"Get off!" Erin cried.

"Make me."

"Darrell, stop!"

Shad made no sounds. Erin wasn't sure if he was still conscious.

"I like it up here," Darrell Grant chirped. He balanced on Shad's skull as if it were a cypress stump.

"Don't," Erin pleaded.

"What's it worth to you? How about a twenty?"

Erin looked at Shad's face under the boots. His eyes were closed but his jaw was set.

"Twenty bucks," Darrell Grant repeated. "Hurry, hurry."

He had tossed Erin's purse under the car. She had to crawl for it. Darrell Grant leered as he watched her down on all fours. "I like that," he said. "Brings back memories."

Mechanically Erin fumbled in the purse for her cash. She found a twenty-dollar bill and handed it to her ex-husband. He sniffed it as if it were cognac. "Amazing," he said. "All you gotta do is flash your twat and men throw money. Isn't it a great country, Erin? Aren't you proud to be an American?"

At that moment, the only person she hated more than Darrell Grant was herself, for marrying him. "Get off the man," she said coldly. Darrell hopped from Shad's head.

"Where's Angie?"

"Safe and sound," said Darrell Grant. "If you're a good mummy, I'll let her call on Christmas Day."

"We're going back to court." Erin's voice trembled. "You've already violated the judge's order."

"Back to court!" Darrell Grant's hooting filled the night. "Back to court! I love it."

"What's happened to you, Darrell?" She really wanted to know. He was worse than she'd ever seen him.

He yanked the knife from his belt and bent over Shad. For a moment Erin feared that he would slit Shad's throat. She had an image of herself hanging on Darrell's back, digging her fingernails into his eye sockets.

"Don't do it," she said.

"Do what?"

Using the dagger as a pen, Darrell playfully etched the letter G into the crown of Shad's naked scalp. Blood trickled down his head and puddled in the folds of muscle at the base of his neck. Erin felt woozy and chilled. Shad remained silent, although his eyes had opened.

"There." Darrell Grant stood back and admired his work.

Erin said, "What does that prove?"

"We're not going back to court."

"You're wrong, Darrell."

"I won, sweetheart. All the marbles, remember?"

"What'd you do with my shoes?"

Again came the hooting laughter. "Wake up, little Dorothy," he said. "You're not in Kansas anymore!"

Darrell Grant circled Erin's car, puncturing each tire with a thrust of the knife. Then he kicked each of the soda cans and sauntered off across the parking lot. As he disappeared in the darkness, Erin could hear him singing, "Somewhere Over the Rainbow."

At her feet, Shad rolled over and blinked up at the stars.

"Nice guy," he said. "Too bad it didn't work out for you two."

7

The next night, Erin danced to ZZ Top.

Her record store didn't stock the band's first album, so she bought one of the newer releases. Kevin, the club's disc jockey, was pleased with the hard guitar and fast bass beat. Her regular customers didn't seem to mind the change of pace.

The one she called Mr. Peepers was not in the audience. Erin feared that Shad had scared him away from the Eager Beaver forever. Either that, or he'd given up the hustle.

So much for love.

Against her better judgment, Jerry Killian had become a reed of hope for Erin in her battle for Angela. Dealing with Darrell Grant was impossible, but maybe Killian could get to the judge. Maybe political pressure was the way to go. Erin needed to know more about Killian's connection, the congressman.

His name, for starters.

She danced out of the spotlights long enough to shield her eyes and scout the back rows. The judge was in his customary booth near the Foosball machines. Monique Sr. was on the tabletop, bouncing up a storm. The judge watched droopy-eyed and inert. Erin figured his hands were busy under the table.

After the set, Mr. Orly came to the dressing room and announced that he approved of the new music. "Faster the better," he said.

Urbana Sprawl said ZZ Top was hazardous to her health. "My tits are killing me."

"Hey," Orly said, "we put up with your rap crap. Ice Puke or whatever."

"Ice Cube!"

"Bottom line is, you can tolerate eight minutes of hard rock."

"Instant stretch marks," Urbana complained.

Erin said, "I'll find some slower cuts."

"Don't!" Orly protested. "Fast is good. Everybody sweats, everybody drinks."

"And everybody tips," said Monique Sr., waving a fifty. The other dancers whistled.

"Case closed," said Orly, and he was gone.

When the shift was over, Erin scrubbed off her makeup and dressed quickly. Urbana asked what was the hurry.

"I've got an errand."

"Three in the morning?"

"Meeting somebody."

"Tell me it's not Darrell." Urbana and the other dancers knew about the harrowing incident at Erin's car. They'd seen the dagger cuts on Shad's bald head.

"Don't worry," Erin said. "It's only Jerry Killian." She zipped her jeans and stepped into a pair of sandals.

"Mr. Peepers?" Monique Jr. said. "Why?"

"To talk."

"Bad idea," said Monique Sr.

"Not many good ones at three in the morning." Erin checked herself in the mirror. "Desperate times call for desperate measures."

"Be patient," Urbana Sprawl advised. "He'll be back. Especially you keep playing his songs."

"I can't wait," Erin said.

"How you gonna find him?"

"He's found."

Urbana Sprawl smiled. "The phone book!"

"Nope," said Erin. "Unlisted, unpublished."

"Then how'd you find him?"

"Research," Erin explained, enigmatically. Erin couldn't tell them the truth. One phone call had sent Agent Cleary to the computer keyboard. He was glad to help, and asked few questions; he still felt bad about her dismissal.

Monique Jr. told Erin that it was crazy to call on Mr. Peepers in the middle of the night. "He could be a psycho slasher for all you know."

"Oh, I believe he's harmless."

"That's what they said about Ted Bundy."

"Thank you," said Erin, gathering her purse and dancing clothes, "for the peace of mind."

Without much effort, Urbana Sprawl blocked the door. "Give him till the weekend," she said.

Erin felt a wave of fatigue. She was losing the energy to argue. Her friends were right: it was craziness.

"Patience," Urbana said.

"Until the weekend," Erin promised. "If you can stand the new music that long."

Monique Jr. said the ZZ Top was dynamite. She said she'd never dance to rap again. She wanted a white top hat and tails as a costume for "Sharp-Dressed Man."

Frowning, Urbana hoisted a titanic breast in each hand. "Try jumping around with *these* suckers and you be in traction. So screw your ZZ and gimme that slow Cube."

Erin was sympathetic. She couldn't imagine going through life with a bosom so large. None of the dancers doubted the rumor that Urbana had once smothered a man on a convertible sofa. It was completely plausible.

"See you tomorrow," Erin told her friends.

"You headed home?" Monique Sr. asked. "Be honest."

"Home," Erin said.

Shad followed in his own car, just to make sure.

Moldowsky found the congressman in a state of massage. A redheaded woman in a gold tank suit straddled his back, chopping at his pale shoulder blades. The woman had very long fingernails for a masseuse.

"Say hi to Eve." Dilbeck's words thrummed comically with each chop.

"Hello, Eve," Moldowsky said. "We need a moment of privacy. Do you mind?"

Eve said that was perfectly fine. She spoke with a light British accent.

"Go hop in the shower," Dilbeck told her. "I'll be there in a flash."

When she was out of the room, Moldowsky said, "David, where is your wife?"

"Shopping, I think."

"You think?"

"Yes, shopping. I told Pierre to drive slow."

Moldowsky said, "You are a hopeless shithead."

Dilbeck sat up and covered himself with the towel. "What'd I do now, Malcolm? Hell, you're acting like my mother."

They heard the faucets turn in the shower down the hall.

Moldowsky motioned with his chin. "Is she a hooker?"

"I don't know yet," said the congressman. "And even if she is, so what? She's got no earthly idea who I am, Malcolm. She just moved here from London."

"Beautiful. Hands across the water."

"What's the matter with you?"

"The sugar bill, Davey. Your colleagues are playing it tough, and my clients are deeply concerned. They want to know if they've got their money on the wrong horse."

"Relax. I'm entertaining young Christopher tonight."

Relax? Moldowsky thought. The moron has a prostitute in the tub, an assault victim in the hospital and a blackmailer who's ready to call the newspapers. "Did you speak with the judge?" he asked.

Dilbeck nodded. "Yes, we had lunch."

"Well?"

"He was grateful for my interest in his career. He does, as you say, have his heart on the federal bench." Dilbeck stood up and adjusted the towel. He looked longingly down the hall, toward the gentle sounds of the shower.

Moldowsky said, "And what about *Grant* versus *Grant?*"

"Oh, we talked it over." Dilbeck began to move around the room, trying to get upwind of Moldy's cologne. "The judge is deeply religious," Dilbeck said, "or at least he pretends to be."

"Born again, I suppose."

"Several times. He feels strongly that he made the correct decision in the custody case. He seems to have a personal interest in the situation."

"True enough," Moldowsky said.

"He said the mother is a harlot. Is that right, Malcolm?"

"I haven't the faintest idea."

"There's something you're not telling me."

"There's lots I don't tell you, David."

"I've got a soft spot when it comes to harlots."

"Don't even think about it." Moldowsky wasn't giving Dilbeck anything. The less he knew, the better. "So what's the punch line? What did the judge say?"

"He doesn't need me, Malcolm. He plays golf with a fucking senator."

Moldowsky cursed dispiritedly.

"—a senator on the Judiciary Committee. The next time there's an opening in our district, the judge has got it locked. He doesn't need us, is what I'm saying."

"So he won't fix the case," Moldowsky said, "even as a favor."

" 'The woman is a tramp and a sinner. She is unfit to raise a child.' Those are his words, Malcolm. Plus he quotes the Bible."

"This is bad news."

"Yes," Dilbeck said. "It was not a productive lunch."

Moldowsky ground his knuckles together in agitation. "Would he go for a bribe? Straight cash?"

"It's against his principles," David Dilbeck said. "But he's amenable to a free blowjob."

A pulse became visible in Moldowsky's neck. "Let's see if I understand: only if the lady goes down on the judge does she get custody of her child—"

"He says he'll consider it. That's all. 'Brownie points' is the way he put it."

"David, I'll say this. You're one terrific negotiator. They needed you at the fucking SALT talks." Moldowsky began to pace and rant. "Who is this jizzbag judge? Bible quotes—from what, the Book of Dick?"

"Hey," the congressman said, "we're talking one lousy blowjob."

Moldowsky cornered David Dilbeck and seized him by the arms. "Killian won't go for it. The mother won't go for it. Hell, Davey, I got no morals whatsoever and *I* wouldn't go for it. It's the worst goddamn thing I ever heard."

The vapors from Moldy's cologne made the congressman's eyes water. "The judge won't take cash, Malcolm. I tried."

"That's a disgrace."

"Not even for his campaign," Dilbeck said. "I offered to funnel it through a PAC but he said no. See, that's the main reason he's angling for a federal gig, so he won't have to run for office anymore. He has a very shitty opinion of politicians."

The plumbing emitted a metallic screech as the shower stopped. Dilbeck turned sharply at the noise. His expression was a familiar glaze of sexual distraction.

"You're hopeless," Moldowsky grumbled.

"What?" Dilbeck licked his lower lip.

"I said you're hopeless. Go check on your friend. I'll let myself out."

"Thanks, Malcolm."

"And stay out of trouble tonight."

"Of course," said the congressman. "Erb will be there."

"Fine," said Moldowsky. Erb Crandall was good, but he was only one man. On some nights Dilbeck needed double-teaming.

As Moldowsky stalked down the hall, the bathroom door flung open and he was enveloped in a cloud of sweet-smelling steam. Eve stood there, sleek and wet and flushed in the cheeks. If Moldowsky was the least bit dazzled, it didn't show. He courteously stepped to the side and motioned for her to pass.

"You've got soap on your ears," he said.

Less than two hours later, Congressman David Lane Dilbeck was a portrait of male contentment and relaxation. He smiled, he blew smoke rings, he tapped his shoes, he hummed to the music. A fresh rum-and-Coke appeared inches from his fingers, further improving his mood. Sitting to his right was Erb Crandall, who was huddled anxiously over an orange juice. Every so often he glanced toward the door in anticipation of a raid. Sitting to the congressman's left, a man named Christopher Rojo folded a fifty-dollar bill into an airplane and sailed it toward the stage, where a woman danced cautiously with a nine-foot Burmese python. The reptile's jaws were secured with Scotch tape, and someone had painted a bottlebrush mustache on its snout. Erb Crandall figured it was some kind of Hitler joke.

"This is so wonderful," said Dilbeck. "Isn't she something, Erb? How about that damn snake!"

"Yeah," Crandall said, "what a life."

The woman, whose stage name was Lorelei, had arranged the python in an intriguing way. The tail followed the crease of her bare buttocks downward through her legs, curling out to the crotch.

"That's a well-trained animal," the congressman observed.

Christopher Rojo was similarly impressed. He was making a new paper airplane with a one-hundred-dollar bill. Rojo was a wealthy young man with few ambitions and plenty of spare time. His family owned a large sugar-cane operation on the southern shore of Lake Okeechobee. Christopher had never been to the farm, but he'd seen photographs. The cane fields looked like a stinking hellhole; he was astounded at the fortune they produced. There was so much money that one couldn't possibly spend it all. Heaven knows he was trying.

"Here, Davey," he said. "Your turn."

Dilbeck took the paper airplane and tossed it toward the python dancer. It landed between her feet. She gave the men a slow wink, and scissored elegantly into a split. Picking up the money, she pretended to show it to the snake. Dilbeck laughed and laughed. Lorelei sprung to her feet, waved once and disappeared offstage. The set was over.

Erb Crandall sagged with relief. Maybe they'd get through the evening without incident.

Rojo said to Dilbeck: "What's your bet?"

The congressman sipped his rum thoughtfully. "Thirty-eight B," he said. "Nature's own."

"And I," said Rojo, waving more cash, "say she's thirty-six inches of plastic fantastic." He smoothed a fifty on the table. David Dilbeck did the same. They turned toward Crandall, who signaled himself out of the wager. They'd been at it all night, every time a new dancer came on stage. There were two parts to the bet: the size of the breasts, and whether or not they were surgically enhanced. Rojo was getting creamed, and Crandall wasn't surprised. The congressman had an unfailing eye for the female form; it was his life's passion, graft being a close second.

Rojo rose drunkenly and called for a man named Ling. Soon a small Oriental in a black tuxedo and a Yankees cap appeared at the table. He didn't look like the co-owner of a strip joint, but he was.

"Mr. Ling!" Rojo said, opening his arms. "Give us the scoop on Python Lady."

"Her name is Lorelei," said Dilbeck. "Have some respect."

Rojo sat down. Dilbeck pointed at the cash. "Mr. Ling, you see what's at stake."

Ling nodded tolerantly. "You want the knocker report?"

"Indeed we do."

"Miss Lorelei is a 38-B."

"Ha!" Dilbeck crowed.

He grabbed for the money but Christopher Rojo caught his arm. "Implants!" the young man hissed. "Tell him, Mr. Ling. Tell him it's implants, and we halve the bet."

"No, sir," Ling said. "Lorelei is all Lorelei."

"Mierda," said Rojo.

The congressman gloated as he scooped up the cash.

Ling said, "Only the best at Flesh Farm. Only the finest."

"Top of the line," agreed Dilbeck.

"Where else you see a snake so big?" Ling bragged. "Snake like that could eat a pony."

"So could Lorelei, I'll bet." Dilbeck chuckled at his own incredible wit. It wasn't a light breezy chuckle, though. It was deep and ominous. Erb Crandall went on full alert.

He said, "Davey, it's getting late."

"Nonsense." The congressman lit a cigarette. "Mr. Ling, I would like to meet the python princess."

"Me, too," said Christopher Rojo.

Ling shrugged. "With or without the snake?"

"Without," Dilbeck said. "Tell her I've got one of my own."

Rojo busted a gut. Erb Crandall shifted uneasily. This wasn't a smart idea, not at all. He said, "Come on, Davey, you've got a speech in the morning."

The congressman postured idiotically. "Four score and seven years ago, our foreskins brought forth a new nation . . ."

Crandall didn't smile. Dilbeck said, "All right, Erb, who the hell is it?"

"Chamber of Commerce."

"Shit." Dilbeck slapped Rojo's shoulder. "Chris, you've never seen such stiffs. The Chamber of Cadavers is more like it."

"Still," said Crandall, "it's for seven-thirty sharp."

"We'll get him there," Rojo promised.

"So," said Ling, mildly impatient, "you want a friction dance or what?"

The congressman spread his arms. "Sounds enchanting, Brother Ling. Go fetch what's-her-face."

"Miss Lorelei?"

"Absolutely."

Crandall edged closer to Dilbeck and spoke sternly into his right ear. Dilbeck shook his head back and forth, keeping the drink to his lips the whole time. "One little frictionating *lambada*," he said with a slurp. "What harm could it do?"

"Yeah," said Rojo. "Let the poor man have some fun."

It was useless to object. Crandall removed all loose bottles and other potential weapons from the table. Then he made a slow pass through the club to see if he recognized anyone. He wasn't worried about the press, because reporters didn't make enough money to hang out in places like the Flesh Farm. Republicans were what Erb Crandall feared—all it took was one, spying from the shadows, and the Hon. David Lane Dilbeck was cooked. The crummy wig and dark glasses only made him more conspicuous; the chauffeur's cap, borrowed from the taciturn Pierre, was at least three sizes too small. To keep it from falling off, Dilbeck had pinned it to his wig; every time the cap moved, the hair moved with it. Not even Christopher Rojo seemed to notice. That was one good thing about Dilbeck's little problem; customers in nudie joints didn't spend much time scrutinizing each other. The dancers got all the attention.

Tonight the club was scarcely half full, and Crandall spotted no one from the wonderful world of politics. When he returned to the table, the congressman's chair was empty. Rojo pointed to the rear of the club, where a row of gilded booths lined one wall. The booths were reserved for friction dancing and other private interludes.

"I slipped him two hundred," Rojo said. "He wanted three but I made it two."

"Two's plenty." Crandall sat down and checked his wristwatch. He'd give it ten minutes.

Rojo said, "I'm tired, man." He reached into his coat and took out a tiny foil packet. "You want some blow?"

Erb Crandall felt exhausted. "That's brilliant, Chris. What a nifty idea. May I?" He unfolded the foil and examined the powder. Rojo smiled encouragingly. Crandall smiled back. Then he hawked up a glob and spit all over Christopher Rojo's dope.

"Jesus!" Rojo cried.

Crandall pushed the foil across the table. "Get rid of it," he said, "on your way out the door."

"You crazy mother!"

"Chris, listen. You're not gone in thirty seconds, I'll tell your old man about this. First thing *mañana.*"

Rojo saw the family trust fund evaporating before his eyes. He hastily wrapped the spit-soaked cocaine in a monogrammed handkerchief. "There," he said to Crandall. "You happy now?"

"I said get lost."

"But what about my turn?"

Crandall didn't understand the whining.

"With the snake lady, Erb. I'm next after Davey!"

"Take a rain check," Crandall told him. He got up to search for the congressman.

Nothing took David Dilbeck's mind off his troubles like friction dancing. The sugar vote, the reelection campaign, the wife, the blackmail—
who cared? He was alone with the python princess. They were swaying
to imaginary Johnny Mathis tunes. The congressman had his hands on
Lorelei's bottom. She was rubbing her delightfully natural protuber-
ances against his middle-aged flab. Her voice sounded sweet and sincere. Her hair smelled like orchids. Dilbeck was getting hard. Life was
good.

When he tried to unsnap Lorelei's top, she blocked the move.

"That's a no-no," she whispered.

"What!"

"It's the law, baby."

"Don't worry about it," he said.

"Look, if you want to slow dance, I can't be naked. That's the law.
I'm naked, you can't touch me anywhere."

Dilbeck had a passing knowledge of the county obscenity ordi-
nances.

Lorelei said, "I'm sorry, baby." She moved her hips against him in
sinuous rhythm. "That's not so bad, is it?" She had him pinned against
the door to the booth.

"I've got an idea," Dilbeck said.

"Yeah?"

"What if you get half naked? Then I can touch the part that's not."

"Nice try," Lorelei said, "but it's all or nothing."

So they continued dancing until Dilbeck felt himself poking her
through his pants. In a low voice, he said, "And what are we going to
do about *him?*"

"Admire it," Lorelei said, "but that's all."

Dilbeck gazed at his groin forlornly.

"Look," she told him, "you could be a cop for all I know."

He whipped off the cap and the hairpiece, and presented his true self
to the python lady. "I'm not a policeman. I'm a United States congressman."

"Yeah, and I'm Gloria Steinem."

Dilbeck sensed from Lorelei's demeanor that the friction dance
would soon be finished.

"How much time do we have?" he asked.

"About forty-five seconds, baby."

David Dilbeck hurriedly unbuttoned his shirt, dropped to the floor and lay on his back. Lorelei studied him guardedly.

"Dance on me," he said.

"How much?"

"Two hundred bucks."

"Heels or bare feet?"

"One of each," said the congressman, shutting his eyes.

Carefully, Lorelei stepped on his chest. "What's that scar?"

"Double bypass," Dilbeck replied with a grunt. "Don't worry, I'm good as new. Now dance, please."

"Jesus," mumbled the python woman.

"Oh yeah. Good girl."

"Let me know if it hurts."

"I'll let you know if it doesn't," said the congressman.

Lorelei had difficulty keeping her balance, as Dilbeck's topography was spongy and uneven.

"You're a wonderful talent," Dilbeck said, groaning pleasurably under the weight. His hands crept spiderlike toward his crotch.

"Oh, no you don't." Lorelei stepped hard on his wrists. "That's not allowed."

"Stop, mommy."

"You wanna play with yourself, go home and do it."

David Dilbeck cried out once. Next came a series of wet suckling noises. Then he began to thrash epileptically beneath the astonished dancer; legs kicking stiffly, mad-dog eyes rolling back and forth.

Lorelei was afraid to take her feet off the man's arms. Inwardly she berated herself for not demanding payment up front; if the jerk croaked, she'd have to go through his pockets.

Dilbeck began to buck as if jolted by a hot wire. To keep from falling, Lorelei braced both arms against the walls of the booth. The door flew open and a stranger took her under the arms. He carried her out and asked if she was hurt. She said she'd left a shoe inside. The man said she probably wouldn't want it back, all things considered. He handed her three hundred dollars.

"Thanks," Lorelei said. "Will he be OK?"

"Don't you worry."

The dancer's hands were shaking as she folded the money. "You know what he told me? He told me he was a congressman."

Erb Crandall laughed. "Some guys," he said, "will try anything." He dug into his pocket for another hundred-dollar bill.

The next day, Malcolm Moldowsky made the call. The meeting was set at a bowling alley on Sunrise Boulevard. "Grab any lane you can," the man said. "It's League Night."

Moldowsky's feet were so small he had to rent women's shoes. He got a nine-pound ball and tried to clean the germy holes with his monogrammed handkerchief. He willed himself to not think about those who had fingered the ball before him.

He bowled alone for an hour until the man showed up. He was as big as a wine keg, and wore a brown UPS shirt. He scanned Moldowsky's scores and said, "Not bad."

"I cheated," Moldy said, tossing a gutter ball. He had knocked down maybe forty pins in all. On the score pad he had given himself a 164.

The man put on his bowling shoes and bowled strike–spare–strike. "You picked a good lane," he said to Moldowsky.

A waitress came by and the man waved her away. Moldowsky handed him a thick brown envelope. "It's all there," he told him. "The tickets, too. Check for yourself."

"Nuh-uh," said the bowler. "I don't care what's inside. I'm just the delivery boy."

He rolled a snapping curve that left the seven-ten combination. "Are you a gambling man?" he asked Moldowsky. "Wait, that's a dumb question. Of course you're a gambling man. Otherwise you wouldn't be involved."

"Good thinking."

"Five bucks says I make this split."

"Sure," said Moldy. "Five it is." His lack of interest would've been obvious to a three-year-old.

The big man made it look easy, nicking the seven-pin just enough to kick across and take out the ten. "That's the toughest split in bowling," he said. "Did you know that?"

"Amazing," said Moldowsky with a yawn. He gave the man five ones. "Ask your people to move as quickly as possible. We're up against a deadline."

"I don't know what the hell you're talking about," the man said, "but I'll be happy to pass it along. Your turn, sport."

Unhappily, Moldowsky positioned himself at the head of the lane. He made three tiny, stiff steps and heaved the ball down the alley. Somehow he got a strike.

"Pure luck," Moldy admitted.

"The best kind," said the man in the UPS shirt. "You go on home now, OK? Everything's under control."

A single piece of rotten news affirmed the leaden sense of futility that had burdened Mordecai every day since his graduation from law school, 207th in a class of 212.

The setback was especially cruel, coming at a rare moment of optimism. A lawyer from the Delicato Dairy Company had arrived at Mordecai's office to discuss a possible settlement in the case of the roach-tainted blueberry yogurt. For Mordecai, the company's willingness to negotiate (without the customary exchange of nasty correspondence) was a glorious surprise. An out-of-court agreement would have spared him long hours of excruciating preparation for a trial; it would also have saved him from exposing a jury to the sight of his client, Shad the bouncer.

The informality of the meeting had sent Mordecai's hopes soaring. The attorney from the Delicato Dairy Company had been civil, sensible and not given to bluster. He was keenly aware of the public-relations consequences of a high-profile insect trial. The central concern was television: in Florida, TV cameras are allowed in court. The two men agreed that color videotape of a cockroach being plucked from a Delicato container could have a negative impact on consumer confidence. The extent of damage, sales-wise, would depend on how many major markets picked up the satellite feed from the courtroom. The attorney's eagerness to avoid such a risk was obvious by the size of his initial offer—a settlement in "the mid-six figures." Mordecai struggled to mask his elation.

Of course, the Delicato attorney requested to see Shad's roach. Just a formality, he assured Mordecai. The attorney had brought a 35 millimeter camera to document the contamination. Photographs would be important, he explained, should his clients challenge the wisdom of settling. A brief slide show in the boardroom would turn them around.

Mordecai was impressed by the attorney's thoroughness. He could see how product liability might be an attractive field of practice, if one could avoid the courthouse.

He wished Beverly were there to share the triumph, but she was out with one of her three-day migraines. Mordecai was using a temp named Rachel, whose unflagging bubbliness compensated for her lack of shorthand skills and slothful pace at the typewriter. Mordecai called Rachel into his office and told her to fetch the blueberry yogurt from the refrigerator. The smile left her face instantly, and Mordecai knew.

"I'll get some more," she said quickly, "on my lunch hour."

Mordecai found no words to express his dismay. The Delicato attorney politely excused himself to use the telephone in the other room.

"Oh Rachel," said Mordecai, abjectly.

"I'll buy the variety pack. Eight kinds of tropical fruit."

"Rachel!"

"Yes, sir?"

"What possessed you?"

"I was hungry."

"Did you not notice that the carton was open?"

"I thought it was Bev's. I didn't want it to sit there and go sour."

"Rachel," said Mordecai. "You don't understand."

"I'm very, very sorry." She began to weep.

"Shut up," Mordecai said. "Shut up this instant." When he thought of Shad, the flesh on his neck got damp. How would he tell him? What bloody havoc would ensue? Mordecai also mourned his own financial loss: forty percent of zero was zero. His vast stomach pitched.

"I didn't know it was yours," Rachel slobbered. "I didn't know you liked yogurt."

"I hate yogurt. It gives me the runs."

The secretary's remorse clouded with confusion. "Then why are you so upset?"

"Because you swallowed my evidence." Mordecai spoke in an odd singsong voice. "So how was it, Rachel?"

"The yogurt?"

"Yes, the yogurt. A little chunky, perhaps?"

"Now that you mention it." She sounded worried. "Are you going to fire me?"

"Oh, worse than that," said Mordecai. "Please sit down."

"What are you going to do?"

"Something that will give me great pleasure. I'm going to tell you exactly what you ate."

Visitation day.

Erin waited under cloudy skies at Holiday Park. She chose a bench near the public tennis courts where Chris Evert had learned to play. Today it was a doubles match among French Canadian tourists. They had the whitest skin and the bluest veins that Erin had ever seen.

Darrell Grant always kept Erin waiting because it gave him a feeling of power, knowing how she lived for these afternoons. Today he arrived forty-five minutes late, pushing Angela in a wheelchair.

"Momma, look what we got at the hospital!"

Erin lifted her daughter to the sidewalk and told Darrell Grant to get lost.

"How's your butt-ugly boyfriend?" he said.

"Momma's got a boyfriend?" asked Angela.

"No, baby, I don't."

Erin was furious that Darrell was using Angie in his wheelchair heists. If he were caught, the consequences would be terrible—the state authorities would take the little girl for good. Erin felt perfectly entitled to scream at Darrell and tell him what a reckless idiot he was, but she didn't want to spoil her brief time with Angela.

Darrell Grant said, "I see you got new tires."

Erin ignored him. She checked her daughter's dress and socks and underpants, to make sure they were clean. For a sociopath, Darrell was good about doing the laundry.

"Take care of my pretty little partner," he said, and pushed the empty wheelchair back to his van, where he waited. On visitation days, he never let Erin and Angela out of his sight. Given an opportunity, Erin surely would try to run away with the girl. Darrell knew it for a fact.

Erin held her daughter's hand and they began to walk.

"How are you, baby?"

"Just OK."

"Are you making new friends?"

"I spent Friday at Aunt Rita's. She's got a real wolf!"

Terrific, thought Erin. Crazy Rita and her cuddly carnivores. "Stay away from the wolf, Angela. They can be mean sometimes."

"She said I can have one of the babies, Momma."

"No, we'll get you a real puppy—"

"But Daddy said no. He said maybe a bird."

"A bird?" Erin said. Just what every four-year-old wants.

"A talking one," Angie said. "Like Big Bird, only littler."

"Would you like that?"

"He said we can call it Humpy. Is that a good name?"

"No," said Erin. "Not really."

They walked the perimeter of the park. Darrell Grant followed slowly in his van. Erin fixed a picnic under the trees. She and Angela ate peanut butter sandwiches and sang songs from "The Electric Company." A gray squirrel appeared and they fed it Cheese Doodles.

At ten minutes to three, Darrell began honking the horn. When Erin didn't react, he leaned on it annoyingly. The blare drowned the gentle sounds of the park. The Canadians stopped playing tennis and began cursing at Darrell Grant in French.

"For God's sake," said Erin.

"Is Daddy making that noise?"

"I'm afraid so." Erin gave her daughter a hug and a kiss. She smelled Darrell's goddamn cigarettes in the girl's hair.

"Momma, I forgot to tell you."

"What, honey?"

"I lost all my dolls."

"I'm so sorry."

"When we moved. Daddy said he couldn't find them."

"I'll get you some new ones," Erin promised. She would never reveal to Angela what her father had done. Such a thing could not be explained.

"I love you, Angie."

"Love you, too, Momma. Can I tell Daddy about the new dolls?"

"Let's keep it a surprise."

.   .   .

From Agent Cleary, Erin had learned the following basic information about Jerry Killian: he was five-foot-nine, 140 pounds, 48 years old and divorced. He worked as a videotape editor at the local CBS affiliate. He was a registered Democrat. He drove a 1988 Chevrolet Caprice. He purchased his eyeglasses from a discount optician. He subscribed to *Newsweek, Harper's, The New Yorker, Rolling Stone, Consumer Reports* and *Hustler.* His ex-wife recently opened a macramé shop in a suburb of Atlanta, and he co-signed the loan. They had two daughters at Georgia State University. He owned season tickets to the Miami Dolphins. He rented every movie that Debra Winger ever made. He carried a $3,000 credit limit on his Visa card. In the fall he went trout fishing in western Montana, and always rented a compact car. In his entire life he had never been arrested for anything.

And he lived in Apartment 317 at 4566 Green Duck Parkway, Fort Lauderdale, Florida.

Erin phoned ahead. Killian was flabbergasted to hear her voice. He put on a coat and a tie to meet her at the door.

"In my purse," said Erin, "is a loaded gun."

"So be it."

"I'm here on business only."

"Understood," Killian said.

She had expected his apartment to be tidy, and it was. The place smelled of Lemon Pledge. They sat in opposing chairs at an oval-shaped dining table.

"I just wanted to thank you," she said. "That music you suggested is great for stage dancing."

Killian glowed. "You tried it? I'm so pleased."

"You should come by the club to see. I told Shad it's fine if you do."

"Really?" He looked wistful. "Maybe later down the road."

"Why later? Why not now?"

"The deal is cooking. Part of the agreement is for me to steer clear of the Eager Beaver." Killian paused. "It's the hardest thing I've ever done. I miss you so much."

Here we go, Erin thought. Get the hose.

She said, "May I call you Jerry?"

"I'd be in heaven if you did—"

"Jerry, look. I need to know more about this so-called deal. It's my life we're talking about. My little girl."

"Naturally you don't trust me."

"I don't *know* you."

"Erin," he said, "I would do nothing to put you or your daughter in jeopardy. My devotion is complete and enduring and pure. I am consumed by it, day and night. I am lost in love."

Erin's heart didn't flutter even slightly. She said, "Jerry, who is this congressman?"

"His district is elsewhere. You wouldn't know his name."

"Try me. I read the newspapers."

"The name is unimportant," Killian said. "The key fact is, he's got a serious problem with the ladies. I'd feel uncomfortable going into details."

"Oh please."

"I'm a gentleman. That's how I was raised."

"And I'm a stripper, Jerry. Once I had a customer eat the G-string off the crack of my ass—chew it up, swallow it, wash it down with Southern Comfort. Then he burped the elastic."

Killian's ears turned red.

"The point is," Erin said, "nothing a man does can shock me. I have an ex-husband who carves his initials into other people's scalps. Is your congressman that much fun?"

"I'm not protecting him," Jerry Killian said. "I'm protecting you."

"In case there's trouble?"

Killian got up and said, "Come with me."

Erin followed him through the apartment. The purse was tucked tightly under her left arm, so she could feel the gun through the fabric. Killian opened the door to a small guest bedroom, which he had converted to a private hall of fame. The walls were decorated with publicity pictures of local nude dancers. Interestingly, the photographs were all standard head-and-shoulder shots; one could have shown them to a kindergarten without fear of corruption. Erin's publicity photo was framed in wood and centered prominently in the pantheon. It was illuminated by its own brass lamp.

Scanning his collection, Killian said, "Nothing is more beautiful than a woman's smile."

"Oh really," said Erin. "That's why you come to the Eager Beaver—for our smiles?"

"It's the portal to true love and serenity. Without a smile, what's the rest of it? Just boobs and a patch of hair."

"Jerry?"

"Yes."

"You're giving me the creeps."

"Well, Erin, I'm lost. I admit it."

"You know all these girls?"

"I knew them. Befriended them. And whenever I could, I helped them." He pointed to a platinum blonde with a sharp nose and spiky greased eyelashes. "Allison had a substance problem. I got her into a very fine program, and today she's clean."

Erin asked if she was still dancing.

"No, she's not." Killian stepped close to the photograph, contemplating each detail as if it were a Monet. "A week after she got out of treatment, she married a tree surgeon and moved to Tallahassee. I never even got a postcard." He turned to Erin and brightened. "But that's all right! I ask for nothing."

"Except a smile."

"When it's from the heart."

Erin turned off the light and directed Killian back to the living room. She sat beside him on a deacon's bench, and spoke to him as if he were a small boy.

"This is not a game," she said.

"I heard they call me Mr. Peepers."

"We all like you, Jerry. It's an affectionate nickname."

"I do have a frail and bookish appearance."

"Scholarly is the way I'd describe it."

"Don't be fooled, Erin. I can play hardball."

She took both his hands—a standard move, to keep them from wandering. "Exactly what've you got on the congressman?"

Killian said he couldn't tell her. He pulled one hand free and made a zipping motion across his lips.

"It must be good," Erin coaxed, "to make him lean on a judge."

"I can't discuss it," Killian repeated. "It's man's work."

Erin sighed and relaxed her grip. "Here's my problem, Jerry. Do I believe your story? Do I get my hopes up for nothing? The whole thing with Angie and Darrell has been a nightmare."

"I understand," he said. "I read through the files at the courthouse. That's how I got the judge's name."

"If I knew more, maybe I could help set this up."

"It's set up just fine," said Killian.

He wouldn't budge. Usually a soft hand-holding would do the trick, but not this time. Erin rose and said, "All right, Jerry. How long will it take?"

"I'm expecting a phone call this afternoon."

"Congressmen work on Sundays?"

"They do when their careers are at stake."

Erin stood at the door, searching for a humane way to say what had to be said. "If this works out, if I get Angela back . . . well, I can't give you anything, Jerry. You should know that."

"By anything, you mean—"

"You know what I mean," Erin said. "I'll be eternally grateful for your kindness. That's the most I can promise."

"Do I look crushed?"

"Slightly."

"Well, who wouldn't be?" He chuckled softly. "I bet you'll quit the club, too."

"Absolutely. Once I get Angie back, I'm gone."

"Then there's one thing you can do for me." He went to the stereo and picked through a stack of CDs. "Just a second," he called to Erin. "Please!"

Soon the apartment filled with heavy rock—"She's Got Legs," by ZZ Top. Erin gave Killian a look of mock disapproval.

"Let me guess," she said.

"Do you mind?"

"Just one dance," Erin said. Urbana would've wrung her neck.

The first time she went on stage at the club, Erin vomited before and after the performance. Urbana Sprawl took her aside: "It's like wing-walking, OK? You're fine, long as you don't look down." Monique Jr. hugged her and whispered: "It's a slumber party, hon. That's how come we're in our nighties." And Monique Sr. said: "Quit crying, for God's sake. Bobby Knight is at table nine!"

It had taken Erin a week to find a method that worked. Whenever she froze and found herself asking why—why am I doing this!—she thought of Angie. Once on stage, the trick was to dream herself away with the music. That's why she was so picky about the selections: the songs had to mean something. If things felt right, the awful anxiety would melt away and Erin would become wondrously detached from the surroundings. She'd forget she was jumping around in her birthday suit before a roomful of drunks. In Erin's fantasy, the men in the audience were cheering the high kicks and fluid turns, and not the shape of her ass.

Smiling was a struggle at first, because Erin wasn't particularly ecstatic about the work. Morever, she'd noticed that many of the customers didn't smile, either. Instead they watched with studious and impassive expressions, like judges at a cattle auction. Again, Urbana had offered valuable counsel: "A nice smile beats forty-inch jugs any day!"

So Erin made herself smile, and the money got better. The men came forward and folded ten-dollar bills into her garters or the elastic of her G-string. Many customers were nervous about standing so close, and plainly terrified of touching a foreign thigh. Erin was constantly reminded of the ridiculous power of sex; routine female nakedness reduced some men to stammering, clammy-fingered fools. For the bolder clientele, Shad's spooky presence discouraged groping and crude solicitation.

Erin had conquered her shyness in about a month. Unlike some of the dancers, she would never be totally comfortable on stage. There was a small thrill to the tease, but no hot rush from the cheers and whistles of strangers. By contrast, the two Moniques loved the boisterous attention, because it made them feel like glamorous stars. The wilder the audience, the wilder their performance. Erin didn't play to the crowd. The music was her master, and also her escape. When Van Morrison sang, Erin *was* dancing in the moonlight.

But that was in the club, not in a customer's apartment.

Still, she wasn't afraid. Mr. Peepers obviously was helpless in her presence; he would have inserted his tongue in a light socket if she'd told him to. Erin further neutralized the man by asking about the sepia portrait of a curly-haired woman, gazing up at them from the credenza. It was, as Erin had surmised, Jerry's dear departed mother. Erin felt safer under the late Mrs. Killian's watchful eye.

Killian cleared the oval table and helped Erin climb up. She handed him her sandals and her purse. By then Killian had already forgotten about the gun, the congressman, the blackmail, what day it was . . .

The wood was slick and cool under Erin's feet. She danced for four minutes and never even removed her sweater. Killian was dazzled. "Splendid," he said over and over, to himself.

As the song ended, he tucked something into the back pocket of Erin's jeans. It wasn't a tip.

At the door she gave him a sisterly peck on the cheek. Killian jumped at the moment of contact. He said, "If I have good news, you'll see me outside the club."

"Be careful," said Erin, although she wasn't seriously concerned. The worst that could happen was that the congressman would tell Killian to blow off.

He waved fondly from the doorstep as Erin walked to her car. She waved back and gave him one of her best smiles. She had decided that he was basically a good person.

When Erin got home, she took the note from her pocket and unfolded it on the kitchen counter. It said:

Thank you for saving my soul.

That night, Erin worked a double shift at the Eager Beaver in the hopes that Jerry Killian would show up. He didn't. The following morning, she phoned his apartment and got no answer. When she tried the TV station, the news director told her that Mr. Killian had gone on vacation. He was expected back in two weeks.

At the club, Erin switched back to her familiar dancing routines—Clapton, Creedence Clearwater, the Allman Brothers. Soon she got lost in the blues guitar, and the world seemed like a better place, even though it wasn't.

She never saw Jerry Killian again.

9

On the evening of September sixteenth, at a tavern called the Lozeau Lounge in western Montana, the Skyler brothers drank six beers apiece, threw darts at a stuffed elk and argued over the cosmic meaning of a Randy Travis song.

Then they headed for home, which was a valley in the Bitterroot Mountains. Johnny Skyler drove because brother Faron's license had been suspended four times and revoked twice permanently. That was no small achievement in the great and free state of Montana, where driving and drinking are regarded as inalienable rights.

Johnny Skyler followed the dirt road toward the Clark Fork River and the one-lane steel bridge that would carry them to their respective wives and children, waiting in identical doublewide trailers that had been purchased for twenty percent off at a spring trade show in Spokane. The money that the Skyler brothers saved on the mobile homes had been put to good use: a large satellite dish was wired to the earth on a flat clearing between the two doublewides. A parabolic eyesore among the regal vectors of Douglas firs and Ponderosa pines, the TV dish was still the finest investment that Johnny and Faron had ever made: Wrestlemania! Japanese game shows! One night, flipping channels, they'd stumbled onto a guy talking with real Playboy bunnies! The interviewer was so tan that the Skylers speculated he might be an Indian, except he talked too fast and laughed too loud. Around the man's neck hung a gold medallion as thick as a goose turd. Johnny and Faron couldn't get over it.

No doubt about it: satellite TV preserved the Skyler family units. In the long bleak stretch of winter, it was all that kept the men from going mad with boredom. In the summer, it entertained the wives and kids so that Faron and Johnny could stay out extra late: crack open another

Rolling Rock, kick back, watch the sun drop down over the mountain-tops.

On this night, though, a storm was rolling in hard from Idaho. There would be no sunset, just an ominous and sudden darkening. Bruised clouds stacked up over the Bitterroots, and a cool wind chased down the river. It rattled the tin price sign that hung over the gas pump outside the Lozeau Lounge. Inside, Johnny Skyler reared back and heaved one more dart at the taxidermied elk, yanked his brother off the bar stool and said they'd better get on home, while they could still see the way.

The dirt road fed straight downhill to the old steel span across the river. Fat raindrops began to slap against the Bronco, dimpling the chalky brown dust on the tinted windshield. Mindful of the strong wind, Johnny Skyler took it slowly. First gear. High beams. Both hands on the wheel. Approaching the bridge, he was careful to line up the truck's wheels on the twin wooden planks, already slickened by the drizzle.

Halfway across, Faron Skyler said, "Hold up."

His brother braked the truck to a stop, idling.

"Out there," Faron said.

"On the river?"

"Yeah. I seen a raft."

"No way," said Johnny Skyler. He lowered the window. It was too dark to see anything on the Clark Fork.

His brother said, "Wait for the lightning."

Up the valley it came, an ultraviolet burst that illuminated the river for a fraction of a second. In that blink of a moment, Johnny Skyler spotted the raft, twenty yards downstream from the bridge.

"There—against the gravel bar," Faron said.

"Yeah, I saw it."

"Did you see the guy?"

"No." Johnny dimmed the headlights and squinted into the thickening night. The rain was coming down pretty good, soaking the sleeve of his left arm. Johnny spit hard, and the wind hurled it back in his face.

Another rip of lightning, high and far away. A purple strobe brightened the valley, then it was dark again. But the scene was stamped in Johnny's eyes: a red raft, oars askew, gliding sideways along a narrow gravel spit that briefly split the river in two. The man in the raft had his back to the bridge. He wore an olive vest and an updowner-style cap, either of which marked him definitively as an out-of-towner. His arms were straight at his sides. A fishing rod lay across his lap.

"Crazy bastard," said Faron Skyler.

"Think he needs help?"

"Hell, yes, he needs help. He needs his damn head examined. Crazy bastard trout fiend."

Johnny wasn't sure what to do next, wasn't sure what could be done. As the sizzling electrified maw of the storm boiled down on them, a steel bridge seemed not such a smart place to be. Thunder had begun to shake the struts.

"He better get off the water," Johnny Skyler remarked, staring at the place where the rafter had last appeared in a blast of light. Johnny briefly considered the logistics of a rescue, then pushed the notion out of his head. Here the banks of the Clark Fork were rocky and steep, and of course the Skyler brothers were full of beer. Disaster was the word that came to Johnny's mind.

He cupped his hands to his mouth and shouted against the wind: "Hey out there!"

Faron said, "Forget it, man. He can't hear you."

Johnny tried again: "Hey you!"

Another flash, another glimpse of the raft, slipping farther downstream. The fisherman appeared not to have heard the shouts. The rod still lay across the man's lap; the oar handles remained unattended—one pointing upriver and the other pointing the opposite way.

"There's one crazy bastard," Faron reiterated.

"Somethin' ain't right."

Lightning exploded nearby, and the brothers covered their heads. They heard the crash of a lodgepole pine, breaking in three pieces.

"Time to go," Faron said. "Would you agree?"

Johnny Skyler had a bad feeling in his gut. He gazed down the Clark Fork, waiting for more lightning, for one more look at the lunatic trout fiend.

"He'll be all right, Johnny. The river slicks out for the next mile. A blind dog could make it to shore."

"I suppose." Johnny had never seen a raft on this leg of the Clark Fork so late in the evening. The next takeout was twelve miles downriver. And who the hell goes fishing at night in a thunderstorm?

"Would you please fucking step on it?" Faron Skyler was saying. "I don't feel like gettin' barbecued up here on this damn bridge. Besides, we're missing the ballgame."

Ever since Denver had gotten a major-league franchise, Faron had become a baseball fanatic. His brother could take it or leave it. Football was something else. With the dish they could even pull in the Argonauts.

"It's nine-thirty," Johnny Skyler noted. "Game's almost over."

"Well, shit."

"Faron, I can't see him no more."

"Maybe he turned the big bend."

"Not without rowing he didn't. Not unless he's got an Evinrude on that raft."

Faron said, "All he's got to do is hang on, he'll be okay. Now let's go."

"Just a minute." The rain came down in sheets, thrumming on the roof of the Bronco. Johnny finally rolled up the window but he didn't take his eyes off the water.

Sky crackled and the river became a pink mirror. This time the brothers had no difficulty spotting the small red raft, turning in the slow current as it floated downstream.

"Oh my Lord," Johnny Skyler said.

Faron grabbed the dashboard with both hands. "Crazy goddamn bastard," he said.

The raft was empty. The man was gone.

The Skylers hopped from the truck and ran for the river.

The rain stopped two hours later. By then the Mineral County Sheriff's Office had arrived with a motorboat and a bona fide scuba diver. The U.S. Forestry Service had promised to send four rangers and a helicopter, providing the weather didn't act up again. A few residents turned out with rafts, rowboats and waterproof flashlights. The small riverside campground at Forest Grove served as headquarters for the search, which by local standards was heroic and exhaustive.

By dawn, the raft had been found, wedged sideways under a piling of the I-90 bridge, due west of Lozeau. The oars had been lost, and the raft contained no clues to the identity of the missing angler. An empty can of Colt 45 and a crumpled Snickers wrapper were the only evidence of a human passenger.

The search for the body lasted eighteen hours, and proved fruitless. A reporter from the *Missoulian* arrived at Forest Grove and interviewed the Skyler brothers, who gave a richly embroidered account of what they'd seen on the river during the thunderstorm. Then they posed for pictures next to the Forestry Service helicopter. For the next several days the brothers faithfully watched C-Span on the satellite dish, but saw no mention of the Clark Fork rescue effort or their role in it. Fame embraced the Skylers in more modest ways: it was years before they had to pay for their own beers at the Lozeau Lounge.

The children of Al García's second wife called him Al, and that was fine. "Dad" was out of the question. The kids already had a dad, who was in prison because of Al García.

That was how García had met his second wife—while arresting her husband for a drug murder. There were no hard feelings. Six months after the trial, she filed for divorce and married Al.

From hash dealer to homicide detective, García had told her, you're moving up in the world. Not by much, Donna had said. Quick on the draw, that was Donna. The children were all right, too: a boy and a girl, ages eight and nine, or nine and ten—García had trouble remembering. Overall he was very fond of the kids, and didn't feel the least bit guilty about the circumstances.

The first time the boy asked when his real dad was getting out of jail, Al García took the small hand and said: "Never, Andy." When the boy asked why, García said: "Because your daddy shot a man between the eyes." Andy appreciated the seriousness of the situation. His sister, Lynne, who was either a year older or a year younger, said maybe her dad had a good reason for shooting the other guy. A hundred thousand reasons, Al García had said, but none good enough. Just then Donna had come storming in from the kitchen and ordered them all to hush up, or else.

When it came time for their first family vacation, Donna chose western Montana because she and the kids had never seen mountains. It sounded fine to Al García. He made a few calls and found out that Montana, for all its Wild West lore, was a safe and tranquil place; there were traffic intersections in Dade County with higher murder rates.

Donna arranged to rent a small log house on the Clark Fork River, about sixty miles outside of Missoula. García was no outdoorsman, but a cabin on the water seemed like a splendid idea. He promised Andy and Lynne he would help them catch a big rainbow trout and they could fry it up for supper. He promised Donna he wouldn't talk about his job and wouldn't call Miami, not even once, to check on his open cases.

In fourteen years as a homicide detective, Sgt. Al García had personally investigated 1,092 murders. It was his curse to remember every one; the oddest details, too. "Rescue 911" playing on the television while they chalked the body. The counterfeit Rolex worn by the victim. The smell of burned biscuits in the kitchen. A photograph in the hall, the dead man whooping it up at Disney World. Al García hated the unfailing thoroughness of his memory; it made him an excellent detective but a deeply troubled person.

Montana turned out to be better than he had expected; wide-open and friendly, with a few exceptions. A desk clerk at the motel in Missoula shot him a hard look when she saw the name on the credit card. Being a García from Miami wasn't easy these days. Some people automatically assumed you had six kilos in the trunk and a loaded Uzi under the front seat.

The next day, when they got to the log house on the river, Al García nearly forgot where he'd come from and what he did for a living. Standing on the wooden deck, he thought the river valley was the most peaceful place he'd ever seen. He drank the piney air, closed his eyes and easily lost himself in the silence of the surrounding woods. The first day, Andy spotted two deer. The second night, Lynne found a small bleached skull from a dead skunk; she wanted to take it home to Florida, but Donna said no, give it a decent burial in the garden.

On the third day, Andy came running up the bank so fast that García thought a bear was chasing him. The boy was shouting: "Al, you better come! You better come fast!"

García told him to slow down, take a breather. Andy grabbed his arm and tugged hard. "Come on. Down to the river."

"What is it, son?"

"A floater!" Andy exclaimed.

García felt a sour knotting in his gut. Living with a homicide cop had given Donna's youngsters a gruesome vocabulary. They knew all about trunk jobs, John Does, Juan Does, gunshots, accidentals and naturals.

And floaters, of course.

García followed the boy down the hill to the river's edge. The detective waded into the water, skating his tennis shoes across the gravel bottom. The body floated face-up, tangled in a shallow brushpile. The face was violet and bloated, the eyes springing out in a cartoonish way.

"Is he dead, Al?" Andy stood on the bank; he folded his small arms across his chest, looking very serious. "He's dead, isn't he?"

"Extremely," García said.

"I told you!"

The dead man wore heavy rubber trousers and an olive vest with many small pockets. García unzipped the one over the left breast, and removed a wallet. The wallet held three one-hundred dollar bills, a half dozen traveler's checks and a laminated driver's license with familiar colors.

García said, "Goddammit to hell."

The boy shouted, "Who is he, Al?"

"Go tell your mother to call the police."

The boy ran off. The dead man's face stared up googly-eyed from the hissing river.

"You're a prick," Al García said to the corpse. "You're a prick for spoiling my vacation."

He looked again at the dead man's license and cursed acidly. The sonofabitch was from Fort Lauderdale, Florida.

Why? García wondered. Why won't they let me be?

Shad was intrigued by the psychiatrist's eyebrows, lush and multi-hued.

"Those real?" he asked.

"Please," said the doctor, recoiling. "No touching."

It was Shad's first visit to a shrink—Mordecai's man. His name was Vibbs, Palm Beach sharpie and plaintiff's best friend. A laminated diploma from Yale University hung on one wall. Shad was more interested in a jar of hard candy on the doctor's desk. He filled his cheeks and began to chew.

"Tell me about the roach," Dr. Vibbs said.

"Big fucker." The words crackled out of Shad's mouth.

"Did it upset you?"

Shad's laugh exposed a wet maw of peppermints and butterscotch. "Upset? Hell, I'm traumatized. Write that down."

Dr. Vibbs was rattled by Shad's hairless, hulking presence. Most of Mordecai's referrals had nothing wrong with them; this one was different. When the hairless man bent to pick up a candy wrapper, the psychiatrist noticed a "G" carved into his scalp. He assumed that Shad had done it to himself.

Vibbs probed with caution. "I need to ask some personal questions—it's standard for these evaluations."

"Evaluate away," said Shad. "I told you I was fucking traumatized. What more do you want?"

"Are you having bad dreams?"

"Nope."

"Not even about the roach? Try to remember."

"Ah," Shad said. He was catching on. "Now that you mention it, I been havin' fearsome nightmares."

"That's understandable," said the psychiatrist, scribbling up a storm. "Tell me about them."

"I get chased down Sunrise Boulevard by a giant cockroach with yogurt dripping from its eyeball sockets."

"I see," the psychiatrist said. He scarcely glanced up from his notes. Shad took this as a signal to try harder.

"Yeah, so this monster roach is chasin' me back and forth, drooling and growling like a thousand tigers. The fucker's as big as a tanker truck. Plus it's got a dead baby in its teeth."

"I see."

"And when it gets real close . . . it turns into my mom!"

"Good," said Dr. Vibbs, without emotion. "So tell me more about your mother."

"Eh?"

"Please. I'm interested in your relationship with your mother."

"You are?" An odd light flickered in Shad's eyes. He dragged Dr. Vibbs out of the chair and put him face down on the floor. Then he took a handsome pair of wood-handled scissors and sliced the psychiatrist's clothing from neck to buttocks. On the desk Shad found a rotating tray of rubber stamps. He selected a red one that said NO INSURANCE, and stamped it all over Dr. Vibbs's naked torso. It was quite some time before Shad ran out of ink. Meanwhile, sad puppy noises rose from the doctor's throat.

"What a phony," Shad complained. He tossed the stamp on the desk and grabbed a handful of hard candies, for the road.

"You're disturbed!" Vibbs cried.

"I ain't disturbed. The word is fucking traumatized. You should've wrote it down."

"Go away," said Vibbs.

Shad stood over him. "Not until you spell it."

"What?"

"Come on, wigpicker. *Trau-ma-tized.* I'll even spot you the goddamn T."

In a shaky but defiant voice, the psychiatrist spelled the word perfectly.

"Proud of you," Shad said, stepping across him. "And forget that business about my mom. I don't know what got into me."

To quell employee unrest at the Eager Beaver, it was Orly's custom to pound on the desk and invoke the Mafia. He would brag of lifelong bonds with Angelo Bruno, Nicky Scarfo, Fat Tony Salerno and other famous gangsters whose names he'd clipped from crime magazines. He would talk of blood oaths, and the certain death awaiting those who violated them. Orly's performance usually had the desired effect of stanching demands for pay raises, health benefits or the slightest improvement in work conditions at the club. In truth, he had no connections whatsoever to organized crime. The mob wasn't interested in the Eager Beaver because strip joints got too much heat from police. Orly heard this first-hand from the only genuine Mafioso he'd ever met, a loan shark on trial for breaking the thumbs of a delinquent Chrysler salesman. Orly had gone to court as personal research, to learn how the mob actually operated. During a recess he approached the loan shark and struck up a friendly conversation. When Orly asked if the loan shark knew anyone in the market for a nude dance club, the man frowned and said no fucking way, there's too much heat. Now video arcades, the mob guy said, that's a whole other deal. A video arcade would be very attractive, investment-wise. Orly was disappointed, but out of politeness he hung around to hear the verdict. Not guilty, it turned out. The jurors (among them, several recent purchasers of Chrysler products) were visibly unmoved by the victim's tale of woe. Orly noticed a few of them smiling as the salesman described his hands being placed in the doorjamb of a steel-blue New Yorker sedan. All that muscle over a six-hundred-dollar debt! Orly was impressed. He clung to his dream that someday the Mafia would make him a partner.

For now, though, the illusion would have to suffice. Orly faced a roomful of disgruntled dancers. As usual, Erin spoke for the group.

"Item Number One," she began. "The air conditioning."

Orly scowled. "So what about it?"

"It's way too cold," said Erin.

Urbana Sprawl spoke up. "Thermostat's on sixty-eight degrees. That's awful cool."

Orly turned to Shad, who stood expressionless in a corner. "You chilly?"

"No," said Shad, "but I don't feel much in the way of hot and cold."

"Well," Orly said, "I'm quite comfy at sixty-eight."

Because you're a reptile, Erin thought. She said, "You're wearing a cardigan, Mr. Orly. We, on the other hand, are freezing our bare butts."

Orly rubbed his palms together. "The cold makes you look sexier. Makes those nipples good and hard. Customers go for that, am I right?"

The room got tense. Erin said to Orly, "Congratulations. You've hit a new low."

"Watch it," he warned. "You just watch how you talk."

Monique Jr., normally timid, said: "I don't believe it—that's why you made it so cold? So we'd get hard?"

"Nipples," Orly declared, "are a mighty important part of this enterprise."

In the corner, Shad muffled a laugh.

Erin said, "Turn up the thermostat, or we don't dance."

"I'll pretend I didn't hear that," said Orly.

Erin picked up a ballpoint pen and wrote on the blotter: 72 DEGREES OR NO DANCING!

Orly said, "I'll pretend I didn't see that." He was waiting for Erin to back down. So were the other dancers. Orly adopted a menacing tone: "Insubordination can be dangerous, young lady. Remember what happened to poor Gonzalo."

Poor Gonzalo was the Eager Beaver's previous owner, whose bullet-riddled corpse had been dumped on the interstate—punishment, Orly claimed, for filching from the coin boxes on the Foosball machines.

"Bottom line is, Fat Tony likes things to run smooth," Orly said.

Erin suspected that Fat Tony and the Mafia had nothing to do with Gonzalo's death. More likely, it was a dispute between Gonzalo and one of his many PCP suppliers.

"Tell you what," said Erin. "Why don't you ask Fat Tony to stop by the club tonight?"

Orly was dumbstruck. He rocked precariously in his roost.

"I want him to strip down," Erin said. "See if he doesn't freeze his saggy old Mafia tits."

The other dancers murmured in amazement. What had gotten into this girl?

"Well?" Erin said. "Give the man a call."

Orly looked whipped. "You're on very thin ice," he said weakly.

Erin smiled. "I bet it's warm and cozy down at the Flesh Farm."

"Oh Christ," said Orly. "Don't even think about it."

She turned to the other dancers. "Show of hands?" One by one, the women joined up.

"No!" cried Orly. "You stay away from those fucking Lings!"

"Then turn up the damn thermostat," said Urbana Sprawl, freshly emboldened. "Fat Tony don't want his dancers out sick with a chest cold."

The two Moniques began to giggle. Shad turned toward the imitation red velvet wall, to hide his grin. He knew there was no Fat Tony and no mob connection. The principal investors in the Eager Beaver were a group of relatively harmless orthopedic surgeons from Lowell, Massachusetts.

A reluctant Orly said he'd raise the temperature in the main lounge to seventy degrees. Erin held out for seventy-one.

"All right," Orly agreed, "but I want to see some rock-hard cherries. I mean it!"

Erin proceeded with Item Two on the agenda. "We've been kicking around some ideas for a new name."

"Forget it," Orly sniffed. "I already said no."

"Something classy."

"You want classy? Teach these fucking bimbos how to dance. *Then* maybe we'll talk about a classy name. For now, the Eager Beaver is perfect."

"Candy Rockers," Erin said. "Sexy but not crude. What do you think?"

"I think," Orly said, "that I give these girls a video from only the hottest joint in Dallas, right? All they gotta do is pop it in the VCR and watch the motherfucking tape. I mean, a chimpanzee could pick up some a these steps—"

"It takes time," said Erin.

"Like hell." Orly pointed at Sabrina, who was absorbed in polishing her toenails. "You watch that tape?"

Sabrina bowed her head and said no.

"Case closed." Orly slammed his hand on the arm of the chair. "Case closed. We'll switch to a classy name when I see some classy dancing."

Urbana Sprawl waved. "Mr. Orly, I looked at that video. I believe those Dallas girls were high on crank."

"Oh, is *that* it?" Orly laid on the sarcasm.

"Candy Rockers," Erin said again. "Think about it, OK?"

Someone knocked quietly on the door. Orly motioned to Shad, who went to the back of the office and positioned himself strategically at the doorway.

"Who's there?" he asked.

A thick voice on the other side said: "Police."

Shad looked to his boss for instructions.

"Shit," Orly said. "What now?" His face turned the color of spackle.

. . .

Erin wasn't sure what to make of Sgt. Al García. She didn't know if he was a good policeman or a lousy policeman, but she knew he'd never make it in the FBI. He was not an assiduous note taker.

However, other factors worked in his favor. Eleven whole minutes had passed and Al García hadn't yet propositioned her, or even asked if she was married. That set him apart from most cops who dropped by the Eager Beaver.

He sat across from Erin in a back booth. Orly, citing phony flu symptoms, had slithered out the front exit. Shad was at the bar, haggling with a wholesaler over two cases of Haitian rum. On stage, Urbana Sprawl danced to a dirty rap song.

Erin wore a lace teddy, a white G-string and high heels—not ideal attire for a police interview. García smoked a cigar and paid no attention to the perfumed surroundings. He handed Erin a Xeroxed copy of a Florida driver's license. When she saw the photograph of Jerry Killian, she knew she was looking at a dead man. García had already told her.

"Exactly what happened?" Her mouth had gone dry and her eardrums buzzed faintly.

"Drowned," the detective said. "Your picture is hanging in his apartment."

"Mine and a dozen others."

"I found a stack of cocktail napkins on the bedstand. Did you know about that? Eager Beaver cocktail napkins."

With extreme firmness, Erin said: "I never saw his bedroom."

"He wrote notes on these damn napkins. Notes to himself, notes to his kids, notes to you." García paused. "Is the smoke bothering you?"

"No," said Erin, "it's my all-time favorite aroma. That and gum turpentine."

Without apologizing, the detective extinguished the cigar.

"Tell me what happened," Erin said. It was still sinking in—Mr. Peepers was dead. This was too much. "I want to know everything," she said.

"What happened is, your friend floated up deceased in the Clark Fork River and spoiled my trout fishing. You ever been there—the Clark Fork?" García reached in his jacket and took out an envelope of family snapshots. He found one photo showing the river and the mountains, and he handed it to Erin. "Mineral County, Montana. Beautiful country, no?"

Erin agreed. In the foreground of the photograph was an attractive woman and two children. They looked perfectly normal, Al García's family.

"Not many homicides in Mineral County," the detective was saying. "The coroner takes one look at Mr. Tourist, all dressed up in his L.L. Beans, and says Accidental Drowning. Being the hardass ill-mannered big-city Cuban that I am, I politely request to peek inside Mr. Tourist's chest. The coroner, nice guy, says sure. Unzips 'em right on the spot."

Erin's low-cal lunch did a slow somersault in her stomach. She asked García what was found inside Jerry Killian.

"Not much." García held his dead cigar poised, like a paintbrush. "A little water in the lungs. That's to be expected. But when a man drowns in a lake or a river, he also tends to suck up grass, bugs, sand—you'd be surprised. One night we got a floater off Key Biscayne, had a baby queen angelfish in his bronchioles!"

Al García spoke loudly to be heard over the dance music. "You don't look so hot. Want me to come back some other time?"

"Could you get to the punch line," Erin said, impatiently. "In ten minutes it's my set."

"Sure," said García. "Here's the deal. The Clark Fork was full of bugs and leaves—dip a bucket in the river and you'd see what I mean. But the water in Killian's body was amazingly clean."

"Tap water," Erin said.

"You're a smart girl."

"So somebody killed him?"

"Probably in a bathtub," García said, "if I had to guess."

"Can we go outside?" Erin asked.

"Only if you let me smoke."

Shad followed them to the parking lot. Erin motioned him to go away. Al García acted as if he didn't care one way or the other. He lit his cigar and leaned up against his car, an unmarked blue Caprice.

Erin said, "You're serious about Jerry being murdered?"

"His ex says he went fishing out West every year. This time was different in one respect: when he got there, he never took out a fishing license. That's damn strange." García turned away and blew smoke into the darkness. "Two local boys saw him going downriver on a raft, alone in a rainstorm."

"Alive?"

"I doubt it. You got any ideas, Mrs. Grant?"

Erin said, "Let me think on it. Things are complicated." Maternal instinct told her to avoid the subject of Angela, and Jerry Killian's promise. It was possible that García already knew.

"For the record," he said, "you didn't kill him, did you?"

Erin laughed in bitter astonishment. "No, sir. I didn't love him, I didn't sleep with him, and I most definitely didn't kill him."

"I believe you," García said. "But I'm a sucker for high heels."

He gave her his card. She studied it curiously. "This says Dade County."

"Yeah, that's a problem. We're in Broward, aren't we?" García rolled the stogie back and forth in his mouth. "Montana's a long way off, Mrs. Grant. It may take me a while to drum up local interest."

"But technically it's not your jurisdiction."

"That's right," he said, agreeably. "I'm meddling, pure and simple."

"Why?" Erin asked.

"Because my boy is the one who found him." García took out his car keys. "You got children, you'll understand."

"Is he all right—your son?"

"Sure. He just wants to know what happened, and I'd prefer to tell him the truth. Anyway, floaters happen to be right up my alley, I'm proud to say."

Al García's voice trailed off. He looked tired and preoccupied and ten years older than he probably was. Erin fought back an urge to tell him everything.

"I'd like to help," she said, "but I doubt if I can. Mr. Killian was a customer, that's all. I hardly knew the man."

García flicked the cigar. It landed with a hiss in a puddle.

After he got in the car, Erin motioned him to roll down the window. She stepped up to the door and said, "If it's not an official investigation, how'd you get inside his apartment?"

"All I did was ask the super." García winked. "A badge is a badge." He started the car. "Get back inside," he told Erin, "before you catch cold."

"Will there be a service?" she asked.

"For Killian? Not for a while. The coroner promised he won't sign the papers for a week or so, until I check around."

"So where's Jerry's body?"

"In a freezer in downtown Missoula," García said. "Him and two tons of dead elk."

.   .   .

Cousin Joyce wasn't the very last person in the world that Mordecai wanted to see, but she was high on the list.

"Disaster," she said, dropping a stack of color slides on his desk. "I found these in Paul's underwear drawer."

"And how is Paul?" asked Mordecai.

"Feeling better," Joyce said. "Temporarily."

"Any luck locating the phantom synagogue?"

"There was no synagogue," she said. "Look at the slides, Mordecai."

They were the photographs taken by Paul Guber's friend at the ill-fated bachelor party. The lawyer went through the slides methodically, holding each one up to a gooseneck lamp.

Joyce sat down and began to sniffle. "That's the man I wanted to marry."

As Mordecai peered at the pictures, he longed for a projector and a screen. The women were happy-looking, gorgeous and nude. The lawyer pitied Paul Guber, for there was no mistaking his youthful face, buried serenely in the bare loins of a brunette. The effect was to give him a curly goatee.

"Obviously alcohol was involved," Mordecai said. "Too much alcohol."

"Don't make excuses. I want you to sue the bastard."

"For what? You're not married yet."

"Some lawyer," she said, blowing her nose.

"What's this?" Mordecai was examining the last slide, which differed in content from the others. In it, a paunchy silver-haired man loomed over the still-kneeling Paul Guber. With both hands the stranger was raising a green bottle over his head, as if swinging an ax. His face was twisted with rage. Behind the stranger was the figure of a larger man lunging with outstretched arms, trying to stop the attack.

"Dynamite," Mordecai said. He took a magnifying glass from the top drawer and hunched over the slide.

"I'm so glad you're amused," said Joyce. "My future is in shambles, but thank God you're enjoying yourself."

"Joyce?"

"What?"

"Shut up, please."

The sniffling stopped. His cousin's expression turned cold and spiteful.

Mordecai glowed as he looked up from the pictures. "I *know* these guys!"

"Who? What are you smiling about?"

"Joyce, go home immediately. Take care of your fiancé."

"I can't. He's playing golf."

"No!" Mordecai exclaimed. "He can't possibly be playing golf. He's a very sick man. He's got cluster migraines. Blackouts. Double vision. Go find him, Joyce. Tend to him."

The lawyer hustled her toward the door. "I'll be out to see you tomorrow. We've much to talk about."

Joyce balked. "And what about me? I'm expected to forget what I saw on those pictures? My fiancé, the man I planned to marry, licking at the belly of some sleazy whore. I'm supposed to put that awful image out of my mind!"

"If you're smart, yes," the lawyer said, "because we've still got one hell of a case."

"Suing a nudie bar?"

"Don't be silly." Mordecai held his cousin by the shoulders. "First rule of torts: always go after the deepest pockets—in this case, the fellow who assaulted Paul."

"So who is he?" Joyce demanded.

"We'll discuss it later."

"A celebrity?" She was hoping for a movie star. "Let's see that picture again."

"Later," said Mordecai, aiming her toward the door.

"He's got money? You're absolutely sure?"

"Oh, I'm certain he can get it," the lawyer said. "I'm as certain as I can be."

Mordecai thought: Finally it pays to be a Democrat!

CHAPTER 11

Midnight found Congressman Dilbeck and Christopher Rojo in high spirits at the Flesh Farm. They were celebrating Dilbeck's good news, as related by Malcolm Moldowsky via Erb Crandall: the blackmail threat was vanquished! The elated congressman sought no details, and none were offered. Moldy was a magician, his tricks meant to be secret and mystical. Dilbeck and Rojo drank a toast to the greasy little rat-fucker, then turned their attentions toward the dance stage. Soon the blue haze filled with paper airplanes made from U.S. currency. By closing time, Dilbeck and Rojo were fast friends with two of the Flesh Farm dancers.

Dawn found the foursome eighty miles away, on a levee on the southeastern shore of Lake Okeechobee. Wearing only knee socks and Jockey shorts, Chris Rojo was orating the history of sugar cultivation and Congressman Dilbeck's role in it. The dancers complained of being chewed by fire ants, and retreated on four-inch heels to the air-conditioned comfort of the limousine, where Pierre prepared Bloody Marys.

Rojo paced the dike and chattered nonstop, a typically brilliant cocaine monologue. "Two hundred thousand acres of muck, glorious muck," he said. "Sweet sugar cane, far as the eye can see . . ."

Dilbeck's gin-clouded retinas barely saw past the laces of his shoes. The first rays of sunlight warmed his bare shoulders and ignited an itchy prickle of insect tracks. Dilbeck rocked from one leg to the other, as if he'd spent the night on a very small boat. "I may puke," he announced to Rojo.

It was the young millionaire's first visit to the fields where his family fortune was sown. He raised lean brown arms to the sky and cried: "Twenty-three cents a pound!" The bleating caused Dilbeck to wince. "Twenty-three cents!" Rojo yowled again. "Thank you, *Tio Sam!* Thank you, Davey."

Twenty-three cents per pound was the average wholesale price of the sugar grown by Christopher Rojo's family corporation. The inflated figure was set by the United States Congress and monitored by the Commodity Credit Corporation, an arm of the Department of Agriculture. Rojo had good reason to be thankful: Cane sugar from the Caribbean sold for only twelve cents per pound on the world market. Strict import quotas kept most foreign sugar out of America, thus allowing the Rojos to maintain their fixed price and, thus, their grossly excessive life-style. Whenever the import quotas came under attack from international trade groups, Congress charged to the rescue. Dilbeck was one of Big Sugar's best friends, and Chris Rojo never missed an opportunity to demonstrate his gratitude. Now, standing on the levee, he locked the congressman in a ferociously sloppy embrace.

Dilbeck felt himself teetering, and pulled free. "I don't feel so good. Where are the girls?"

"Who knows," said Rojo. "Relax, my friend. There will always be girls."

The congressman squinted into the sun. "Did we get laid last night?"

"I haven't a clue."

"Me neither," Dilbeck said. "I'm assuming we did."

"For a thousand dollars, I certainly hope so."

Dilbeck grimaced at the sum. "That's what you paid?"

"Five hundred each. So what?" Chris Rojo's voice was dry and high-pitched. "It's nothing to me," he said. "Just money."

Dilbeck felt his body heat rise with the sun. He touched the back of his neck and found it damp. He wondered what had happened to his shirt. He hoped that one of Mr. Ling's dancers had chewed it off in a sexual frenzy.

Rojo said, "It's a crazy world, Davey. I give some girl five hundred bucks just to go for a ride, OK? The poor fucks who cut this cane"—he waved toward the fields—"that's three week's pay."

"Are you serious?" Dilbeck said.

"This is some country, my friend. Now I must find my pants."

By the time they returned to the limousine, Christopher Rojo had come down hard from the coke, and David Dilbeck wobbled on the brink of heatstroke. Pierre held the door as the two men tumbled into the backseat. The dancers were asleep, a bright tangle of blonde, lace and Spandex. Dilbeck's shirt and Rojo's trousers lay crumpled on the floor of the car. The congressman dug a handful of ice from the portable refrigerator and packed it to his forehead.

"It's so fucking hot," he said.

Chris Rojo grunted. "Florida, man."

In the driver's seat, mute Pierre turned to receive directions.

"Civilization," Rojo commanded. "And step on it."

Dilbeck watched the flat brown acres fly by at ninety miles an hour, tall stalks of cane stretching to the horizon. He couldn't believe that human beings worked in such suffocating heat from dawn to dusk. He'd heard it was bad but, Christ Almighty, he'd never imagined it like this.

"How much do you pay them?" he asked Rojo.

"The girls? I told you, Davey—five each."

"No, I mean the migrants."

"Oh, that." Rojo was struggling to fit his legs into the wrinkled trousers. "My father says it's up to thirty dollars a day. All depends if the foreman's in a good mood. But when you subtract room and board, booze and smokes—who knows? And medical care isn't cheap, either."

"Jesus," said the congressman.

"Hey, they keep coming back. Compared to Santo Domingo, this is fucking Club Med."

"How long do they work?"

"Until it's done," Rojo said. "My father says a good hand cuts a ton of cane every hour. You believe that? A whole goddamn ton—amazing what a man can do when he's properly motivated."

David Dilbeck turned from the window and closed his eyes. It made him dizzy and sick, just thinking about it.

The judge was startled when Erin sat down at the table.

She said, "You remember me? The unfit mother."

The judge stiffly drained his Jack Daniels. "I was hoping this was a social visit," he said.

Erin fought to steady herself. She'd had two martinis during her break—a rare indulgence while performing. The problem was Jerry Killian being dead. Even peripheral involvement with a murder could ruin her chance of getting Angie back. In his lovestruck quest to help, Killian might've provoked the wrong people. How far had he taken his screwball scheme? Had he actually tried extortion on a U.S. congressman? Erin needed to know more, before she told Al García about her own supporting role. The judge was her strongest lead, and also the riskiest.

Erin feinted in the obvious direction. "I'd like you to hear my side of the case."

"I already have," the judge said, "in court."

A waitress brought a fresh drink, which the judge eyed longingly but did not sip. Erin wondered if Shad had defiled it in the usual way.

"Thanks to you," she said, "my daughter is in the custody of an incorrigible felon."

"The record reflected no such thing."

"The record was sanitized, Your Honor. Darrell Grant is a paid informant for the Sheriff's Office, and you know it. They purged his rap sheet."

Fidgeting in a dark booth, the judge wasn't nearly as imposing as he was in the courtroom. Here at the Eager Beaver, he was just another horny old fart with impossible fantasies.

Erin said, "My ex-husband deals in stolen wheelchairs. He's made an accomplice of our daughter."

The judge told her that he based his opinion on the known facts of the case; that's the law. "But it's also true that a decision can be reversed." He twirled the ice cubes counterclockwise in the bourbon. "Are you going to dance on my table?"

"I don't do that."

"The others do."

"Not I," said Erin.

"Then perhaps something else?" The judge clutched his glass with both hands, as if it were a sacred chalice. His voice took on a sly tone: "I mentioned one particular idea to your friend."

"Which friend was that?"

"Your 'special' friend."

Naturally, Erin thought. "I've got lots of special friends," she said, "with lots of special ideas."

The judge pursed his wormy lips and said: "You're playing games." He fumbled under the table as if scratching himself, but brought forth a Bible. "I come here often, to pray for sinners like you."

"Oh, that's a good one."

"I keep the Good Book on my lap at all times."

"I'll bet," Erin said. "Levitating?"

"Fighting the devil on his own turf."

"Whatever," she said.

"Good versus evil, evil versus good. It's an eternal struggle." The judge found a dry corner of the cocktail table and placed the Bible there. Then he treated himself to a noisy gulp of bourbon. On stage, the two Moniques danced as gunslingers: fringed boots, Stetsons, holsters and a silver star on each bare breast. The judge was briefly transported.

"Time to get ready," Erin said, slipping out of the booth.

The judge snapped to attention. "Does this mean the answer is no?"

"What did my special friend say my answer would be?"

"Mr. Dilbeck wasn't sure."

Finally, Erin thought: Jerry's congressman.

"We talked about your custody case," the judge said. "I suggested an oral settlement. Didn't he tell you?"

Oral settlement. How incredibly clever! A regular Noel Coward, this one. "Your Honor," Erin said, "I don't know anyone named Dilbeck. And whatever you suggested to him, I promise that my answer would be no."

The judge seemed more perplexed than humiliated. "All right," he said, stirring the ice, "but perhaps we could pray together some fine Sunday morning."

The lawyer, grinning like an imbecile, was waiting at the door. "Come in, come in, come in!"

Shad distrusted joviality. "I heard you the first time. What's the news from Delicato Dairy?"

Mordecai led him to the conference room. "Coffee, Mr. Shad?"

"Answers, Mr. Mordecai."

From his waistband Shad pulled a Black & Decker cordless drill with a ¼-inch steel bit. Without a word he began to put numerous holes in Mordecai's favorite Matisse print. "The new pointillism," Shad explained to the stupefied lawyer.

Soon the painting fell off the wall, exposing an identical pattern of fresh holes in the plaster. Mordecai's secretary pounded urgently on the door and Shad instructed her to go away. Mordecai dropped to his knees and began begging for mercy. He'd been rehearsing ever since Dr. Vibbs had phoned, weepy on Nembutals. His session with Shad had gone quite badly.

"Don't kill me," Mordecai pleaded. "I'll do anything."

Shad tucked the drill under his arm. "Start at the beginning, fuckhead."

The lawyer's story came out in whimpers: The yogurt had been stored securely in the office refrigerator. One day Beverly was out sick. The temp helped herself, never asked . . . ate the whole damn thing, roach and all. You believe that dumb twat?

Shad's amphibian eyes closed slowly, and remained that way for a long time. He was thinking that he should have left the warning note on the yogurt carton.

The lawyer's knees ached, but he was too frightened to move. Beverly rapped on the door again, and this time Mordecai was startled to hear his own voice telling her to relax, everything's OK.

Just another narcoleptic sociopath in need of legal advice.

"You all right?" the lawyer asked Shad.

The hairless giant opened his eyes. His face showed nothing. From a breast pocket he scooped a handful of crispy dead insects—cockroaches, grasshoppers, june bugs, Japanese beetles, even a scorpion—which he organized on the table for Mordecai's inspection.

"This time," Shad said, "no fuckups."

The lawyer rose to his feet. He circled the table slowly, pretending to admire Shad's collection.

"We should discuss this," Mordecai said.

"Nothing to discuss, partner. Send your girl off to the supermarket. Fruit flavors only."

"You don't understand—"

"And tell her to check the date on the cartons. I ain't stickin' my pinkies in expired yogurt. No way." Shad sat back and waited for Mordecai to get rolling.

The lawyer said, "But this is fraud. I could be disbarred."

"You could be dis*membered,*" said Shad, "if you don't move your fat ass."

Mordecai felt the blood rush from his legs. Soon he lost all feeling below the waist. His throat tightened. "I . . . have . . . another plan."

"Sure you do."

"I . . . d-d-do!"

With a single punch to the shoulder, Shad knocked the lawyer down. Mordecai wailed. Shad told him to shut up, don't be such a pussy. Mordecai wailed louder.

Shad stood over him, taking aim. All he said was: "Pitiful." Then he dropped the dead scorpion into Mordecai's open mouth. Instantly the lawyer stopped crying, in order to gag.

"There's more where that came from," Shad said.

Suddenly Mordecai's secretary came through the door. It was a half-hearted charge. For a weapon Beverly had chosen a cheap gold-plated letter opener, which crumpled like foil against Shad's massive rib cage. He calmly disarmed the woman, and directed her to fetch a glass of water for the boss.

Later, after Mordecai had regurgitated the scorpion and everyone had settled down, Beverly confirmed the lawyer's version of what had happened to Shad's evidentiary cockroach: the temp had scarfed it down.

"Mmmmm," Shad said, "I smell malpractice." He arranged the other dead insects in military formation on the table.

Mordecai said, "Please. It was an accident."

"That fucking roach was my retirement. Understand?"

"You want to retire a rich man, Mr. Shad, then listen to my offer." Mordecai signaled for his secretary to leave the room. "Please pay attention," he said to Shad.

Shad held a grasshopper and a Japanese beetle delicately in between the thumb and forefinger of each hand. He was making the dead bugs dance a little jig on the table. "Go ahead," he told the lawyer. "I'm perfectly tuned in."

Mordecai unveiled the color slide from Paul Guber's bachelor party. "Take a look."

"What is it?"

"Here. Hold it by the corner."

Shad put the insects back in formation, and turned his scrutiny to the slide. He held it to the lamp, and squinted with one eye at the stamp-size image.

He said, "Well, lookie there."

"Do you know where that photo was taken?"

"Sure. At the club."

"And who's in the picture?"

"Me and Erin and a couple asshole drunks."

"Erin would be the stripper?"

Shad's head turned slowly. "She would be a dancer. The best."

His voice was murderous. Mordecai thought: Good Christ, now I've insulted the monster's girlfriend. Can anything else possibly go wrong?

The lawyer hesitantly moved on: "The young man's name is Paul Guber. He's my client."

"Then God help him."

"The older man, the one swinging the wine bottle—do you recognize him?"

Shad glanced at the picture again. "Nope. And it's a champagne bottle. Korbel, I would guess."

"The man's name is David Dilbeck. Do you follow politics, Mr. Shad?"

"Do I *look* like I follow politics?"

"Mr. Dilbeck is a United States congressman."

Shad thought about that as he studied the slide once more. He said, "Man's put himself in one helluva posture. I'm guessing you're gonna sue his ass."

"It may come to that," Mordecai said. "However, I'm hoping the matter can be settled privately, in a reasonable atmosphere."

" 'However?' " Shad disapproved of snooty verbiage. He pinched one of Mordecai's plump cheeks and said: "I liked you better with the scorpion in your gullet."

"Quit!" the lawyer cried out.

Shad released him. "So how do I fit in? And no more shrinks. I've had it with phonies."

Mordecai rubbed the sting from his face. "You saw everything, Mr. Shad, the entire assault. When Dilbeck's people learn I've got an eye-witness, they will—pardon the expression—shit a brick."

"Tell me," Shad said. "How much money can a lousy congressman have?"

"Trust me. The lousier they are, the more they have." Mordecai eased himself out of Shad's lunging range. "The thing to remember, always, is that we're not after Dilbeck. The serious money is with the men who own his soul."

Shad was toying with his dead insects again. "I should try this on a chessboard," he remarked.

"Please," said Mordecai. "Trust me. I know about Dilbeck—both of us were Mondale delegates back in '84."

Shad said, "I may just cry."

"We're talking millions of dollars!"

The man appeared to be serious. Shad postponed his decision to stomp the shit out of him.

"Millions," Mordecai repeated, huskily. "The people who own David Dilbeck, the people who'd do *anything* to keep him in office—they're some of the richest bastards in Florida. They've got money to burn."

"In that case," Shad said, "let's burn some."

12

Orly hired a new dancer whose stage name was Marvela. She was a tall strawberry blonde with a lovely figure, and she knew how to move. On her first night working the birdcage, she doubled Erin in tips.

Later, over a tub of vanilla Häagen-Dazs, Urbana Sprawl told Erin that it was about time she had some competition.

"An off night," Erin muttered. She had danced poorly, with a smile so forced and insincere that only the drunkest customers wouldn't have noticed. "My concentration's shot," she said.

"You wanna talk about it?"

"Mr. Peepers is dead."

Urbana whispered, "Oh my Lord."

"Possibly murdered."

"Sweet Jesus."

Until now, Erin had told no one the true reason for Sgt. Al García's visit to the Eager Beaver. The other dancers had assumed that the topic was Erin's ex-husband, in whom many police agencies had expressed interest.

Urbana Sprawl begged for the details of Jerry Killian's death.

"It's a long story," Erin said, "and I think I'm in the middle." She reached back and locked the dressing room door. "Apparently somebody drowned the little guy."

"Because of you?"

"Indirectly."

"Then you'd better hide, girl. Come stay with me and Roy." Urbana's boyfriend, Roy, was a mechanic for an outlaw motorcycle gang. He and Urbana specialized in unexpected house guests. Erin said thanks, anyway.

"I was you, I'd be on the first plane out."

"Not without Angela. And first I need more money." Her options were limited, and all were expensive.

Urbana suggested table dances and private parties. "You're the only one who won't."

"It may come to that."

"There's other ways, too," Urbana said, gravely. "I know you wouldn't, but some girls do. It's all according to what you need, and how bad."

Erin patted her friend's hand and told her not to worry. "I'll rob Jiffy Marts before I'll turn tricks. Urbana, would you tell Mr. Orly I'm knocking off early tonight?"

Erin was too tired to scrub her makeup or take off the dancing clothes. Over the red teddy and G-string, she put on gray sweats and a baggy T-shirt. She tied her hair in a loose ponytail, folded the tip money in her purse and put her pumps in a Penney's bag. She looked at the hollow-eyed face in the mirror and said, "What a hot number I am."

"Anything I can do to help," Urbana said, "you name it."

"Break Marvela's legs?"

"Go home now, honey. Get some sleep."

"Sleep? What's that?" Erin said goodbye and unlocked the dressing room door. Monique Sr. was in the dim hallway, struggling to repair a broken garter.

"Of all nights," she said. "John Chancellor's at table eleven."

"Yeah?" Erin said. "I'm a Brokaw fan, myself."

Erin went home and fixed herself a martini. She put Tom Petty full blast on the tape deck and took off her clothes. Lying on the bed, she contemplated familiar gaunt faces on the wall—posters of legendary rock stars, including a few who were still alive. The posters were a gift from one of Erin's ardent customers, a concert promoter. He was so eager to impress her that he once forged Peter Frampton's autograph on a compact disc. It was beyond pathetic.

Erin's apartment was decorated minimally because it was a temporary stop. She refused to invest in anything that wasn't plastic and portable and couldn't be moved in one day by a woman laboring alone. Even the sound system, Erin's only extravagance, broke down into four lightweight boxes.

Nothing connected her soul to the place, not even memories. The three men who'd been in the bedroom were as forgettable as the discount decor. One of them hadn't gotten his pants off before Erin told him to get lost. She'd been watching "60 Minutes," her favorite TV program, when the young visitor remarked that he didn't like the show because "there was too much talking." Erin ordered him to button his trousers and hit the bricks. Never again would she date a baseball player—at least, nothing below Triple A.

She bunched a pillow under her head. Acidly she thought: Quite a life I've made for myself!

The telephone looked red-hot on the bedstand; so many possibilities. Call Mom and borrow money for more lawyers? Perhaps when Biscayne Bay freezes over.

Call García and spill everything? Erin doubted the detective would be moved to tears by a recounting of her domestic problems. He would, however, be greatly intrigued by the weird details of Jerry Killian's blackmail plot. A homicide with political connections would be a welcome break from the drudgery of domestics and drug murders.

Maybe that was the phone call to make, Erin thought. Get it over with.

She changed her mind and put the empty martini glass on the floor. Jimi Hendrix loomed over the headboard, tonguing his left-handed Stratocaster. Dead at twenty-seven. Erin thought: Not me, buster.

She took the telephone off the bedstand and balanced it on her tummy. She punched a number in Deerfield Beach and closed her eyes, thinking *please, please, please.*

Angela answered on the third ring.

"Baby?"

"Momma?"

"It's me. Did I wake you?"

"Where are you, Momma?"

"Is your father there? Talk softly if he is."

"Can you come see us? Every day we go for rides in the hospital."

"Which hospital, baby?"

"Different ones. Daddy dresses up like Doctor Shaw."

"Oh God," Erin said.

"Then he puts me in a wheelchair and pushes real fast. Can you come see us? We go real fast—you can push, too."

"Angela, listen to me."

"I think I gotta go. Love you, Momma."

"Angela—"

Long silence. Somebody breathing. Then a wet cough.

"Angie?"

Darrell Grant laughed, high-pitched and juiced by speed. "I gotta get this number changed."

Erin said, "You are one dumb shit. If you get caught using that little girl—"

"Hell, I won't get caught. It's a dream setup, didn't she tell you? I stole a doctor's jacket, a real stethoscope, the works. Man, I look so legit! Fact, I'm thinking seriously about trying some gynecology on the side—"

"Darrell, they'll take her away! The HRS will take her away from both of us. Forever."

"Lord, you *do* worry. I already told you, I won't get caught. The setup is, I dress Angie in pajamas so she looks like a real patient. Her Cookie Monster pajamas, remember? The ones with the little feetsies in the bottom—"

"You asshole."

"Now, don't be judgmental. You, who flashes her tits for a living. Don't fucking judge me, sweetcakes—"

Erin hurled the phone to the floor. She was too mad to cry, too upset to sleep. She pulled on a sweatshirt and blue jeans, and grabbed her car keys off the dresser.

Special Agent Tom Cleary wore a burgundy bathrobe and brown floppy bedroom slippers. To Erin, he looked practically adorable. She'd never seen him rumpled and ungroomed. Sleep had sculpted his sandy hair into a sharp peak, like the crest of a cardinal.

"Coffee?" he croaked.

They sat in the kitchen and spoke in low tones while Cleary's wife heated a bottle for the baby, who was yowling upstairs. It was the couple's fourth child in six years and the stress of fecundity was taking a toll. When Erin apologized for the lateness of the hour, Mrs. Cleary said it was no problem. No problem at all! She was about to explode with artificial politeness. The moment she went upstairs, her husband sagged with relief.

"I need some help," Erin said, leaning forward.

"Darrell again?"

"Naturally." She told him about her ex-husband becoming a police informant, about the expensive court fight, about Darrell Grant's wheelchair scam with Angela as a human prop—

"Back up," the agent interjected. "He's got custody? That doesn't seem possible."

Erin's throat felt chalky. "The judge says I'm an unfit mother. How 'bout them apples?"

Cleary was incredulous. "Unfit?" The word came out in a horrified whisper, as if he spoke of a dreaded disease. "What in the world . . . Erin, did something happen?"

She thought: I can't tell him about the job. The Eager Beaver he would never understand.

"It's a long story," she said.

"Darrell got to the judge?"

"Well, something did."

The coffee was ready. Cleary poured. Upstairs, the baby finally stopped crying. Erin said, "Tom, he's turning my daughter into a gypsy."

The FBI man nodded soberly. "The problem is, we can't stretch jurisdiction." She started to say something but Cleary cut her off. "Let me finish, Erin. Your divorce, that's a civil matter, totally out of our scope. But if you've got proof the judge is corrupt, then maybe we can do business—"

"I don't have proof," Erin said sharply. "I thought that was your department."

Cleary's eyes flashed but he continued: "The wheelchair racket— now I agree it's despicable. But basically you're talking grand larceny, which the Bureau won't touch."

"But the locals have Darrell on the damn payroll!"

"Listen," Cleary said, "if I tried to run this one past my supervisor— well, there's no chance in hell. He'd throw it right back in my face."

The agent was rueful but unwavering. Erin felt whipped. "A phone call from you and the cops would drop him like a rock," she said. "One lousy phone call, Tom."

"I don't work that way. Rules are rules."

"But you helped me before."

"I ran a name. That's easy, Erin." Cleary took off his glasses and kneaded his temples. "What I cannot do," he said wearily, "is open a federal case on your ex-husband. I'm very sorry."

"Me, too," Erin mumbled into her coffee cup.

The agent asked if the information about Jerry Killian had been helpful. Oh yes, Erin said, very helpful. She thanked him for the coffee and rose quickly to leave, but not before Cleary asked: "How does he fit into all this? Killian, I mean."

"Another long story," Erin said. Cleary would panic if he knew Jerry Killian was dead. Automatically he would connect the murder to his own leak of the computer check. Next he'd feel compelled to confess the breach of regulations. Several cubic yards of paperwork would accumulate before an actual field investigation of Killian's drowning began. Meanwhile, Tom Cleary most certainly would be transferred to the FBI equivalent of Siberia, where his wife would ponder a future of frigid winters and limited day-care possibilities. Eventually the Bureau might sort out the facts of Killian's death and exonerate the exiled Cleary. By that time, though, Darrell Grant could be safely in Tasmania, or anywhere, with Angela.

Erin had no time to wait for the FBI. And she wanted Agent Tom Cleary in Miami, in case she needed him.

As he walked her to the door, Cleary asked where she was working.

"A dive," Erin replied, "tending bar." Not an unmanageable lie. The same one she told her grandparents.

Cleary said, "Which dive?"

"You don't know the place, Tom. It's definitely not in your jurisdiction."

The agent accepted the sarcasm impassively. He said he hated to think of her slinging drinks. Erin said the money wasn't bad.

Cleary, his voice heavy with guilt: "On this Darrell thing, I wish I could bend the rules, but I can't. I simply can't."

"I understand, Tom." Erin checked discreetly for the wife, then pecked him on the cheek. "Thanks, anyway," she said.

When she got home, Mexican championship boxing was on ESPN. The face of one fighter was purple and pulped, blood trickling from what appeared to be three nostrils. The other boxer aimed meticulous jabs at the man's fractured nose, until the bleeding got so bad that the referee lost his footing on the slippery canvas.

At one time in her life, Erin couldn't have comprehended how a human being could inflict such misery on an opponent he scarcely knew. Now, thinking of her ex-husband, Erin began to understand the boxer's drive: a simple transfer of aggression, from real life to the ring.

By morning, she had cooled off. She did one hundred sit-ups, reassembled the telephone and tried another phone call. This, too, was a long shot.

Erb Crandall noticed something new in the front hallway of Malcolm J. Moldowsky's penthouse. It was a color portrait of John Mitchell, former attorney general and convicted felon.

"A dear friend and mentor," Moldy explained. "Savagely maligned, long before your time. An American tragedy."

"I know all about him, Malcolm."

"Political genius," said Moldowsky. "Misplaced loyalty was his fatal flaw. He took the fall for Nixon."

"Who didn't?" Erb Crandall had been in college during the Watergate hearings. He remembered John Mitchell as a surly old dog who couldn't lie his way out of a paper bag.

"The ultimate insider," Moldy said, aglow. He stroked the frame of the portrait in a tender manner that worried Crandall.

"Don't you have a hero?" Moldowsky asked.

"Nope."

"That's very cynical, Erb."

"People with heroes usually believe in something. How about you?"

Moldy thought about it while he poured two cognacs. He handed one to Crandall and said, "I believe in influence for the sake of influence."

"Pushing buttons."

"It's a kick—wouldn't you agree?"

Crandall said, "To be honest, some days it sucks."

"You're still in the trenches, Erb. Be patient."

"You mean someday I could end up like . . . *him?*" He pointed at John Mitchell's toady visage. "Gee, Malcolm, I can hardly wait."

"You are one cynical fuck."

They sat in Moldowsky's plush living room, which featured a panoramic vista of the Atlantic Ocean. Distant lights of freighters and cruise ships winked at them from the Gulf Stream. Crandall was soothed by the view and warmed by the cognac.

Moldowsky asked for an update on the reelection campaign. He was pleased to hear that David Dilbeck's Republican opponent, a right-wing appliance dealer, had raised only sixty thousand dollars to date. The hapless yutz was spending most of his days fending off the press, and trying to explain two long-ago convictions for mail fraud back in Little Rock, Arkansas. Moldy himself had unearthed the obscure rap sheet, and passed it along to a friendly Miami columnist.

On the home front, Erb Crandall reported that every living Rojo, including scores of far-flung cousins, had dutifully sent cashier's checks for the maximum allowable contribution to the Re-Elect Dave Dilbeck Committee. Additional thousands of dollars were pouring in from supposedly ordinary citizens wishing to support the congressman's exemplary work. Cross-checking those contributors' names with voter rolls, or even with the telephone book, would have been useless. The names belonged to Caribbean farm workers, imported by the sugar industry to work the cane fields. It was Moldowsky's inspired idea to use the untraceable migrants as a cover for illegal Rojo donations.

"Davey still doesn't know," Crandall said.

"Don't tell him," said Moldy.

"He thinks he's adored by the masses."

"Encourage that notion, Erb. We like a candidate with confidence."

"Oh, he's confident," Crandall said. "He's so goddamn confident I can't control him." He handed Moldy the congressman's most recent tab from the Flesh Farm. Mr. Ling had boldly tacked on forty bucks for "replacement of damaged pasties."

"And where were *you?*" Moldowsky demanded of Crandall.

"He went out the back door, Malcolm. Chris Rojo sent the car."

"I said, where were you?"

"Asleep in the living room."

"Nice work."

"Fuck off," Crandall said. "Tonight *you* can tuck him in. That I'd pay to see."

Moldowsky was disturbed to hear that Dilbeck was up to his old licentious tricks. Obviously the idiot had learned nothing from the Eager Beaver episode.

Erb Crandall said, "Can we put something in his food? I was thinking saltpeter."

"Yeah? I was thinking thorazine." Moldowsky was astounded by the congressman's stupidity. Didn't he realize how close he'd come to disaster? Jerry Killian was gone, but there would be other Killians, other dangerous blackmailers, if Dilbeck didn't steer clear of the tittie bars.

"There's something else," Crandall said.

Moldowsky loosened his necktie vigorously, as if escaping a noose.

"Let me guess: he's gone and knocked up a cheerleader. Make that an underaged cheerleader. Catholic girl's school?"

"You told me to keep you posted in the weirdo department."

"So post me, Erb. Before I die of fucking suspense."

Crandall popped a cough drop into his mouth. "The congressman got an unusual phone call this morning."

"Here, or in the Washington office?"

"Washington. One of the secretaries took the message." As he spoke, Erb Crandall clacked the lozenge from cheek to cheek. He said, "It was a woman calling."

"There's a shocker."

"Said she was a friend of Jerry Killian."

"You're shitting me." Moldy's jaw hung. "Erb, this better be a joke."

"You see me laughing?"

"What else?" Moldowsky barked. "What else did she say?"

"That's it, Malcolm. She didn't leave a name or a number. Very polite, according to the secretary. Said she'd call back another time, when the congressman was available."

Moldowsky ran his fingernails raggedly through his hair—that's how Crandall knew he was upset. Impeccable grooming was one of Moldy's trademarks.

"Did you tell Davey?" he asked.

"Of course not."

"Which secretary took the call?"

"The older one—Beth Ann. Don't worry, she doesn't know a thing. The name Killian meant zero to her." Crandall noisily chewed the cough drop and washed it down with cognac. "Malcolm, it's about time you filled me in."

"Be glad I haven't."

"But you said it was taken care of."

Moldowsky stared out to sea. "I thought it was."

At the moment his pager beeped, Sgt. Al García was sitting on a meat freezer, chewing gum, filling out paperwork. Inside the freezer were Ira and Stephanie Fishman, ages eighty-one and seventy-seven, folded up like patio furniture. They had passed away within two days of each other in the month of July during the first full year of Gerald Ford's presidency. Daughter Audrey, their only child, had placed the dead

Fishmans in a Sears industrial-size deep freeze, which she'd purchased especially for that purpose. Between them, Ira and Stephanie Fishman had been collecting about $1,700 a month in Social Security, disability and veteran's benefits. Being chronically unemployed and without prospects, Audrey felt no urgency to inform the government or anyone else that her parents had died. Friends assumed that the couple had grown tired of the hot weather and moved back to Long Island. No one but Audrey knew that Ira and Stephanie lay perfectly preserved beneath three dozen Swanson frozen dinners, mostly Salisbury steaks. The Social Security checks kept coming, and for all these years Audrey cashed them.

Her secret was safe until this day. She got up early and took the church bus to Seminole bingo, as usual. At about noon, a young outlaw named Johnnie Wilkinson broke a bedroom window and entered the Fishman residence in search of cash, handguns, credit cards and stereo equipment. Curiosity (or perhaps hunger) attracted Johnnie Wilkinson to the big freezer, and his subsequent screams were heard by a passing postal carrier. Audrey returned to find the small house swarming with cops. She was immediately taken into custody, but detectives were unsure what charges should be filed.

Days would pass before the Fishmans defrosted enough for a proper autopsy, although it appeared to García that they'd died of natural causes. Florida had no specific law against freezing one's own dead relatives, but Audrey had committed numerous misdemeanors by failing to report her parents' deaths, and by storing the bodies in a residentially zoned neighborhood. As for her Social Security flimflam, that was a federal crime. Al García had no jurisdiction, or interest. He was rather pleased when his pager went off.

Erin met him at a Denny's on Biscayne Boulevard. They took the farthest booth from the frozen pie display. When García attempted to light a cigar, Erin plucked it from his mouth and doused it in a cup of coffee.

"Unnecessary," the detective groused.

"Get out your notebook," she said.

Al García smiled. "Good old FBI training."

"You know about that?"

"I'm not as slow as I look." A waitress appeared, and García ordered a burger and fries. Erin asked for a salad.

She said, "What else do you know?"

"You went through a blonde phase."

Erin laughed. "God. Not my driver's license!"

"You look better as a brunette." Al García took out the notebook. He clenched the cap of his pen in his teeth, to compensate for the missing cigar. He said, "All I got really is the basics. Height, weight, marital status. Big fat zilch on the FCIC, which is good. Oh yeah, you're overextended about a hundred bucks on your Visa card. Boy, do I know *that* drill."

"I'm impressed," Erin said.

"Don't be."

"You know about Darrell?"

"He's a hard one to miss. But let's hear about the late Mr. Killian."

The more Erin talked, the better she felt. García acted as if he believed every word, although she wondered if it was part of the routine. The detective was non-threatening to a fault. He made notes in sloppy cop shorthand, careful not to let the transcribing interfere with the eating of his hamburger. Predictably, he perked up when he heard that Killian had boasted of a pipeline to a congressman. "I got the name from the judge," Erin said. She watched as the detective printed the word DILBECK in neat block letters in his notebook.

She added: "Whatever Jerry tried, I'm praying that it isn't what got him killed."

"Love can be a dangerous item," García said.

"I didn't stop him because—OK, I figured there was an outside chance to get my daughter back. I know it sounds a little crazy."

"Not to me," said García. "I read the divorce."

"Wonderful," Erin said. The file was a trove of slander. Darrell Grant had invented lurid lies about her sexual appetite, and bribed two of his pals to corroborate the fiction. Then there were the cutting words of the judge himself, pontificating on Erin's unfitness for motherhood. She looked hard at García. "I wouldn't hurt my daughter for the world."

"I know you wouldn't."

Erin went for the salad with a vengeance. It tasted like wet napkins.

"What I meant," García said, "is it doesn't sound so crazy, your going along with Mr. Killian's scheme. Your ex-husband is a shitbird, if I can be blunt. He's got no business raising the girl. It's Angela, right?"

"What he told the judge, the stuff in the files—"

"Forget about it," García said.

"It's lies."

"I said don't worry. How about some Key lime pie?"

Erin had a piece. Al García ate two. Then he unwrapped a fresh cigar, holding it safely out of Erin's reach. "Please," he said, "I beg of you." She found herself smiling. As García clipped off the butt, Erin picked up his lighter and flicked it open. She reached across the table and lit the cigar.

"They shipped the body back from Montana," García said, puffing out the words. "Back to Atlanta, I should say. Killian's ex-wife wants to bury him up there."

"What about the murder investigation?"

"They don't like that word out in Mineral County. *Murder*, I mean. *Unclassified* was the best they could do. The coroner says he'll reopen the case if I turn up something new. Something besides a few drops of tap water in the lungs."

"You'll keep at it?"

"In my spare time, sure." García leaned back in a pose of total relaxation. He asked Erin if anything unusual had happened at the Eager Beaver lately. "Think hard," he said.

"Things stay quiet. We've got a pretty large floor manager."

"No incidents? No bad fights?"

Erin mentioned the lunatic drunk with the champagne bottle. "He sent a young man to the hospital," she said. "I'm sure there's a record."

"So where was your bigshot 'floor manager'?"

"He couldn't do much. They had a gun on him."

"Don't stop now," García said.

"It wasn't the guy swinging the bottle. It was his bodyguard who had the gun."

"You get lots of bodyguards in the Eager Beaver?"

"No shots were fired," Erin said. "The whole thing was over in five minutes."

"And you didn't recognize this particular drunk."

"I had another one attached to my thigh. The guy with the Korbel came out of nowhere."

García leaned forward. "Did you see his face? Would you know him if you saw him again?"

"Maybe." Erin paused. "Shad got a better look than I did."

"The bouncer?"

"Don't ever call him that. 'Floor Manager' is the title."

García said, "I need to chat with him."

Erin was skeptical. "He's the strong, silent type." She chose not to burden García with Shad's opinion of cops.

"I'll come by the club some night," the detective said. "You make the introductions and we'll play it by ear. All he can do is say no."

Wrong, thought Erin. That's not all he can do.

García asked if Jerry Killian had been in the audience on the night of the champagne-bottle attack. Erin didn't remember; she said she'd check with the other dancers.

"This is probably a dumb question," Al García said, "but it'll save me some time: Was anybody arrested?"

Erin giggled. She couldn't help it.

"I'll take that as a no," said the detective. He signaled for the check.

Erin said that there was something else he should know. "Today I called the congressman's office. I told them I was a close friend of Jerry Killian."

"Cute," García said. "I'm guessing he didn't take the call."

"Right."

"And I'm praying you didn't leave your name."

"Right," Erin said. "Want me to try again?"

"Please don't." García slid out of the booth and went to pay the bill. Erin waited by the front door, then followed him out. A light summery rain was falling. The palm trees along the boulevard looked droopy and anemic.

García stood beneath the Denny's awning and jotted on a piece of paper. He gave it to Erin and said, "My home number. Guard it with your life."

Erin put the number in her purse. "Does your wife know what you're working on?"

"Don't worry about it. You call anytime." He shielded his cigar from the rain and walked Erin to her car. "Donna'll understand. Trust me."

Erin said, "I'll bet she had a Darrell, too."

"A world-class Darrell. Makes yours look like an altar boy."

"What happened?"

"First, I put his ass in jail," García said, "then I married his wife."

"Now that's style," said Erin.

"Yup. That's what Donna says, too."

13

On the morning of September twenty-fifth, a breezy autumn day, Jerry Killian was laid to rest at Decatur Memorial Gardens, a few miles outside Atlanta. Burial followed a small ceremony attended by Killian's ex-wife, his daughters and nine friends from the television station in Florida. All who came to the funeral were secretly photographed by a man concealed forty-five yards away in a vale of young Georgia pines. The man wore the drab overalls of a gravedigger, but he worked for Malcolm J. Moldowsky. He used a Leica 35-millimeter camera with a long lens and a motordrive, and bracketed the exposures just to be safe. By midafternoon, six strips of black-and-white negatives were sitting on Moldowsky's desk in Miami. Every person in every frame had been identified; none seemingly could have connected the late Mr. Killian to Congressman David Lane Dilbeck.

Moldy was convinced that the woman who'd phoned Dilbeck's office was not present at the funeral. Who was she—a mistress? A secret partner in the blackmail scheme? Finding her wouldn't be easy. Had Killian worked any place but a TV station, Moldowsky could've sent a discreet private investigator to chat up his pals and colleagues. In this case it was too risky. Press people tended to be cranky and suspicious, and a visit from a PI would only stir things up. The safest strategy was to wait. Maybe the mystery woman would call again, maybe she wouldn't.

Either way, Malcolm J. Moldowsky couldn't relax. It was like having a cobra loose in the house. Eventually you're bound to step on it. The only question was: when?

Darrell Grant was loading wheelchairs when Merkin and Picatta arrived, unannounced. The Broward robbery detectives got out of the unmarked car and walked slowly around the U-Haul three times. Finally one of them asked Darrell Grant what the fuck he was doing.

"Business," he said.

"You steal these?" Merkin asked.

"Of course not." Darrell Grant was twitchy and freckled with sweat.

Picatta said, "What's the substance of the day, tiger?"

"Folger's," Darrell Grant said, rolling an Everest-and-Jennings up the ramp. "You wanna move please so I can finish here? Please?" He was worrying about something Erin had said—about what might happen to Angie if he got popped again.

Picatta and Merkin were exchanging cop-style glances, which increased Darrell Grant's nervousness. He ran a long bungie cord through the spokes of the stolen wheelchairs, and hooked it to a ring on the wall of the U-Haul; that way, they wouldn't roll all over creation every time he took a corner.

Picatta said, "What about your van?"

"What about it?"

"Why rent the truck, is what I mean."

"Van's too small," Darrell Grant said. "That should be obvious."

"Yeah," said Merkin. "This broken wheelchair business is going gangbusters. Pretty soon you'll be franchising."

Picatta laughed. Darrell Grant locked up the U-Haul and sat down on the bumper.

"Ain't like stealin' cars," Picatta said. "Cars got a VIN number you can check."

"And registration," said his partner.

"And a license tag, too," Picatta said. "That's the beauty of wheelchairs. They're pretty much untraceable."

Darrell Grant took out the dagger and began cleaning his fingernails, wiping the blade on his jeans. The cops couldn't believe the balls on this guy.

"You think I stole these?" Darrell said. "Let me put it another way: Do you want the honest-to-God truth? If I did steal these goddamn chairs, would you guys really want to know?"

"No," Merkin said. "We wouldn't."

"Then stop these bullshit head games, OK?"

Picatta said, "Funny, we were about to make the same request of you."

Darrell Grant looked up, feigning innocence.

"You gave us a grand total of three tips this month." Picatta paused.

"Three red-hot leads. You ready for the box score, tiger? No hits, no runs, nobody left on base."

Darrell tapped the knife on his kneecap. "You know how it goes," he said. "Win some, lose some."

"You," Merkin said, "are a fucking fountain of wisdom."

The detectives ran through a list of Darrell's bum tips: An alleged coke peddler turned out to be dealing uncut grams of Tide laundry detergent. An alleged big-time bank robber turned out to be a teenager who vandalized (but seldom penetrated) suburban ATM machines. And a ring of allegedly sophisticated foreign-car thieves turned out to be a trio of hapless hubcap boosters.

"Bad luck streak," said Darrell Grant, pondering his sneakers.

Picatta crouched down to eye level. "Look at me, handsome, I'm speaking to you."

"I got lousy information, that's all."

"We stuck our necks out for you, tiger."

"And I appreciate it—"

"Not once, but twice we stuck our necks out. Where's your little girl?"

Darrell Grant went rigid. The knife fell out of his hand. "None a your goddamn business," he said.

Merkin grabbed him roughly by the forelock. "Blondie, lemme 'splain de facts o' life. Everything you do is our business: What you drive, what you eat, where you sleep, what you steal or don't steal. Whether you wipe your ass with your left hand or your right hand. It's all our business."

"She's in the day care," Darrell Grant said. "She's fine." He knocked Merkin's hand away and smoothed his hair. When he bent down to pick up the knife, Picatta kicked it away.

"We could always call that judge."

"Fuck the both of you," said Darrell Grant.

"Then give us some cases," Merkin said. "*Good* cases."

"Which means," Picatta said, "you need to be out on the street, with those pretty blue eyes wide open. Lay off the wheelchairs, tiger."

"And the dope," Merkin added. "Think of it like this: What if that judge suddenly hauls you in to drop urine? You want to keep custody of that little girl, you better clean up."

"Speed freaks make lousy parents," Picatta said. "That's a well-known fact."

Darrell Grant stood up. "Thank you, Dr. Spock." Sullenly he picked up the dagger and climbed into the cab of the U-Haul. "I'll be in touch," he said.

As the truck pulled away, Merkin frowned. "You hate to see that— so much bitterness in such a young man."

"What'd you expect from a career asshole."

"Yeah," Merkin said, "but he's *our* asshole."

Shad was short-tempered and withdrawn. Undoubtedly it was the job— the drunks, the unpredictable girls, Orly, the whole damn shooting match. Now Kevin, the disc jockey, was on a Hammer spree: twenty solid minutes of the most annoying music Shad had ever heard. Finally he couldn't stand it. He vaulted into the booth, knocked Kevin aside and tore the compact disc from the CD player. The Eager Beaver was plunged into silence—the dancers stopped moving, mid-thrust. Customers murmured worriedly. A Peruvian tourist, anticipating a raid, bolted for the door; from his abandoned tabletop came a curse of self-pity from Monique Jr. The fleeing Peruvian had been trimming her garter with twenty-dollar bills.

Shad chewed up the Hammer CD like a big shiny wafer, never feeling the sharp pieces cut his tongue and gums. He spit the whole bloody mess on Kevin's mike stand, and commanded him to play Bob Seger or die. Watching from the rear of the club, Orly silently retreated to his imitation red-velvet sanctuary.

Erin waited about an hour for Shad to settle down. When she approached him, he was sitting alone in a corner booth, reading a large-print edition of Kafka's "The Metamorphosis."

"Good book?" she asked.

Shad looked up. "I'm startin' to feel sorry for cockroaches."

"I've been meaning to ask," Erin said. "How's the lawsuit?"

Shad shook his head glumly. "On to other projects, babe."

"Like what?"

How Shad had fretted over this moment: should he include Erin in Mordecai's scheme? She was Shad's friend, or the closest he had to one. Wouldn't she be surprised to learn that the drunk lunatic with the champagne bottle was a congressman! It was almost worth telling her, just to see that beautiful smile.

On the other hand, a potentially mountainous sum of money was at stake. The more participants in Mordecai's shakedown enterprise, the smaller everyone's cut. There were times, Shad reasoned, when financial exigencies overshadowed friendship.

"I'm sworn to secrecy," he said. "Nothing personal."

"Is there a yogurt angle?"

He laughed, loosening up. "No yogurt, no fucking insects."

Erin inquired about the scalp wound. Shad lowered his head to show her how Darrell Grant's dagger mark was healing. "The scar's fading," he said. "I'm a little disappointed."

For the fiftieth time, Erin apologized for what happened.

"Forget it," Shad said. "I imagine we'll meet again, me and your ex."

"Not if I can help it," said Erin. She had a fleeting image of Darrell Grant being loaded into an ambulance.

The new dancer, Marvela, came out on the main stage. With both hands she seized one of the gold poles, straightened her long legs and leaned back at a languorous slant. She began tossing her head like a mop, around and around in time to the music. The men in the front row crowed enthusiastically.

"What do you think?" Erin asked Shad. "Is it the boobs or the hair?"

"Hair, definitely."

"Supposedly she cleared four hundred the other night."

"Oh yeah?" Shad made a mental note to speak with this upstart Marvela; she'd only tipped him out five bucks. "You're still the best," he told Erin.

"I don't know. She can really dance."

"Not like you." He went back to his Kafka.

Erin knew she should've been up dancing, making a few bucks, but it felt good to take a break. She was comfortable sitting in the dark booth with Shad.

"I've got a small problem," she told him.

"What'sa matter?" He glanced up from the book.

"I need you to talk to somebody."

"Who?"

"He's all right. I think he can help me."

"I said, who?"

When Erin told him it was a cop, Shad snorted. "You got more than a small problem."

"Well, yes. It's a homicide detective."

"Christ Almighty."

"It's not as bad as it sounds." But when Erin related what had happened to Mr. Peepers, it sounded bad indeed. Shad didn't understand why anyone would bother to kill the little guy, and he didn't honestly care. He was more worried about Erin.

"Aren't you due for a vacation?" he said. "I recommend Mars."

"The detective wants to know about that night a few weeks ago, when the guy pulled a gun on you."

"I don't remember. Sorry."

"Come on," Erin said, pinching his arm. "It'll help with Angela. Everything's connected."

"How?" Shad asked. "Your daughter's involved—how'd you manage that?" He couldn't believe Erin had dug herself into such a mess.

"Shhh," she said.

Monique Jr. approached the booth and said Mr. Orly wanted to speak with Shad. She said Kevin was demanding an apology. Shad said he'd be glad to apologize as soon as Kevin displayed a trace of good taste in music. Monique Jr. cheerlessly agreed to take that message back to Mr. Orly.

After she was gone, Shad turned to Erin and said the floor manager's job was getting to him. "I definitely need a new career."

"Me, too," Erin said. "A job where I could wear underpants again."

Shad put his hands on his head and squeezed lightly, as if testing a cantaloupe for ripeness. He squinted hard, then blinked repeatedly. "I ain't noticing ordinary things anymore, that's what's got me worried. For instance, it just now hit me that your boobs are hangin' out."

Erin covered up. "Jeez, I'm sorry. I was in the middle of a set—"

"Point is, I should've picked up on that. Don't you agree?"

"But you see so much of it—"

"Exactly! Too much of it. I need to get out." Shad pointed at the book on the cocktail table. "The guy in this story, he turns into a motherfucking centipede. Wakes up one morning and bingo, he's a bug. Sounds asinine but it sure makes you think. People change overnight, they're not careful."

Erin said, "Maybe *you* need the vacation."

"Yeah, maybe so." Shad drummed his fists softly on the table. "OK, I'll talk to your damn detective. But as I mentioned, my memory ain't so hot."

Erin leaned over and kissed his vast forehead.

Shad said, "Hey, that's a new G-string."

"Sure is."

"Very snazzy."

"Look here. Velcro instead of snaps." Erin demonstrated how it worked.

"I'll be damned." Shad studied the plastic patch thoughtfully. "Whoever dreamed that up, he probably made a bundle."

"*She* probably made a bundle."

Shad shrugged. "One thing's for sure, we're in the wrong end a this business."

"Amen," said Erin.

When David Dilbeck heard the latest fund-raising figures, he told Erb Crandall to summon the limousine. It was time to celebrate! Crandall said absolutely not, tonight we stay home.

"Erb," said the congressman, "look at the day I had. *Three* goddamn anti-Castro rallies. Fidel is a tyrant. Fidel is a bum. Fidel is a monster—"

"Every politician's got to sing that tune."

"It's tiresome, Erb. A man needs to unwind."

"Out of the question, Davey."

"I've bought a new wig—"

"Forget it."

"We'll sit way in the back, Erb. No friction dancing, on God's word. Call the Lings and get us a table."

Crandall offered an alternate plan. The congressman looked intrigued.

"Where's Pamela?" Crandall inquired.

"In Virginia. One of the Kennedys is having a benefit for some disease. I'm not sure which one."

"Which Kennedy?"

"No, which disease," Dilbeck said. "Some kind of anemia."

"But Pamela definitely won't be home tonight?"

"Not until Sunday."

"So it's safe to have visitors."

The congressman beamed. "The more, the merrier."

At half-past nine, the dancers from the Flesh Farm arrived. They brought their own music. Erb Crandall directed the two women toward a teak coffee table in the den. Dilbeck appeared in a loose white robe and sat cross-legged on the floor. He asked Crandall to fetch a bottle of

Korbel from the refrigerator. The dancers expressed concern about damaging the fine wood, so Dilbeck encouraged them to remove their high heels and go barefoot. Erb Crandall returned with the champagne. He poured three glasses, iced the bottle and left the room. He pulled a chair into the hallway, and positioned himself near the doorway of the den. The music throbbed through the walls, unbearably monotonous. After about an hour, Erb Crandall went to Pamela Dilbeck's medicine cabinet in search of migraine relief. He lucked into a bottle of Darvons, and swallowed two with a glass of bitter orange juice from the kitchen.

When he got back to his post, the dance music seemed louder than ever. Crandall noticed that the door of the den was ajar. Before he could peek inside, one of the dancers emerged from a bathroom across the hall. In one hand she carried a curly black wig, in the other a damp towel. She seemed in a hurry.

"Everything OK?" Crandall asked.

"Peachy," the dancer said. "I hope you know CPR."

In the den, there was no sign of the second dancer. The congressman lay unconscious next to the teak coffee table. His robe was open, exposing pink belly lard and silk paisley boxer shorts. Erb Crandall knelt down and placed a hand on David Dilbeck's chest, which rose and fell rapidly.

"Heart attack," Crandall speculated.

"Wrong," said the wigless dancer. She told Crandall what had happened.

He said, "Jesus Christ. Where'd she hit him?"

"Between the eyes."

"With what?"

"Right cross."

"Her fist?" Erb Crandall found this amazing. He carefully examined Dilbeck's pallid face. A nasty blue knot was rising between the congressman's eyebrows. In the center of the bruise was a microscopic indentation, perfectly rectangular.

"She's wearing a ring," Crandall observed.

"Aquamarine," the wigless dancer said. "Her birthstone."

Erb Crandall placed a pillow under Dilbeck's head, and fashioned the damp towel around his neck. The dancer offered to call 911, but Crandall said no.

"Where's your partner?" he asked.

"Out in the car. She's scared shitless."

Dilbeck stirred slightly, emitting a gerbil-like squeak. Crandall put his lips near the congressman's ear and said: "Davey, wake up!" Dilbeck grew quiet again. Crandall went to the desk and found the number of Dilbeck's private physician. He dialed rigidly, leaving an emergency message with the service.

The wigless dancer said, "Better get him to a hospital."

"Sure," Erb Crandall said, caustically. Show up at Mt. Sinai and tomorrow it's all over the papers:

CONGRESSMAN INJURED BY MYSTERY BLOW TO HEAD
Aides Mum Over Late-Night Incident—
Dilbeck Reelection Campaign on Hold.

Crandall gazed at the coldcocked candidate with alternating fury and panic. Whether Dilbeck lived or died, Malcolm Moldowsky would be enraged—and the blame would again fall on Crandall. It wasn't fair. Short of house arrest, it seemed impossible to control Dilbeck's carnal appetites.

"He looks bad," said the dancer, now dressed in street clothes. "What if he croaks?"

"Then the country loses another great leader. How much do we owe you?"

"Mr. Ling said five each."

Erb Crandall got two thousand cash from an envelope locked in the usual place, the bottom-right drawer of Dilbeck's desk. Crandall gave the money to the wigless dancer and said: "You weren't here tonight, you never saw me, you never saw him. Same goes for the other girl, OK? You don't know this man."

"But I *don't* know this man. I really don't."

"God bless you," Erb Crandall said.

"He shouldn't have done what he did. No matter who he is."

"For that, we're truly sorry. If you count the money, I think you'll see how sorry we are."

Something moved on the floor: the congressman's right leg, kicking out at unseen demon dogs.

The wigless dancer put the money away, strapped the purse over her shoulder. She said, "There's no call for what he did. Everything was going fine, a nice little party. I don't know what got into him."

"Beats me," Crandall said. Where was the doctor?

"Maybe he should lay off the champagne."

"Yeah, that's it. The champagne."

The dancer stepped closer for a final look at the bruise between Dilbeck's eyebrows. "Damn," she said. "That's a big stone she's wearing."

"Goodbye," said Erb Crandall.

"Can we take the limo back to Lauderdale?"

"Sure," he said. "Take the limo. Have a ball."

14

Paul Guber wasn't gushing enthusiasm about Mordecai's plan. "I want no part of it," he said.

The lawyer clucked disapprovingly. "This is a rare opportunity."

"I heard you before. The answer is no."

Joyce, sitting with her fiancé, prodded forcefully. "It's our future we're talking about, Paul. We'll be set for life."

From the young man's bleak expression, it was plain he didn't wish to be set for a life with Joyce. Mordecai sensed his gossamer skein unraveling and acted swiftly to save it.

"Come," he said to the troubled couple. "Let's go for a ride."

An hour later, they were in a northbound Lincoln on a two-lane truck route known as Bloody 27. Mordecai maintained a steady monologue to mask his nervousness on the highway. Joyce had forgotten what a terrible driver her cousin was; poor vision, sluggish reflexes, and limited range of motion behind the wheel due to excessive girth. Paul Guber was a basket case by the time they reached Clewiston. Mordecai parked the car with a jolt and extricated himself from the front seat.

"Where are we?" Paul asked.

"Sugar mill," said the lawyer. "Ever seen one?"

The mill was a sprawling collection of irregular barns, smokestacks and warehouses. Harvest season was weeks away, so the millworks were quiet except for the clatter of pneumatic wrenches; groups of shirtless mechanics worked on tractors, flatbeds and migrant buses. A flaking blue-and-white sign, planted by the road, said ROJO FARMS. In smaller letters:

Division of Sweetheart Sugar Corp.

"Well," Mordecai said. "Shall we request a tour?"

"We shall not," Paul said. Joyce concurred, fearing that offensive agricultural aromas might taint the fabric of her imported blouse.

The lawyer sagged heavily against the fender of the car. "Fine," he said. "As you wish."

Joyce crossed her arms impatiently. "It's sticky out here. Can you get to the point?"

Mordecai sighed like a tortoise. "The purpose of this field trip was to illustrate the financial dimensions of your case. The Rojo family"— nodding toward the sign—"is worth approximately $400 million."

"Hmmmm," Joyce said.

"Conservatively."

"We aren't suing the Rojos," Paul Guber noted.

"True," the lawyer said, "but we're suing their favorite congressman, the fellow who makes all this wealth possible. Are you beginning to understand? Sugar money."

"Look, I got clobbered in a strip joint. That's all."

"The short view," Mordecai scolded.

"I'm damn lucky my boss hasn't found out. If this thing goes to court, I'm out of a job."

"Paul, you won't need a job," the lawyer said. "You'll need a Brink's truck. Tell him, Joyce."

The sting of the bachelor-party photos had apparently abated, for Joyce wholeheartedly supported her cousin's scheme. "Mordecai swears it'll never get to trial. Remember, darling, this is an election year."

"Which means," the lawyer cut in, "the settlement will be timely, substantial and extremely secret. The congressman, too, has much to lose."

Paul Guber replied with a skeptical grunt.

"We're talking two, three million dollars," Mordecai said. "That's a handsome nest egg for two young newlyweds." He chose not to mention Shad's role in the enterprise, or his percentage.

Paul kicked idly at pebbles while a big jet passed overhead, drowning the conversation. When it was quiet again, he turned to Joyce and Mordecai. "The answer is still no," he said.

"Sleep on it," the lawyer advised. He winked instructively at Joyce. "You two should discuss it alone."

Paul said he didn't need to sleep on it, didn't need to discuss it: he flatly refused to sue anybody. "What happened just happened. There's no permanent damage—heck, my insurance covered the hospital bills." He broke into a series of jumping jacks, causing Joyce to gasp in concern.

"See?" said Paul, breathless. "I'll be back at the brokerage house next week."

In exasperation, Mordecai slapped a fleshy hand on the hood of the Lincoln. "There's a legal term for your condition," he told Paul. "It's called 'diminished capacity.' Which means the injury to your head is affecting your judgment."

Joyce nodded. "He hasn't been sleeping well."

Paul Guber stopped jumping and let his arms fall slack. "You two are incredible," he said, panting. Joyce's glare failed to intimidate him. "It must run in the family," he said, "this conniving."

"Is that what you call it?" Joyce's voice was taut.

Mordecai moved between them. "Come now. Let's have a nice peaceful ride home."

Joyce insisted on driving. Mordecai wedged into the Lincoln beside her. Paul Guber rode in the backseat alone; he fell asleep before they got to the I-595 interchange. His snores brought a mirthless chuckle from Mordecai.

"Young Paul is being foolish," he said.

"Tell me about it."

"This is such an opportunity," the lawyer said. "Such a rare, rare opportunity."

Joyce glanced back at her snoozing husband-to-be. It was not a look of pure, unconditional love.

She said, "I was thinking . . ."

"Go on."

"Do we need him? I mean, when all is said and done . . ." She pretended to concentrate on the highway. "Supposing they agree to a settlement right off the bat—then you wouldn't even need to file court papers, is that right?"

"Correct. A few phone calls, a few meetings, a cashier's check made out to a trust account—that's the simplest way, for all concerned."

Joyce lowered her voice. "So . . . do we really need him?"

The lawyer fingered the multiple clefts of his chin and pondered the innocent snores of his client. "That's a good question," he told his cousin. "A very good question."

When Erin arrived at the Eager Beaver, she saw a crew of workmen on the roof, dismantling the fluorescent sign. Orly and Shad stood in the parking lot, deep in discussion. As Erin got out of the car, Orly waved for her to join them.

"Well, you get your wish," he said.

"You're changing the name?"

"Got to," Shad said. He seemed to be enjoying himself.

Orly told Erin not to get a swelled head. The decision had nothing to do with the dancers' complaints; it was strictly a legal matter.

"Don't tell me," said Erin. "There's another strip joint with the same awful name."

"Not a strip joint," Orly said, "a chainsaw."

Shad bit his lower lip, trying not to laugh. Erin was on the verge of exploding. With a straight face, she said, "Mr. Orly, I've never heard of Eager Beaver Chainsaws."

He sneered. "Me, neither. Apparently they're very big in New England, like I give a shit."

Shad said, "They sent a registered letter. Threatened to sue."

"You believe that?" Orly threw his hands in the air. "They said I'm hurting their corporate image, on account a using the name to promote sex and nudity. Fucking asshole lawyers!"

A liquor truck pulled in, and Shad excused himself to check the shipment. Up on the roof, the last plastic vestige of BEAVER fell to a workman's wrench. Orly winced at the sight, as he still had three remaining payments on the lettering.

"How," he mused, "can you slander a fucking garden tool?"

Erin said she was impressed that the Eager Beaver Chainsaw company had heard about Orly's club, so far away. Orly said it was reported by a vacationing chainsaw salesman: "Supposedly he just drove by and noticed the name."

"Oh sure," Erin said. "He just drove by."

"Anyway, my asshole lawyers talked to their asshole lawyers and the upshot is, it's easier to switch the goddamn sign than go to court."

Erin couldn't resist a Mafia dig. "I never imagined the mob would be scared off by a lawsuit."

"Scared's got nothing to do with it," Orly grumped. She'd nailed him good this time. "Little Nicky, guys like him, they don't like publicity. Case like this could wind up on the front page."

"I hadn't thought of that."

"So their attitude is screw it, just change the name."

"The end of an era," Erin said, with mock wistfulness.

"You know me. I'd love to fight the bastards!"

"But they could drag it out for years," she said. "It's best to be practical."

Orly rubbed his nose fiercely, as if trying to dislodge a bumblebee. "Anyone tells you it's a free country, they're full a shit. That's all I can say." He trudged toward the entrance of the lounge. Erin stayed at his side. She asked him if he'd given any thought to a new name.

"Yeah, as a matter of fact. And I don't want to hear boo about it, OK?"

"Let's have it," said Erin.

Orly shuffled into the club. Erin wasn't offended that he didn't hold the door. The man was a pig. He couldn't help it. In the office, he went directly to the refrigerator and got a cold Dr. Pepper. The thought of offering one to Erin never crossed his mind.

"Tell me the new name," she said.

"You'll be a big girl? No whining?"

"No whining."

"All right," Orly said, slurping his soda. "'Tickled Pink.' How about that?"

"You're joking."

"I think it's fine." Orly smacked his lips. "Feminine. Funny. I like it."

"It's dreadful," Erin said. She got up to leave.

"Now don't go making trouble out there—"

"Tickled Pink?"

"Hey, this ain't the Christian Science Reading Room, it's a tittie bar. I got a product to sell."

Erin said, "You're the boss."

"Sometimes I think you forget what you do for a living, which is take off your clothes for money. Or maybe it's just you prefer to forget." Orly rocked back and forth behind the desk. "It's only a name, honey. Doesn't change the merchandise."

Erin didn't back down. She wanted to keep Orly on the defensive.

He said: "Both Moniques love 'Tickled Pink.' They said it sounds like the name of a French boutique."

"No," said Erin, "it sounds like a gynecologist's yacht."

Orly slammed the soda can on his desk. "That's all in your head!" he snapped. "I can't help it you got a filthy mind."

As Erin walked down the hall, she heard Orly shouting: "Hell, it's classier than 'Flesh Farm'! It's classier than those fucking Lings!"

Sgt. Al García spent the morning at a rockpit on the outskirts of Hialeah. He was searching for Francisco Goyo's head. Goyo was a gun dealer who'd been kidnapped on Key Biscayne, murdered in Carol City and dismembered in Homestead. Body parts were turning up from one end of Dade County to the other. Al García had put hundreds of bitter miles on the Caprice, collecting Francisco Goyo's hands, feet, torso and limbs. García hated dismemberments because the paperwork multiplied in direct proportion to the number of body parts; it took hours to write up a simple severed thumb. Naturally, the Goyo case had spawned an office pool. To win, one had to match a particular component of Francisco Goyo with the date of discovery. When an anonymous caller reported a possible floating head in Hialeah, a detective named Jimbo Fletcher let out a jubilant roar—if the head was that of the murdered gun dealer, Fletcher stood to make sixty-five bucks. As much as García disliked Fletcher, he found himself hoping that the floating head did belong to the late Señor Goyo. García wanted the case to be over. He had a suspect and a motive; what he needed was a semi-assembled corpse.

While police divers probed the milky depths of the rockpit, García walked the shoreline. It was so windy that he couldn't light a cigar. Sand from the mountainous limerock dredgings whipped across the wide water, stinging the detective's eyes. Trudging through the chalky dirt, García turned his thoughts to Jerry Killian, and the nearly impossible obstacles to solving that murder. Jurisdiction was a tangle, and it depended on where Killian had died. If he was killed at his apartment, the case belonged to the Fort Lauderdale police. If he was murdered near the river in Montana, the investigation fell to authorities in Mineral County. And if Killian was abducted from Florida to Montana against his will, the FBI should get a piece of the action.

García himself had no jurisdiction whatsoever, no legitimate excuse for pursuing the case except one: nobody else seemed interested. The detective was nagged by an old-fashioned belief that no one should get away with murder so easily. He also wanted to punish the creeps who ruined his family's vacation. The possible involvement of a bigshot politician added urgency to the quest. In fact, García had become so fascinated with the Killian case that he was tempted to take extended sick leave from his Dade County homicide duties. He resented every minute wasted on mundane murder chores, such as bagging fragments of Francisco Goyo. Here was a common shitbird felon with a five-page rap sheet. The world was enriched by his sudden passing. Why, García wondered, am I out here hunting for the man's head? The cosmic purpose eluded him.

At noon, one of the police divers surfaced with a splash. As he paddled to shore, he held an object high out of the water. The object was the shape of a large coconut. Assuming the worst, García retrieved the voluminous Goyo paperwork from the trunk of the Caprice. Returning to the shore, he found the divers gathered around the severed head of a large brindle hog. The hog was wearing a baseball cap: Atlanta Braves.

"Fletcher'll be pissed," García said.

The divers debated the significance of the find. Animal sacrifice was common among worshipers of Santería, a black magic popular in parts of South Florida. Chickens, goats, turtles and other creatures were slaughtered to appease specific gods; depending on the ceremony, it wasn't unusual to find these grisly offerings in public places. The baseball cap was a riddle, though; none of the cops knew what to make of it. Was the hog beheaded as a curse on the Atlanta Braves, or as a tribute? For guidance the divers turned to Al García. As the senior Cuban, he was presumed most knowledgeable in matters of the occult.

"It's not a religious sacrifice," García said, winging it. "It's a family pet."

"No way," scoffed the diver who'd found the head.

"Didn't you ever watch 'Green Acres'? They had a helluva pig."

The diver said, "Come off it, Al. What kind of people kill their own pet?"

"Hey, *chico*, we're in a recession. All bets are off." On that somber note, García departed the rockpit. Instead of driving back to the station, he took the turnpike north toward Broward County. On the way, he stopped at a toll plaza, phoned Donna and told her he'd probably be late for dinner.

"What's up," she asked.

"The usual," García said. "Murder. Topless babes. Nude oil wrestling."

"You poor thing."

"See you around nine."

"Good," Donna said. "I expect to be regaled."

Shad was everything that García had expected, and more. The man's musculature was enormous, but typical for his line of work. The detective was more impressed by the cumulative balefulness of Shad's presence—gleaming smooth pate, ferocious overbite, engorged but expressionless eyes. The man's age was impossible to guess. He was not a freak so much as a living dinosaur, slow-blinking and fearless. When he spoke, the voice was low but the tone was hard. When he smiled, which was seldom, he showed no teeth.

Still, Erin Grant seemed to trust him. From this García concluded that, for all his brutishness, Shad was a gentleman toward the dancers. It was a hopeful sign.

They'd found a relatively clean booth near a dance cage. Erin asked Kevin to drop the volume a couple notches so that García wouldn't have to holler over the music. The detective spread several black-and-white photographs on the table. Without prompting, Erin immediately identified the drunk with the champagne bottle.

"Except he had a mustache," she said, pointing.

García looked positively delighted. "Know who that is? That's our famous Congressman Dilbeck!"

Staring at the picture, Erin thought: Perfect. This is just my luck. "But he was a maniac," she said. "A drunken nut case."

The detective nodded enthusiastically. "Is it making sense yet? Your little pal Jerry witnesses the assault, recognizes Dilbeck on stage and immediately grasps the wonderful possibilities. Yet of all the blackmail options available, he chooses the most unselfish of all: arranging for you to get your child back. Or so he thought."

Erin couldn't take her eyes off Dilbeck's photograph—the starched smile, the smug eyes. He had not looked so dignified while bashing Paul Guber's skull. "Sonofabitch," she said.

Al García awaited Shad's confirmation of the lecherous drunk's identity. None came. "Ring a bell?" he asked.

"Nope," Shad replied. He would need to consult with Mordecai as soon as possible. Police involvement could screw up the lawyer's plan, and seriously interfere with Shad's retirement.

García selected a picture of Erb Crandall. "How about him?"

Shad's brow crinkled. "I'm not sure."

"I am," Erin said. "That's the one who had the gun."

"Very possible," García said. "Mr. Crandall is licensed to carry a concealed weapon. Him and seventy-five thousand other upstanding Floridians."

Shad asked if Crandall was a professional bodyguard. García said his official title was Executive Assistant to Representative Dilbeck. "Meaning babysitter," the detective added, tapping a finger on Crandall's unsmiling face. "Bagman, too, according to the rumors. But that's of little interest to us."

García quizzed Erin about the other photographs—assorted aides and cronies of David Dilbeck—but none looked familiar.

"So here's our scenario," García said, steepling his hands. "Ms. Grant has positively identified Congressman Dilbeck and Mr. Crandall as being in the Eager Beaver on the night of September sixth. She's also identified the congressman as the man who jumped on stage and assaulted another customer. The attack ended when Mr. Crandall displayed a handgun and escorted Mr. Dilbeck out of the club. Is that correct?"

"Right," Erin said. She shot a suspicious glance at Shad, who shifted uneasily. It bothered him to hold out on Erin. If she and the cop only knew about Mordecai's incriminating photo!

García said, "It's all right, Mr. Shad. If you don't remember, you don't remember. Think on it is all I'm asking."

"I see assholes every night. They start to look the same."

"Christ, I know exactly what you mean. Erin, can I have a Diet Coke?"

"She ain't a waitress," Shad said.

"I'm sorry, you're right. I'll get it myself—"

García started to rise, but Erin motioned him down. "I've got to dress, anyway. I'll bring three on my way back."

As Erin headed for the dressing room, Shad began sliding out of the booth. Al García grabbed his elbow and told him to sit tight. He wasn't sure if Shad was stunned or amused by the command.

The detective leaned close. "Listen, Mr. Floor Manager, I don't know your angle, why your memory suddenly is so shitty. That's your business and you sure don't owe me a goddamn thing. But I know you care about that pretty lady, am I right?"

Shad's huge neck throbbed, all veins.

"Here's the deal," García said. "She got herself tangled in a black-mail. Not her fault—just some love-crazed customer trying to play hero, trying to get the lady's daughter back from her ex. You're familiar with Mr. Darrell Grant, no?"

Shad nodded, barely.

"Ha! Your recall's improving every second." García let out a grand laugh. "Anyway, the idea was to put the arm on the congressman, make him pull a string with the divorce judge. The lady gets her little girl, the customer gets to be Sir Galahad. Except somebody whacks him first, which is why I'm sittin' here."

"You're saying Erin's in trouble."

"Could be," the detective said. "It's an election year, which is no time for a sex scandal. They might figure, hell, who's gonna miss a dead stripper?"

"She ain't a stripper. She dances."

"Point is, you don't want her to die. Me, neither. She's a nice person, works hard, loves her kid, et cetera. So if anything important shakes loose inside that incredible bulbous noggin of yours, gimme a ring." García stacked the photographs and slipped them into his coat. He said, "In case you didn't notice, I need all the fuckin' help I can get."

Shad's expression was stone, but his gut was churning. A keen judge of cops, he knew this one was no bullshitter. Erin might be in real danger, and over what—politics? The woman was a dancer, for God's sake. All she wanted out of life was her daughter.

Insanity is what it was. A world gone mad. Shad felt a strange fever in his breast.

García stood up and laid a five-dollar bill on the table. "Have my soda," he said. "You look thirsty."

15

Congressman Dilbeck was revived by the sharp tang of Malcolm Moldowsky's cologne. He sat up coughing in spasms. At the foot of the bed stood Moldy and Erb Crandall, appearing dour and unsympathetic.

Moldowsky's greeting confirmed the mood: "Good morning, shit-for-brains."

"Hello, Malcolm."

"Erb told me about your evening."

"I'm sorry, Malcolm. I got swept away."

"Know what we need to do? We need to teach you to masturbate creatively. Then maybe you wouldn't bother women."

Crandall said, "Those blow-up dolls might do the trick. We'll order him an assortment, all shapes and colors."

Dilbeck felt dizzy. Slowly he lowered his pounding head to the pillows. He was relieved to see that he was in his own bedroom, not a hospital. From this he concluded, perhaps prematurely, that his injury wasn't so serious. Touching the bruise, he moaned melodramatically; the knot was huge.

He said, "Don't I need a doctor?"

"Been here and gone," Crandall reported. "You're a very lucky man—no concussion, no brain damage."

"As if we could tell," Moldy said.

The congressman pleaded for them to lay off, his head was killing him.

"But you've got a fund-raiser tonight, David."

"No way, Malcolm. Look at me. *Look at me!*"

Moldowsky moved to Dilbeck's side and hovered gravely, like a dentist. "Under no circumstances will you miss this function, understand? The marquee is Bradley, Kerry and Moynihan, who don't wish to be stood up. More important, we've got six potential sugar votes coming down from the Hill."

"Those fellows, they're still pissed about the pay raise—"

"Extremely pissed," said Moldowsky. "That's why we're flying them first-class. That's why we've got Dom and fresh citrus waiting in their suites. It's suck-up time, Davey. Everyone's counting on you to make things right again."

"What's that supposed to mean?"

"It means the senior Rojos called, among others."

Overwhelmed by Moldowsky's musk, Dilbeck began to sneeze violently. Moldy backpedaled, shielding his mouth and nose from flying germs. When the congressman regained normal respiration, he announced that he wouldn't be seen in public looking as pitiable as he did.

Erb Crandall said, "It's not the public, David, it's thousand-dollar-a-plate suckers. Tell them whatever you want. Tell them you got hit with a fucking golf ball."

"We're locking out the media," Moldy added. "Feel free to lie your ass off."

David Dilbeck grimaced as he fingered the bruise. "What about X-rays?" he asked. "How can they be sure about concussions if they didn't take X-rays?"

"The doctor checked your ears," Crandall explained, "for fresh blood."

"Jesus, Mary and Joseph!"

Dilbeck's whining grated on Moldowsky's nerves. "We'll ice your fucking head, all right? Spend the day on your back, and by tonight the swelling's gone."

"Exactly," Crandall said. "You'll be as dashing as ever."

"Stop making light of the situation."

Moldowsky twisted the cap off a pill bottle and tapped out two orange tablets. He instructed Dilbeck to swallow them for his headache: "Erb told me what happened. In my view, you're lucky that girl didn't stomp on your balls."

As usual, the congressman remembered almost nothing of the incident. He asked, "What was her name?"

"Jeanne Kirkpatrick," said Erb Crandall. "A very hot number."

"Seriously, I can't recall a damn thing. Her name. What she looked like. Was she blonde or redheaded, Lord, it's all a blank."

"Keep it that way," Moldy said. He closed the drapes to darken the room. "Get some rest. You've got a big night."

"Malcolm?"

"What is it, Dave?"

"This is the last time, I swear to God. I'm cured."

"I'd love to believe you, I dearly would."

"On my mother's grave, Malcolm. Never again. Never! I hurt so damn bad."

Moldowsky said goodbye and left the room. His aroma, however, lingered like an industrial smog. Crandall packed a towel with ice cubes and placed it on the congressman's forehead.

"Erb, you believe me?" Dilbeck asked. "It's out of my system for good."

"Sure, it is," said Crandall. "I'll be in the hall if you need me. Try to sleep."

As David Dilbeck slept, psychedelic visions flashed and popped behind twitching eyelids. Eventually, jumbled starbursts gave way to soothing scenes. The congressman dreamed of a lovely dancer with rich brown hair and small round breasts and a smile that could stop an executioner's heart.

When Dilbeck awoke, the ice in the towel was melted and the pillowcase was soaked against his cheek. His breathing was hot and irregular, but his head no longer throbbed. He bolted upright, energized by the knowledge that the woman dancing in his sleep was real, that he couldn't have dreamed such a smile.

He had seen that dancer somewhere: a radiant moment, buried deep in submemory by a drunken blackout.

Yes, he'd seen her. And she most definitely smiled.

"What did she mean?" In a sing-song tone, the congressman addressed silent walls. "Who is this lovely?" He shook off the sheets and hopped from the bed. The room rolled under his legs. He stumbled to the bathroom and flipped on the lights. Anxiously he examined both ears for signs of blood, but found nothing but clotted wax.

"Who is she?" he cried to the mirror. "What does she want with me?"

After less than a week, Marvela quit the club and defected to the Flesh Farm. The enticement was a $500 signing bonus, Mondays off and a new wardrobe. Orly was livid. To all who would listen, he declared that the Ling brothers henceforth were dead men—gator bait, orchid fertilizer, breakfast sausage, D-E-A-D. Orly said he was calling Staten Island and arranging a murder contract. Nobody stole his dancers and got away with it!

The next day, he installed a wind machine among the footlights on the main stage. He said it was part of a new campaign to make the Tickled Pink a classier joint—new name, new spiffy image. Erin and the other dancers suspected that Orly was upgrading mainly to compete with the hated Lings.

The wind machine was a hooded electric fan, aimed at an angle to blow and swirl the dancers' hair. The desired effect was an untamed, sultry look. "I got the idea from Stevie Nicks videos," Orly told Erin. "You go on and try."

She danced a short set in front of the wind machine. The air hitting her face made her blink continually. She didn't feel particularly sexy.

Afterwards, Orly said, "It's your hair."

"Oh, here we go."

"Just listen for once. Would it kill you to grow it down past the shoulders? Or at least get a perm?" He knew better than to suggest a dye job.

Erin said, "Stevie's got her look, I've got mine."

"I also bought smoke cannisters and a neon blue strobe."

"You're really trying," Erin said, "and we all appreciate it." Now if he'd only eighty-six the damn oil wrestling.

Orly opened a box of the new cocktail napkins—pink, naturally. "Notice anything?" he said. "Lookie: No tits. No snatch."

The club's previous napkins had featured drawings of saucy nudes in feathered hats and spiked heels. Erin favored the plain pink. "These are elegant," she said, "relatively speaking."

Orly was pleased. "It occurred to me, why overdo it with the tits and so forth? No sense staring at poon on a napkin when the real McCoy is wiggling right in front of your nose."

"Good thinking," Erin said. Orly was hopeless, but at least he was making an effort. In fact, the long-haired dancers and those with lush wigs did seem to enjoy performing in front of the wind machine. Only Urbana Sprawl declined to use it, complaining that the fan aggravated her allergy to dust mites. She said there was no tactful way for a naked person to cope with a runny nose, especially while dancing. Orly grudgingly agreed.

Discussion of the new wind machine continued all evening in the dressing room. Most of the dancers considered it a worthwhile investment; it was heartening to see Orly spend on capital improvements. Preliminary feedback from customers was positive, too, judging from the tips. For club regulars, windblown hair was an exotic diversion from leaden footwork and half-hearted pelvic thrusts.

"Speaking of customers," Erin said, "remember Mr. Peepers?"

The two Moniques said they did. Erin asked if they recalled seeing him on the night of the champagne-bottle attack. Monique Jr. said yes, she was giving him a private dance at table three when the fighting broke out. She remembered it well because Jerry Killian had scurried to the main stage to see the commotion, leaving her unpaid and dancing on an empty table.

"I was pissed," Monique Jr. said, "but he came back later and gave me a whole ten dollars." She rolled her eyes in disdain.

"Did he say anything?" Erin asked.

"He said I had bold nipples, whatever the hell that means."

"No, did he talk about what he saw—the fight?"

"He asked did I know the guy with the bottle, and I says no. Then he asked do I know what chivalry is, and I said sure I know what chivalry is. 'Well,' he goes, 'you'll be glad to know it's not dead.' And I said great, glad to hear it. Then he started on again about my nipples."

Urbana Sprawl was impressed by the junior Monique's detailed recollection of a three-week-old conversation; most dancers ignored the idle babble of customers.

"I always remember the shitty tippers," Monique Jr. explained, "just like I remember the good ones."

Erin fluffed her hair, touched up her lipstick and headed for a three-dance set in the cage. Kevin cued up one of her favorite Allman Brothers cuts, and Erin blew him a kiss. Long songs were bad for business, but occasionally she needed one to help her disconnect from the routine, drift away with the music.

Tonight she used the time to think about murder. The facts seemed to fit Sgt. Al García's scenario: Killian was in the audience when the horny congressman sailed off the deep end. The little guy probably recognized Dilbeck, ratty mustache and all, and hatched the idea for a blackmail.

And days later he was killed . . .

Erin was so absorbed that she didn't spot the customer right away. He stood below the cage, staring at her bottom, waiting for her to spin in his direction. Finally he called Erin's name, and she danced up to the bars. He reached up and folded some money in her garter. It was a fifty-dollar bill. Erin smiled and crossed her arms over her breasts, teasingly lovestruck. Later she sat down at his table to say thanks, a strip-joint ritual when a customer gives an exceptional tip. A three- or four-minute visit was considered sufficient; any longer took precious time off the dancer's clock. Chatty friendliness inevitably gave way to salesmanship, and experienced strippers were masters of the blend. A good table dancer could work the same customer for a half-dozen private numbers between performance sets. That was how most of them made their money; Erin was the only one who got by on stage tips alone.

This big tipper was in his mid-fifties, and dressed like a senior loan officer. He was sipping a Jack Daniels too carefully, and hadn't bothered to loosen his necktie. Obviously he had plans for the evening. When Erin thanked him for the money, he reached for her hand: "If that's how much I'll pay just to look, imagine how much I'll pay to touch."

Another smoothie, Erin thought. She tried to pull away, but the man wouldn't let go. She said, "Obviously this is your first time here."

"How'd you know?"

"I'm guessing the Midwest—Chicago, Minneapolis?"

"St. Paul," the man said. "You're pretty good, honey pie."

"Honey Pie? That's the best you can do?" Erin wasn't in the mood for dumb banter. It had been many months since she'd been groped by an out-of-town creep—Sweetie Pants, he'd called her. That one was from Syracuse; the hairiest arms she'd seen outside a zoo.

"Please let go," she said to St. Paul.

"Dance for me."

"I did."

"Not here. I've got a room on the beach." His grip was dry and firm. "A room with a sauna."

"No, thank you."

"For two thousand dollars?"

"I'm not worth it, believe me." Erin dug her fingernails into the soft underside of the man's wrist. He yelled angrily and let go. As she pushed back from the table, the man's leg shot out and kicked her chair. Erin went over backward.

The customer's laughter died with an epiglottal peep. Erin rose to see the man's face pinched in the crook of Shad's arm. The face was bloody and full of deep remorse. Shad was punching in his usual calm and methodical way, but in his expression Erin saw genuine rage, which was rare.

"That's enough," she told him.

Shad let the man fall, face-down. The customer rolled onto his back and blubbered something about a lawsuit.

"Really?" Shad said. "You wanna call your wife? I'll bring the phone." He nudged sharply with a boot. "Well?"

Ten minutes later, the man from St. Paul was strapped in his rented black Thunderbird. He adjusted the rearview mirror to check the condition of his nose and lips, which were swollen to the size of wax party gags.

Shad propped himself on the door of the car. "Don't ever come back," he advised.

"I meant no harm."

"She look like a hooker?" Shad's barren orb filled the window. "Answer me, bud. Did the lady look like a whore?"

The man from St. Paul was shaking. "I'm really sorry."

Shad called Erin to the car and told the man to apologize again, which he did with all his heart.

Erin said, "You should learn some respect."

"I'm so sorry. I swear to God."

Shad said, "What kinda place you think this is? Does it look like a whorehouse?" The man shook his head tensely.

"This is a classy operation," Erin chimed in. "Surely you noticed the napkins."

The man from St. Paul drove swiftly into the Florida night. Erin put an arm around Shad's waist. "You're in a lousy mood tonight," she said. "What's the matter?"

"I'm just worried about you is all."

"Why?"

"There's bad people in the world, that's why."

She laughed. "But you're here to protect me."

"Right," Shad said. First thing tomorrow he would go see Mordecai and tell him the deal was off. The stakes had gotten too damn high.

Down the street came the wail of sirens. Soon a police cruiser raced past the Tickled Pink; then an ambulance, two more police cars, another rescue truck. Shad and Erin walked to the curb to see if there was a traffic accident. Moments later they were joined by Orly, bubbling with mirth.

"There *is* a God!" he said.

"Now what?" Erin asked.

"Just listen."

As if on cue, the sirens began winding down, one at a time. The flashing lights had converged a half-dozen blocks away, on the opposite side of the highway.

"Must be some wreck," Shad said.

Orly giggled. "Ain't no wreck. It's the Flesh Farm!"

"What'd you do?" Shad asked. "Did you pull something?"

"Wasn't me, it was Marvela. She just called, bawling her pretty eyeballs out." Orly was jubilant. "She wants her old job back. Haw!"

Shad said, "Something bad happened."

Orly grinned. "Yeah, very bad. Guy dropped dead at the table."

Erin thought: Poor Marvela.

"And not just any guy," Orly said. "A goddamn judge."

Erin heard herself say: "Which judge?"

"Who cares? A dead judge is a dead judge. Those fucking Lings, I hope they're pissing razor blades . . ."

Erin started down the road toward the winking blues and reds. Orly called her name but she kept walking. Traffic slowed and a few drivers honked salaciously. Erin clicked along in her tall heels, sequined G-string and black lace bra, aiming for the flashing lights, walking faster, telling herself: maybe, maybe, oh maybe Mr. Orly is right.

Maybe there is a God.

The judge considered Marvela a sleek and delicious archangel. She was the only one at Orly's club who flirted properly. The other dancers were detached, perfunctory, even chilly; some refused to perform for him at all. The judge suspected that Erin had poisoned the others against him—they probably despised him for separating their friend from her only child. How unfair! The justification was there in the Bible, plain as day, but none of the dancers wanted to hear him explain it, no matter how heavily he tipped. Everybody had a gift, the judge would say. Everybody had a special purpose on this earth. Motherhood was one, he would say, dancing naked was another.

Being new, Marvela wasn't aware that the judge had been unofficially ostracized. She gave him some terrific table dances, and in a matter of days he was infatuated. When she quit Orly's club, the judge eagerly followed her to the Flesh Farm and the brave new world of friction dancing.

The distance between the clubs was half a mile, but the drive seemed to take forever. The judge found a parking spot far from the streetlights, to avoid being recognized by a passing motorist. Discretion was extremely important until he was confirmed for the federal bench. After that, he was free to recreate as he pleased; to his knowledge, no one had ever been impeached for patronizing a tittie bar.

As the judge turned off the ignition, his heart hammered against birdlike ribs. He felt light-headed, but attributed the feeling to raw excitement. Before entering the steamy house of Ling, he recited a silent prayer, thanking God in advance for the blessings he was about to receive. To be able to lay hands on the beautiful Marvela, to feel her rub those velvet loins against him—these would be fantasies come true!

Sadly for the judge, they did not. Anticipation killed him moments before friction was to begin. He died with his tongue on the table, the Bible balanced on his knees. One hand was fastened to his crotch like the claw of a lobster; it remained attached throughout vigorous rescue maneuvers, including cardiopulmonary massage.

Death had taken the form of a massive cerebral hemorrhage: A significant part of the judge's brain had more or less exploded when the prancing Marvela had draped her *bustier* across the crown of his head. A quick-thinking bouncer had removed the garment before paramedics showed up.

Considering the traffic, their response time was outstanding. The frantic Lings had no opportunity to move the corpse off the premises; all they could do was whimper at the mayhem. Within moments of the first policeman's appearance, the Flesh Farm emptied as if there were a toxic gas leak. The bartenders and dancers were the last to flee.

When Erin arrived, she saw an old man stretched out on the floor. He was surrounded by young medical technicians in blue jumpsuits. One of them knelt beside the lifeless form, thumping the man's chest in perfect time to Janet Jackson's "Rhythm Nation," which was playing on the club speakers. The Lings stayed well back from the scene, yammering about bad publicity, loss of revenue and a possible visit from state beverage agents.

Erin casually walked up and positioned herself between paramedics. Lifesaving efforts were winding down, along with the music. The man on the floor was plainly deceased. Erin leaned over to examine the face; he looked like the right judge, but she wasn't certain. "Can you take off the oxygen mask?" she asked.

One of the paramedics, smitten by Erin's attire, cheerfully obliged. He asked if she knew the victim.

"In passing," she replied.

Marvela, who had changed into street clothes, was being inter-viewed by two uniformed officers and a detective. She chain-smoked furiously, tapping her ashes into a beer stein. Erin sat at the bar and waited for the cops to finish. Shad came in and joined her. He said, "You oughta see the helicopter outside."

"Waste of fuel," said Erin. "He's dead as a flounder."

"It's not from the hospital. It's from Channel 7."

"No kidding?" Erin laughed darkly. "Shad, I'm enjoying this. I hate to admit it, but I am."

"Well, the guy was a prick."

"And such a hypocrite."

"Maybe now you can get your girl back."

Erin said, "That's what I'm thinking. It's awful, I know, under the circumstances—"

"Forget it. The man was puke." Shad reached behind the Lings' well-stocked bar and got two glasses. He unhooked the fountain gun and squirted each of them a Coke. Erin watched the paramedics place the dead judge on a stretcher, strapping him under a brown woolen blanket.

"My lawyer," she said, "will be amazed."

"So will your ex." Shad's lips cracked into a cold smile. "I'd love to be there when you tell him."

"I doubt if I'll get that pleasure," Erin said.

When the police were done with Marvela, she came to the bar and sat with Erin. "I never even touched him," she confided, her voice raw with disbelief. The weeping began, and Erin gave her a hug. She didn't know Marvela well, but she could appreciate the trauma of seeing a customer keel over.

Shad hopped the bar and fixed a Dewar's for Marvela, who con-tinued sobbing intermittently. She said she didn't know what hap-pened—she'd barely gotten her top off. "I can't believe he fucking died. *Died!* I wasn't even down on his lap—"

"That's enough," Erin told her. "It wasn't your fault." She stroked Marvela's hair, which smelled like Marlboros and mousse. Marvela's tears dripped freely on Erin's bare shoulder.

"Look at it another way," Shad said. "The man died staring at pussy. There's worse ways to go."

Marvela was not consoled. She drained her drink and fumbled for another cigarette. "I should've stuck to straight modeling. Swimwear and teddies, that's it."

Shad held out a lighter and said, "For Christ's sake."

"It's all my fault. He's dead because of me!"

"Hush," Erin told her. "You were only doing your job."

16

Rita and Alberto Alonso agreed to keep Angela while Darrell Grant drove a load of stolen wheelchairs to St. Augustine. Alberto was fond of the girl, but Rita preferred the company of canines; Lupa's pups were getting big and frisky. Darrell Grant told his sister to keep Angie inside the trailer, away from the damn wolves. Rita asked where was the kid's toys, and Darrell said there wasn't room in the van for no toys. Alberto said don't worry, there's plenty around here for a girl to play with. He brought out a bag of golf balls and dumped them on the floor. Angela amused herself as best she could.

Alberto slept all day while Rita spent much of the time in the yard with the animals. Angela was fascinated by her aunt's eccentric appear-ance—catcher's mask, cigarette, logger mitts, baggy housedress. The little girl sat for hours at the window, watching Rita work with her high-strung pets. Once, alone in the trailer, Angela picked up the phone and dialed her mother's number, which she had memorized. There was no answer, but Angela let it ring for twenty-five minutes. Rita came inside and pitched a fit. She snatched the telephone and placed it on top of the refrigerator, out of the little girl's reach.

Darrell Grant was glad to leave town, even for a short time. Free of parental responsibility, he no longer had to be discreet about gobbling speed, upon which he was increasingly reliant. The drugs gave him the nerve to steal, and the guile to lie about it. They also helped him cope with Merkin and Picatta, who hassled him relentlessly. The detectives were vicious nags, always after hot tips. Darrell didn't mind snitching on other criminals, especially since the alternative was prison, but sometimes there simply was nothing to snitch. Merkin and Picatta didn't seem to understand that many crooks were chronically lazy; weeks, even months might pass between crime sprees. Yet the detectives were always demanding fresh stats and warm bodies. If there were no serious felonies afoot, they expected Darrell Grant to hit the streets and get the ball rolling.

The trouble was, Darrell didn't have time to hang out with dirtbags. Dealing wheelchairs was a fulltime gig. The St. Augustine run, for instance, promised to net three grand—a nursing home was waiting, C.O.D. Then Merkin and Picatta called, harping at him to go see some Cuban bartender in frigging Hallandale who might or might not be dealing kilos. Darrell Grant needed to think fast, and that's where the speed saved his ass. It helped him remember the name of Tommy Tinker, the heroin man. Darrell knew how much the cops in South Florida loved a scag case. Not only was it a refreshing change of pace from crackheads, it was a guaranteed commendation, usually officer-of-the-month. So Darrell pitched Tommy Tinker as the Number One Heroin Dealer east of I-95, and told Merkin and Picatta exactly where on Sunrise Boulevard they could find him.

"Grams or ounces?" Picatta asked.

"Ounces," Darrell Grant said quickly, "but he don't sell to white guys. Otherwise I'd be happy to make the score."

And off went the two detectives in search of a black snitch, while Darrell made tracks for St. Augustine. He was passing the Vero Beach city limits when his brain decelerated just enough to remember that Tommy Tinker had been fatally firebombed in New Orleans back in 1987. Darrell Grant experienced a brief flush of panic, but at no time considered turning back or making a call. He popped three more beauties, and stepped on the pedal. Soon the van was racing as fast as his heart, and life seemed fine.

The congressman rallied in time for the gala fund-raiser. He was able to dress without assistance, shave with a dull blade and comb his own hair. Tan makeup camouflaged the bruise, which had shrunken to a greenish marble in the center of his brow.

Erb Crandall drove him to the hotel, and hung near his side throughout the evening. The dinner was well-attended and the speeches flattering. The most effusive testimonial came from Senator Moynihan, who'd never met David Dilbeck and was therefore unencumbered by sour memories.

After dessert, Dilbeck himself rose to the podium and managed to speak for eleven minutes without repeating himself. He was careful to lavish absurd praise on colleagues whose votes were crucial to renewing the price supports for domestic sugar. Dilbeck inwardly prayed that his remarks would begin to thaw the ill feelings—after all, how often did such small-timers get compared to the Roosevelts and Kennedys! Erb Crandall said the other congressmen seemed genuinely moved. Dilbeck hoped so, since he'd practically gagged on the compliments he'd dished out.

Later he pinballed from table to table, thanking the paying guests for their generosity. Normally Dilbeck adored being the center of attention, but tonight the limelight was excruciating; the vision in his left eye was blurry, and both ears pounded with an invisible orchestra of steel drums. He sustained himself by silently repeating Erb's mantra: each handshake is worth one thousand dollars.

At a far table, the congressman was greeted by a rotund fellow with flushed cheeks and jumpy rodent eyes. The man was dressed for a funeral. He said he was a lawyer, and introduced a stern female companion as his cousin. Dilbeck noticed a slight family resemblance.

"Remember me?" said the lawyer.

"Well, you certainly look familiar," Dilbeck lied.

"San Francisco. The Mondale Express."

"Of course, of course." Dilbeck didn't have the faintest recollection; he'd spent much of the convention on a barstool at Carol Doda's topless revue. "I saw Fritz about three weeks ago," Dilbeck improvised. "He looks absolutely fantastic."

The lawyer invited the congressman to sit for a few minutes, but Dilbeck said no thanks, they've got me on a tight schedule. That's when the lawyer handed him the photograph.

"For your album," he said.

"Jesus, Mary and Joseph!" said the congressman.

Dilbeck cupped his bad eye and gazed at the color print of his drunken self, swinging a bottle at a stranger's head. Dilbeck had no distinct memory of the raunchy scene, except for the woman on the stage. It was the dancer in his dream—by God, she was real! The congressman experienced a tingle that was grossly inappropriate for the moment.

The lawyer said, "We had the photo enlarged from a slide, which I'm keeping in a very safe place." He paused, running a finger along his upper lip. "If I may say so, sir, you look better without the mustache."

Dilbeck smiled anemically. Erb Crandall, craning over the congressman's shoulder, was comforted not to see his own likeness in the background of the photograph. He wondered, though, if there were other pictures in sequence—pictures of him pointing the gun, for example. Jesus, what a lousy night that was.

"It's peculiar," Dilbeck said, "how I don't remember this."

"But it's you, isn't it?" The lawyer gloated.

Crandall curtly demanded to see identification. Mordecai handed him a business card and said, "I'm sure you're curious about Joyce's interest. The fellow being assaulted is her betrothed."

Crandall put his lips to Dilbeck's ear. "Don't say another word."

"It's all right, Erb. I honestly don't remember."

The lawyer went on: "You're probably wondering about the young man's condition. Unfortunately, the news is not good. He suffered grievous injuries in this attack."

Dilbeck slumped. "What can I say? I'm terribly sorry."

"Shut up," Crandall hissed.

Joyce spoke up. "Sorry is fine and dandy, but my Paul will never be the same."

"Severe head trauma," the lawyer added. "That's a champagne bottle you've got there. Korbel, if I'm not mistaken."

The congressman gave the photograph to Crandall and said, "You were there, Erb. What the hell happened?"

From the corner of his eye, Crandall spotted a ragged line of well-wishers, including several prominent Rojos, moving across the ballroom toward David Lane Dilbeck. Crandall deftly concealed the dangerous photo in his tuxedo jacket, and told Mordecai to meet him upstairs in the hospitality suite.

The lawyer said, "Good, we were hoping for some privacy."

"Fifteen minutes," Crandall said. Then he rushed off to find Malcolm J. Moldowsky.

Strength fading, David Dilbeck managed to finish his rounds—shaking hands, feigning recognition, chuckling at lame jokes, bowing at banal flattery ... and thinking only of the sleek dancer whose honor he'd so nobly defended that night at the Eager Beaver. Did she think of him, too?

Joyce paced the lobby while Mordecai met Moldowsky alone, in the hospitality suite. There were no formalities. The lawyer stated his demands; Moldowsky took a few notes. The photograph, creased by Crandall's tuxedo, lay on the coffee table between them.

"Extortion," Moldy said, thoughtfully.

"In my game, it's called negotiating a settlement. Do you suppose I'm joking about filing a civil action? The picture speaks for itself, Mr. Moldowsky."

"I disapprove of shakedowns."

Mordecai shrugged. "Other attorneys would've sued first, then offered to settle. Of course a lawsuit instantly puts the matter in the public eye. Considering Mr. Dilbeck's position, I assumed he wished to avoid the publicity."

"Thanks for being so damn considerate." Moldowsky got up and fixed himself a drink. His eyes flickered toward the incriminating photo of The Honorable David Lane Dilbeck—homicidal, out-of-control, crazed by lust. It would make quite a splash on the front page of the newspapers.

The lawyer said, "I'll understand if you need some time. It must be quite a shock."

"Not really," Moldy said. "The man's name is Paul Jonathan Guber. He spent five days at Broward General with cuts, bruises and a mild concussion. He's doing just fine now, but I guess that's beside the point. Right?"

Mordecai was stunned into a momentary silence. After a few seconds, he said, "Am I to assume that you called the hospital out of concern for my client's health?"

Malcolm Moldowsky tapped his polished fingernails on the side of his glass. "We look out for the congressman," he said. Erb Crandall had been keeping tabs on young Mr. Guber since the night of the assault.

"I'm impressed," said Mordecai. "However, your interest in my client's medical condition could be perceived as an acknowledgment of responsibility. A jury might be curious to know why Mr. Dilbeck never voluntarily came forward. So might the State Attorney."

Moldy was amused. "Who do you think you're dealing with?"

"That's what I came to find out. I was hoping for a civilized discussion." Mordecai rose and smoothed the wrinkles from his suit. "I'll be at the courthouse first thing in the morning. Prepare the congressman for the worst."

Moldowsky said, "Sit down, hotshot."

"No, sir. I've said my piece."

"Three million is too high."

"Really?" Now it was Mordecai's turn to be amused. "Do you know what Sweetheart Sugar grossed last year?"

Moldy made a sucking noise through his front teeth. In slow motion he placed his glass on the table. The lawyer remained smug. He wished that Joyce could see him in action, cutting the nuts off the big boys.

Moldowsky said, "You know a man named Jerry Killian?"

The lawyer said he'd never heard of him. Moldy could tell he was being truthful. Leave it to Dilbeck to get blackmailed twice for the same fuckup—three times, if you counted the mystery woman who phoned his Washington office.

"I need to know who else is involved."

Mordecai said, "My clients are Joyce and Paul." He didn't mention that Paul Guber, having disassociated himself from the scheme, would never be told about the money. Nor did Mordecai reveal that a modest slice of the settlement would be shared with a violent bouncer named Shad.

"The check," the lawyer said, "should be made out to my firm's trust account."

"A check?" Malcolm Moldowsky laughed harshly.

"Surely you don't intend to pay in cash."

"No. Wire transfer."

"From overseas?"

"Nassau," Moldy said. "Possibly the Caymans. Is that a problem?"

"Not as long as it's U.S. dollars." The lawyer fancied himself the portrait of slick.

Moldowsky said, "Three million won't fly. Try two-point-five."

"You're playing games, Mr. Moldowsky. We both know the price of sugar, and how it stays so high."

"Don't push your luck, hotshot. According to my information, Paul Guber is completely recovered."

"Never know about the human brain," Mordecai mused. "One day the man could be fine. The next day it's intensive care."

"Oh, you're a pistol."

"The prospect of a trial would be most stressful for the young man and his bride-to-be. I'd recommend some long-term counseling."

Moldy flicked a hand in the air. "Cut the bullshit. I'll talk to some people and get back with you."

"Of course."

"In the meantime, have a chat with Joyce. Explain the importance of confidentiality."

"Don't worry," Mordecai said, "she's a smart lady."

And soon to be a rich one.

The Rojos' boat was called the *Sweetheart Deal*. It was ninety feet long, made in the Netherlands. All three staterooms had wet bars and Dolby sound.

The yacht was docked at Turnberry Isle, on the Intracoastal Waterway. By the time Moldowsky arrived, it was almost two in the morning. The elder Rojos, Joaquin and Willie, offered a cup of Cuban coffee to their guest. Moldy didn't need it; he was wide awake. Two young women were taking a bubble bath in the jacuzzi. Christopher was passed out on the carpet, next to a spotted ocelet in an emerald-studded collar. The wild cat groomed its paws and rumbled.

The Rojos led Moldowsky upstairs to a small sitting room on the captain's deck. Willie asked about Erb Crandall.

"I didn't invite him," Moldy said, "for his own protection."

"Tell us the problem, Malcolm."

He kept it simple: The congressman had gotten himself into an unsavory situation. A compromising photograph had been taken. Now a lawyer had come forward, demanding three million dollars.

The Rojos were deeply concerned, and conferred quietly in Spanish. Moldowsky noticed that the brothers wore matching robes with the name of the boat stitched over the left breast. One of Joaquin's earlobes was white with dried soap bubbles.

Moldy said, "The options are limited."

"Three million dollars," said Willie, "is not possible."

"I'm sure he'll settle for two."

Joaquin Rojo whispered a curse. The timing of the lawsuit threat couldn't be worse—Dilbeck should hustle the sugar legislation out of committee immediately, so that the full House of Representatives could vote on it before the November election.

Impossible, Moldowsky said. "Those jerks couldn't pass a kidney stone right now. Everybody's home campaigning." Besides, he added, the Speaker didn't want the bill on the floor so soon—too controversial. Ralph Nader had gone on "Nightline," making a stink about subsidies for Big Agriculture. The tobacco and rice lobbies panicked, which caused their stooges in Congress to do the same. A House vote now would be dicey; the smart thing to do was to wait. Which meant the Rojos were forced to rely on David Dilbeck for several more months—and they needed him squeaky clean.

Willie asked, "How bad is the photograph?"

"Fatal," said Moldy.

"*Mierda*. Let's pay the goddamn money."

"No!" Joaquin said. "I will not be blackmailed."

"Do we have a choice?" Willie turned to Moldowsky. "Well, Malcolm?"

Without mentioning Jerry Killian by name, Moldy confided that a similar problem had arisen a few weeks earlier. "I handled it myself. But this one is more complicated."

"Because of the photograph?"

"And the fact it's a lawyer."

Willie Rojo nodded. "That's what worries me, too. Let's just pay the bastard and forget it."

His brother rose, shaking a pale fist. "No, Wilberto. You want to pay, do it with your own children's inheritance. I'm out!"

Spanish erupted again, and this time the brothers' voices escalated in argument. Moldowsky picked up a word here and there. Finally, Joaquin Rojo sat down. "Malcolm," he said, "how much do you know about cane farming?"

Moldowsky shrugged and said he didn't know much.

"We plant in muck," Joaquin said. "Mostly sawgrass muck, sometimes custard apple. They call it black gold because it produces such rich sugar. A farmer might get ten good seasons out of a field, then the tonnage starts to drop. Why? Because with each crop, the layer of muck shrinks." He dramatized with a thumb and forefinger. "Eventually the soil isn't deep enough for cane, and the land becomes useless. Underneath is solid limestone."

Willie said, "When the muck is gone, Malcolm, it's gone forever. Our people are telling us five, maybe six more seasons."

"Then what?"

Joaquin turned up his hands. "Rock mining. Condominiums. Golf resorts. That's not important right now."

"Later, yes," said his brother. "But for now, our business is sugar cane. We need these last few years to be good ones."

"A legacy," Moldowsky agreed.

"Please make Mr. Dilbeck's problem go away."

"I assume you're not paying off the lawyer."

"My brother and I have decided against it."

The emerald-collared ocelet trotted up the steps and crouched at Willie Rojo's slippered feet. The old man dug into the folds of his monogrammed robe and produced a gooey chicken drumstick. The brothers watched fondly as the animal devoured the piece, bone and all. The crunching bothered Malcolm J. Moldowsky, who was not much of a cat person.

Joaquin yawned and announced it was time for bed. "Call us when it's done," he told Moldowsky.

"This'll still be expensive."

Willie Rojo giggled as he let the ocelet lick chicken grease off his fingers. "How expensive?" he asked. "Not three million dollars, I'm sure."

"Not even close," Moldy said, "but there's a certain risk."

"Not to us, I hope."

"No, gentlemen. Not to you."

Darrell Grant sold the wheelchairs for $3,200 cash and drove straight from St. Augustine to Daytona Beach. There he purchased an assortment of colorful pills, and picked up two prostitutes on the boardwalk. Later, when they thought he was asleep, the hookers let their pimp enter Darrell's motel room and pick through his belongings. Darrell waited a suitable interval, then slipped his hand under the pillow where he kept the dagger. With a ghoulish screech, he sprung from the bed and stabbed the pimp in the fleshy part of a thigh. While the man wriggled on the floor, the hookers straddled him and frantically tried to stanch the bleeding. Darrell Grant calmly yanked the sheet from the bed and sliced it into long strips. Then he tied up the thrashing pimp and the two hookers, and stuffed dirty socks in their mouths. The women didn't struggle, as they had gotten a close-up glimpse of Darrell Grant's microdot pupils.

As he worked on the pimp, Darrell hummed a tune from *The Jungle Book*, which Angela had on video cassette. Gaily, he lathered the man's curly black hair and shaved him bald. Then he took the dagger and cut a perfect capital G on the scalp. The pimp moaned and grunted into the filthy gag. Blood trickled in twin rivulets down both sides of his head. The women watched silently, fearing they were next.

Darrell Grant said: "Now I'm going to teach you people a lesson." He got his keys and ran to the van. Two minutes later he returned, carrying an electric staple gun that he'd stolen from a construction site in Boca Raton. At the sight of the stapler, one of the hookers began to sob. Darrell Grant walked over to the pimp and untied one of his arms.

Still panting, he said, "Were you going to rob me?"

The pimp shook his head violently.

"Liar, liar, pants on fire," Darrell sang.

He plugged the staple gun into a wall outlet, and said, "Next time you want money, ask polite." He grabbed the pimp's hand and stapled a one-dollar bill to the palm. He held the trigger down a long time— ping ping ping—until the staple gun was empty. The pimp's eyelids fluttered and he lolled unconscious. The women shivered with fright.

Suddenly Darrell Grant felt spent. He stretched on the bed and dialed Rita's house. She growled at him for phoning so late, three-goddamn-thirty in the morning!

Her brother apologized and said, "Listen, I might take a few extra days up here. That OK?"

"Suit yourself. Erin's coming tomorrow."

"What?"

"Visitation day," Rita said.

"No!"

"That's what she told us."

"Jesus, Rita, did you tell her Angie was there? How the hell did she know?"

"I can't help it your daughter knows how to use the phone. And she climbs, too, like a little monkey."

"Angie called her?" Darrell Grant pounded a fist on the bare mattress. "Goddamn, I can't believe you let this happen." He was too overmedicated to concentrate on two crisis situations simultaneously. He didn't notice that one of the tied-up hookers had managed to twist an arm free, and was working covertly on the other knots.

Darrell choked the telephone receiver and cried: "Don't let that cunt in the house, you understand?"

"It's visitation day," Rita repeated.

"It ain't fucking visitation day!"

"Then *you* come back and deal with it. I got wolves to train."

"Lord Christ."

"Another thing, it was on the news—what's the judge that got your divorce?"

Darrell Grant told her the name.

"Yep, Alberto said it was him. He's dead, Darrell."

"Now hold up—"

"It was on the TV," Rita said. "He died last night at a nudie joint."

Darrell Grant rested his cheek on the foul-smelling mattress. It was definitely time for more pills.

On the other end of the line, Rita was telling the story. "His family said he went there to preach gospel at the naked girls. You believe that shit? They found a Bible on his lap—it was all on the television."

"I'll be home by morning," Darrell Grant said thickly.

"What about Erin?" Rita asked. There was no answer from Daytona Beach. "Darrell? Whoa hey, little brother, wake up!"

But he was out cold, sapped on the skull by a hooker swinging a staple gun. They made off with the cash, the drugs, the dagger, and of course the van. They did not take Darrell Grant's dirty socks, which were the first things he tasted when he regained consciousness four hours later.

17

On the morning of September twenty-eighth, Sgt. Al García drove through a light drizzle to the Flightpath Motel, two hundred yards due west of the main commercial runway of Fort Lauderdale–Hollywood International Airport. The motel manager, an amiable Greek named Miklos, led the detective to Room 233. As Miklos fit the key in the door, García said, "I bet the carpet is brown."

"How you know that?"

"It came to me in a dream," García said. Miklos opened the door and pointed gleefully at the carpet, which was a cocoa-brown shag.

The detective said, "Sometimes I scare myself." The Mineral County coroner had found three brown carpet fibers under Jerry Killian's left thumbnail.

"What else you dream?" Miklos asked.

"A man named Killian was murdered in this room."

"Oh no," Miklos said. "Don't tell me." He said the maid found Killian's checkbook beneath the bed.

"He probably threw it there on purpose," García said, "so the bad guys wouldn't get it." People did weird things on the verge of dying.

Miklos said, "I send it back right away, next day."

"You did the right thing."

"Who called the police?"

"Nobody," Al García said. "I opened Mr. Killian's mail. There was the checkbook, and your note."

Miklos frowned. "Is that OK? To open his letters?"

"Oh sure. I'm an officer of the law." García got on his knees and crawled under the bed. His fingers probed the ratty shag in search of other clues. All he found was a petrified pizza crust and a nickel. García got up and brushed the fuzz off his trousers.

Miklos said, "Since I work here, seven people die. It is very sad. Seven in seven months."

"Guests?"

"Yes, sir. Drugs, guns, stabs, problems with the heart. The police come many times. Always we are replacing carpets and sheets."

"Maybe it's the location," García said, his voice rising over the roar of an incoming jet. The place was ideal for customers wishing not to be overheard. He took out a photograph of Jerry Killian.

"I never see him before," Miklos said. "You say this man was a murder?"

"Yeah. In the tub is my guess."

"The bathrooms we clean three times a week."

"Wow," García said. "Your Lysol bill must be outta sight. Can I have a look?"

Miklos sat on the bed and waited. He heard the detective fiddling with the faucets in the bathtub. "Mr. Miklos, what happened to the hot-water knob?"

"Somebody broke."

"How?"

"I dunno. Maybe two weeks ago."

The detective came out, drying his hands on a towel. Another jet howled overhead. García said, "Looks like somebody kicked that fixture right off the wall." The drowning Jerry Killian had put up a pretty good fight.

Miklos said, "You say murder but the maid didn't find no dead body."

"That's because the killer drove the dead body to Montana and dumped it in a river."

"Why?"

"To mess up my vacation," Al García said. "Can I see the guest register?"

Miklos took him back to the office, which wasn't much larger than the bathroom. Killian's name did not appear on the check-in sheets; García would've been shocked if it had. He made notes on everyone who'd rented Room 233 during the previous two weeks. One name showed up five times.

"He's a local," Miklos said.

"Local what?"

"Businessman. He entertains."

"Oh," said García. "You mean he's a pimp."

Miklos squirmed. "Boy, I dunno."

The detective asked if any of the other guests in 233 had made an impression. Miklos said yes, one man checked in with a bag of live gerbils and a video camera.

"And you find that unusual?" García smiled. "Go on."

"Another night was three Jamaicans. I tell them there's only one bed but they say it's OK, *mon*. Three big guys in that room—you saw how small it is."

García tapped the guest register. Miklos found the name: "John Riley." Conveniently generic. The address was a post-office box in Belle Glade, of all places. Lake Okeechobee.

"Big strong guys," Miklos reported. "They check out before midnight."

"Paid cash, I'm sure."

"We don't see many credit cards," Miklos said.

"Remember what they were driving? Was there anybody else in the car?"

"Boy, I dunno."

"What else?" García asked. "You said they stood out."

"They all have scars. Very bad scars."

"On the face?"

"Legs."

"Do tell," García said.

"They were in short pants. Red, green, I dunno, but was very bright colors."

"Gym shorts," the detective said.

"That's how I saw the scars." He reached down and patted his shins. "All down here."

"You've been a big help, Mr. Miklos."

The friendly motel manager offered to show Al García the other rooms where guests occasionally died. The detective said no thanks, maybe another time.

"So maybe it was Jamaicans who killed the man who lost his checkbook."

"It's a thought," García said.

Miklos winked. "Maybe your dreams will tell you who did it."

The detective laughed. "I deserve that."

The motel manager accompanied him to the car. Miklos said he'd applied to be night clerk at a Ramada near the beach. He said the waiting list was two pages long.

"But I got more experience than most."

"You're not kidding," García said. "Good luck with that job."

"Thank you," said Miklos. "Good luck with your murder."

Erin got to the trailer park at seven. Rita was already out in the backyard, yelling at the wolf dogs. It was Alberto Alonso who opened the front door. He'd just returned from the nuclear plant, and still wore his gabardine security-guard uniform. Erin was shocked that he was allowed to carry a gun.

"Coffee?" Alberto said. He unbuckled his holster and casually hung it over the back of a chair. Erin felt sick to her stomach; she had a flashing image of her daughter picking up Alberto's pistol, thinking it was a toy.

"Where's Angela?" she said tensely.

"Asleep, I think."

Erin checked both bedrooms, which were empty. She returned to the kitchen, where Alberto was tending the coffee maker.

"Where is my daughter?" Erin said.

"Better touch base with Rita."

"No, I want an answer from you." She felt her arms shaking with anger. "Alberto, it's visitation day."

He poured a cup of coffee at the dinette. "I remember last time you stopped over. Took off without even saying so long."

Erin said, "I didn't feel so well."

"Rita sure was pissed about the mail."

"I sent it all back."

Alberto Alonso eyed her over the rim of the coffee cup. "You look good in blue jeans," he said. "How's the job? I hear they changed the name of the place."

Erin felt short of breath. What had these two cretins done with her daughter? She said, "OK, I'll go ask Sheena of the Jungle."

"Hold on there." Alberto snickered nervously. "Maybe we can work something out, just the two of us."

They heard Rita shouting curses outside. It sounded as if she was being dragged through the shrubbery. "Lupa don't take to the leash," Alberto explained.

Erin steadied herself; outmaneuvering Alberto shouldn't be hard. He moved to a window and peeked through the blinds. "Rita's got her hands full," he reported in a furtive voice. He hustled back to the kitchen, and swept the dishes and silver off the table.

"How about a little show?" he whispered to Erin. "Just like you do at the club, only private."

She thought of that final night, dancing on the table at Jerry Killian's apartment—he'd been so sweet and shy about it. Alberto Alonso was a different story.

He said, "One little number, OK? Then I'll show you where Angie's at." He sat on a stool, and excitedly motioned for Erin to climb on the dinette.

"Music would be helpful," she said.

"Just pretend," said Alberto. "Rita hears the stereo, she'll want to know what's up."

Erin wasn't sure she could dance just then, with or without her songs; all she could think about was finding Angela. Darrell Grant must've called and warned Rita to hide the child. If he knew that the judge was dead, then surely he knew Erin's plan. That he would disregard an emergency injunction, or any court order, was a foregone conclusion. The man would skip the country before surrendering custody of his daughter. To Darrell, it wasn't an issue of rightful parenthood, it was competition—a game of keep-away, with Angela as the prize. Erin knew she had to strike fast, before her ex-husband got back to town.

Stepping up on the table, she almost bumped her head on the drop-ceiling of the trailer. She began humming "Brown-eyed Girl," slowly moving her hips, waiting for Alberto's inevitable grope.

"Faster," he said.

Erin put on her stage smile. As she danced, her sneakers skated on the Formica. After a minute or so, she started to hear the music, clear and tender, in her head. Alberto's coffee-stained leer seemed far away and harmless. She didn't flinch when he clamped his hands around her ankles.

"Go faster," he said again.

Erin thought: Everything will be all right. Softly she sang the first verse.

"Not too loud," said Alberto, glancing toward the screen door.

"It's such a great song," Erin said, to no one.

Alberto dropped his voice. "How about some titties?"

Erin raised her eyebrows.

"Just a peek," he said. "Maybe take off your top."

Still smiling, Erin undid the top two buttons. Then she said, "You do the rest, OK?"

A blissful glow came to Alberto Alonso's face. He rose off the stool and reached for her, his fingers wriggling like night crawlers. Erin knew that Alberto would never locate, much less master, the tiny buttons of her blouse; in such extreme states of desire, men tended to lose their fine-motor skills. Alberto's paws ultimately settled upon Erin's chest, and began to massage in rhythmic circles. His coarse touch gave her an ugly chill, but Erin kept dancing like a pro. Alberto's groans intensified with the pace of his fondling; the tip of his tongue emerged between his teeth, a sluglike sentinel of arousal.

Erin's next move was to tousle Alberto's hair, which was more than he could stand. He got a clumsy grip on her breasts and tried to pull her down, toward his waiting mouth. It presented Erin with an irresistible target. She brought her right knee up, majorette-style, high and hard against the point of Alberto's unshaven chin. The crack was like a rifle shot.

Suddenly Alberto lay flat on his back, gargling blood. Erin stood over him. The stage smile was gone. Her blouse was fully buttoned. In one hand she held the coffeepot; Alberto could see steam curling off the sides.

"I intend to pour this on your balls," Erin said.

Alberto attempted to speak, but the words came out in bubbles.

"I'm not sure this'll kill you," Erin said, taking aim, "but you'll wish it had."

A squeal rose from Alberto: "Neth doe! She neth doe!"

"Next door?"

He nodded hysterically. Erin put down the coffeepot and dashed out of the trailer. Alberto began gagging on the severed chunk of his tongue. Rita burst in the screen door; at her heels stood Lupa, ears pricked.

"Aiyeeee!" cried Alberto, shielding himself with both arms. But the wolf dog had already picked up the primal scent of the freshly wounded.

Erin held Angela's hand the whole way back to Fort Lauderdale.

"What's wrong?" the girl asked.

"I'm just glad to see you, baby." It had been fourteen months since she and her daughter had been alone, without Darrell Grant hovering nearby—the worst year of Erin's life. She wondered what had been lost.

Angela said, "Mrs. Bickel has an aquarium. She let me feed her eels."

Mrs. Bickel was the elderly next-door neighbor of Rita and Alberto Alonso. She had been microwaving glazed donuts for Angela's breakfast when Erin arrived to collect her daughter.

"I didn't notice an aquarium," Erin said.

"It's in the bedroom near the TV. The eels are green and they ate all her pretty fish."

"I see," said Erin. It sounded like Mrs. Bickel fit perfectly in the demographic strata of the trailer park.

Angela said, "Are we going to your house now?"

"We sure are. *Our* house."

"For all day?"

"Better than that," Erin said.

Angela looked worried. Erin's heart sank at the thought that her daughter might rather be with Darrell, or Rita, or the old lady with the eels. It was Erin's most dreadful nightmare, a year's worth of nightmares. Now she felt paralyzed, afraid to say something that might prompt a lacerating burst of candor from Angie. *I want Daddy!* Erin couldn't have endured it.

The little girl broke the silence with one word: "Pajamas."

She was wearing her favorites, starring Big Bird and the Cookie Monster. "But they're dirty," Angela said. She pinched a sleeve to show her mother. "All my clothes are at Daddy's. And what about clean underpants!"

Erin said, "We're going to buy you some new clothes."

"Good!"

"You like to shop?"

"I don't know. Daddy only takes me to hospitals."

"Right. To ride in the wheelchairs." Erin thought: How will I ever explain that man to his daughter? At what age is a child capable of understanding that her father is irredeemable scum?

Angela said, "One time I saw a boy riding a wheelchair."

"At a hospital?"

"Yep. Daddy said the little boy was very sick, so we couldn't race."

"Your daddy was right," said Erin.

"When they put the boy back in his room, Daddy got the wheelchair and took it home."

"Oh?"

"To fix it," Angela said proudly. "It needed a new brake."

"Is that what Daddy said?"

"And new wheels. Wasn't that nice of him?"

Erin sighed. "Angie, I'm glad you called last night."

"Me, too."

To Mordecai, the term "blackmail" was a melodramatic way to describe what he was doing to Congressman David Lane Dilbeck. Playing hardball is what it was. Strip away the tedious formalities of a lawsuit and the essence was no different: give me money—or else. In or out of court, the seminal element of negotiation was the threat. It was an art, the core of Mordecai's chosen livelihood.

Man falls in supermarket, hires attorney; supermarket settles for six figures. Happens all the time and nobody calls it blackmail. Here an innocent man gets mauled by a drunken congressman, hires an attorney—and they're calling it a shakedown! Mordecai was amused by the double standard.

The attack on Paul Guber was vicious and indefensible; any personal-injury lawyer would've jumped at the case. Of course, most lawyers wouldn't have arranged a secret settlement against their client's wishes, or devised to keep the bulk of the money for themselves. It wasn't Mordecai's proudest moment as a member of the Bar, but these days a fellow did what he must. In fifteen years of practice, youthful fantasies of immense personal wealth had evaporated in disappointment. The Delicato cockroach fiasco was a prime example of his recurring foul luck. Now, the horny congressman loomed as Mordecai's first realistic chance at collecting a seven-figure lump. He proceeded on the assumption that it would be his only shot.

In the early 1970s, Mordecai was among the hundreds of idealistic young law-school graduates who rushed to South Florida with the dream of defending drug smugglers for astronomical cash fees. He'd even studied Castilian Spanish in anticipation of his Colombian clientele! But Mordecai arrived in Miami to discover a depressingly small number of imprisoned South American drug barons; defense lawyers seemed to outnumber the defendants. An attorney of modest talents stood little chance of landing a billionaire narcotrafficker as a client; Mordecai was lucky to get the occasional mule or offloader. Before long, he moved to Fort Lauderdale and opened a personal-injury practice.

The strategy had seemed sound: Broward County was growing much faster than Dade County, and most of the new arrivals were elderly. The elderly tended to fall down more often than younger people, Mordecai noticed, and their injuries usually were more complicated. Better still, there was an inexhaustible supply of old folks, thousands upon thousands, with more on the way each winter. Condos sprouted from the beach to the edge of the Everglades—high-rise bank vaults, in Mordecai's view.

He set up shop and made plans to become absurdly rich. It didn't happen. Mordecai's income was respectable but not profane. He got by on minor negligence cases, insurance litigation and probate, which he hated. He told his secretary that they could both retire to Bermuda if his clients spent half as much time falling down as they did drawing up new wills.

Still, Mordecai was in no position to be picky. South Florida was swarming with young lawyers who prowled the courthouses in a feral hunger, scrabbling like jackals for the tiniest morsel. Competition in all specialties was savage because there wasn't enough work to go around. Desperation was manifested in an epidemic of oily late-night advertising. Once the exclusive province of negligence lawyers, television now attracted all fields of the profession: immigration, divorce, adoption, even traffic violations. One of Mordecai's former classmates had become famous touting himself as "Doctor D.U.I." It was survival of the slickest.

Mordecai refused to make a commercial, as it involved the unpalatable prospect of trimming down for the cameras. His mother nagged doggedly—she was dying to see her son on television!—but Mordecai held firm against it. Maybe that had been a mistake. Maybe his career would've taken a loftier trajectory had he chosen the glitter of self-promotion. Then again, what was worse: shaking down a sleazy politician, or putting drunk drivers back on the road?

"I've got to live with myself," he confided to Joyce.

"You did the right thing," she said.

They were going to see Malcolm J. Moldowsky, who had called first thing that morning. Moldowsky said there was good news; he wanted to meet both of them in an hour. Mordecai told Beverly to reschedule his morning appointments, and euphorically thundered from the office. Crossing the lobby, a flash caught the lawyer's attention—a ray of sun, glinting off Shad's enormous head. The bouncer was waiting tight-lipped at the west elevator. Mordecai nearly stumbled: What did the lunatic want today? Had he somehow gotten wind that a deal was imminent? The lawyer slipped unseen through the easternmost exit.

When he picked up Joyce, she said, "You're excited. Let me drive."

"No, I'll be fine."

Joyce warned him about the wet roads and checked the fit of her seatbelt. "Are you sure you got this right?"

"House of Pancakes. That's what he said."

"In Davie? Why so far?"

"I don't know, Joyce, but that's what the man said." Mordecai's voice was tight. "Do you seriously think I wouldn't write it down—something this important?" He pulled the note from his pocket and thrust it toward her.

"Eyes on the road," she said. Then, skimming her cousin's scribble: "All right, so it says pancake house. We'll see."

Mordecai was silent for several miles while Joyce searched for a radio station that suited her taste. Mordecai wondered why Moldowsky had requested her presence at the meeting.

"Joyce, I'm going to ask a favor. When we get there, let me do the talking."

"You don't have to get nasty."

"Now listen—"

"Besides, it was my idea. Cutting Paul out."

Mordecai took a deep breath. "So it was."

"Maybe I'm not so stupid then?"

"I didn't say you were stupid. It's a delicate situation, that's all. These are serious people, and we both need to be mindful of what we say."

Joyce flipped the visor and examined her makeup in the vanity mirror. "I'm a serious person, too," she said. "Slow down, there's the exit."

They pulled off the interstate at Davie Road and quickly spotted the International House of Pancakes. In his excitement, Mordecai mistakenly parked the Lincoln in a handicapped zone. Before he could back out, a man in blue tapped on the windshield. Mordecai rolled down the window.

"I work for Mr. Moldowsky," said the man. The blue was a bowling shirt. "He's waiting at the country club."

"Who are you?" the lawyer asked.

"Messenger," the man replied. "Part-time. You want to see an ID?"

Mordecai shrugged and said, "Hop in."

The man told Mordecai to take Orange Drive west to Flamingo Road. "How far?" asked the lawyer.

"Not far."

Joyce wore a cocky smirk. She reached across and poked her cousin in the arm. "I told you," she said. "House of Pancakes! I knew that couldn't possibly be right."

"Enough," said Mordecai.

Joyce turned to the stranger in the backseat. "What's the name of the country club? Is it Brook Run or Pine Abbey?"

The man hesitated, but not long enough for Joyce to notice. "Brook Run," he said.

"I hear it's just lovely."

"Yeah," the man said. "That's what I hear, too."

"Do they have a brunch?"

Mordecai said, "Joyce, for God's sake."

The man in the bowling shirt sat forward. "Yeah, they got a helluva brunch," he said. "Slow down and make the next turn."

18

Erin moved out of her apartment on the same day that she snatched Angela. She found a place in a suburban development called Inverarry, where Jackie Gleason once lived in a luxury mansion with a billiard room. Erin was in a bind, so she took what was available—a two-bedroom town house that was too expensive. The security deposit was a thousand dollars plus first and last month's rent. She paid in cash and signed the lease under her maiden name. She and Angela relocated the entire household by themselves in three trips. The only casualty was the Jimi Hendrix poster, which ripped when Erin removed it from the wall.

The next day, she withdrew another two thousand dollars from her savings account, drove to her lawyer's office and gave him the money— which (by his secretary's tabulation) reduced Erin's outstanding balance from eleven thousand to nine thousand dollars. That afternoon, the lawyer asked the new judge in Erin's divorce case to remove Angela from Darrell Grant's custody because he had dumped the child with dangerously unreliable relatives. Alberto's pistol and Rita's wolves figured prominently in the judge's decision. Neither Darrell nor his attorney showed up to argue. The judge ordered a full hearing on the case in four weeks. He was curious to know more about Erin's occupation.

The other dancers congratulated Erin and doted on Angela in the dressing room of the Tickled Pink. They took turns playing with the little girl until she dozed off on the floor. Erin wasn't happy about the arrangement; the club was no place for a child. The new judge would take a dim view.

Dancers with children customarily worked the day shift so they could be home at night. Erin couldn't afford to work days because the money was lousy, and she was now nearly broke—the apartment, the lawyer, Angie's new wardrobe.

"The shoes are adorable," said Urbana Sprawl, fingering the tiny Reeboks. "Where'd you find these?" She spoke in a whisper, trying not to wake the girl.

Erin said, "I'm doing tables tonight. So don't fall off the stage when you see me."

"Damn, you *must* be tapped." Urbana knew how Erin hated table dances. "But you'll make money," she told her. "Real good money."

"First one that touches me—"

"No, girl. You call Shad. That's what he's there for." Urbana removed her top and studied her breasts critically in the mirror. "Mosquito got me on the left one," she reported.

Erin said you could hardly see it.

"Hardly ain't good enough." Urbana found a jar of dark makeup and touched up the bite. "Don't you worry," she told Erin. "Everybody does tables. Fact, you're the only one I ever knew who didn't. That's how fine a dancer you are. Most girls'd starve to death on stage tips."

"Well, now I'm dancing for two," Erin said.

Monique Sr. came in and announced that Keith Richards was sitting at table five. "I told Kevin to play some Stones," she said excitedly. "Next set, I'm gonna knock his socks off."

"Keith Richards," Erin said, failing to conceal her amusement.

"What—you don't believe me?"

Urbana asked what he was drinking.

"Black Jack and water."

"Then it ain't Keith. What he drinks is Rebel Yell, straight up." Urbana was an encyclopedia of trivia when it came to the Rolling Stones.

Monique Sr. looked crestfallen. Erin, feeling guilty, said: "Hey, maybe he switched labels."

"It's *him,*" Monique Sr. insisted. "Come see for yourself."

Erin said, "We believe you."

"No, we don't," said Urbana. "Anyway, what's the difference? The Stones don't use dancers. What could he do for us, even if it was really him?"

Monique Sr. started to tell Urbana to go fuck herself, but then she spotted Angie, sleeping. She would not swear in the presence of a child.

"Now, say it was Rod Stewart," Urbana went on, "then we got us some possibilities. He uses dancers in all his videos. That's when you got my attention, when Rod the Bod takes table five."

Erin cut in: "Monique, you want us to come look?"

"Keith would be thrilled," she said icily.

"Let's go then." Erin opened the door and there stood Orly, looking gassy and dour. Monique Sr. curtly excused herself and hurried back to the lounge.

Orly trudged in and closed the door. He glared at Angela, curled on the carpet. "I could lose my license," he said to Erin. "Tell me that's not a minor on the premises. Tell me it's a midget stripper in tennis shoes. Otherwise I lose my fucking liquor license."

Erin apologized for bringing Angie to the club. She told Orly it was a family emergency.

"Shit," he muttered, and sagged down in a folding chair.

Urbana Sprawl said: "Don't you wake that child, Mr. Orly."

"Don't worry," Erin said. "She doesn't sleep, she hibernates."

Overcome by cosmetic fragrances, Orly immediately fell victim to an allergy attack. He stifled his sloppy sneezes as best he could.

"Hush," Urbana said. "You ain't even supposed to be in the dressing room. Or did you forget?"

"Forgive me," Orly said. "See, I couldn't control myself. It's been at least ten whole minutes since I seen your fat ass naked, so I snuck back here to cop a peek. You don't mind if I whack off now, do you?"

Erin said, "God, you're in a lousy mood."

"Damn right." Orly grabbed a handful of tissues from a box on the vanity. "The Ling brothers are doing standing-room, on account of that old judge croaking in their club. They got so much business, they're takin' reservations. *Reservations*, at a goddamn tittie bar!"

Erin said, "The TV news is what did it. You can't buy that kind of publicity."

Orly began to fulminate obscenely, then caught himself. He glanced irritably at the sleeping girl. In a bitter rasp: "We're talking about a dead body, a stiff—just about the worst thing you can imagine. And people are lined up around the block to see where it happened. I don't understand human nature, I honestly don't."

Urbana's eyes were full of mischief. She said, "Let's keep our fingers crossed. Maybe somebody famous will die here, too."

"Not the way these girls dance," said Orly. "The only thing my customers might die of is sheer goddamn boredom."

"That's enough," Erin said sharply. "I mean it."

Urbana hustled off to do a set in the cage. Orly shrunk deeper in the folding chair, which pinched his torso like an oversize clothespin. "Even Marvela's cashing in," he complained.

"She's overcome her grief, has she?"

"The Lings got her name in big letters on the marquee: come see the pussy that killed the judge!"

"Is that what it says?"

"I'm paraphrasing," Orly admitted. "Bottom line, my business is down fifteen percent."

Bracing for the worst, Erin said, "So what do you want from us?"

"Reconsider friction dancing."

"Absolutely not. We took a vote, Mr. Orly."

"Yeah, yeah." He dismissed the idea with a brusque wave. "Then how about this: creamed corn."

Erin said nothing. She wanted him to choke out every depraved detail, with no help or encouragement. She wanted him to be as uncomfortable as possible.

"Instead of Wesson oil," he said. "What do you think?"

Erin's face gave nothing away; she didn't even blink. Orly's hands fidgeted on his belly like two fat crabs.

"Wrestling!" he blurted. "For God's sake, that's what I'm talking about. Creamed corn instead of oil. There's a place in West Palm where it started. First the girls do some—you know, roll around, put on a show—then the guys climb in and wrestle the girls. I'm thinking twenty bucks a pop."

Finally Erin spoke. "Just so I understand. You want me to jump into a puddle of creamed vegetables and roll around nude with a bunch of drunk slobs."

"Not nude. Topless." Orly gnawed off a hangnail and spit it on the floor. "Health department won't go for nude. Not with food products."

"What happened to classy?" Erin demanded. "New name, new image—what happened to that?"

"Those fucking Lings is what happened to that." Orly looked despondent. His words carried a tinge of genuine shame. "You want the truth, I'm hurting. I need a goddamn gimmick, Erin. This creamed corn thing is what they call camp. I'm told the yuppies are suckers for it."

She said, "So it's come to this."

"I can't force you to do it."

"No shit," she said. "With a shotgun you couldn't force me to do it."

Orly straightened and put on his businessman's face. "What's the part that gripes you—is it the wrestling or the corn itself? Because something else occurred to me."

"I can hardly wait," Erin said.

"How about this? Forget the creamed corn—"

"Bravo."

"Consider pasta." Orly's eyebrows danced. "You mention class, well, there you are. What's classier than pasta?"

"Pasta wrestling?" Erin was tumbling through space.

"Egg noodles, linguini, take your pick."

"I've got to undress now, Mr. Orly. Could I have some privacy please?"

When he stood up, the chair fell off his ass with a clatter. Angie stirred but did not awaken.

"Think about it," Orly told Erin. "Like I say, it's a smash in West Palm."

In the mirror she watched him go out the door. "What happened to just plain dancing?" she said.

Sabrina came in to keep an eye on Angie while Erin performed. "I heard you're doing tables tonight," Sabrina said, combing a jet-black wig. "It's not so bad."

"Unless they grab you," said Erin.

"They won't grab tonight. Shad's in one of his moods." Sabrina's hairbrush hit a snag and the wig jumped off her lap. "Damn," she said.

Erin fastened her G-string and checked her butt in the mirror, to make sure the strap was lined up. She said, "The thing is, I need the money."

"You'll do good," Sabrina said. "Just be careful not to fall."

Kevin was playing "Honky Tonk Woman" when Erin went on stage. The song brightened her mood nearly as much as the sight of Monique Sr. dancing wildly on the table of a man who actually looked like Mr. Keith Richards, if you used your imagination.

Which is all that was keeping Erin sane.

Visions of Valium tablets danced in Beverly's head. The phones were beeping off the hook, the mail had piled up, and that horrid bald man was reading *National Geographic* in the waiting room, for the second straight day—the same man she'd tried to stab with a letter opener! Seeing him again was awkward; in sixteen years as a legal secretary, she'd never assaulted a client. Half in terror, Beverly had offered a meek apology.

For what? the bald man said. He'd already forgotten about it. Beverly felt more afraid of him than ever.

"I do need to see the boss," Shad had said.

"You just missed him."

That was yesterday. The lawyer had rushed to a meeting and failed to return. He hadn't even phoned in for messages. Today, Beverly's exasperation was turning into concern: Mordecai could not be found. So far he'd skipped four office consulations, two depositions and an important hearing in Circuit Court. The court hearing was significant because it involved the awarding of attorney's fees, an occasion that Mordecai never missed.

Beverly was mystified. Now a bank officer was on the line, seeking to verify the number on Mordecai's client trust account. The officer recited the account number and Beverly told him it was correct. "All deposits usually go through me," she said.

The bank officer said it wasn't a deposit, it was a withdrawal. A substantial withdrawal. He said Mordecai had called with instructions to close out the account immediately.

Beverly didn't like the sound of that one bit. Another line lighted up—Paul Guber, mildly worried. He hadn't heard from his fiancée in two days. It was unlike Joyce not to pester him hourly. Did Mordecai happen to know where she was?

Poor Beverly had no answers. Now Shad loomed in front of her desk. Today he wore camo fatigues. "This is getting ridiculous," he said.

"I know, I know," the secretary agreed. "I can't imagine where he's gone."

Shad said, "Let me check around." He stepped past her and opened the door to Mordecai's office. Afraid to protest, Beverly followed.

"Did you turn all these lights on?" Shad asked.

The secretary said no, the lights were on when she got there. "He might've worked late last night," she said. The phones resumed beeping, but she didn't pick up. She was determined not to let Shad out of her sight.

He circled the desk, touching nothing. "Someone's been through this."

"How can you tell?"

"It's too damn neat," Shad said. A man working late hours would leave some clutter, but Mordecai's desk was abnormally tidy, not a pencil out of place. Even the trash can looked as if it had been vacuumed.

Shad asked if there was a drop safe. Beverly said no—Mordecai kept all sensitive files in a lock box at a bank.

"How many keys?" Shad asked.

"Two, I think."

"Where are they?"

"I don't know," said Beverly. "He won't tell me."

"This is good," Shad said.

"He won't even tell me which bank."

"Figures."

Beverly speculated that maybe the janitors had left the lights on. That might explain why the place was so orderly.

Shad shook his head. The place had been gone over by pros. "I seem to remember a Rolodex."

Beverly scanned Mordecai's desk. "A locked Rolodex, yes. He kept it by the telephone."

"Well, somebody got it," Shad said. Damn, this was shitty news.

"Shall I call the police?"

"Suit yourself," he said. "My guess is, they'll be calling *you.*"

A man followed Erin home from work. It was three in the morning and the streets were empty. The man was careful to keep a distance of three or four blocks between his car and Erin's smoky old Fairlane. He did a good job, because Erin never suspected that she was being trailed.

She parked beneath a streetlight and led Angela across the lot toward the town house. The man parked not far away, turned on the car radio and napped until dawn. He kept watch on the apartment until ten in the morning. When Erin didn't reappear, the man drove away.

This happened two days in a row. On the third morning, Erin came out of the town house carrying a basket of laundry, Angela scampering close behind. Together they got in the Fairlane and went to a laundromat off Oakland Park Boulevard. Again the man followed, parking at a video store directly across the street. Through binoculars he watched Erin loading the washing machines. An hour later, he watched her loading the dryers. After she was done, the man didn't tail her back to the apartment. Instead he hurried on foot across the street to the laundromat. He was thinking: This is the sickest thing I've ever done. . . .

The congressman had been adamant.

"Erb," he'd said, waving the photograph of the stripper, "I want her."

"No, you don't," Erb Crandall said.

"I've never felt like this before."

"Yes, you have."

"I want her in all the wondrous ways that a man can want a woman."

"Give me a fucking break," said Erb Crandall.

"If you don't help me find her, I'll do it myself."

"After the election."

David Dilbeck said, "I can't wait that long. I'm under a spell, Erb. I am . . . driven."

"Sorry," Crandall said, "I've got my orders."

They were riding first-class on a Delta flight from Miami to Dulles; a one-day quickie. Somebody was giving a bullshit party for Tip O'Neill. Dilbeck paced the aisle, clutching the incriminating photograph to his breast. He simply would not shut up and sit down.

"Did you see the picture? Did you see what she looks like?"

"Very attractive," Erb Crandall said.

"I want you to find her and offer her a job on my staff."

"Have some breakfast," said Crandall. Other passengers were starting to murmur. The next time Dilbeck came within range, Crandall grabbed the Eager Beaver photo and stuffed it inside a flight magazine, which he placed in his briefcase.

Soon Dilbeck tired. He sat down and said, "Erb, I won't get through the campaign without her. She haunts my dreams."

"Really. You know who haunts *my* dreams? Malcolm J. Moldowsky."

"I need to learn everything about her. Everything."

"We don't even know her name," Crandall lied.

"Find out, dammit. Find out everything." Dilbeck's eyes were on fire. "Erb, she's not like the others."

"Yeah, I can tell from the picture. For a minute I thought it was Julie Andrews, dancing in the Alps. Except she was naked with some guy's face between her legs."

The congressman seized Erb Crandall's arm and said, "God, I am hopelessly possessed."

You're half right, thought Crandall. The hopeless part. "Eat your omelet," he told David Dilbeck.

"After the election, you said?"

"Right."

"Maybe I can endure it, Erb. Maybe I could get by if I had something of hers. Something to cherish!"

"Keep your voice down," Crandall said. "I'll see what I can do."

The congressman tugged his arm again. "No, not like the others. No panties or garters or bra cups."

"What then?"

He couldn't believe it when Dilbeck told him. "You are deeply warped," Crandall said.

"Now, what harm could it do? Seriously, Erb."

So Crandall found himself in a laundromat, surreptitiously scraping the lint from the filter of a dryer. Not just any lint—the lint from the beautiful nude dancer's personal laundry. Crandall wrapped the sheath of pink fuzz in a handkerchief. He saw a customer peeking over a stack of folded linens, and flashed a phony FBI badge that he kept handy for odd occasions.

When Crandall returned to the house, the congressman met him in the foyer. Dilbeck's hair was freshly combed and his cheeks shone. He received the lint gratefully, in cupped hands. "My God," he said. "You did it." Then he disappeared into the master bathroom for a long time.

Erb Crandall locked the front door, went to the den, and lay down on a sofa. He turned on a game show and got drunk on gin. He closed his eyes and tried to remember when politics was fun.

19

Shad called Sgt. Al García and said it was time to talk. García picked him up at noon and took the new interstate west, out of the city. Shad wondered where they were headed. He told the detective about Morde-cai's plan to shake down the congressman. García wanted to hear about the photograph.

"Who's in it, besides Dilbeck?"

"The guy he's whaling on," Shad said, "then me and Erin."

"Where's the original?"

"It's a color slide. The lawyer's got it, probably in a bank box but I don't know where. Not even the secretary knows."

García asked about Mordecai. How had Shad met him? What was he like? Shad recounted everything, starting with the cockroach scam. The detective chuckled at the business about the temp eating Shad's yogurt, but otherwise listened seriously. He said: "So it's your guess the lawyer braced Dilbeck with a copy of the picture."

"That's the way he laid it out."

"And he promised you a cut of the payoff?"

"Yeah. Because I was a prime witness."

"And because he screwed up your roach case."

"Royal," said Shad, spitting out the window.

"Now he's missing and you're finally worried. You think maybe the same thing happened to your lawyer that happened to poor Jerry Killian. And you're thinking you might be next."

Shad said, "It's not me I'm worried about."

"Me neither, Cueball. It's your stripper friend."

"Dancer friend."

"Right. She's a nice lady."

Shad blinked straight ahead. "She got her daughter back. That ups the stakes."

"I see your point."

They came to a tangle of converging highways. García bore north on U.S. 27. On both sides was a rolling horizon of water and sawgrass.

"The hell are we going?" Shad asked.

"Beautiful downtown Belle Glade. How about a cigar?"

Shad said sure. Al García was pleased. They both lit up and the car filled with smoke. The detective rolled down the windows.

"Good?" he asked.

"All right," Shad said.

"Hey, *chico*, you inhaling?"

"Yeah. I like it."

"Damn," García said. "That doesn't burn like hell?"

Shad said he didn't feel a thing. "I got what they call a high threshold."

They rode about ten miles working on their cigars, not saying a word. Eventually García asked what it was like to work at a nude dance club.

Shad puffed out a heavy grunt. "After a while, you don't notice."

"Come on."

"Really. I'm to the point where I get excited when they put their clothes *on*. That's what happens after too long."

García said, "I know guys would kill for your job."

"They can have it. Being around naked women all day is bad for your outlook. After a while it's just tits and ass and nothin' special. Like if you worked an assembly line making Ferraris—before long, they're just cars and that's all. You understand?"

"Everything gets boring."

"Damn right," Shad said, teething the cigar, "and when pussy gets boring, it's time for a career move."

"I know exactly how you feel." Al García jerked a thumb over one shoulder. "Guess what I got in the trunk? An Igloo cooler. And guess what's in the cooler? A human head."

Shad violently expelled the cigar out the window. He wiped his mouth on the sleeve of his camo jacket.

"No joke," García said. "Property of one Francisco Goyo, deceased. I can't begin to tell you how much gas I've wasted on the case. The fat prick got dumped in a dozen different zip codes."

"Why," Shad asked, "do you got his head in an Igloo?"

"So it won't stink up the car."

"That ain't what I mean."

The detective said that a windsurfer on Key Biscayne had found the gruesome item by accident that morning. "I gotta drop it by the morgue on the way home. They got a Frigidaire full of Señor Goyo."

"Goddamn," Shad said, gravely.

"But I know what you mean about boring. Same old shit, day in day out." García flicked the ash from his cigar. "You want to trade jobs?"

"Goddamn," Shad said again.

García drove directly to the Belle Glade post office. He asked Shad to wait in the car so as not to terrify bystanders. At the desk, García showed his police badge and asked about the box number given by the three mysterious Jamaicans at the Flightpath Motel. The clerk, a handsome woman with thick gray hair, said the box indeed belonged to a Mr. John Riley, but that Mr. Riley had not picked up his mail in six months. There was an excellent reason.

"He's passed on," the clerk said.

"I'm very sorry."

"Then you're in the minority."

García said, "Who could tell me about it?"

"Anybody," the clerk replied. "Riley was a crew boss at Rojo Farms. He was shortin' his cutters and they all knowed it. One morning he got runned over by a migrant bus." The clerk paused. "It was a accident, accordin' to the state patrol."

"But maybe not," García said.

"Misself, I lean toward a act of God. Riley was a bad man. Bad things happen to bad men."

"And this was six months ago?"

"At least. And they still curse his name, the cutters do."

"Anybody curse it more than others?"

The clerk said, "I don't follow."

"Did any of the men have a special reason to hate Riley, besides the money he was stealing?"

The clerk was greatly amused. "What other reason would they need?" She began sorting the mail, arranging it in neat stacks. Many of the envelopes bore scriggly printing and foreign stamps; Belle Glade was a migrant town. The clerk said, "Sounds like you're after somebody in particular."

"Don't laugh," García said. "It's three Jamaicans."

"Oh my."

"I asked you not to laugh."

"But his whole crew was Jamaicans."

"I figured," García said. "And they all hated him, right?"

"Worse than a snake."

Back in the car, García asked Shad if he wanted to ride over to Clewiston and see a sugar mill. Shad said he had no earthly interest.

"It'll help make sense of all this," García said.

"Save your gas and tell me about it on the way back to Lauderdale."

"Why the hurry?"

Shad's neck inflated. "Because there's a goddamn Cuban head in the trunk!"

"Señor Goyo was Panamanian."

"Jesus!" said Shad.

A marsh rabbit appeared in the middle of the road. Al García weaved around it without braking. "This congressman," he said, "his balls belong to the sugar companies. They need him up in Washington, to keep things right. So when dorky little Killian threatens a blackmail, the sugar people's people get nervous. You with me?"

Shad pointed ahead and said, "Speed trap."

García said, "For Christ's sake, I'm a cop. Remember?" He blinked his dashboard light at the state trooper as they flew by. "You aren't even listening," he said to Shad.

"Yeah, I am. Sugar money."

"Killian makes his demand, which is so weird it probably freaks out Dilbeck's people. Fix a custody case? they're thinking. Lean on a judge? We're dealing with a crackpot, they're thinking. So somebody—not Dilbeck, but somebody close—makes a phone call."

"And so long, crackpot."

"Right. Three cane cutters show up and snatch Killian, probably out of his apartment."

"How do you know they're cane cutters?"

"Scars, man. They've got the scars on their legs. Cutters are always whacking themselves by accident with those damn machetes; even the good ones do it. Anyway, they haul Killian to a cheap motel and—as a sick joke—register in the name of a dead boss man. The motel is where they drown him. Then they put him on ice—"

"Don't tell me," Shad said. "Another fucking Igloo."

"Not likely," said García, steering with one hand, waving the dead cigar stub with the other. "Anyway, they ice him down and drive straight to Missoula, Montana. Or maybe they use the Rojo corporate jet, who knows—"

Shad said, "Why Montana?"

"That's where Killian vacations. See, it was set up to look like a fishing accident."

Finally Shad cracked a smile. His colossal white dome bobbed as García heard him swallow a laugh.

"What is it?"

"Man," Shad said, "three Jamaicans cruising through Montana."

"Yeah, I know."

"Holy Christ. Is that a riot? Jamaican cowpokes."

"They had nerve," Al García said. "Whoever it was."

"You'll never get 'em."

"You're right."

"Never in a million years."

"I'm quite sure," García said, "they're already back in Kingston. Or dead."

The temperature light on the dashboard flashed red, so he steered the Caprice to the shoulder of the road. He opened the hood and checked the hose fittings, which seemed tight. There was no sign of a leak from the radiator. "Wires," the detective muttered, and slammed the hood.

Shad was gone from the car. Al García found him forty yards away, three rows deep in a field of tall cane.

"So this is it," Shad said. A fat blue horsefly gorged on his gleaming scalp. The fly was so big it looked like a tattoo.

García snapped off a stalk of cane and sniffed it. "What a deal these bastards get. All the water they want for practically nothing. Imported slave labor for the harvest. Then they get to sell the crop at jacked-up prices, courtesy of the U.S. Congress. And when they're all done, they're allowed to dump the stink straight into the Everglades."

Shad was impressed. "Land of opportunity," he said, probing the black muck with the toe of his boot.

"Millions and millions of dollars," García said. "Killian had no idea what he was dealing with. Same goes for your ace attorney."

They got back in the car. Shad declined the offer of another cigar. The horsefly remained attached to his head. García reached over and brushed it away.

Five miles later, Shad said, "So where's your jurisdiction on this deal? I don't see a Miami connection."

The detective smiled ruefully. "Dilbeck's congressional district is in Dade County. That's the best I can do."

"Pitiful," Shad remarked.

"Nobody else is much interested. I can't just let a homicide slide."

"Other words, you're doing this off the clock."

"That's why I need your help," García said.

"Think they'll come after Erin?"

"I think they'll come after everyone in that photograph, if necessary. I think they won't even hesitate."

Shad turned to look out the window. They were out of farm country now. The Everglades shimmered west to the horizon. "She's got her little girl back."

"So you said."

"I guess that don't count."

"Not with these people." García stopped at a fishing camp to buy another bag of ice for Francisco Goyo's severed head. Shad frowned when he heard the trunk pop open, the cubes pouring out of the plastic. He hoped García wouldn't try to show him the damn thing. Some cops got off on shit like that.

When they were back on the road, Shad told the detective that he'd done some state time.

"Oh, I know. Manslaughter."

"Manslaughter *two*," Shad said.

"That was the plea. The crime was manslaughter." García saw that the temperature light had come on again. He thumped the dashboard with a fist, and the light went out. "God bless General Motors," he said.

Shad asked if he knew about the agg assaults, too. García said sure.

"My boss, Mr. Orly, he'd hit the fucking roof," Shad said. "Hiring a felon and all. He could lose his license."

García kept his eyes on the road. "Don't worry about your boss," he said. "I needed to know. He doesn't."

"I appreciate that."

"Here's another thing: I'd prefer not to be informed if you've got a piece, OK? Because if I see it, then I gotta do something. Like arrest your ass, OK? That's the law, felons can't carry a gun. So don't feel obliged to take it out and play, because then we got a problem."

Shad said, "I'm with you. Let's talk about Erin."

"Yeah." The detective drummed his fingers on the steering wheel. "We gotta figure something out."

"Shouldn't be hard," said Shad. "With my good looks and your brains."

Malcolm J. Moldowsky prowled the penthouse restlessly. The ocean view did not soothe him, nor did the fine cognac. He was a resentful man, deeply resentful that a person of his stature should be forced to worry.

Moldy was at the top of his game: insidiously powerful, obscenely wealthy and largely untouchable. Up until now. Lately his hard-earned arrogance had lost some of its starch. He was feeling vulnerable, even shaky. Others were to blame. Free-floating incompetence threatened to destroy an artifice that Moldowsky had spent years constructing. He knew how his hero, John Mitchell, must've felt when those idiots bungled a simple burglary. A life's work destroyed by unspeakable stupidities.

In protecting David Dilbeck's career, Moldowsky had breached a realm far beyond the mere peddling of influence. Committing illegal acts was nothing new. It was the nature of the recent felonies that concerned Moldy: a superb white-collar criminal, he'd been forced out of his element. Diverting election funds was a breeze. Unlawfully compensating an elected official was child's play. Falsifying campaign finance reports was a routine chore.

But this! Goddamn that Dilbeck.

For the first time in many years, Moldowsky was second-guessing himself. He hated the feeling because he hated all forms of introspection. In Moldy's line of work, a man's worst enemy was a functioning conscience. He poured another cognac and resumed his idle pacing through the apartment. Passing a mirror, Moldowsky saw that he'd skipped a belt loop in the back of his pants. Also, he had misbuttoned the cuff of his left sleeve. God, was he rattled!

It was the sudden death of the divorce judge that did it. The judge who couldn't be persuaded to help a congressman and fix a lousy custody case. The judge who didn't need a favor because he was already coasting on his merry way to the federal bench.

Jerry Killian was killed because the judge wouldn't budge. Moldowsky had seen no other solution; eliminating the blackmailer removed the threat to David Dilbeck. It was simple, logical, expedient—but had it really been necessary? Moldowsky was annoyed at himself for fretting about it. The Killian decision made perfect sense at the time. Who could've predicted that the judge would obligingly croak?

Moldy was a man who appreciated cruel irony. Normally he would've been amused by the seedy circumstances under which the pious little shit had expired—his brain detonating in a sea of bare breasts. The TV crews swarming the Flesh Farm had left little to the imagination.

Yet the only thing that had entered Moldowsky's mind was an unfamiliar stab of doubt: Maybe I acted too precipitously. If I'd stalled Killian, jerked him around for a couple weeks, then the judge would've solved both our problems by dying. *Grant* v. *Grant* automatically would've been reassigned, and Killian would've backed away from David Dilbeck.

Oh well, Moldy thought. What's done is done. The three Jamaican cane cutters have gone home. Next month there would be a terrible truck accident near Montego Bay; no survivors. And the flight logs for the Rojos' *Gulfstream II* would show a trip to Aspen, not Missoula. Push came to shove, the FAA would back him up with tower tapes. The daughter of a deputy assistant administrator owed her job to Malcolm J. Moldowsky . . .

The phone beeped twice and Moldy picked it up. He stood at the broad window and gazed across the Atlantic. Under cloudy skies, the water was foamy-gray and unalluring. Just over the horizon, in Nassau, was the man on the other end of the phone call. He was a banker who'd been educated in London, but whose speech had retained its soothing island cadence. He told Moldowsky that the wire transfer had been completed.

"What shall we do with the balance?"

"It's entirely up to you," Moldowsky said.

"We can put it in trust," the banker suggested.

"Hell, you can keep it, for all I care. Buy yourself a new Hatteras."

The banker chuckled nervously. "Certainly Mr. Mordecai left some instructions."

"As a matter of fact, he didn't."

"But, sir, the account is in excess of eighty thousand dollars. I'm sure he expects the money to be properly invested." The banker paused. "Is there a problem I should know about?"

"Not that you should know about, no. A trust is fine, Mr. Cartwright."

"Unless he needs frequent access."

"No," Moldy said. "That's one thing he definitely won't need."

He thanked Cartwright and hung up. Immediately the phone rang again. It was the lobby—Erb Crandall was coming up for a visit. Moldowsky took out another glass, just in case the bagman was in a mood to unwind. He wasn't. He said he was ready to quit David Dilbeck's campaign.

Moldy said, "Now slow down, Erb."

Crandall stood rigid, arms folded. "I've been telling you he's a time bomb. Well, the fuse is finally lit."

Moldowsky was glad he'd had the foresight to start drinking early. "What's he done?" he asked.

Crandall told him about the clandestine lint mission to the laundromat.

"Lord," Moldy said. "That *is* bad."

"It's only the beginning, Malcolm. He wants more."

"More what?"

"He's crazy for this stripper. The one in the picture."

Moldowsky squinted. "So he wants more lint?"

"Not just lint."

He described the congressman's current fantasy. Malcolm Moldowsky rocked on his heels, the brandy boiling up in his throat.

"He's off the deep end," Moldy said hoarsely. "Completely insane."

"Thank you, Dr. Freud." Erb Crandall went to the bar and got an ice-cold can of ginger ale, which he rolled back and forth across his throbbing forehead. He slumped in an armchair, his back to the ocean. "What now, Malcolm?"

"The girl," Moldowsky said. "Obviously."

Urbana Sprawl was right about the money. Erin made an extra ninety bucks on her first night of table dancing. Shad stayed close, and nobody touched her. Still, she hated it. The tables at the club were so small that the dancers couldn't move their feet without kicking the customer's drink in his lap. The performance itself wasn't dancing so much as wiggling in place, which was fine for the girls with large breasts— gravity did all the work. But Erin's strong suit was choreography, and there simply was no room to show off. On the tables she was just another stripper, bouncing up and down for tips.

Another drawback was the music. The dancer on the main stage got to pick the songs, which was only fair, but it meant that the table dancers never knew what was coming next. Most of Kevin's play list was disco, techno, fusion, dance-club, hip-hop and rap, all of which Erin detested. There was no heart to any of it, and pretending otherwise was an ordeal. She smiled so intractably that her facial muscles soon became numb; toward the end of the shift, she looked in the mirrored walls and saw a rictus grin, earnest but unsexy. The tabletop customers never noticed, since their eyes were riveted on her crotch.

On the second night, Erin made two hundred and ten dollars on the tables; the third night, one-eighty-five. On the fourth night, the homicide detective showed up. He and Shad sat down and began to talk. Erin watched curiously from table five, where she was dancing against her better judgment to an extremely long number by Paula Abdul—or, as Mr. Orly called her, Kareem Abdul Paula. Erin was eager to finish the dance so she could find out why Al García had come to the club. As the song thumped to an end, the customer reached up and folded a bill into Erin's garter. She thanked him as he helped her step off the table. While reattaching her G-string, Erin saw that the man had given her a hundred-dollar bill. She thanked him again, this time with the standard hug and peck reserved for overly generous customers.

"How about another one?" the man said. He was a handsome young Latin, doing his smoothest Jimmy Smits. His clothes were expensive and his hair was raked back and there were knobs of gold on both hands. He wasn't yet drunk enough to present a problem, so Erin said sure and got back on the table. Shad and García were still hunched in conversation at the bar—she hoped they'd be there for a while. A smart dancer didn't walk away from a heavy tipper, not when she still owed her lawyer nine grand.

Erin did five table dances for the young Latin, and he gave her a hundred each time. She was excited about the money, but also suspicious. The guy wanted something else. Had to.

Eventually it came her turn to dance on the main stage. Kevin put on a cut by the Black Crowes, which woke up the whole joint. The song was fast and nasty, and Erin loved it—she kicked and whirled and double-clutched, working out lots of unspent energy. At the bar, Shad sat alone; Al García was on the pay phone near the front door, with his back to the stage. Oblivious, Erin thought, thoroughly unmoved by my spirited performance. It was funny.

The young Latin customer came to the footlights and waved Erin over. He slipped two hundred dollars in her garter. When Erin leaned down to thank him, he put a hand on her shoulder and whispered something.

Shad tensed, watching Erin's expression. He was ready to move fast, if the creep made a grab. Erin seemed puzzled, but not upset, by the young man's words. When she moved back to the middle of the stage, her smile looked solid and her eyes were calm. She even took a languid, Stevie Nicks-style twirl in front of the wind machine. Shad held steady.

After the set, Erin returned to the young Latin's table. Shad didn't see her stand up for another dance. Before long, the Latin man rose and left the club. Erin appeared at the bar and said: "I would like a martini."

Shad asked what was wrong.

"Nothing," Erin replied. "Show business."

"Quite a fan there." It was Al García. He sat down on the other side of Erin. "You know who that was?"

"Said his name was Chris."

"Christopher Rojo," the detective said. "Of the sugar Rojos."

Erin said, "That would explain all the money. But it doesn't explain this." She spun on the stool, and swung her right leg across Shad's lap.

"Where's your shoe?" he asked.

"Young Christopher just purchased it," Erin said, "for one thousand dollars."

The bouncer's vast brow crinkled in astonishment. Erin herself was in a mild daze. The money was a godsend, but it wasn't the career of her dreams—selling used footwear to wealthy perverts.

"A fucking shoe," Shad muttered. "What for?"

Erin covered her face. "I don't want to think about it."

"Love," said Al García. "Ain't it grand?"

Merkin cupped the receiver and asked Picatta if they should accept a collect call from Darrell Grant.

Picatta said, loudly, "I don't know a Darrell Grant. How about you?"

"Never heard of him."

"Where's he calling from?"

"The Martin County jail," Merkin said. He grinned and held the phone away from his ear. Darrell could be heard, pleading with the long-distance operator to put him through.

Picatta leaned close to the receiver and boomed: "The only Darrell Grant I know is a lying cocksucker who's getting his probation yanked the second he's back in Broward County!"

Merkin said, "Is that the same misfortunate Darrell Grant that's about to lose custody of his kid, due to his felony records suddenly showing up on the courthouse computer after being lost all those years?"

"The damnedest thing," said Picatta, "after all those years. That new judge was real surprised, is what I heard."

On the other end, Darrell Grant fell silent. The long-distance operator, an angel of patience, again asked if Detective Merkin would accept the call.

"No, ma'am," he said. "You tell Mr. Grant if he needs to chat, he should phone up Mr. Thomas Tinker, that so-called big-time heroin dealer he told us about. The switchboard at the graveyard will patch you right through. Goodbye now."

Merkin hung up. The operator clicked off. Darrell Grant glumly handed the telephone to the patrolman, who put it back on the jailhouse wall.

"They're playin' a joke," Darrell Grant said.

"Didn't sound like a joke." The patrolman pulled Darrell's arms behind him and snapped on the handcuffs.

"You're makin' a big-time mistake. I work for those boys."

"Really? They told you to come all the way up here and steal Miss Brillstein's wheelchair?"

The cop marched Darrell Grant to the holding cell. He said someone from the Public Defender's Office would stop by later to discuss a plea.

Darrell Grant found an empty place on a steel cot, between two sleeping drunks. "You let me know when Merkin calls back," he told the patrolman.

"In your dreams."

"I work for the goddamn Broward County Sheriff!"

"Maybe once upon a time," the cop said, disappearing.

Darrell Grant rocked miserably on the cot, grinding his molars, picking his cuticles, tapping his feet. Was Merkin bluffing, or had they really cut him loose? Worse, had they given his rap sheet to Erin's lawyer? Darrell couldn't believe the detectives could be such bastards. He had to get back to Lauderdale and see what's what. Meanwhile, he needed something to clear the brain and settle the nerves. He asked the other prisoners where he could score some crank. They were not particularly helpful.

A burly redhead with twin cobra tattoos stepped forward. "Hey, beach boy. True you stole a wheelchair off a cripple?"

"I didn't know she was a cripple," Darrell said. "I thought she was just old."

The Palm Lake Rest Home—he'd cased it pretty carefully, considering he was still foggy from when the hooker had clobbered him . . .

Noon sharp. There's the cute Filipino nurse wheeling Miss Elaine Brillstein down the driveway toward the van. Nurse chatting as she pushes Miss Brillstein, who squints into the sunlight and clutches a fuzzy white sweater across her lap. 'Scuze me, ladies. Who's that? says Miss Brillstein, squinting harder. Excuse me, y'all need a hand? Well, all right, says Miss Brillstein, thank you very much. I'll get the door. Hold my sweater, please. Here, let me help with that. My, what a nice young man . . .

Soon as Miss Brillstein's up in the van—the nurse half in, half out, wrestling with the old lady's seat belt—Darrell Grant hijacks the wheelchair and off he runs. Two blocks later, the brake switch drops a bolt and Darrell goes ass-over-teakettle in the middle of a school zone. There's a black-and-white parked on the median, clocking speeders. Darrell Grant can't fucking believe his lousy luck.

From the redheaded prisoner with the snakes on his arms: "The cop said the old lady had polio."

Darrell Grant's eyes felt raw and swollen. He experienced an urge to sleep. "I thought polio was extinct," he said.

The redhead moved closer. "My aunt's got polio."

"Yeah?" said Darrell. "Is her name Brillstein?"

"No, it ain't."

"Then mind your own goddamn business." Without his drugs, Darrell often got pissed at the whole universe.

The redhead said, "I bet you'd look good in a wheelchair."

"Not as good as you," said Darrell Grant, "with a two-foot donkey schlong up your ass."

Later, when he awoke in the county hospital and saw that they hadn't bothered to cuff him to the gurney, Darrell Grant congratulated himself for such a bold and brilliant plan.

In South Florida, the disappearance of a lawyer was seldom front-page news. It happened often enough, usually coinciding with the theft of a client's money. The man from the Florida Bar used the term "misappropriation" when he described the scenario to Beverly.

"How much?" the secretary asked.

"Approximately eighty-five thousand dollars."

"No way," she said. "I can't believe it."

"Then what do you think happened? Where is he?"

"Maybe he was kidnapped." Beverly told him that burglars had gone through Mordecai's office one night—even the Rolodex had been stolen! The man from the Florida Bar asked if she'd called the police. Beverly admitted that she hadn't.

"Because you were afraid," the man said, "that the clues would point toward Mordecai himself."

"I kept hoping he'd show up."

The man from the Florida Bar was sympathetic, but firm. "The trust account was emptied on his direct instructions. The assets were transferred out of the country three days ago."

"Yes," she said glumly. "The bank called."

The man from the Florida Bar sat before an open briefcase at Mordecai's desk. The law office was closed—temporarily, according to a note on the front door. Beverly wasn't optimistic. She let the answering service take all the angry calls.

The man from the Bar asked, "Do you know the number-one cause of disbarment in Florida?"

"Moral turpitude?"

"Good guess, but no. Misuse of client trust funds. Some lawyers simply cannot resist."

Beverly was in the high-backed chair where Mordecai's clients normally sat. She tolerated the arrangement only because she was curious about what the Bar might know of her boss's whereabouts.

The man said, "Did he have many elderly clients?"

"Not enough," Beverly said. "Why?"

"It's part of the pattern. Older clients tend to be conservative with their money. They put it somewhere and let it sit. Years and years might go by."

Beverly said, "Like in their lawyer's trust account."

The man from the Florida Bar nodded. "Meanwhile the balance keeps growing. Some lawyers dip in, call it borrowing. Some even go through the motions of trying to pay it back. Others just flat out grab it all."

Beverly didn't particularly like Mordecai, and had no illusions about his sterling character. But she'd never pegged him as the sort to skip town with clients' money. He seemed more of a small-time chiseler and cutter of corners. Embezzlement seemed too ambitious for Mordecai.

The man from the Florida Bar said, "Who knows what triggers the impulse. A financial setback, gambling problems, a secret love affair. Which brings us to the obvious question—"

"We were *not* involved," Beverly cut in. "Give me a little credit, please."

"Looks aren't everything. Even a physically . . ."—the man groped for the right word—"*daunting* fellow can have his charms."

"Not Mordecai," Beverly said. "Believe me."

"Tell me: How did he feel about his cousin?"

The secretary acted confused. "Which cousin—Joyce?"

"Yes. We believe they're together. Did he ever discuss an attachment?"

"Joyce and Mordecai!" It was so twisted that Beverly almost hoped it was true. Joyce was an avaricious bitch, always angling for the big score. Maybe she'd romanced Mordecai into the swindle. No man was immune to seduction, but Mordecai (who hadn't dated in years) was exceptionally vulnerable. Beverly imagined the two cousins entwined, and it made her shiver.

The man from the Florida Bar said: "Joyce's fiancé doesn't think much of the theory but, I must tell you, stranger things have happened."

"Maybe it wasn't a love affair," Beverly said. "Maybe it was a straight business deal."

The man from the Bar folded his hands across his chest. "What would he need her for? Mordecai alone had access to the trust account. He didn't require an accomplice."

"No, I suppose not."

"In many of these cases, these sudden disappearances, the lawyer brings a woman along on the adventure. Frequently, it's his own secretary."

"Well, I'm still here," Beverly said sourly. "And he owes me two weeks' pay."

"Could be worse. You could be one of those clients."

"Is that who called you? Was it a client?" The investigator's arrival at the law office had surprised Beverly. The Florida Bar was not renowned for swift and aggressive pursuit of errant members.

The man said, "We received a tip. That's all I can say." He gave her a business card with an 800 number in Orlando. "If you should hear from him, please encourage him to return swiftly and make restitution. The longer he's gone, the worse it will be."

Beverly felt more abandoned than ever. "What do I tell everyone about the office being closed? What should I put on the door?"

The man from the Florida Bar shut his briefcase and crisply snapped the brass locks. "We recommend 'Death in the family.' Most clients won't press the issue."

They moved from the lounge to Orly's office: Orly, Al García, Shad, and Erin. Angela was in the dressing room with one of the fully-clothed Moniques.

García had Orly in a sweat. "I want to know more about the phone calls."

"Me, too," said Erin.

"Some guy, I don't know." Orly was slurping a Dr. Pepper. "He's asking about a certain customer—"

"Jerry Killian."

"Yeah, so big deal. There was a fight on stage and this Killian is in the audience, like I give two shits. Man calls and I tell him what he wants—"

"How'd you know Killian's name?"

"Credit card slips," Orly said. "Anyway, this guy who calls, he says to keep him posted if the customer shows up again."

Al García said, "Why'd you agree?"

"Because I got a license to consider, and this guy says he can give me problems. Says he works for a congressman. So . . . a few nights later, Killian shows up again. This time he's outside, hanging around Erin's car. You remember?"

Shad and Erin nodded together.

"See," Orly continued, "I can't have customers hassling my dancers. The guy on the phone says he'll make sure it doesn't happen again. That's it. End of story. I don't hear from him anymore, until today."

García had a notebook in his hand, but he wasn't writing much. "Why won't you tell me the man's name?"

"Because you don't understand. The nature of my business, I don't need any grief. I got a liquor license to protect."

Erin told Orly that Jerry Killian had been murdered.

"Shit," Orly said, sucking air. He looked at García. "Is that why you're here?"

"What a sharpie you are. Now give me damn name."

Orly looked cornered. "Maybe I should check with my lawyer. Maybe you should come back tomorrow."

García said, "If I have to come back tomorrow, I'm bringing beverage agents. You follow? We'll board the place up, *chico.*"

"Screw you." Orly was feeling worn out and reckless.

Shad stirred. "Mr. Orly, you better listen. This is no bullshit."

Al García tapped a ballpoint pen on his knee. "The deal is, Erin's life is in danger. I've advised her to get out of town, but there's a complication."

The new judge had forbidden Erin from taking Angela out of Florida. "As long as I'm stuck here, I might as well work," she said, "considering I'm broke."

Orly's puzzlement deepened. "Who'd want to kill *you?* I mean, besides your ex."

Someone knocked sharply on the door. Before Orly could respond, Sabrina burst in. She wore a thin sleeveless T-shirt and pink bikini bottoms. She was splattered with yellowy goop that Erin despondently recognized as creamed corn. Random kernels clotted Sabrina's platinum wig, which she clutched in one fist.

"I can't do this!" she cried.

"Later," Orly said. "We got a meeting here."

"But it got up my nose—"

"Later, I said."

The dancer ran out. A brief silence followed. Finally Orly said, "Erin's the best of the bunch."

"So you wouldn't want anything to happen to her," García said.

"No, I sure wouldn't."

Erin said she was deeply touched. Orly scratched at a scab on his arm. "Plus your little girl. That's a factor."

"You're all heart," the detective said.

"The guy's name is Moldowsky. And don't ask me to spell it. Melvin or some damn thing."

García said, "Excellent. What did he want today?"

Orly jerked a thumb toward Erin. "He asked about her. What kind of person she is. Has she got a drug problem. Is there a boyfriend."

Erin felt a bolt of fear. She'd never heard of this person.

"Another thing," said Orly. "He knows about the kid. Knows there's a problem with your ex-husband. The guy, he knows lots."

"He mentioned Angie?" Erin's voice cracked. She sat forward, balling her fists. "What did you say?"

"Not a damn thing," he said. "I swear, I told him zippo." Erin's glare was scalding. Orly angrily jabbed a finger in the air. "You tell her, Shad. Tell her how I handled it."

Shad backed up Orly's version. "I was there when the asshole called. Mr. Orly didn't give him shit."

"Okay," Erin said, leaning back. "I'm sorry."

"He's a heavy hitter," said Orly. "He dropped a few names to get my attention. Otherwise I'd say fuck off." His piggy eyes narrowed on García. "I lose my license and there's hell to pay. Bottom line, there's some serious people I answer to."

"Don't worry, Mr. Orly. You cooperate and everything'll turn out just beautiful."

"Cooperate?" Orly sprayed the word. "Sweet Christ Almighty, what more you want? I gave up the goddamn name."

"Yeah, you did," García said. "If only there was a phone number to go with it."

Orly adopted the impatient pose of a man with better things to do. "Yeah, Moldowsky left a number. I got it here somewheres." He pawed halfheartedly at the clutter on his desk.

The detective said, "Excellent. I want you to call him."

Orly frowned. "What the hell for? I'm not callin' nobody."

"Come on," said Al García. "Let's find that number."

Shad winked at Erin, as if to say: This part might be fun.

García stayed at the club until closing time. He waited in the parking lot until Erin came out with Angie. The detective tried to make friends, but the little girl was tired and cranky. She climbed in the backseat of the Fairlane and lay down. García said it was a lousy arrangement, letting Angie stay at the club.

Erin said, "Sorry you disapprove." She was in no mood for a male lecture. "The other girls are terrific with her. And, no, she's not allowed in the dance lounge to see what her bimbo mom does for a living."

"Easy now," García said. "I'm not talking about the atmosphere, I'm talking about the child's safety."

He held the door while Erin got in the car. She turned the key and revved the engine noisily. "I want her near me at all times," she said, "as long as Darrell's out there."

From the backseat: "Momma, can we go home now?"

García lowered his voice to a whisper. "Think about it. If someone's after you, where's the first place they're gonna come? Right here. Say the shit hits the fan—you want that little girl asleep in the dressing room?"

"Fine," Erin said. "Then you find me a kindergarten that's open at three in the morning." She slipped the car in gear. "Besides, what's there to worry about? We got you and Shad to protect us."

Erin drove away fast, burning rubber on the corner. Very childish, she thought, but wonderful therapy. She gunned it all the way home.

When Al García arrived at the town house, twenty minutes later, Erin and Angela were still sitting in the Fairlane. Erin's face was taut as she stared at the front of the apartment. When the detective approached the car, he saw a small pistol on the dash. In the backseat, Angela was as still as a porcelain doll.

García asked Erin to put the gun away. She pointed at the second-story window and said, "The bedroom light's on."

"You didn't leave it that way?"

"No lights," Erin said. She'd shut off everything before leaving for work. It was an old habit; the electric bills were murder.

They watched the window for signs of a shadow. Nothing moved behind the half-drawn drapes.

"Give me the key," García said.

"It's probably open."

"And the gun, please."

Erin gave him the keys and the .32. "The safety's on," she said.

"Thanks. If things break loose, lean on the horn."

The front door was locked. The detective opened it softly and went inside. For several interminable moments, nothing happened; it was as if Al García had been swallowed up in the darkness. Erin scanned the windows and braced for the sound of a muffled gunshot, but all she heard was Angela's gentle breathing in the backseat. Eventually the other windows lit up, one by one, as García moved from room to room. When he reappeared at the front door, he waved for Erin to come in.

The place looked untouched. The detective accompanied her and Angela through the kitchen, the living room, up the stairs to the bedrooms. Nothing seemed to be missing.

So I made a mistake, Erin thought. I left the damn light on.

"This is all your stuff?" García asked.

"Angie and I travel light." It felt strange to have the detective in her bedroom. Erin caught him smiling at the rock posters on the wall.

She said, "I'm saving for a Van Gogh."

"No, I like it."

Angela ran down the hall and returned with a crayon drawing. "I drew this myself," she said, thrusting it at García.

"What a pretty dog."

"No, that's a wolf. Aunt Rita's." Angela traced the outline with a finger. "See the bushy tail? And here's the baby wolves under the tree."

"Right," said the detective. "Wolves."

Erin took the drawing from his hands. She said, "That's Darrell's side of the family. I need some aspirin."

The bathroom was the last place she expected to find signs of an intruder. At first she didn't notice. She got a bottle of Advils from the medicine chest and swallowed three. Standing at the sink, looking in the mirror, Erin sensed something was out of place. She turned and saw what it was.

"God," she said. A prickle went down the back of her neck.

García walked in. Erin told him to look at the shower curtain, which was pulled open along the length of the bathtub.

"You didn't leave it that way?"

"Never," Erin said.

Angie squeezed between the grown-ups' legs and said: "Because of mildew."

"That's right," said her mother. "It mildews if you leave it bunched up that way."

García smiled. "Every day I learn something new."

Erin gave Angie a glass of chocolate milk and put her to bed. Then she and the detective went through the medicine chest, the cabinets, the vanity. They found nothing missing or even disturbed, yet Erin was sure that someone had been there.

Inside her house.

Not Darrell Grant, either. He wouldn't have come and gone without leaving tracks. His ego couldn't abide an anonymous entry. No, Darrell would've mangled something intimate and left it on display.

Erin sat on the edge of the tub and fingered the shower curtain, as if it held the clue.

"Weird," García said. "Not your average burglar."

"I can't afford to pack up and move again. I just can't."

García leaned against the bathroom sink. He was dying for a cigar. "I wonder what he wanted," he said.

Erin said she was too tired to keep looking.

"One more try," the detective said. "I got an idea that might help. Tell me everything you do to get ready for work."

"Please," said Erin.

"I'm serious. Everybody's got a routine when they get up in the morning. Tell me yours."

"I'd say the high point is flossing my teeth."

"Whatever. Walk me through it."

Erin agreed, out of pure exhaustion. "Well, first I shower, do my hair, shave my legs. Then I touch up my nails . . . Wait a second." She was looking at the window sill where she kept her bath articles.

"God, this is sick. Now I know what's missing." She stood up, shaking. "Angela can't stay here," she said, "not another single night!"

The detective put an arm around her. "Tell me what they took."

"You won't believe it," Erin whispered. "*I don't believe it.*"

The congressman lay flat on the bed. He wore a black cowboy hat, a white towel around his waist and a pair of green lizardskin boots. The surgical scar on his breastbone pulsed like a worm in the ultraviolet light.

Erb Crandall said: "What've you done here?"

"Created a mood." David Dilbeck opened his eyes. "Did you get what I wanted?"

"Yeah, I got it. Where's the wife?"

"Ethiopia, courtesy of UNICEF. Then Paris and probably Milan. Do you like the black lights?"

"Brings back memories."

"Pierre found them at a head shop in the Grove. Let me see what you've got, Erb."

Crandall stepped tentatively through the purple glow. He said, "Geez, look at you."

Using handkerchiefs, the congressman had tied one arm and both feet to the bedposts. Above the boots, his pale shins gleamed, as if shellacked.

"Vaseline," Dilbeck explained. "First I warmed it in the micro-wave—it's best to use the sauce setting." Erb Crandall's disgusted expression prompted Dilbeck to add: "This is what happens when you won't let me go out and play."

"David," Crandall said, "tell me you've been drinking."

"Not a drop, my friend."

So he was insane, Crandall thought; downhill from downhill. He wondered what the chairman of the Florida Democratic Party would say if he could see the senior congressman at this moment.

Dilbeck thrust out his free arm. "Come on. I've been waiting all night."

Crandall dropped it—the thing he had stolen from the stripper's apartment—in Dilbeck's open palm. The congressman squirmed on the bed as he examined the illicit treasure: a pink disposable razor.

"Now, this is the genuine article?"

"From her very bathroom," Crandall said, listlessly.

Dilbeck twirled it between his fingers. With an edge of excitement, he said, "I bet she used it this morning."

"I wouldn't know."

"I can see the little hairs!"

"Be careful, Davey." With any luck, the dumb shit would slice his own wrists.

Dilbeck's chest rose and fell heavily. "Erb, do you like Garth Brooks?"

"Is that who you're supposed to be?"

Dilbeck smiled dreamily. "My boots are *full* of Vaseline."

Well, thought Crandall, enough's enough. He took one of the burglar tools from his pocket—a small screwdriver—and put the blade to Dilbeck's neck. The congressman seemed surprised, but not particularly afraid.

Crandall pressed firmly and said, "I'd be doing us both a tremendous favor."

"Erb, please. This is harmless sport."

"You're a sick puppy."

Dilbeck said, "Stop that right now."

"This isn't why I went into politics, David—to pimp and steal for a perverted old fuck like you. Believe it or not, I once had ideals."

Crandall was romanticizing; he was not a man of ideals so much as a man of instinct. He had been drawn to politics by the sweet scent of opportunity. The bitter backlash from Watergate had guaranteed a landslide for the Democrats, so that's when Crandall invested his loyalty. The choice was not between good and evil, but between winning and losing. Occasionally Erb Crandall was compelled to question the wisdom of his allegiance, but never had it been so tested as it was now.

"Know what?" he said to the prone and bound congressman. "Even that jizzbag Nixon wouldn't have pulled something like this."

"Maybe he'd have been a better President if he had." Dilbeck arched his silvery eyebrows. "Ever think of that?"

Dispiritedly, Crandall put the screwdriver away.

"That's a good boy," David Dilbeck said.

"Moldy's coming in an hour. If I killed you, there wouldn't be time to clean up the mess."

Dilbeck studied the plastic razor from all angles, as if it were a rare gem. "What's her name?"

"Erin," Crandall said.

"That's beautiful. Irish, obviously. Erin what?"

"Never mind."

"Come on, Erb. I won't try to find her, I promise."

Crandall walked to the door. "I need a drink. By the way, you look absolutely fucking ridiculous."

The congressman paid no attention. "Erb, one more small favor."

"Let me guess. You want me to tie your other arm to the bed."

Dilbeck cackled. "You better not!"

"What then?"

He wiggled the pink razor in the air. "Shave me, Erb. Shave me all over."

Crandall glared loathesomely as he stalked from the room.

David Lane Dilbeck was the only son of Chuck "The Straw" Dilbeck, once the foremost pumper of septic tanks in Dade, Broward and Monroe counties. In the early boom days of South Florida, before sewers were available, nearly every family relied on a septic tank buried in the backyard. The massively squat cylinders were vital components of the average household, and a frequent source of whispered anxiety. A septic-tank backup was the secret nightmare of every rural husband, as dreaded as a hurricane or a heart attack. Cleaning clogs was a vile business, and only a few hardy entrepreneurs had the will to compete.

The Dilbeck name was widely known in the solid-waste industry, and its prominence endured long after most South Florida septic tanks had rusted out. Young David never spent a day pumping sewage (he insisted it gave him a rash), but early on he recognized the value of having a notable father. In 1956, at the age of twenty-four, he boldly announced his candidacy for the Hialeah city council. Many of the town's citizens were lifelong customers of Chuck Dilbeck, and were glad to support his son's ambitions. Speedy response was critical in a septic-tank crisis, so it was important to stay on The Straw's good side. Hundreds of local septic-tank owners enthusiastically volunteered to help in young David's first political campaign, which he won handily.

Even by Florida standards, Hialeah was—and remains—egregiously corrupt. For council members, the easiest graft was the fixing of zoning cases in exchange for cash, real estate and other valuables. David Dilbeck was fortunate to be in Hialeah during the salad years, when there was still plenty of land to be carved up and paved. He spent four fruitful terms listening, learning and successfully avoiding indictment. He excelled at negotiating bribes, and carried the skill with him when he went to Tallahassee as a junior member of the state Senate.

The atmosphere in Florida's capital was different, and the pace of life was faster. Corruption was a sociable affair, rich with tradition; the stakes were higher, as well. Because of occasional scrutiny by pesky news reporters, it was unwise for legislators to be seen drooling openly on the laps of private lobbyists. David Dilbeck worked hard to polish his rough edges. He learned to dress and talk and drink like a country gentleman. The senate was loaded with self-cultured rednecks, and most were unabashedly crooked. But the pecking order was rigid, and newcomers who ignored protocol paid dearly for the mistake. Dilbeck adapted smoothly, and was soon studying at the knees of some of Florida's most prolific thieves. He was rewarded in the usual ways.

It was in Tallahassee where he first learned that some women were attracted to politicians and would actually have sex with them. Dilbeck gained this pleasant knowledge episodically, and with each conquest he became more obsessed. He'd always anticipated that public service would make him wealthy, but he never dreamed that it would get him laid. For eight years Dilbeck wallowed promiscuously and then—in fine Southern tradition—married a phosphate tycoon's gorgeous, semi-virginal daughter, who seldom consented to sleep with him. Pamela Randle Dilbeck was more interested in new fashions and social causes. Her husband encouraged her to travel often.

By the mid-1970s, Dilbeck's career had stalled in the halls of state government, where he had authored exactly two pieces of legislation. Neither could be described as landmark. One of the bills made it illegal for sporting-goods stores to sell machine-gun clips to minors on Sunday. The measure passed narrowly, despite staunch opposition from the National Rifle Association. Dilbeck's only other achievement was a joint resolution naming the Okaloosa dwarf salamander as Florida's official state amphibian; a special limited-edition license plate was made available to the motoring public for thirty-five dollars, plus tax. The salamander tag was designed by a vivacious art instructor from Florida

State University, who was paid $40,000 from the general revenue fund, and who also happened to be screwing a certain senator on Thursday afternoons.

Dilbeck's big break was the passing, at age eighty-two, of Congressman Wade L. Sheets of South Miami. The venerable old Democrat had been mortally ill for the better part of three terms, and was rarely seen on Capitol Hill. Those close to Sheets sadly reported that his numerous health problems were complicated by fast-advancing senility; toward the end, he refused to wear pants and demanded to be addressed as "Captain Lindbergh." By the time Sheets died, a score of local politicians had positioned themselves to make a run for his seat in the House of Representatives. Among the hopefuls was David Lane Dilbeck.

At Sheets's funeral, Dilbeck delivered a eulogy that was uncharacteristically graceful, bringing fond laughter and tears from the huge assembly of mourners. The emotional speech was even more remarkable, considering that Dilbeck had met Wade Sheets only twice in his life and on both occasions the ailing congressman appeared not to be conscious. Dilbeck's remarkable panegyric (written by an eager young staffer named Crandall) borrowed heavily from old John F. Kennedy scripts, which had borrowed heavily from everybody else. No one in the hushed church picked up on the plagiarisms. The other candidates for the dead Sheets's seat also presented eulogies, but none were as moving or as memorable. The others knew they were sunk when all the TV stations led the news with a video snip of David Dilbeck in the pulpit. That single maudlin oratory ensured his selection as Wade Sheets's successor. Hands down, Dilbeck had given the best damn sound bite at the funeral.

He was thrilled to travel all the way to Washington; the farther one got from one's constituents, the harder it was for them to keep an eye on you. Again, Dilbeck modified his style of larceny to fit local custom. Outright cash-in-a-bag bribery was rare on Capitol Hill; special-interest groups were more subtle and sophisticated. A compliant congressman might receive four skybox seats to a Redskins game in exchange for a key vote. Such arrangements were virtually impossible to trace, much less prosecute. Another quick way to a politician's heart was by exorbitant campaign donations; in this manner, David Dilbeck was seduced by the powerful sugar lobby. Other industries found him equally receptive to their attentions. For two decades he was content to coast along as a well-lubricated lackey. He weathered several stiff Republican challenges and numerous negative news stories, but always managed to get reelected. Those who owned Dilbeck's soul remained silent because they were satisfied with his favors. Consequently, he was never threatened by a scandal.

Until now.

"Good evening, deacon."

"Hello, Malcolm." The congressman shrank in Moldowsky's presence. Erb Crandall could be handled, but Moldy was something else. The man held no loyalties beyond the contractual.

He said, "Where's the cowboy suit, Davey?"

"So Erb told you." Dilbeck had ditched the boots and the cowboy hat for a maroon jogging suit. He stood casually in the den, sipping an iced tea.

"Erb is concerned," Moldowsky said. "Frankly, so am I."

As always, Dilbeck found himself admiring Moldy's elegance. He wore a gorgeous dove-colored Italian suit with an indigo necktie. Tonight's cologne was particularly memorable; Moldowsky smelled like an orange grove.

"David," he said, pacing, "I hear talk of Vaseline."

"I'm trying to cope—"

"—and laundry lint. Is this possible?" Moldy's fulsome pucker suggested that he was about to spit on the carpet.

"Malcolm, I wish I could explain. These are forces rising up in me, animal urges . . . and it's simply a matter of coping."

"Sit down," Moldy barked. No taller than a jockey, he hated staring up at the person he was berating. "Sit, goddammit."

Dilbeck did as he was ordered. Moldowsky moved slowly around the den, occasionally pausing to scowl at the photographs and laminated press clippings that hung on the wall. Without glancing at Dilbeck, he said, "Erb found a lady's shoe in your desk. Where did that come from?"

"Chris bought it for me."

"From this stripper?"

"Yes, Malcolm." Dilbeck took a gulp of tea. "These little things— they help me get by. It's harmless sport."

Moldy felt a jolt of desperation. Insanity was one thing he could not fix, spin, twist or obscure. And David Dilbeck was plainly nuts.

"What did Erb do with the shoe?" the congressman demanded. "He didn't throw it away, did he?"

Unbelievable, thought Moldowsky. He's like a damn junkie.

"My inclination," Moldy said, "is to haul your ass back to Washington and lock you in my apartment until the sugar vote. Unfortunately, we've got a campaign to worry about. It would be poor form for you to vanish."

"I suppose," Dilbeck said, absently.

"David, you do understand what's at stake?"

"Of course."

"What if I brought in a woman, to be here just for you—for when you got in these moods. Maybe two women . . ."

Dilbeck thanked Moldowsky for the offer but said it wouldn't solve the problem. "Love has swept me away," he said.

"Love?" Moldy laughed acerbically.

"It's frightening, Malcolm. Haven't you ever felt so passionately about someone?"

"Never," Moldowsky said, truthfully. He stuck to call girls. They spoke his language.

"Don't worry, it'll be all right," Dilbeck told him. "I'll make it to the election just fine." He rested his glass on the arm of the chair. "Erb says Flickman wants a debate. I'm ready."

"Ignore the little fuck," advised Moldowsky.

Eloy Flickman was Dilbeck's hapless opponent in the Congressional race. Under ordinary circumstances, a debate might've been productive, since ideologically Flickman stood slightly to the right of Attila the Hun. Among his campaign promises: televised executions of drug dealers, free sterilization of welfare mothers and a U.S. military invasion of Cuba. Even the state GOP was leery, providing the shrill appliance salesman with only nominal support.

Dilbeck said, "I could destroy him, Malcolm."

"Why bother. He's destroying himself."

"I worry about that Cuban thing. It's loony enough to catch on."

"No debate!" Moldowsky said. He stopped pacing and planted himself in front of Dilbeck's face. "Davey, we've got a more pressing matter—this goddamn stripper you're so taken with."

The congressman bowed his head. "What can I say? I'm no longer in control of my impulses."

In Malcolm Moldowsky's grand vision of the future, David Dilbeck already was a goner. The day the sugar bill moved out of committee, he was finished. A stiff. Moldy and the Rojos would get him dumped from the chairmanship. Other congressmen would be elated to assume

Dilbeck's special role; surely not all of them were so conspicuously deranged. In the meantime, Moldowsky had formed a plan. It was not without risk.

"I'll make you a deal," he told Dilbeck. "First you've got to promise: no more collecting her laundry lint and razors and her goddamn shoes. Is that understood?"

"All right. But what do I get?" The congressman sounded skeptical.

"A date."

Dilbeck rose slowly, eyes widening. "God, you're serious."

"Her boss called me tonight. He said she might be up for it, if the price is nice."

"When?" Dilbeck's voice jumped. "You mean, right now?"

Incredible, Moldowsky thought. He's about to come in his pants. "Tie a knot in it," he told the congressman.

"A date, you said."

"I'm working out the details."

Dilbeck showed no curiosity about Moldy's relationship with the owner of a nudie bar. He held Moldowsky by the shoulders. "If you can arrange this, honest to God—"

Moldy brushed Dilbeck's hands away. "Then you'd behave until the election? This crazy shit'll stop?"

"On my father's grave, Malcolm."

"Very funny."

The Straw—a showman to the end—had been buried in a silk-lined septic tank. Moldowsky thought: His lunatic son should have so much class.

Dilbeck rubbed his damp palms on the knees of his jogging suit. "Malcolm, are we talking about a *date* date, or the other kind?"

"Meaning, do you get to screw the girl? That's between you and her. Hell, I can't do everything—"

"You're right, you're right—"

"—I can't get it hard and put it in for you. Some things you've gotta do for yourself."

The congressman was on a cloud. "My friend, you've got no idea what this would mean to me." He raised his glass to Moldowsky. "Another coup, Malcolm."

"Try miracle," Moldy said. "A fucking miracle."

"Your specialty!"

"Oh yeah," Moldowsky mumbled. Rep. David Dilbeck had no inkling of the drastic steps that had already been taken to save his worthless hide.

By the 1970s, the once-dazzling underwater reefs of Miami and Fort Lauderdale were dead, poisoned by raw sewage dumped into the ocean from the toilets of swank waterfront hotels. Submerged pipes carried the filth a few hundred yards offshore, so beachgoers wouldn't see the billowing brown spumes. It was assumed that even the most dogged tourist might think twice about snorkeling in a torrent of shit.

Decades of rancid outfall eventually killed the delicate corals and drove the glittering fish away. The reefs became gray escarpments, barren and manifestly untropical. Drift-boat captains and dive-shop operators complained of losing customers to the Florida Keys and the Bahamas, where the water was still clear enough to see one's hand in front of one's face. A few South Florida coastal cities took modest measures to reduce the offshore pollution, but the reefs failed to regenerate; once dead, coral tends to stay that way.

Biologists theorized that it was possible to attract fish without real coral, and thus was born the concept of "artificial reefs," which was neither as exotic nor as high-tech as it sounded. Artificial reefs were created by sinking old ships; once nestled on the bottom, the ghost hulks attracted schools of baitfish which in turn attracted barracudas, jack crevalles, sharks, groupers and snappers. The drift boats and scuba captains were happy, as they no longer had to travel forty miles to find an actual fish to show their customers.

From a public-relations standpoint, the artificial reef program was a grand success—a sort of living junkyard of the deep. For once, human practices of waste disposal could be passed off legitimately as a benefit to the environment. Every few months another derelict freighter would be towed offshore and blown up with dynamite. Local TV stations swarmed the event, as it gave them an opportunity to use their expensive helicopters for something other than traffic reports. Predictably, the highly publicized demolitions became a regular South Florida tourist attraction, attended by hundreds of boaters who cheered wildly as the rusty vessels exploded and disappeared under the waves.

On the morning of October second, an eighty-six-foot Guatemalan banana boat called the *Princess Pia* was towed from Port Everglades to a pre-selected site off the Fort Lauderdale coast. The *Princess Pia* had been salvaged meticulously from the inside out: gone were the melted twin diesels, the corroded navigational gear, the radio electronics, the bilge pumps, the ropes, the hoses, the pipes, the fixtures, the hatch covers, the windshield, even the anchor—every item of value had been stripped from the boat. What remained essentially was a bare hull, degreased to minimize the purple slick that inevitably would form when the *Pia* went down.

The preparation of the ship had taken nearly a month, and was supervised by a Coast Guard inspector, a Broward County environmental engineer and an agent from the U.S. Customs Service, which had seized the vessel fourteen months earlier. Once the Customs agent was satisfied that the *Princess Pia* had no more hidden cargo compartments and carried no more hidden hashish, he signed off on the project. The Coast Guard inspector and the county environmental expert walked through the old heap one last time on the evening of October first. Much later, both men would testify that, except for the explosives, the *Pia* was empty that night; specifically, the aft hold was bare.

A single guard, hired by the demolition company, was posted at the ship's mooring to prevent the dynamite from being stolen from the hull. The guard kept watch dutifully until approximately three in the morning, when a group of friendly stevedores invited him aboard a Japanese lumber barge to play cards and watch pornographic videotapes. In all, the *Princess Pia* was unguarded for at least three and possibly five hours, depending on whose testimony one believed.

This much was undisputed: At dawn the next day, two tugs hauled the *Pia* out to sea on a falling tide. Three Florida Marine Patrol boats and a Coast Guard cruiser led the way, positioning themselves between the celebratory armada and the dynamite-laden freighter. The site for the new artificial reef was only three miles offshore, but it took a full hour for the *Princess Pia* to get there. The ocean was choppy, with northeast winds kicking to twenty knots; the tug captains kept a cautious pace.

By 9 a.m., the *Pia* was tethered in place, bow facing into the breeze. The police boats raced in widening arcs, clearing a buffer zone. At precisely 10 a.m., a radio signal detonated twin explosions in the ship's hull and stern. Tall blasts of dirty smoke rose from each end, and the ship listed dramatically starboard. She sunk in nine minutes flat. Boaters clapped and howled and sounded air horns.

Nobody suspected that there was a 1991 Lincoln Continental chained to the beams of the aft cargo hold. Nobody knew, until much later, what was in it.

22

The wrestling pit was in the back room, which had its own stage and a small horseshoe bar. Erin was dancing tables while Urbana Sprawl wrestled members of a bachelor party in ninety gallons of Green Giant niblets. The bachelor of honor was a young mortgage banker with many pallid, out-of-shape companions. They stood no chance against Urbana, who played rough and employed her formidable cleavage to maximum advantage. She specialized in pinning opponents without using her arms.

Erin remained baffled by the success of the nude wrestling exhibitions, which had become a red-hot fad in upscale strip joints. There was nothing erotic about grappling with a topless woman in a vat of cold vegetables, although the sodden realization came too late for most customers. By the time the bell rang, few were able to climb from the ring without assistance. The young bankers appeared especially whipped after their sessions with Urbana Sprawl.

Working table to table, Erin paid little attention to the comic slaughter in the wrestling pit. She was thinking about politics, which suddenly had touched her life in a dramatic way. Erin couldn't remember the last time she'd stood in a voting booth. Campaigns bored her. Every politician wore the same horseshit smile and gave the same horseshit speech. Erin was amazed that anyone would believe a word. She recalled being stricken by severe intestinal cramps while trying to watch the Bush–Dukakis debates.

Agent Cleary, bless his buttoned-down heart, used to scold her for being so cynical. On election day he'd lecture the office staff, telling them that democracy is futile without "an informed and participatory electorate." He'd say that people get exactly the kind of government they deserve, and those who won't vote have no grounds to complain.

He was right, Erin thought. This is what I get for not paying attention. Thieves like David Lane Dilbeck couldn't get elected dogcatcher without the gross apathy of the masses.

And this is my punishment, Erin thought. I've got to date the asshole.

Al García had laid out the situation in his maddeningly laconic way. Erin, who was seldom shocked at the depth of human sordidness, found herself stunned by what she heard: Jerry Killian had been murdered over *sugar*. The lovestruck little nerd was killed because he'd threatened the career of a crooked congressman. According to García, the congressman's principal contribution to the governing of the republic was to direct jillions of dollars in aid to the sugar cartels. Poor Mr. Peepers jeopardized that arrangement, so he was swatted as dead as a fly.

García said he wanted to catch the killers before they came looking for Erin. She said that was an excellent idea, and agreed to help in any way possible. Self-preservation was the main motivation; guilt was another. Erin couldn't forget that it was her sexy dancing that had fatally infatuated Jerry Killian.

Men were so helpless, she thought, so easily charmed. Monique Jr. was right: they'd do anything for it. Anything.

That's what Erin's mother didn't understand about yuppie strip clubs: it wasn't the women who were being used and degraded, it was the men. Her mother thought these places were meat markets, and indeed they were, the meat being the customers. Experienced dancers always kept one eye on the front door, scouting for the next mark. If you knew your stuff, you could work a guy all night and get every last dollar out of his wallet. You didn't have to blow him or screw him or even act like you might. A girlish smile, a sisterly hug, a few minutes of private conversation—Urbana Sprawl said it was the easiest money in the world, if you could get past being naked.

Because men were so easily charmed. That was a fact.

But Erin was apprehensive about the congressman. He wouldn't be shy and polite like Killian and the other regulars. No, Dilbeck would be pushy and crude and probably kinky. Al García warned her to be prepared.

"You think he's the one who took my razor?"

"Ask him," García had said.

Fear wasn't the worst part for Erin; the worst part was sending Angela away. It was the sensible move, because certainly Angie couldn't stay in the new apartment—couldn't stay anywhere near her mother—

until the danger was over. Erin felt terrible about it. She didn't like being alone again. She dreaded the silent afternoons, the dinners for one. Angie was safe, and at least Darrell Grant wouldn't find her. But still . . .

"Hey, babes."

A hand clamped on Erin's leg. She snapped back to reality—Urbana rolling in the creamed corn, Aerosmith blaring on the speakers, her own bra and G-string in a lacey mound between the Michelob bottles at her feet. Three young bankers sat at the table, trying to appear cool and unimpressed. The drunkest of them kept snapping Erin's garter, where the cash tips were folded. She asked him to stop but he didn't. She brushed his hand off her leg and spun a circle on the table, making evasion part of the dance; when she stopped spinning, the banker's hand returned, crawling like a mantis up her thigh. Erin looked across the room for Shad, but couldn't see him.

"That's enough," she told the banker.

The next thing she felt was his tongue. He was licking vertically from ankle to knee, long, sloppy Popsicle licks.

Erin snatched the man's hair and lifted his head. "You behave," she said sharply.

But he wouldn't.

That morning, a small item had appeared on page 6-D of the Fort Lauderdale *Sun Sentinel,* under the headline: BAR TO PROBE MISSING LAWYER. The four-paragraph story said the Florida Bar was investigating whether a lawyer named Mordecai had looted his client trust account and fled the country. The article said the man had not been seen for several days, and was believed to have flown to the Bahamas with an unnamed female companion.

Sgt. Al García clipped the story and put it with his homicide paperwork in his briefcase. Then he drove to a street corner in Liberty City, where two crack dealers had done the planet a tremendous favor by killing each other in a pre-dawn shootout. Witnesses were as scarce as mourners, but García took out his notebook and went to work.

Another man who clipped the *Sun Sentinel* item was Erb Crandall, sitting in the lobby of the Sunshine Fidelity Savings Bank on Galt Ocean Mile. Crandall was about to commit a minor crime for major stakes. He was about to forge a false name on a vault-room ledger, and use a stolen key to open a stranger's safe-deposit box. Crandall was searching for a Kodak color slide that Malcolm Moldowsky urgently sought to possess. The slide was the original photograph of Congressman David Lane Dilbeck assaulting Paul Guber with a champagne bottle on the stage of the Eager Beaver lounge. Erb Crandall's plan to obtain the incriminating picture began smoothly in the vault room. He signed a well-practiced version of Mordecai's name to the ledger, and handed the key to the clerk. The clerk pulled the steel box from the wall and unlocked it. He led Erb Crandall to a windowless cubicle and left him alone.

When Crandall opened the lid, he found no Kodak slide. Mordecai's box had been cleaned out. In the bottom, face up, lay only a business card:

Sgt. Alberto García
Metropolitan Dade County Police
Homicide Division (305) 471-1900

Erb Crandall's fingers were shaking as he carried the safe-deposit box to the clerk's desk. It was all he could do not to run from the bank.

That evening, over dinner, Sgt. Al García took out the news clipping and read it again. He was impressed that anyone would go to the trouble of framing a lawyer who most likely was dead. The trust account ruse was very nifty.

Andy asked: "Al, did you catch 'em yet? The guys who killed that man in the river?"

"Not yet," García said. The boy talked about the floater all the time; it was the highlight of the family vacation.

"Any suspects?"

"No, Andy. It's a tough one."

Donna said: "That's enough, both of you. Remember our rule."

The rule was: no talk of dead bodies at supper. Al's work was to be discussed only after the dishes were cleared.

"Sorry, Mom," Andy said.

Lynne, the little girl, asked if they could go to Sea World next summer. She wanted to see some turtles and sharks. Andy said he'd rather go back to Montana and hunt for clues.

Donna chased the children from the table and brought her husband a pot of coffee. He said, "Look what I've gotten you all into."

"It's all right. She seems like a nice person."

"Of course she's a nice person. Next question: how come she's working at a nudie bar? Right?"

Donna shrugged. "It's no great mystery. Have a slice of pie."

García was intrigued. "Could you do that—take off your clothes in front of all those drunken strangers?"

"If I had to," Donna said. "For the kids."

"Jesus, there's only about a million other jobs. The girl's not stupid. She can type seventy words a minute."

"You said she owes her lawyer."

"Yeah," García said. "Who doesn't?"

"So maybe she wants a nest egg. Where's the crime in that?"

"You're right, sweetheart."

"I like her."

"Me, too," he said. "But it's the job that's got her into so much damn trouble."

"No, honey, it's the men." Donna cut a piece of apple pie and put it on a plate. "So what does she look like, Al?"

"You saw her." He teased with a long pause. "Oh, you mean with her clothes off? Tell you the truth, I didn't notice."

Donna smiled. "You are a pitiful liar. Eat your dessert."

The phone rang. Donna didn't bother to get up. Only cops called at dinner time. García went in the kitchen to take it. He looked grim when he came back.

"That was the Broward sheriff's office," he said.

"They still don't want the case?"

"I knew they wouldn't." García sat down heavily. "Hell, I can't even get that cowpoke coroner to say Killian's death was a homicide. Meanwhile I got no weapons, no witnesses and no suspects." He took a large bite of pie. "I don't blame BSO for taking a pass." Another huge bite. "Least they were decent about it. I mean, they didn't laugh too hard."

Donna said, "Slow down. You'll choke to death."

"It's good pie."

"Not *that* good. Now tell me what else is wrong."

"I end up on a speaker phone with two brain-dead detectives. See, the girl's ex was a C.I. for Broward robbery." García didn't need to translate police jargon for Donna. She'd learned plenty from her first husband, the dope dealer.

"The ex is still an informant?"

García, chewing mechanically: "Nope, they cut him loose after he got busted for grand theft up the coast."

Donna shook her head. "I don't get it. If the ex got arrested, isn't that good news for Erin?"

"Oh, great news," García said, wiping his mouth, "if they'd managed to keep the bastard in jail."

"You're kidding."

"Nope, he escaped. From a county hospital! Stole a wheelchair and rolled out the fucking door!"

Donna told her husband to keep his voice down. "We've got company," she reminded him. "Where's your cigar?"

"Wait, there's more." García slashed the air with both hands. "The girl's ex-husband—the kid's father—he's not only mean, he's not only violent, he's got a frigging drug problem. Isn't that a hoot!"

Andy dashed into the dining room and asked what Al was hollering about.

"Work," Donna said. "What else."

Andy clambered up on García's lap. "Maybe you need another vacation."

Donna turned away, smothering a laugh. "So everybody's a smart-ass," García said, tickling the boy until he howled.

Shad was at the bar in the main lounge. He was distracted by a management problem.

Orly had connived to hire Lorelei, the fabulous python princess, away from the Ling brothers. Tonight was to be her first stage performance at the Tickled Pink, but she'd arrived in puffy-eyed hysterics. Orly could not decipher the problem, and delivered the distraught dancer to Shad, who was on break, reading a large-type edition of *The Plague* by Albert Camus. The book made Shad feel slightly better about living in South Florida.

He was interrupted by Lorelei's convulsive sobs. Her snake was missing, and she suspected the vengeful Lings of abduction. When Orly was informed, he ordered Shad to find another snake for his new star. Shad noted there were no all-night reptile stores in the neighborhood. Unfortunately, Lorelei refused to dance without Bubba, which is what she called her nine-foot Burmese python.

"She says they're a team," Shad reported. "She says the snake is trained."

Orly crumpled an empty can of Dr. Pepper and lobbed it grenade-style behind the bar. "First, there's no such thing as a trained snake, OK? And Item B, did you see the fucking marquee? LORELEI in great big letters—I got customers drove all the way from Miami. Tell her she's got ten minutes to get her boobs on stage."

Shad glanced toward the hallway, where the weeping python princess now huddled in grief. "She'll need more than ten minutes," he said. "She looks like hell."

Orly cursed and hacked and massaged his nostrils. "You don't know anyone with a goddamn snake?"

"Not a big snake," Shad said. "I know some guys who breed diamondbacks."

"Sweet Christ Almighty."

"They're not much good for dancing."

"OK," said Orly. "Here's what you do. Go see those fucking Lings. Find out how much they want for the girl's python."

"Bubba is the name."

"Whatever. Offer five hundred."

Shad said the Lings likely would tell him to fuck off and die. "They hate your guts," he told Orly.

"No, this is business. Now hurry it up."

Shad put the book by Camus behind the bar, under the popcorn platters. Then he drove up to the Flesh Farm, where the Ling brothers kept him waiting an hour—a nervy move. Shad passed the time drinking Virgin Marys and surveying the dance talent in case Orly demanded a scouting report. Shad's ominous bald presence quickly thinned the audience and further irritated the Lings. Shad finally got his meeting, but the brothers reacted to the python proposition more biliously than anticipated.

He returned to find the Tickled Pink in an uproar. Erin seemed to be in the thick of it. Paramedics were fitting a neck brace on a pale and dazed young man. The victim was encircled by a dozen equally wan companions with corn kernels stuck in their hair. From a distance it looked as if they'd been bombed by sparrows. The men shouted high-pitched questions at the paramedics, over the jackhammer music. As a protective measure, Urbana Sprawl had stationed her insurmountable breasts between Erin and Orly, who was red-faced and raving.

"Damn," said Shad, and waded into the chaos.

Later, in the office, Orly blustered about liability and lawsuits and his liquor license.

"You aren't listening," Erin said. "The man touched me."

Urbana Sprawl, showered and fully dressed, spoke out in support of her friend: "I saw the whole thing, Mr. Orly. He got what he deserved."

Orly snorted. "A sprained neck. Is that what he deserved? A trip to the hospital, for copping a feel!"

"He touched me," Erin said, "between my legs."

"Aw, he was drunk."

Erin turned to Urbana. "This is why I hate table dances."

Orly said, "You could've crippled the guy, kickin' him in the head like that."

"And what's she supposed to do?" Urbana said. "Give him a nice friendly finger fuck?"

Orly flinched, turning his head. "Christ, that's enough. No more a that talk."

"So it's OK for Shad to beat a customer's ass, but not us. Is that the deal?"

"I said, that's enough."

"Urbana's right," Erin said. "It's not fair."

"Screw fair," said Orly, puffing his cheeks. "Shad's job is keeping the peace. Your job is to dance. That's the bottom line."

Standing by the office door, Shad reluctantly abandoned his silence. "I got sent up the street," he said. "Otherwise it wouldn't have happened."

Orly gave a corrosive laugh. "Wonderful. Now it's all my fault. Well, fuck the whole bunch a you."

Urbana was livid. She leaned her double-wide bosom across his desk and shook a Day-Glo fingernail in his face. "Nobody touches me 'less I wanna be touched, especially down there. I don't care who it is or how shitfaced they are or how much money they got, I won't stand for it. That little shit's lucky to get out with a sprained neck, because if it was me, I'd rip his damn balls off with my bare hands, just like this—"

Orly gaped as Urbana simulated her technique, snatching imaginary testicles off an imaginary oaf.

"—and don't think I can't!"

Then she was gone. Nobody moved for several moments.

Orly said: "That girl gives big tits a bad name."

Erin stood up. "Well, I'm through for the night."

"Now wait a second—"

"No. I'm going to visit my daughter."

After Erin left, Shad came to her defense. He told Orly that Erin had many good reasons to be jumpy—the custody case, the burglary of the apartment, and now a congressman in hot pursuit. "It's a bad time for her right now. That's how come she blew up tonight."

Orly wiped his neck with a soiled handkerchief. "You and me are the only ones in this joint that don't get PMS, and sometimes I'm not too sure about you."

"It's the music," Shad said. "It makes my head hurt."

"Talk to Kevin."

"Kevin says talk to you."

Orly said, "I don't know rap from reggae. You know my secret? I don't even listen." He twisted an invisible knob at his right earlobe. "Just turn it off. I don't hear a damn thing." He asked how it went with the Lings.

"Lousy," Shad said.

"They don't have the girl's snake?"

"Yeah, they got it. They just won't ransom it."

Orly raised his palms. "Why the fuck not? Business is business."

"Mainly because they hate your guts."

"Because of me hiring Lorelei?"

"Because of everything," Shad replied.

"So the answer is no. It took you two damn hours to get a simple N-O from those jerkoff Japs. Meanwhile I got a crazed stripper doing a Chuck Norris routine on my customers—"

"The answer wasn't only no," Shad said. "It was this, too." He placed an oblong package on Orly's desk. "The Ling brothers wanted you to have it."

Orly eyed the crude parcel, wrapped in Flesh Farm cocktail napkins and bound with masking tape. "What the hell is it?" he asked Shad.

"About twelve inches of dead Bubba."

Orly yelped and pushed away from the desk, away from the unopened package. "Did I tell you they were animals! Did I! Jesus, what else did they say, those goddamn Lings?"

"They said there's plenty more where that came from."

23

On the morning of October third, under a hard blue sky, Perry Crispin and Willa Oakley Crispin went down to the beach.

The attractive young couple spread out towels from their suite at the Breakers Hotel, and lay side by side in the bleached sand. They took turns smearing number 29 sunblock all over each other: Perry spelled out "I Luv You!!!" on his wife's tummy. Willa drew an oily heart on the small of her husband's prodigiously freckled back.

A strong breeze put a salty tang in the air, and made the waves bite raggedly against the shore. The Crispins planned a brief swim later, when they were sweaty. They wore matching black Ray-Bans and pink terrycloth tennis visors. They smiled and whispered and touched each other frequently, as is the habit of newlyweds. Willa and Perry were from large, wealthy families in Connecticut, so the wedding had been suitably extravagant. Palm Beach was the first leg of a four-week honeymoon that would take them to Freeport, St. Bart's and finally Cozumel. The sun was high and bright, and the Crispins glistened on their towels. They were unabashedly romantic, totally relaxed and not at all apprehensive about their future together. Substantial trust funds awaited both of them.

By noon, Willa's adorable nose had turned pink. Perry noted it with alarm; his father was a limited partner in four dermatology clinics, and skin cancer had been a recurrent topic at family gatherings. From an early age, Perry showed an eagle eye for discolored moles and suspicious lesions. He told his bride that it was time to get out of the U.V. rays.

"I came to get a tan," she protested.

"Darling, we've got four whole weeks."

As they crossed the beach toward the hotel, the Crispins were followed by a slender blond man in dirty jeans and cowboy boots. Perry and Willa didn't notice the stranger—they were engrossed in discussing the poor quality of the sunblock ointment, and the possibility of trying zinc oxide instead, at least on their noses.

The man behind them said, "Scuze me, folks."

Perry and Willa turned. The man wasn't dressed for Palm Beach. His blue eyes were bloodshot and jumpy. His hair was matted on one side, as if slept on.

"You got a car?" he said.

Willa looked frightened. Perry sized up the stranger and took a small step forward. The man displayed a rusty steak knife and said, "Don't make me ask twice."

The Crispins led Darrell Grant to their rental car, a candy-apple Thunderbird. Darrell Grant said he approved. He took the keys from Perry and ordered the couple to hop in the backseat.

"Why?" Willa asked.

"Till we get across the bridge," Darrell said.

The Intracoastal Waterway separated the town of Palm Beach from West Palm Beach. Two more disparate worlds would be hard to find; West Palm was for normal humans, Palm Beach for the eccentric rich. The cops on the island were notorious rousters of unwanted visitors—blacks, Hispanics, and anyone not wearing Polo. If you worked in one of the mansions, fine. Otherwise, get your ass over the bridge. Darrell Grant figured he might need the Crispins to talk him out of a Palm Beach traffic stop.

"You got a purse?" he asked Willa.

The newlyweds squeezed each other's hands. Perry was relieved to see that Willa had left her two-carat diamond wedding band in the hotel room. He hoped she'd done the same with the traveler's checks.

"Halloo?" Darrell Grant said.

"Yes, I've got my purse."

"Thatta girl."

"All I carry is forty dollars."

Darrell snorted. "How about you, sport?"

"Credit cards is all I've got," Perry said.

"Figures." Darrell barreled through a red light on Worth Avenue. He liked the way the T-bird handled. "All right, honey, gimme the cash. And your medicines, too."

Willa looked confounded. Her husband motioned gravely at her purse. She took out two twenties and nervously extended them over the headrest, as if feeding a bear at the zoo.

"I don't have any pills," she told Darrell Grant. "Except my birth control."

"That'll do fine." He grabbed the money with his steering hand. The other hand held the steak knife, running the stained blade through the stubble on his jawline.

From the backseat, Willa said: "I'm sorry but you can't take my pills."

"Oh yeah?" Darrell was heartily amused.

"You'll get sick," said Willa. "They're not made for men."

"Sick?"

"They're made of hormones!"

"No shit," Darrell Grant said. "So, like, I might grow knockers. Is that what you mean? Or maybe even a love muffin."

"No, I didn't—"

"Be a good girl and hand over the fucking pills." Darrell's arm came down and speared the rusty knife into the white upholstery. He ripped a long sibilant gash in the stiff vinyl.

Perry Crispin said: "Willa, give the man what he wants."

"No."

"My God," said her husband. "Don't be foolish."

"Fine, Perry. And what're we supposed to do for the next four weeks—hold hands?" Willa protected the purse with both arms. "Our pharmacy is in Westport, remember?"

Perry Crispin said: "I'm not believing this."

"What—you want me to get pregnant?"

In the front seat, Darrell Grant was humming the theme from *The Sound of Music*, which was his sister Rita's favorite movie of all time. Or maybe that was *Mary Poppins*, he always got the two mixed up. "Which is the one with Dick Van Dyke?" he asked. "Did I get it right?"

The Crispins had no clue what he was talking about. A dope fiend, jabbering. Willa leaned forward to plead her case. "Please, don't take the birth-control pills. It's our honeymoon."

Ahead was one of the drawbridges leading to West Palm. Finally, thought Darrell, I can dump these brainless puppies. He goosed the accelerator.

"My sister's a nurse," Willa was saying. "These pills are very strong. They *will* make you sick."

Ahead, the crossing gates swung down and a tinny bell rang. The bridge began to rise. Darrell Grant cursed vehemently and hit the brakes.

Perry Crispin's feeble voice: "It's just a sailboat going through. It shouldn't take long."

Darrell Grant whirled in the driver's seat. He thrust a calloused palm at Willa and said: "The pills."

She shook her head adamantly. Her husband was dumbstruck.

Darrell said, "Listen, you silly cunt. I ain't gonna eat the damn things, I'm gonna sell 'em. You understand? I'm gonna go acrosst this bridge and scam me some stoners who don't know birth control from LSD. Get it?"

Tears appeared in Willa's eyes. She blinked downheartedly at her husband. "Perry, he called me a cunt."

Perry Crispin felt horrible. He felt he should attack the crazed dope fiend in defense of his wife's honor. On the other hand, he was crippled with terror. He expected his bladder to fail at any second.

"Don't you worry," he told Willa. "We'll get more pills."

"How? My prescription is in Westport." Despair fogged her voice.

"FedEx, darling. Now do as the man says."

The drawbridge began to go down, one side at a time. Darrell Grant announced that he would count to five, then hack out Willa's heart and make Perry eat it on a hoagie for lunch. Willa immediately opened the purse and gave the madman her pills. Darrell drove across the bridge and parked at a Mini-Mart. He took Perry Crispin's Ray-Bans and also the hot pink tennis visor. Then he told the couple to get their sorry butts out of the car.

The pavement scorched the soles of the Crispins' bare feet, and they hopped like palsied flamingos to a triangular patch of shade. Darrell Grant adjusted the side mirror of the Thunderbird so he could admire the fit of his new sunglasses. The Crispins watched morosely, waiting for the criminal to drive away. Willa remained very angry. "Thank you very much," she called out acidly, "for ruining our honeymoon."

Darrell Grant scowled and revved the engine. "You people ever heard of rubbers? It's a new thing, sport. Fits right on your dick."

"Perry won't use them." Willa's tone was reproachful. Perry Crispin turned away.

"Figures," Darrell said. He waved tootle-oo with the steak knife before speeding off. It took two hours to find a junkie bent enough to buy birth-control pills and believe they were Belgian Dilaudids. Darrell only got thirty bucks from the scam but, added to Willa Crispin's forty, it was enough to gas up the T-bird and score some reds. He had a good buzz on by the time he made the interstate, which carried him south in blazing pursuit of his precious little girl and her worthless mother.

The Rojos were in Santo Domingo, so Malcolm Moldowsky was given use of the yacht. Erb Crandall dropped off the congressman at nine sharp, and went directly to a dockside bar to drink alone. He had already delivered the bad news about the lawyer's safe-deposit box. Moldy had taken the homicide detective's card delicately, like a butterfly, between two fingers. "This changes things," he'd said, turning the card back and forth, as if marveling at a hologram. "I guess it's time for Plan B." Erb Crandall didn't ask for an explanation. The time had come to forsake party loyalty and begin thinking of one's own situation, and of covering one's own ass. Crandall was grateful that Moldy didn't ask him to stay for the meeting on the yacht.

When David Dilbeck stepped into the master stateroom, the first thing he saw was The Photograph from the Eager Beaver. Moldowsky had tacked it on the wall, over the wet bar.

"A reminder," he said, pouring Dilbeck a drink.

The congressman's eyes riveted on Erin's face. "Isn't she something," he said, breathlessly.

Moldy said, "Don't look at her, David. Look at yourself."

"It was a bad night."

"You don't say." He shoved a tumbler into Dilbeck's gut. "Sit down and have a drink."

The congressman obeyed. "Ginger ale? That's precious, Malcolm."

Moldowsky climbed into a canvas director's chair. He wore rubber-soled deck shoes, pressed white slacks and a navy pullover. It was one of the few times Dilbeck had seen him in casual clothes.

"I want you sober," Moldy began. "I want you to remember every goddamn word I say. Whatever arrangement you and this girl reach, that's fine. But you're to talk to her, David. There are certain things we need to know."

"Good Lord, she's not a spy. She's only a stripper—"

"Bring her here tomorrow night," Moldowsky said. "It'll be safe."

"Safe from what?"

"From blackmailers, David." Moldy pointed up at the photograph. Again Dilbeck's gaze settled on Erin, shielding herself from the bottle attack.

"What if she doesn't like me?" Dilbeck asked.

Moldowsky cracked an ice cube in his molars. "She'll love you, trust me. Two thousand dollars buys serious love."

"And what do I get for that?"

"Two hours of dancing."

"That's all?"

"It's a start."

David Dilbeck sipped at the ginger ale, which tasted flat. "I want sexy music, champagne, candles, the whole nine yards—"

Moldy said it was all arranged. He went through a series of questions that Dilbeck was to ask the nude dancer. Dilbeck said no way, it would spoil the mood.

"Come on," said Moldowsky. "You're the slickest sonofabitch I ever saw. Go easy. Be cool."

The congressman was reluctant. "Malcolm, I do not wish to scare her off. This may be my only shot." Once more his eyes wandered to the grainy photograph on the wall. "Fantastic," he whispered, to no one.

Moldy shot to his feet and tore the picture down. He charged up to David Dilbeck's chair and confronted him, nose to chin. "You *will* do this," he growled at the congressman. "There are things we need to know. It's *essential*, David"—spraying the word *essential*—"considering what's happened the last month."

Moldowsky's breath smelled like bourbon and peppermint mouthwash. The mixture clashed fiercely with his cologne. Dilbeck turned away and huffed for fresh air. The yacht rocked gently on the wake of a passing speedboat.

"You will do this," Moldy repeated in the congressman's ear.

"But I don't understand—"

Moldowsky whirled away. He snatched his glass of bourbon off the bar and took a slug. He noticed a small rectangular outline in the fabric of his pocket—the homicide detective's card, taken from the lawyer's safe-deposit box. Moldy said, "People are trying to harm you, David. We need to be sure she's not one of them."

Dilbeck shook his head. "You're completely paranoid."

"Humor me."

"But she's just a stripper."

Malcolm Moldowsky grabbed Dilbeck's shirt. "Fannie Fox," he said, "was 'just a stripper.' Donna Rice was just a model-slash-actress. Elizabeth Ray was just a secretary who couldn't type. Gennifer Flowers was just a country singer. Don't you get it? Ask Chuck Robb. Or that horny idiot Hart. Teddy Kennedy, for pity's sake. They'll all tell you the same: in politics, stealing is trouble but pussy is lethal."

Moldy released his grip. Exhausted, he wilted on a bar stool. "Those who ignore history," he said, "are doomed to get their nuts cut."

David Dilbeck said, "All right. I'll talk to the girl."

"Thank you."

"I'm smarter than those others."

Moldowsky could scarcely contain himself.

"I'm also stronger," Dilbeck added.

"Yeah," said Moldy. "A rock, that's what you are. A regular Rock of Gibraltar."

The congressman sidled to the bar and disposed of the ginger ale. Keeping his back to Moldowsky, he poured himself a very sturdy rum-and-Coke. "Malcolm," the congressman said, "is it possible she would let me shave her?"

Moldowsky fell to his knees and gagged spectacularly on the Rojos' carpet.

Al García heard music in Erin's apartment. He knocked loudly and rang the bell. When he got no answer, he took out the key she had given him and let himself in. On the bed Erin lay motionless, a pillow wrapped like a helmet around her head. She wore pink panties and a matching bra, and appeared to be breathing just fine. Half a pitcher of martinis perspired on the nightstand, and the stereo was cranked up full blast. García turned it down.

Erin's voice, muffled: "What d'you think you're doing?"

The detective sat on the edge of the bed. "We need to talk."

"Orly won't let me dance to Jackson Browne anymore."

"How come?"

"Or Van Morrison. He says it's too slow. He says I'm pissing off the girls on the tables."

"Erin, how you doin' on gin?"

"That's the first time you called me Erin." Her face peeked out of the pillow. "By the way, I want my gun back."

"It's in the dresser," García said.

"Loaded?"

"Yes, ma'am."

"Good. What time is it?"

"Noon." García tried to cover her with a sheet. Erin kicked it off and gave a gravelly laugh.

"Don't tell me you're embarrassed," she said.

The detective reddened. Erin reminded him that he'd seen her nude several times at the club.

"That's different," he said.

"Oh?" Erin unsnapped her bra and lobbed it at him. It landed on his right shoulder. Then she squirmed out of her panties and tossed them on the floor. "There you are," she said, spreading her arms.

The detective stared at his shoes. "Let me take a wild guess here. You're upset about meeting the congressman."

"Upset is a good word for it. Nervous, disgusted, terrified, and pretty much all alone. The only thing in the world I care about, I can't have—"

"Angela's doing great," Al García said. "You'll be together soon." He took the bra off his shoulder and folded it on the bed.

Erin enfolded herself listlessly in the bedsheets. She looked too worn for her age. "Some guy grabbed me last night."

"Christ."

"I came unglued. Nothing in particular."

"Did you kill him?"

"Nah."

"So what's the big deal." The detective pulled a cigar from his shirt. He put it in his mouth but didn't light it.

Erin stared at the ceiling. "I had a dream about the other man in that picture, the one who's hugging me on his knees. I had a dream they killed him, too, just like Mr. Peepers."

García told her not to worry. "His name is Paul Guber and he's safe and sound. He went to New York for a few weeks."

"At your suggestion?" Erin poked him playfully with a toe.

"His firm's got an office on Wall Street. It seemed like a good time for a visit."

She said, "You take care of everyone, don't you?"

The detective shook his head unhappily. He told Erin about Darrell Grant's ludicrous escape from the Martin County authorities. She received the news more passively than he expected; then again, she'd had the benefit of several martinis.

"Darrell," she declared, "is off the fucking rails."

"Is he crazy enough to show up at the club?"

"Possibly." Erin rolled on her belly. "I can sure pick 'em, huh?"

García left the room to make a phone call. When he returned, Erin had put on a white T-shirt and jeans. She stood at the mirror, brushing her hair. The martini pitcher was empty.

"I poured it out," she said, shooting him a sharp look. "I'm not as bombed as you think."

They went to a Friday's and ordered cheeseburgers. García had a beer. Erin drank coffee. They were conducting a perfectly amiable conversation until the detective asked if she had a boyfriend.

She said, "Shit, don't do this."

"What?"

"You know what."

García chewed thoughtfully. "My interest is purely professional. I need to cover all the angles."

"You're not trying to ask me out?"

"Nope." He raised his right hand, cheeseburger and all. "I swear to God."

"You sure?"

"For Christ's sake, Erin, I took you to meet my wife."

She apologized, sheepishly. She felt like the queen bitch of all time. "It's not that I've got such a red-hot opinion of myself—"

"I understand," García said, "believe me."

"It's the damn job." She was so accustomed to being propositioned that she was automatically suspicious of any man who didn't try. It made for a relentlessly cynical view of the opposite sex. Having Darrell Grant in one's past contributed to Erin's attitude.

She said, "The answer is no, there's no boyfriend. But you knew that, right?"

"Just a hunch."

"At the end of the night, I don't have much energy left for men. Or much interest, for that matter."

"Occupational hazard," said García, attacking a pile of french fries. "Is there any man you trust completely?"

"Don't laugh," Erin said. "I trust Shad."

Al García grinned. "Me, too."

After lunch, he drove out to the ocean. Erin said that she wanted to stand in the sunshine and bleach out the gin. The detective parked at Bahia Mar, and they walked across the overpass to the beach. García wished he'd taken off his coat and tie; people were giving him odd looks.

Erin walked down far enough to get her toes wet. The detective stopped a few feet from the waves. He lit the cigar and blew the smoke over his right shoulder, safely downwind from Erin.

She said, "You think I'm a whore?"

"Don't be ridiculous."

Erin stepped back from the water. "But you wouldn't want your daughter doing what I do."

"My daughter," said García, "is not leaving the house until she's thirty years old."

Erin smiled. "Angie is fascinated by Mommy's costumes."

The detective said, "The time comes, she'll understand."

Erin stretched. The sun felt glorious on her face and arms. She said, "I tell myself it's just dancing."

"And I tell myself I'm an ace crime fighter. So what?"

Erin had an urge to jump in the ocean. She got a running start and dove in. She swam fifty yards and stopped. Floating on her back, she blinked the salty sting from her eyes. The swells lifted the T-shirt, billowing around her breasts. Seagulls kited above the surf and cawed raucously. Silver mullet jumped and skittered toward deeper water. She heard the whoosh of a windsurfer and a lewd whistle from the teenager riding the board. Erin serenely flipped him the finger.

When she waded from the water, Al García offered his coat. Erin thought: How can you not like this guy? She said, "I guess you don't go for the wet look."

"Please." He cloaked the jacket around her shoulders. "Be kind to a shy old fart."

In the parking lot, García searched the Caprice for a clean towel. Erin spotted the Igloo cooler and said she hoped there was a cold six-pack inside. The detective said the ice chest was used for human body parts, not refreshments.

"Yum," said Erin. She picked up a clear bag of blue hospital masks. "I bet you looky snazzy in one of these."

García said they came in handy. He tossed her a striped beach towel that belonged to Donna.

Erin said, "I'll ask you what you've been dying to ask me: How in the world can you do it?"

"Do what?"

"Your job. Dead bodies day after day—I couldn't take it."

The detective said, "Hey, it's a growth industry. The state could sell fucking bonds."

On the drive home, they talked about Erin's date with the congressman. She had plenty of questions. Would he be alone? How long did she need to stay? What should she do if he went crazy again? Some of García's answers were more comforting than others.

The detective's car phone beeped. He spoke for less than a minute and hung up, frowning.

Erin said, "Duty calls."

"Trunk job," García muttered. "Miami International."

"That's ninety minutes away."

"No hurry. The guy's been there since Labor Day." He said the stink wasn't so bad if you dabbed Old Spice inside your hospital mask, before popping the trunk. To Erin, it was the stuff of nightmares.

Back at the apartment, she waited by the front door while Al García checked for signs of intruders. He came back out and told her it was safe. He didn't tell her that he'd emptied her bottle of Beefeater's down the bathtub drain.

At the door, the detective told her to think some more about meeting David Dilbeck alone. If she wanted to change her mind, he'd understand. It was a risky deal.

"I won't change my mind," she said.

"Then be ready for the worst. For two grand, he'll want more than a peek."

"Oh, he'll definitely get more than a peek," Erin said. "Just one thing: can I bring my own music?"

Al García said sure, absolutely.

24

Orly asked Shad where he got the scorpion. Shad said he bought it off a guy at Dania jai-alai.

"Dead or alive?"

"Alive," Shad said.

Orly leaned in for a closer look. "Is it sick or what?"

Shad said, "No, I drowned it."

"How?"

"Johnnie Walker."

Orly laughed, sucking air through his teeth. "Red or black?"

"Red," Shad said. He used his tweezers to lift the dead scorpion from the jar.

"Big fucker," Orly observed. "So the idea is to make it look like the company's fault?"

"Sure." Shad placed the dead scorpion in an eight-ounce carton of cottage cheese. He spooned curds over the soggy corpse except for the stinger, which he purposely left exposed.

Orly said, "And they'll pay off? The company, I mean."

"Wouldn't you?" Shad placed the lid on the container and pressed firmly on the edges. He hadn't yet decided whether to sue the cottage-cheese manufacturer or the national supermarket chain that carried the product.

"The guy who sold you the scorpion, is he the same one that sold you the snake?"

"No," Shad said.

"Because Lorelei ain't thrilled with the snake."

"I heard."

On short notice, Shad had located a half-blind boa constrictor for two hundred bucks. The seven-foot reptile was mean, restless and

extremely difficult to handle on the dance floor. Even with its mouth
taped, the boa intimidated Lorelei.

"She's scared to hang it around her neck," Orly said.

"So tell her don't hang it on her neck."

"Then where? She's buck naked, man."

Shad gave a shrug. "You wanted a new snake. I got one."

"It peed on her," said Orly.

"I heard."

"Now she's threatening to quit on me. Go back to the Flesh Farm."

Shad said, "What the hell, Mr. Orly. Snakes pee." It felt like a
chainsaw was cropping the top of his skull. He placed the cottage cheese
in the refrigerator and wrote a note in block letters warning the dancers
not to touch it. Orly watched quietly, his back to the mirror. Monique
Jr. limped into the dressing room with a broken heel, which Shad fixed
with Crazy Glue. A new hire named Danielle dashed in for a cosmetic
emergency; a sharp-eyed customer had spotted the incision marks from
her recent surgery. While the dancer lifted her round new breasts, Shad
applied Maybelline powder to the scars.

When they were alone again, Orly said: "The Lings don't know who
they're dealin' with."

"I sure told them."

"About Fat Tony? Nicky Scarfo?"

"The works," Shad said. "They don't particularly give a shit. By the
way, Fat Tony croaked. The Lings saw it in *The Herald.*"

Orly planted his elbows on the vanity. "America's going down the
shitter, that's my theory. Why? Because these goddamn foreigners don't
respect our national institutions—not Detroit, not Wall Street, not even
the Mafia."

Shad didn't like the direction of the conversation. Soon Orly would
ask him to sabotage the Flesh Farm; the subject had arisen often.

"I'd like to help," Shad said, "but I can't."

"What's the big deal?"

"I just can't." He was hesitant to tell Mr. Orly about his rap sheet, as the
liquor commission frowned on the practice of hiring convicted felons.
"Call up North," Shad said. "Get a real torch artist." Of course the phone
call would never be made; Orly didn't know a soul in the mob.

The club owner picked up a hairbrush and tapped a beat on the
dressing table. "Those Lings," he said. "I can't believe they'd hack up
a perfectly good snake."

Shad said they were definitely making a statement.

"They broke the girl's heart," Orly said. "Hey, see if there's a cold drink in the fridge."

Shad found him a cream soda.

"I was thinking," said Orly, lapping the rim of the can. "Remember when the business was mainly bikers? Back when we were The Booby Hatch and The Pleasure Palace? Biker girls, biker clientele, biker fights. Those days you knew the rules."

"It was a pit," Shad said, unsentimentally.

"Yeah, but we knew what was what. The strippers hooked. The customers dealt dope. Everybody carried a knife or a piece."

Shad said, "The good old days. I might just cry."

"Bottom line, yes, it was a dive. Yes, it was a sewer. But there was a logical fucking order to things." Orly took a gulp of soda, sloshed it around both cheeks and swallowed. "Those days I never had to worry about crooks like the Lings. Competition? There wasn't none. DJs. Play lists. Wind machines. Trained fucking pythons, forget it! Back then, the girls couldn't dance worth a lick, and I'll also say they were in no danger of getting hired off by *Playboy*. You remember Thin Lizzie?"

Shad couldn't help but chuckle. Lizzie was a biker dancer who stood five-foot-four, weighed a hundred and seventy-seven pounds and had a stock car tattooed on her back. Who could forget? A red-and-blue Dodge, Number 43. King Richard Petty hisself.

"Remember?" Orly said, glowing. "So maybe she did suck off half of Fort Lauderdale in my parking lot. The lady was no trouble to me. No trouble at all. I tell her to dance fast, she danced fast. I tell her to dance slow, she goes slow. That was long before this wrestling thing caught on, but lemme say—if I'd told Lizzie to wrestle in transmission fluid, she'd by God wrestle. The girl was a trouper and she understood the rules."

Shad opened a bottle of Bayer aspirins and chewed up five. Orly offered a swig of cream soda, which Shad declined.

"Now look how the business is changed," Orly went on. "My dancers are practically unionized, thanks to your friend Erin. They pick their own songs, pick their own hours. Meanwhile my liability premiums are tripled on account of all the bankers and lawyers and CPAs hanging out at the joint. Every time there's a fight I nearly have a fucking coronary, wondering which yuppie asshole's gonna sue me next."

Shad said, "One thing about the bikers. They don't sue."

"Damn right."

"On the other hand, you're makin' real good money now. We're selling four, five times the booze."

Orly crumpled the soda can and pinged it off the wall. "Prosperity," he said, "ain't all it's cracked up to be."

Shad was disillusioned, too, but for other reasons. He knew better than to share his innermost feelings with the boss.

Orly said, "I had a chance to get into a Taco Bell franchise up in Orlando. Fifteen minutes from fucking Disney World—did I tell you? This was October last year."

"You told me," Shad said. Orly's wife had vetoed the deal because Mexican food aggravated her colon.

"So there goes my best chance to get out," Orly said, "all because Lily gets the runs from *fajitas.*"

"She'd rather have you runnin' a strip joint?"

"It's crazy, I know, but she's never said a word." Orly lowered his voice. "Between you and me and the four walls, I'm so tired of naked poon I can't stand it. It's been years since I had a serious boner, I swear to God."

Shad agreed it was a draining job. Lord, didn't he know!

Orly said, "I'll ask straight up: What happens you hit it big on this scorpion deal? Say the cottage-cheese company comes through with a couple hundred grand. I guess I'll be needing a new bouncer."

"Maybe. Maybe not. I like you all right, Mr. Orly."

"Hey, you could even buy a piece a this joint. We could be goddamn partners!"

"To be honest," Shad said, "I don't like you that much."

"Whatever. That's okay, too."

In eleven years it was the longest conversation that the two men had ever had. Orly was plainly overwrought about something. Shad asked what had happened to put him in such a mood.

"Not a damn thing," he snapped.

"Moldowsky called again, right? About Erin."

"On top of everything else, yeah." Orly became subdued. "He's looking for a picture of this horny congressman. A picture from right here at the club. I'm sure you wouldn't know anything about that."

"Nope," said Shad. "What else?"

"He had a message for Erin." Orly pulled a shred of paper from his damp breast pocket and gave it to Shad. "Ten o'clock tomorrow night down at Turnberry. Here's the name of the yacht."

Shad struggled to decipher Orly's scribble; his sweat had made the ink run. *"Sweetheart* something," Shad said. He didn't like the idea of Erin meeting Dilbeck on a boat.

Orly said, "So I suppose she's gonna screw this guy."

"Why?"

" 'Cause he's a politician, for God's sake."

Shad said, "You know her better than that."

"A United States congressman, you're telling me it's just a private dance party? No sex is what you're telling me?"

"I'd be very surprised."

Orly did a poor job of masking his disappointment. Shad did an equally poor job of masking his anger; the stare he leveled at Orly was harrowing.

"Fuck the liquor license," he said.

Orly stiffened. "But the guy's busting my balls."

"Then *you* sleep with him."

"Take it easy, take it easy." Nervously Orly chucked Shad on the forearm. "See, this is what I mean. This is my exact point. In the old days we never worried about evil shit like this. Rednecks, bikers and whores—that was the tittie business. Now look out there, you see beepers and cell phones at every fucking table. Blow-dried dorks in designer suspenders, honest to Christ! The parking lot's full of Beemers and Blazers but, shit, I can't sleep nights. No, you keep your fucking upscale clientele."

"And politicians," Shad said. The impulse to choke Mr. Orly had ebbed slightly.

"Bikers are better customers," said Orly. "I swear to God, Shad, I'd rather have a barful of bikers than one shitfaced congressman. The fights we could handle, remember? Hell, I'd take a stabbing every night over evil shit like this. Some guy I never met, busting my balls about the license."

In five minutes Urbana Sprawl was due to wrestle in a vat of cooked linguini. Shad planned to supervise. He stood up and said, "What's done is done. We'll fix things right."

"How?"

"Don't worry about it, Mr. Orly."

They walked through the main lounge together. Rap music pounded pneumatically from the walls. On stage, Lorelei was struggling with the new snake, which had coiled itself the full length of her right leg. Even the most drunken customers realized it was not part of the act.

Orly cupped a hand to Shad's ear and shouted: "Maybe I'll put a sign at the door: No politicians allowed! Ax murderers and perverts welcome, but no goddamn politicians!"

Shad faked a smile. He was grumpy enough to bite the head off a kitten.

"Give me bikers any day," Orly was saying. "No more congressmen in my joint. . . ."

On stage, Lorelei gimped stoically out of the spotlight. She yelled something about her leg turning blue.

Shad thought: I've got to get out soon. Before I do some damage.

Malcolm J. Moldowsky knew that the congressman couldn't be blackmailed by a geek bouncer with a felony rap sheet. More problematic was the young stockbroker, Paul Guber, but he had abruptly left town. It was the third person in the scandalous bachelor-party photograph who most worried Moldy: the stripper.

If so inclined, Erin Grant could singlehandedly destroy the congressman's fragile reputation. Which is precisely why Moldowsky had arranged for the two of them to meet.

Moldy spent the morning of October fourth in a high-level strategy session, by himself. He neither needed nor sought the counsel of others. Silence bred clarity of thinking, and solitude restored one's perspective. It was important to set aside his personal contempt for David Dilbeck and concentrate on the mission for which he was being paid. Many fires burned out of control. It was time to focus.

He needed ammunition, but there wasn't much in Erin's past. The custody file was loaded with juicy accusations, but Moldowsky was skeptical of the ex-husband's veracity; Darrell Grant came off as a despicable creep. No sense opening that particular can of worms.

Moldy decided to treat Mrs. Grant very gently indeed. Look but don't touch, he'd warned the congressman. Do nothing to frighten or anger this woman. If she says no, don't argue. If all else fails, try to make friends.

If only Dilbeck could be trusted to stick to the script! The subject of the deceased Jerry Killian was to be avoided. Subtle inquiries were to be made about the stripper's daughter. If Mrs. Grant complained about the custody litigation, Dilbeck was to offer his assistance. *I know the new judge quite well*—something mild like that, not pushy or boastful.

If Mrs. Grant brought up Dilbeck's bloody outburst at the Eager Beaver, the congressman was to appear remorseful but offer nothing. Moldowsky drilled him on these points. He tried to keep things simple because he knew Dilbeck's brain would be fogged with lust. Precautions had been taken to protect the stripper from lewd assault, but risk was unavoidable. The congressman was coming apart. It was a race against time.

Malcolm Moldowsky studied his reflection in the bay window. He liked what he saw—a portrait of elegant confidence under stress. Even at home, Moldy was rarely comfortable wearing anything but a coat and tie. He'd read that Nixon was the same way, but so what? Casual attire impeded Moldy's genius; he simply didn't feel powerful in a tank top and a pair of wrinkled Dockers. On this morning he wore a three-piece charcoal suit, tailored in Paris. The necktie was burgundy with a gray diagonal stripe.

Moldowsky sat at the cherry desk in his den. The phone rang often, but he let the machine answer. He made notes on a legal pad. He wrote: "What does she want?" Then he jotted a list of possible scenarios, from worst to best.

Worst: The stripper could sink the congressman. She could do it on her own, or at an enemy's behest. She wouldn't necessarily need the photograph, either; an afternoon press conference would do nicely. The revelation would be an instant catastrophe. If it didn't cost Dilbeck the election, it certainly would imperil the sugar subsidies. The Rojos stood to lose millions. Malcolm Moldowsky would do anything to prevent such a calamity. He had painstakingly mended Dilbeck's political fences, and the committee vote was all but nailed down. The single remaining hurdle was a Republican named Tooley from northern Alabama who claimed to be a born-again Christian and railed tirelessly against R-rated movies, all forms of rock music, and the annual *Sports Illustrated* swimsuit edition. Moldowsky happened to know that Congressman Tooley was a syphilitic old fraud, but it didn't matter. The sonofabitch would repudiate David Dilbeck immediately if a seedy sex scandal came to light. Tooley wouldn't vote in the same column as a philandering pagan—not for farm subsidies or any other damn fool thing. If Dilbeck was exposed, the sugar vote would be in grave jeopardy.

At the bottom of Moldy's list was his dream scenario: What if the stripper let the whole thing slide? Maybe she had no hard feelings about the champagne-bottle attack, no interest in blackmailing the hot-blooded congressman, no secret doubts about Jerry Killian's death. Perhaps she just wanted to be left alone to dance her heart out.

Not likely, Moldowsky thought. The woman surely needed money, and surely understood how deeply she could wound David Dilbeck by opening her mouth. Moldowsky guessed that Erin Grant's silence was available for purchase. He figured she'd be content to accept a large sum and leave town quietly with her little girl. That would be fine. A payoff carried its own risks, but arranging a permanent disappearance was no longer viable. Not with a homicide cop hovering in the shadows.

Moldy was vexed by Al García. How did his card turn up in the lawyer's safe-deposit box? Was the detective looking into Mordecai's disappearance? Moldy made a note to check with the Florida Bar. It was he, after all, who had tipped investigators to the missing lawyer's trust-fund "scheme."

There were more riddles: Why would a Dade County homicide cop be snooping around Fort Lauderdale? Was García investigating Jerry Killian's death, too? More important, was it he who removed the Kodak slide from Mordecai's safe box?

Experience had taught Malcolm Moldowsky to brace for the worst. Assume García was hot on the trail. Assume he'd gotten wind of the blackmail plots. Assume he suspected foul play in the death of Killian and the disappearance of Mordecai . . .

Let him assume his fool head off, Moldowsky thought. There's no proof, no evidence, no thread linking these unfortunate coincidences to the congressman. Homicides? A lonely bachelor has a fishing accident in Montana, a slimy lawyer skips town with embezzled accounts. What homicides? What the hell was García doing? Moldy wondered if the detective was playing a little game of his own—maybe the business card was left as bait. If so, the only smart move was to ignore the bastard. Play it cool.

Moldowsky's problem was a pathological lack of restraint. He owned a huge ego, a short temper and no patience. He was unaccustomed to doing nothing. He had so many connections and so much sway that his reflex was to grab the phone and ream some ass. That's what fixers did, they spotted trouble coming and headed it off. But an influence-peddler was only as good as his information, and Moldy didn't know jack about this pushy Cuban cop. It gnawed at him all morning. Two, three phone calls would do the trick . . . but why panic? He'd been so thorough, so careful—a mistake was flatly impossible, ridiculous even. Señor Detective García didn't have squat. Nobody could've put it together so fast.

Yet Moldy found himself eyeing the telephone. Buffed nails tapped restlessly on the cherrywood. He needed to know more. His hand shot across the desk toward the Rolodex. His fingers tripped lightly through familiar index cards. It was an astounding trove of sources. Names and numbers, numbers and names. And they each owed Malcolm J. Moldowsky a favor.

It was like a drug, this power he had.

25

The two goons guarding the Rojo yacht were dazzled by Erin's arrival. She wore blood-red lipstick, gold hoop earrings, a white miniskirt, fuck-me pumps and a sleeveless salmon blouse. She looked great, she smelled great. A walking fantasy. The hired goons envied David Lane Dilbeck.

"You're Mrs. Grant?"

"No," Erin said. "I'm Tipper Gore."

"Who's your friend? He's not invited."

Shad emerged from the shadow. The goons shifted uneasily in their shiny black suits. They clenched their fists and swelled their chests, but the stripper's bodyguard seemed unimpressed. He was as broad as a meat locker, and wore a red beret that barely covered the crown of his lumpy bald dome. His mouth was a cruel-looking beak. He blinked with bulging eel eyes. He had a .38 tucked in his belt, and a South American kinkajou on his left shoulder. The kinkajou was eating a candy bar.

"Relax," Shad told the goons. "He's on a leash."

"Who the hell are you?"

Erin said, "He's a Guardian Angel. Can't you tell?"

"Get lost," said one of the goons.

Erin took Shad's hand. "He goes, I go," she said.

The goons stepped away and conferred briefly. One of them disappeared into the yacht. He returned with a decision: "OK, Mr. Guardian Angel, you can stay out here with us. But your monkey goes back to the zoo."

Shad said, "It ain't a monkey." The kinkajou chittered through a mouthful of nougats. When Shad stroked its neck, the animal turned and bit him on the wrist. The goons jumped but Shad showed no reaction. He wiped the blood on his camouflage trousers and said, "I got him off a guy at jai-alai. He loves chocolate."

"Crazy fuck," muttered one of the goons.

Two couples came strolling down the dock in the moonlight. The men wore white dinner jackets and the women, both blondes, wore shiny evening gowns. They drank Rum Runners and laughed. The women were impressed by the tall fishing boats and gleaming yachts, and the men seemed to be expert mariners. They were much older than their dates. When they reached the slip where the *Sweetheart Deal* was moored, conversation stopped. The men eyed Erin, who smiled tolerantly. On deck the pinheaded Rojo goons stood shoulder to shoulder, steroid bookends. Shad adjusted the angle of his red beret.

One of the blondes: "Say, can I pet your monkey?"

"It ain't a monkey. It's a kinkajou."

"Oh, I love kinkajous."

"Then what the hell. Pet away."

One of the dinner jackets: "He doesn't bite, does he?"

Shad looked insulted. "No, sir, he doesn't."

"See you later," Erin said. She slipped between the two goons and opened the cabin door.

Al García's boss in Homicide was Lt. William Bowman, who once played linebacker for the University of Florida. Billy Bowman hated cigars and was eleven years younger than García, but García didn't mind because Bowman was a decent cop, for an Anglo. Most of the time, he left García alone.

On the night that Erin was to dance for the congressman, Billy Bowman called García into the office. There was the traditional discussion of the wretchedness of the Miami Dolphins offense, followed by a cursory inquiry about the late Francisco Goyo.

"We found everything," García told Bowman, "except four toes and a buttock."

"Nice work."

"Billy?"

"Yeah."

"Why am I here?"

Bowman cracked his knuckles. "Is that a cosmic question? Such as: What's the point of it all? What is God's grand plan?"

García, grumbling: "No, *chico,* I mean why the fuck am I *here?* In your office. Shooting the shit for no apparent reason."

"How about closing that door."

García extended a leg and kicked the door shut.

Bowman said, "I got an interesting phone call from the chief, who had an interesting call from one of the county commissioners."

"Do tell," said García.

"Are you working a case with Broward?"

"Several, Billy."

"A missing lawyer?"

"This is fascinating," García said. "Let's have some coffee."

Over the next half hour, he told Lt. Billy Bowman the whole story, beginning with the floater in Montana. Bowman was a good listener and he asked sharp questions. When García finished, the lieutenant said he was very impressed. "You got 'em to drill a lock box without a court order."

García said, "I knew a girl at the bank, she's a vice-president now. We set a little trap."

Billy Bowman winced. "I didn't hear that."

"Whoever opened the lawyer's safe box found my card. And whoever found my card got on the phone."

"Which is exactly what you wanted."

Al García was generous about handing out his business cards during murder investigations. Frequently he'd give one to a prime suspect, just to gauge the reaction.

"So," said the lieutenant, "under whose ass did you light this particular fire?"

"If I had to guess," García said, "it's Malcolm Moldowsky."

Bowman said he'd never heard of the guy. García told him he wasn't supposed to. Political fixers were like vampires, the way they avoided daylight.

"This is how it went: Moldowsky calls the commissioner, who probably owes him a big favor. Maybe several big favors, who knows. So the commissioner calls the chief and says who's this guy García, why's he mucking around up in Broward? The last thing Metro needs is some jurisdictional beef with BSO."

"Believe it or not," Bowman said, "the commissioner was almost clever about it. He claims to be a dear friend of the missing lawyer. Says they met at a Dukakis fund-raiser and he can't believe—what's the dickhead's name?"

"Mordecai."

"Yeah. The commissioner can't believe Mordecai would take off to the islands with embezzled money."

García laughed. "That's very slick, making it personal. Like he was upset about his pal and that's all."

"Right. And anything we could tell him would be greatly appreciated—and very confidential, of course."

Bowman took a call on the speaker phone while García poured the last of the coffee. A uniformed road officer had shot a burglar after a chase down the Palmetto Expressway. Bowman took notes and said he was on the way. He hung up swearing because the dead burglar was a drag queen, which meant that the local TV stations would go wild. The lieutenant said, "My whole career, I never shot a guy in a strapless cocktail dress. How about you?"

"The world's changing, William." García lifted a salute with the coffee cup.

Billy Bowman swung his size-thirteen Reeboks up on the desk. "About this lawyer—you figure he's dead, too?"

"Most likely," García said.

"And dumped, like the other guy."

"Yeah, but who knows where."

"The Everglades is perfect," Billy Bowman said. "Why go all the way to Bumfuck, Montana, when you got the Everglades in your own backyard? Hell, a dead body decomposes faster here than anywhere else in the country. That's a known fact, Al."

"Don't tell me they've done a study."

"Seriously. Miami's got the fastest rot-rate, because of the heat."

"Really?" García mused. "I thought it was the humidity."

"The point is, Montana makes no sense."

"It does if your victim's supposed to be on vacation. Killian was a trout fisherman, remember? This shitbird lawyer, who knows where they put him. The nearest landfill, probably."

The lieutenant said nothing for several moments. Then: "Al, you can't just go out and bust a fucking congressman."

"I'm aware of that."

"Unless you catch him in the act. Preferably on videotape, with the pope and Mary Tyler Moore as eyewitnesses."

"Bill, I'm aware of that."

"Where's the Kodak slide? I'm curious is all."

García let the question hang. Bowman was a smart guy; it wouldn't take him long to see the problem. About eleven seconds, in fact.

"You're right," he told García. "I don't want to know."

"Tell the chief there's no missing-lawyer case with Broward."

"You were just checking out a tip."

"Right," García said. "Dry hole."

"Sorry we couldn't be more help."

"Yeah," García said. "We're very sorry."

"And this'll go straight back to Moldowsky?"

"You can bet on it."

"Then what happens, Al? Can we look forward to an actual arrest in our lifetime?"

García rubbed his chin. "Frankly, I got shit for evidence. But I got some beautiful theories."

Bowman liked Al García because he was an excellent detective with no ambition to be anything more. Bowman himself wished to be chief some day, and cops such as García often made him look brilliant. Consequently, he wanted García to be happy and productive, not bored or burned out. Al enjoyed challenges, and the lieutenant usually tried to oblige. But this . . .

"Where's our jurisdiction?" Bowman asked.

"It's iffy," García admitted. "Dilbeck lives in Dade County. So does Moldowsky."

"But the crimes took place elsewhere, right?" Bowman cracked his knuckles again. "Al, would you hate my guts if I said you're on your own."

"You'd be crazy not to. Maybe I'll take some sick days."

"But, as your friend, let me also say I'd love to see you pull this off."

"It's a long shot, Billy."

"Yeah, but I got a personal stake here. I voted for the dumb bastard."

"No shit?" Al García couldn't believe that Bowman was a registered Democrat.

The lieutenant pulled his feet off the desk. "I remember what you told me a long time ago—"

"The world is a sewer and we're all dodging shit."

"Very uplifting, Al. I'm surprised Hallmark hasn't bought up the copyright."

"Words to live by," García said.

"You know what's sad? I'm beginning to think you're right. I'm beginning to think there's no hope."

"Of course there's no hope," García said, "but don't let it get you down."

"I'm pissed, Al. I voted for the asshole."

"Here's what you do: First thing tomorrow, sign up for some range time. Check out an Uzi, one of the fully automatics, and go nuts for about an hour. Shoot the living shit outta the place. You'll feel a thousand percent better."

Billy Bowman said it sounded like a good idea. He tossed a notebook and a Pearlcorder in his briefcase. "Well, I better get a move on."

"Good luck with the drag-queen burglar."

"Thanks, Al. Good luck with the degenerate congressman."

David Lane Dilbeck greeted Erin timidly. He wore a blue blazer, a white shirt, pleated camel trousers and expensive cordovan loafers; no socks. His silver hair had a grooved look, as if it had been combed about twenty times in the past hour. Additionally, the congressman reeked of Aramis.

Erin was accustomed to overdoses of cologne, but she wasn't sure if she could hack the comical distraction of a turtleneck.

She said, "This is a gorgeous boat."

"Belongs to a friend," Dilbeck said. "I use it any time I please."

"For this?"

Dilbeck stammered in the negative.

"What's that on the stereo?" Erin asked.

"Dean Martin. Music for lovers."

He's serious, Erin thought. That *is* Dean Martin. "Well, it's pretty," she said, "but I brought my own."

"Fine." Dilbeck sounded disappointed. "It's your show."

Erin had never spoken with an actual United States congressman. She expected a smoother presentation, an air of self-assurance if not downright conceit. But David Dilbeck struck her as just another jittery old lech.

"Let's try this." Erin handed him a cassette. "I put it together my-self." She went to the head and changed to a dance outfit. It wasn't easy; the bathroom was fiendishly small. Erin wriggled into a white teddy. Underneath she wore a lace brassiere and a matching G-string. She was betting that Dilbeck would go for the honeymoon look.

When she came out, ZZ Top was playing on the Rojos' sound system. She balanced the bass and cranked up the volume a couple of notches. The stage was a captain's table that had been moved to the center of the room. The congressman sunk into a canvas director's chair. He crossed his ankles and entwined his hands. A silver champagne bucket sat at his right elbow.

Erin stepped on the table and tested it for traction. As she began to dance, she felt vaguely claustrophobic; the yacht's salon had a low roof, and the paneled walls had no mirrors. Erin never performed without mirrors, and now she was uncomfortable. Mirrors helped her concentrate on the footwork, helped her detach from the stares.

Dilbeck's chin bobbed a half-beat behind the music; he was trying his damnedest to look like a rocker. Erin removed her top and dropped it on his lap. He gazed reverently at the undergarment, his mouth parted. He breathed a low growl. When he raised his eyes, Erin flashed her million-dollar smile. She unsnapped the G-string and slipped it down around the garter. The congressman's neck went limp, and his body swayed.

Scary, Erin thought. A genuine sexual trance. She felt she was witnessing a rare phenomenon, like a total eclipse.

"She's Got Legs" faded into "Brown-Eyed Girl," which blended into "Under My Thumb." With each song the dance tempo slowed, and so did the congressman's pulse. His eyes rolled and his jaw fell open, exposing a fortune in capped teeth. A large man, he seemed to shrink visibly as the music played—a marionette cut loose from its strings. Performing for a catatonic was lonely. Erin missed Orly's mirrors.

When the set ended, David Dilbeck snapped upright and began to clap. Erin was startled at his rapid recovery. The congressman folded two hundred-dollar bills in her garter and offered to pour the champagne. She put on the white teddy and turned off the tape deck. Dilbeck had a chair waiting.

He said, "You are positively amazing."

"So are you."

"The most incredible blue eyes!"

"They're green," Erin said, "but thanks, anyway."

Dilbeck handed her a glass and made a toast to new friendships. "Do you remember me?" he asked. "The last time we met, I wore a mustache." Already he'd deviated from Moldowsky's script.

Erin said, "How could I forget. You nearly bashed me in the skull."

"I'm so sorry."

"What in the world came over you?"

Dilbeck looked away. "Truly I don't remember. It was inexcusable."

He tossed back the champagne. "I hope you can forgive me." It was, he thought, a cunning way to elicit Erin's frame of mind. If she let the subject drop, she probably wasn't planning to shake him down.

"Come on," she said, "how about another number?"

The congressman relaxed. "Wonderful," he said, peeling off his blazer.

By the fourth set, he was helpless, exhausted and bombed. Erin had done some of the best dancing of her life. Dilbeck sat cross-legged on the floor of the salon. He'd kicked off his loafers and unbuttoned his shirt. Erin perched topless on the edge of the captain's table. Dilbeck clutched at her knee but she nudged his hand away.

"I love you," he said. "Desperately I do."

"I love you, too, sweetie."

"Be my girlfriend."

"Your what?"

"How would . . ." His eyes fluttered. "How would you like an apartment on the Intracoastal? And a car—what'd you think of the new Lexus? You can quit your job and live like a queen."

"You're kidding. All that, just for being your girlfriend?"

"Whatever you want."

"Wow." Erin saw an opportunity to have some fun. "Davey, can I ask a question?"

"Anything, darling."

"I wouldn't have to screw you, would I?"

Dilbeck squinted in puzzlement. "Well now," he said, working his lips like a plowhorse.

"What I mean," said Erin, "is you wouldn't expect sex in exchange for your kindness. I can tell you're not that kind of person."

The congressman chuckled wretchedly. He groped for the champagne bottle and took a swig.

Erin let her foot brush against Dilbeck's leg. "You wouldn't believe some men," she said. "They're such pigs. They give you a sports car, they expect at least a hand job. Sometimes two!"

"Huh," said Dilbeck. "Imagine that."

Erin gave a convincing sigh of disgust. "Some guys," she said. "I swear to God."

"But I love you."

"I'm sure you do, Davey. But I couldn't accept an apartment or anything else. It wouldn't be right."

"Please. I want your life to be wonderful."

The congressman watched sorrowfully as Erin put on her bra top. She liked the rush on nights like this, when the dancing was so good. The feeling of control was indescribable. More important, a plan—a wondrously reckless plan—was taking shape.

"What is it you do in Washington?" she asked Dilbeck. "Give me a job description."

Dilbeck took several moments to reassemble his thoughts. "Mainly I help people. My constituents." He paused theatrically. "You may not know this, but I once tried to help you."

"Really."

"Yes, ma'am. With regards to your daughter."

Erin stiffened. She said, "I didn't know."

"Oh yes, oh yes. I spoke to a certain judge. He wouldn't listen to reason."

"My divorce judge?"

"The old man, yes. A difficult fellow, God rest his soul."

Erin said, "Why did you do that? How'd you know about my case?" She tried to sound curious and not accusatory. This was the important part, and Al García would want every detail. Was Dilbeck drunk enough to blab about Jerry Killian?

Apparently not. He said, "A little birdie told me about your case." Erin coaxed but he wouldn't budge.

"I was glad to try," the congressman said. "I have great compassion for working mothers."

"Thank you. I had no idea."

He slid closer to the table. "I know the new judge, as well."

Erin said she was impressed that a man as important as Dilbeck would take an interest in her family problems.

"That's my job," he said. "Helping people." One of the congressman's hands came to rest on Erin's thigh. She gave him three, maybe four seconds of thrill before flicking it away.

She said, "The case is working out fine. My daughter's with me now."

"I'm glad to hear it. But, remember, if you need anything—"

"Aren't you a sweetheart."

"Anything at all—"

"Hey, Davey?"

"What is it?"

"Did you steal the razor out of my bathroom?"

David Dilbeck turned gray. Moldy hadn't prepared him for this. He said, "God help me, I did."

"You're a sick puppy."

"That's what Erb says."

"Who's Erb?"

"Erb Crandall. He works for me."

Erin said, "Why'd you take the razor?"

The congressman's jowls quavered. He appeared on the verge of tears. "That's how much I love you," he said. "I took some lint, too."

"Lint."

"From your laundry. I'm awfully sorry."

Erin stood on the table and put her hands on her hips. Dilbeck was sprawled in a wrinkled heap on the wooden floor.

"Davey, I don't mean to pry. But what did you do with my laundry lint?"

"I'm afraid I made love to it."

The room began to whirl. "Come closer," Erin told him.

Dilbeck gripped the corners of the captain's table and pulled himself to his knees.

Erin said, "Shut your eyes."

"Oh God." The congressman's dreams ran wild.

Erin removed one of her shoes and, with all her strength, hammered the four-inch heel into the bones of David Dilbeck's right hand. So much for García's instruction to remain calm.

Dilbeck didn't scream so much as whinny. Erin snatched a handful of oily silver hair.

"Davey, if you ever come into my apartment again, *ever,* I'll shoot you. Is that understood?"

Through his agony the congressman whispered: "But I love you so much!"

"I know you do, sweetheart."

The two goons asked Shad if he was really a Guardian Angel. He said yes, but he moonlighted nights at a nudie joint. The goons wanted to know all about it. Shad said the music was terrible and the pay sucked.

"Who cares," said one of the goons. "Think of all the pussy."

Shad said, "Pussy don't pay the rent." He plucked an ice cube from his glass and gave it to the kinkajou. The animal snarled as it chewed.

The other goon, who had tiny crumpled-looking ears, asked Shad if he had to pay the dancers for sex. "Or do you get it free? What's the deal?"

Shad said, "They pay *me.*"

"Aw, bullshit."

"It's in my contract."

The first goon said, "Yeah, right."

"Any girl I want."

Shad transferred the kinkajou from one shoulder to the other. His shirt was sticky with blood, from the animal digging its claws. The crumple-eared goon grimaced when he saw the mess. He and his partner had given Shad and his strange pet a wide berth on the yacht's aft deck. Shad knew that the men feared the kinkajou more than they feared him. That was the plan.

The first goon said, "So, like, you get to watch all the auditions?"

"Watch, my ass. I do the hiring."

"Man! So you get to see everything."

"Everything," Shad said with a sly smile.

"And you been at it how long?"

"Ten, eleven years."

"Think of all the titties you've seen."

"Thousands," said Shad. "It boggles the fucking mind." He couldn't believe what morons they were, these hired guards.

The first one said: "When you do the auditions, what do you go by? Is it just size? Reason I ask, once I was with this girl who had gigantic boobs but they didn't look so hot when she took off her top. Know what I mean?"

Shad said, "We got very high standards."

The crumple-eared goon asked: "You ever audition anyone famous? I mean, before they got famous."

"Oh sure," said Shad, thinking fast. These dolts would believe anything. "Kim Basinger danced at the club for a while. So did Meryl Streep, only back then she used a different name."

"No shit?"

"Chesty LeFrance. That's what she went by."

The first goon said, "Kim Basinger, sure. But Meryl Streep, man, she ain't exactly stacked."

"Not now she isn't," Shad said. "You should've seen her before the operation. Awesome."

The kinkajou climbed down his arm and hopped to the deck. Shad gave a sharp tug on the leash. The animal growled and rolled on its back.

"How about that," said the goon with the bad ears.

Shad said, "Yeah, I got him trained good." Truthfully, he wasn't crazy about the kinkajou. He was glad the two hours were almost over, so he could return the animal.

"How about you boys," Shad said. "You like this gig?"

The first goon said he'd rather be down below, doing what the old man was doing. The second goon said yeah, the worst part of the job was trying to stay awake. Shad asked how much the old man paid.

"We don't work for the old man. We work for the Rojos."

"Who's that?"

"Rojo Farms," said the crumple-eared goon. "We get two hundred a day."

"Damn," Shad said.

"And mostly we just hang out."

The first goon said, "They call us drivers but that's bullshit. We're security. The Rojos do lots of entertaining, and we keep an eye on the guests . . . speaking of which." He motioned to his partner, who stepped to the salon door and listened.

"Music's stopped," he reported. "Sounds like they're just talking."

Shad said, "So who's the old man in there—some bigshot?"

"Friend of the family."

The kinkajou began pacing restlessly, tangling the leash around Shad's legs. The Rojo goons were amused by the bald man's efforts to extricate himself. In frustration Shad let go. The kinkajou ambled to a corner and sat down, licking its paws.

One of the goons said, "I never heard of a stripper with a body-guard."

Shad said a woman can't be too careful these days.

The one with the deformed ears motioned toward Shad's gun. "Is that a .38?"

"Special," Shad said.

"That's what I want, too. How long before your license came through?"

"I didn't bother with a license. See, I got a slight history."

"That's rough," said the goon.

"Fucking computers." Shad emptied his glass over the rail.

"But still they let you in the Guardian Angels?"

"No problem. I had references." Shad pointed at his head. "Plus I already had the hat."

Erin came out the door. She looked tired but unmolested.

"All set?" Shad said.

"Fine and dandy."

He held her arm as she stepped from the yacht to the dock.

"Nice night," she said, smiling up at the teardrop moon.

"Very pleasant," Shad agreed. He waved goodbye to the halfwit goons.

"Wait," said the one with the normal ears. "Don't forget your monkey!"

Al García met them at a bagel joint near the jai-alai fronton in Dania. Erin and Shad were late because Shad couldn't find the guy who'd rented him the kinkajou. After twenty minutes of circling the block, he pulled off the road, opened the door and put the animal out. Shad threw a bag of Snickers bars from the car and drove away. When he walked into the bagel joint, a waitress noticed the bloodied shirt and offered to call 911. She assumed that Shad had been stabbed.

García was waiting at a table near the rear of the restaurant. He was mouthing the nub of a very old cigar. He asked Erin how it went with the congressman.

"Piece a cake." She gave a slightly edited account. The congressman's lint confession was the highlight. Even Shad was astounded.

"That's some honor," he said.

García asked Erin if Dilbeck tried anything weird while she was dancing. She said no, just the usual hopeful groping. She left out the part about smashing his hand.

"So what's your impression?" the detective asked.

"One, Davey's not too bright. Two, he probably doesn't know exactly what happened to Jerry Killian."

García concurred. "He doesn't have the nerve to do it himself, and the people who did are smart enough not to tell him."

"In other words," Shad said, "we're wasting our goddamn time."

The waitress brought a platter of bagels and a pot of coffee. Shad took off his shirt and asked the awestruck waitress to please throw it in the garbage. As they ate, Al García peppered Erin with questions.

"Did he say whose yacht it was?"

"A friend," Erin said. "That's all he'd tell me."

García smiled. "Remember the Cuban kid who paid a thousand bucks for your shoe? His family owns the *Sweetheart Deal.*"

"The sugar people?"

"Yeah. They got Dilbeck's balls in a vault somewhere."

Erin drummed her nails on the table. "So the kid bought my shoe as a present for Davey."

"A nice gesture," Shad remarked. "Fetish-of-the-month."

García said, "Are either of you history buffs? Me, I love American history." He leaned forward, dropping his voice. "I'm trying to imagine what Thomas Paine would think of a congressman who has sex with old shoes and laundry lint."

Erin agreed that the republic was doomed. She said Tasmania was looking pretty good as an alternate homeland.

Al García asked if David Dilbeck had mentioned the crucial photograph. Erin said he'd barely talked about that night at the Eager Beaver, except to apologize.

"What about Angela?"

"He offered to help with the new judge," Erin said. "That's the only time I was nervous. He seemed a little too interested."

Shad got up to call the club and make sure no disasters had occurred in his absence. Orly got on the line and bitched about him taking the night off. A British sailor had almost choked to death in the pasta pit—Monique Sr. saved him with a modified Heimlich.

"Sorry I missed it," Shad said. Orly hung up.

Shad returned to the table and said he'd better go, Mr. Orly was pissed. García offered Erin a ride home.

In the car, she said: "So tell me."

"What?"

"You're humming, Al. You never hum. What happened?"

"Progress!" The detective waggled the cigar nub. "A very nice lady at the Missoula Holiday Inn remembers three Jamaicans getting a room and ordering a half dozen rib-eye steaks sent up. This happened a few weeks back. Apparently not a multitude of Jamaicans cruise through Montana this time of year. Anyhow, the nice lady punched their bill up on the computer and read me the charges."

"And?"

"There was a twenty-two-minute phone call," García said, cigar bobbing, "to a certain residence in Miami, Florida."

Erin said, "Dilbeck?"

"God, how I wish," said García. "No, darling. It was Malcolm Moldowsky—the congressman's fairy godfather. The guy who keeps hassling your boss."

So there was no doubt about it, Erin thought. They'd murdered Mr. Peepers.

"I'll never prove it," García said, "but I can sure raise some hell. Did Davey Boy happen to mention Moldowsky's name? Between hard-ons, I mean."

"He talked about a guy named Crandall."

"But no Moldowsky?"

"Not tonight," Erin said. "I'll try again next time."

The detective's foot came off the accelerator. "Did I miss something?"

"I'm dancing for Davey again."

"Like hell—"

Erin cut him off. "He tipped me a thousand bucks, Al. That's three grand I walked with. A couple more nights like this, my lawyer's paid off and I've got cash in the bank."

"Too risky."

"He's harmless. Trust me, he's a little boy."

She didn't tell the detective what she had in mind, because he couldn't help. In fact, he probably would've stopped her from going through with it. Likewise, Shad would be an unsuitable accomplice; too impulsive, too volatile. If things got hot, he'd wind up in the back of a squad car. Maybe Erin would, too. She couldn't take the chance.

"Where," García asked, archly, "is the next rendezvous?"

Erin shrugged. "It's entirely up to him."

"Oh, for God's sake."

They rode in prickly silence for several miles before she said, "Al, tell me what's wrong."

"Nothing." He spit the spent cigar out the window. "I think you liked it. Am I right?"

"It was easy tonight. I like it when it's easy."

He slapped the steering wheel with both hands. "Christ, it's not a game. I pulled your dead pal out of the river, remember?"

She thought: He wasn't there tonight. He didn't see for himself. Dilbeck was completely helpless.

García warned her that it was bound to get hinky. He said she was pressing her luck, seeing the congressman again. She told him he didn't understand.

"Sure I understand," he said. "It's not about the money, is it?"

"Not entirely." Erin's eyes flashed.

"It's about power. Pure and simple."

"Al," she said, "you've been watching too much 'Oprah.' "

26

The next day, Erin took her daughter to see *101 Dalmations* at a mall in South Miami. After the movie, they stopped at an ice cream shop, where Erin ordered two scoops of chocolate pistachio for both of them.

Angela, licking a cone: "Can we get a dog someday?"

"Sure," said Erin.

"Not like Aunt Rita's, either."

"How about a dalmation? Just like in the movie."

Angela said, "No, I want a Great Dane. But not one that bites, OK?"

"Then we'll get a puppy. We'll train it together."

"What about Daddy?"

Erin crunched hard on a pistachio. "Good question," she said.

"He doesn't like dogs. He likes birds."

"I remember," Erin said. "The dog'll be yours and mine."

Angela wore a thoughtful expression. "Is Daddy in trouble?"

"Yes, baby, I'm afraid so."

"Are you in trouble, too?"

"No, Angie, I'm doing just fine."

Later they walked around Burdine's and looked at the clothes. Erin bought her daughter two dresses, two overalls and a pair of white Nike sneakers with pink slashes.

Angela said, "Momma, it's not my birthday."

"I know, honey."

"What's the matter?"

"Nothing's the matter," Erin said. "I love you, that's all."

"I love you, too, Momma. But don't cry."

"I'm not crying. It's my allergies."

Angela looked doubtful. She said, "Allergies make you sneeze, not cry."

"For your information, little lady, there are many different types of allergies."

They held hands, strolling the mall. Coming toward them, a handsome Latin man pushed a girl in a small wheelchair. The girl was pale with jet-black hair, done in braids. She wore a steel brace on one of her legs.

Quickly Erin tugged her daughter toward the doorway of a toy shop. "Remember all those Barbie dolls you lost—"

"But, Momma—"

"Let's pick out some new ones."

"But, Momma, look!" Angie had spotted the wheelchair going by. "It's an Everest-and-Jennings."

Great, thought Erin. He even taught her the names.

Angela said, "That's like Daddy does, pushing me. Only why are they going so slow?"

"Because that little girl is hurt. It's not safe for her to go fast."

"Maybe when she's all better?"

"Yes, baby. When she's all better."

Erin considered explaining to her daughter the saddest of truths— that some sick people never get better. It would've been a convenient segue back to the subject of Angela's father, and why Angela could never be with him again.

But Erin let it slide. The child was only four years old; she had a whole lifetime to learn about sadness. Today was for dalmations, ice cream and new dolls. At the toy store, Erin bought two new Barbies, plus swimsuits and evening gowns. She said no to the fur stoles, but Angie didn't make a fuss.

In the car, she asked, "Momma, when can I go home?"

"It won't be long." Erin prayed that Angie meant "home" with her, not Darrell Grant. "You mean the new apartment, right?"

Angela nodded excitedly. "I liked the stairs. That was fun." She paused. "Where will Daddy go?"

Erin thought: What do I tell her—Daddy's off to prison? No, *prison* is a scary word. How about: a special place for grown-ups who get in trouble. Or better: a big building that looks just like a hospital, except for the barbed wire. Again, Erin chose to dodge the topic of Darrell's fate.

"He'll be taken care of," she said.

"Does he have another girlfriend?"

"I don't know." The question caught Erin by surprise.

" 'Cause I don't want him to be lonely."

"He won't be lonely, baby. I promise." Erin had a depressing vision of Angela as a young woman, loyally visiting her father on weekends at Raiford. Darrell undoubtedly would try to recruit her in the smuggling of cigarettes and pills.

"Where are we going now?" Angie asked.

"Victoria's Secret."

"What's that?"

"That's where Mommy buys her outfits for work."

"Your waitress clothes?"

"Right," Erin said, with a sigh. "My waitress clothes."

It was nearly five o'clock when they got back to Miami. Erin didn't want to say goodbye, but she only had one hour to drive back to the club, and the traffic northbound was hell.

Angela kissed her on the nose and pinched her chin; it was a game they played.

"Momma, thank you for the new Barbies."

"Remember to be nice, and share."

"I promise." Angie hopped out of the car, carefully clutching the shopping bag that contained her dolls. She stood on the sidewalk and waved.

"You run on inside," Erin said. She blew a kiss and tapped the tip of her nose. As Angela started toward the house, Erin slowly drove away. Halfway down the block, she glanced in the rearview and saw her daughter running after the car. Erin braked hard, making the tires squeal.

"Momma!" Angela was on tiptoes at the window. Her cheeks were pink, and she was out of breath. She hugged the bag of dolls to her chest.

Erin said, "What is it, baby?"

"I'm scared."

"Of what?" She opened the car door and Angela clambered onto her lap. Erin turned to see if someone else was on the street, someone who might have frightened the girl. She saw nothing.

"Angie, what's the matter? What are you scared of?"

"Please don't get in trouble like Daddy."

"Oh, honey. Is that it?"

"Please!"

"Don't worry," Erin said, holding her daughter to her breast. "Don't you worry about me."

Darrell Grant phoned his sister from the Wal-Mart and said, "Where's the nearest water from your place?"

Rita said, "Don't tell me you got a boat."

"A car," Darrell said, "but I need to dump it."

"Not in the water."

"Yeah, in the water."

"A brand-new car?"

"Lord Christ, Rita, can't you just answer a simple question!"

Darrell Grant ditched the stolen Thunderbird in a drainage canal at Turkey Point, where Alberto Alonso worked. Then he hitchhiked to the trailer park and enjoyed one of Rita's peanut butter-and-plantain sandwiches.

She said, "They's been cops calling, all hours. Alberto says you must've fucked up."

"You got any Gatorade? The green kind?" Darrell asked.

"It ain't cold."

"That'll do."

Rita poured him a tall glass. "We lost a pup to an eagle."

"No shit," said Darrell. "A real eagle?"

Rita said it damn sure looked like an eagle when it swooped into the backyard. "Also, your wife kicked the Christmas out of Al. Then Lupa got after him, too. . . ."

Darrell Grant waved the sandwich and said, "Hold up now—"

"He's up to the Veterans' Hospital this afternoon. His tongue's all infected."

"Goddamn, Rita, you don't mind if I finish my lunch." Darrell puffed his cheeks to dramatize his urge to vomit.

Rita apologized. Then she said: "You can't stay here."

"I know."

"The cops, they drive by all the time."

Darrell said, "I need to borrow your car."

"The axle's broke."

"What about that Pontiac acrosst the way?"

"Mrs. Gomez," Rita said. "We ain't speakin' on account of the wolves got her Siamese."

Darrell said his idea was to steal the Pontiac, not borrow it. Rita asked since when did he know how to hotwire a car.

"I don't," Darrell Grant said. "But I surely know how to use a key."

From the backyard came a raw chorus of yowls. Rita scooped up her catcher's mask and hurried out through the screen door. Darrell darted to the bathroom and explored the medicine chest; it was cluttered with gauze, adhesive tape and antiseptic ointments. Quickly he spied a bottle of codeine Tylenols, prescribed for the recently mangled Alberto Alonso. Darrell emptied the pills into a front pocket of his jeans.

He was fixing another sandwich when Rita returned. She said, "So what's the plan, little brother?"

"Well, listen," he said, wiping his mouth. "I intend to collect my beautiful daughter and get the hell pronto out of Florida. How's that sound?"

"Start a new life."

"Exactly."

"Because you're too smart for this shit."

"I know it, Rita. I sure do know it."

She always said her brother should've been an actor, he was so handsome. She could easily picture him on one of her soaps—maybe a charming young drifter on "All My Children."

"What about your wife?" she asked.

Darrell Grant laughed caustically. "Erin will be very lucky," he said, "if I don't hurt her before I go."

Rita poured more Gatorade. This time she tossed in a handful of ice cubes. "Raising a child by yourself, I don't know."

Her brother shot her a cold look. "What's your point?"

"I'm just sayin' it might be easier by yourself. To get a fresh start and all."

"I'm a super father, Rita."

"Who said you wasn't."

"And, besides, Angie and I are partners."

"That's the part I don't like," Rita said. "Usin' that little girl the way you do."

Darrell said, "Hey, she has a ball with it. Just ask her if Daddy shows her a fun time."

"Lord, I'm sure. Stealin' wheelchairs."

"Hey, you should hear how she laughs when we're rollin' down the halls. The way her hair flies all back, looks just like silk. Nurses wave and say, 'See that pretty little angel!' " He smiled. "And out the door we go."

Rita said, "You're too good for that, Darrell. That's gypsy shit."

"Well, it works," said Darrell Grant, "whatever the fuck it is. Now—where you figure old Mrs. Gomez keeps her keys?"

The morning after Erin danced on the yacht, David Lane Dilbeck gave one of the most magnificent performances of his political career. It began with a rally in Little Haiti, where the congressman excoriated the U.S. Immigration Service for its heartless treatment of black Caribbean refugees. He declared that America owed its strength and heritage to courageous boat people, and that the Founding Fathers would be shame-stricken to see us now rebuff the neediest and most desperate. The only awkwardness arose when Dilbeck, speaking in fractured Creole, badly mistranslated the Emma Lazarus inscription from the Statue of Liberty ("Give me your oxen, your seedless guavas, your broken truck radiators . . ."). Though perplexed, the Haitian crowd remained enthusiastic.

Next the congressman raced to an American Legion barbecue, where he recounted the Battle of Inchon so vividly that many of the rapt veterans assumed that he'd seen action in Korea. He had not, for an undescended testicle had kept David Dilbeck out of the army. The congressman told his story with chin held high. His voice cracked as he poignantly described a young man's private heartbreak, denied a chance to fight for his nation. Leaving the enlistment center on that sad autumn day in 1951, Dilbeck said, he had vowed to overcome his handicap and serve America as devotedly as any man with two normally descended testicles. Patriotic fervor led him first to municipal government, then to Congress! Let me keep my dream, David Dilbeck boomed. Let me serve again! Cheers rose from the vets, who put down their spareribs and waved, with sticky fingers, dozens of miniature American flags. The congressman placed a bandaged hand over his heart and led the Legion crowd in "The Star-Spangled Banner."

The final stop was the Sunset Bay condominium, and here Dilbeck hit his peak—lucid, heartfelt and damn near eloquent. Erb Crandall was flabbergasted. He called Malcolm Moldowsky from a phone booth outside the rec room, where the congressman was addressing three hundred retirees.

"Malcolm, it's unbelievable," Crandall said. "He's got 'em in tears."

"The Israel thing?"

"Yeah, but he shitcanned the script. It's all off the top of his head."

"Oh Jesus," Moldy said. "You see any reporters?"

"Just Channel 10, but it's all right. He's a major hit, Malcolm. They're bawling all over their bagels."

Moldowsky tried to envision the scene. "Erb, I want an honest answer. Does David know anything at all about the Mideast?"

"He's weak on the geography," Crandall conceded, "but he's gangbusters on the Palestinian question. I counted four standing ovations."

Moldowsky clicked his teeth. "And he looks okay?"

"Like a million bucks. The best part, Eloy Flickman showed up for an ambush debate. That's how come the TV crew was here."

"Sneaky bastard."

"Davey tore him apart," Crandall said. "It was fantastic. Flickman took off like a scalded chihuahua."

"Is that right?" On Crandall's end, in the background, Moldowsky heard a wave of fresh applause. It seemed too good to be true. He thought: What happened last night between Dilbeck and the stripper? She must've screwed him silly.

Moldowsky wanted a full debriefing. "Put David on the line."

"He's on a roll, Malcolm. He's into his Holocaust material."

"I'll wait."

Six minutes and two ovations later, the congressman got on the phone.

Moldowsky said, "So tell me about your hot date."

"A delight," said Dilbeck, short of breath.

"No shakedowns? I want the truth. What about the photograph?"

"The subject never came up. She was a perfect lady."

"And you were the perfect gentleman."

"A monk, Malcolm. By the way, I'll need the yacht again in a few days. Erin's coming back to dance."

"Why?"

"Because she enjoyed herself." The congressman's tone was defensive. "She's very fond of me, Malcolm. Oh, and I'll need more cash."

"David, I want my people there."

"That won't be necessary—" A gaggle of crowlike voices drowned Dilbeck's words. "Malcolm, I've got to sign some autographs. Talk to Erb, OK?"

Moldy fidgeted until Crandall's voice came on the line: "Malcolm, you should see. They got him in a yarmulke!"

"Stick close for a few days."

"No, I'm afraid not." From now on, Crandall was steering clear of Dilbeck's glandular adventures. "I'm going to Atlantic City."

"Like hell," Moldy said.

"Malcolm, let me explain something. I don't work for you, I work for David. And David thinks it's terrific if I take a few days off and fly to Atlantic City."

"That's because David's got big plans."

"Well," said Erb Crandall, "I got front-row seats to see Cher."

"Really? I hope your plane hits a fucking mountain."

"Thanks, Malcolm. I'll be sure to send a postcard."

"Could you at least find out when he's meeting the girl? Or is that too much to ask?"

"I'll see what I can do," Crandall said. "Whatever happened last night, Davey's a new man on the stump. He sparkles, Malcolm."

"I suppose that's good." Sparkles?

"Kennedy-esque, according to the Hadassah ladies."

"Very funny."

"Gee," Crandall chided, "we thought you'd be pleased."

"The man is ill. You know it, I know it."

"He carries her shoe in his briefcase."

"And you're off to the fucking casinos."

"Malcolm?"

"What?"

"I'll miss you."

Erb Crandall reached the parking lot just as the congressman's limousine pulled out. Crandall waved pleasantly. Pierre, the driver, tipped his cap in reply. David Lane Dilbeck remained invisible behind tinted windows.

A nasty canker bloomed on Orly's lower lip. Erin couldn't look at him, even though they were deep in argument. She scanned the imitation red velvet walls while Orly told her no fucking way could she take Saturday night off.

"That's twice this week!"

Erin said, "I can count."

"The answer is no fucking way. I'm thinking maybe you got another gig."

"I do," she said. "Congressman Dilbeck."

"Shit." Orly had no choice but to back down. He didn't want to piss off a congressman, and he definitely didn't want more heat from that ballbuster Moldowsky.

"I'll work a double on Monday," Erin promised.

"Bet your ass." Orly picked pensively at the cold sore. "I'm curious," he said. "What's he like?"

"Nothing special."

"Big tipper?"

"Fair," Erin said. She knew where Mr. Orly was headed. "I didn't sleep with him," she said. "You can ask Shad."

"I already did."

"And what did he say?"

"He said you just danced."

"Don't act so surprised."

Orly shrugged one chubby shoulder. "He's a bigshot. Those guys usually want the full treatment."

Erin's arms began to itch. It happened whenever she sat too long in Orly's office.

He said: "Lorelei's got phlebitis. She's flying home to Dallas."

"I'm sorry," Erin said.

"It was that fucking snake, squeezing on her legs."

Bravely Erin sneaked a glance at Orly's face. He looked downcast and subdued. Of course the canker didn't help. She nearly felt sorry for him.

"How was the yacht?" he asked.

"Fine, except there's no mirrors. I'm dancing blind."

Orly said, "I'll need Shad here at the club. For the noodle wres-tling—last night some guy nearly cacked."

"I'll be fine by myself," Erin said. "Look, I know it's still early but why don't I get started on my sets?"

Orly said great, but no slow stuff. "Not to beat a dead horse, but I'm serious. You can't strip to fucking Jackson Browne."

"Congressman Dilbeck would disagree." Erin stood up and pushed the chair away. "Here's the part he liked best."

Singing now: " 'Down on the boulevard, they take it hard.' " Danc-ing in baggy jeans and sneakers. A kick-boxing move—punch, punch, right leg out, then spin. " 'They look at life with such dis-regard.' " Punch, kick, kick and split.

When she finished, Orly whistled and said, "Damn."

"I told you."

"That's Jackson Browne?"

"The table dancers," said Erin, "don't know what they're missing."

Urbana Sprawl said that there was a guy jerking his weenie in a green Pontiac. Shad went to the doorway and scanned the cars in the lot. The green Pontiac was parked far away, near the road; Shad could make out a silhouette behind the wheel. He went behind the bar to fetch his tire iron, but then Orly called him over to break up a fight between two men at the Foosball table. Men in suspenders! Orly bellowed. By the time Shad got out to the Pontiac, it was empty. He decided to prowl around.

Darrell Grant already had broken into the club through the fire door. He was sitting in the dressing room when Monique Sr. arrived to freshen her makeup. She gave him a radiant smile and said, "Are you Kiefer Sutherland?"

"That's me." Darrell was cooked on codeine and Halcions and some unidentified lemon-yellow capsules that he'd purchased from a newspaper vendor on Dixie Highway. Darrell's eyelids hung half-mast and his tongue stuck to his teeth. He said, "I'm looking for Missus Erin Grant. She works here in a nude capacity."

Monique Sr. told him to put the knife away. Darrell Grant was unaware that he was holding it.

"You lost some weight," Monique Sr. said, "since your last movie. My name is Monique." When she held out her hand, Darrell flicked it with the blade. The dancer cried out and pulled away. A stripe of blood appeared on her fingers.

"Hush up," Darrell said. He grabbed her arm and yanked her into his lap. Monique Sr. told him to stop and balled her fist, to stanch the bleeding.

Darrell Grant rubbed the stubble of his beard on the nape of the dancer's neck. He bounced her on his knees and said, "Here's a news flash, sweetie. I ain't Keith O'Sutherland."

"I kind of figured."

He cut the strap of her bra top, which dropped to the carpet. In the mirror, Monique Sr. studied the man's slack leer and fogged eyes. She felt him getting hard beneath her.

"Let me go," she said. "I'll find Erin."

"What's the hurry." He'd spotted the wad of bills in her black garter. "How much you got there?"

"I don't know. Maybe a hundred."

"Excellent." He slid the flat side of the knife down Monique Sr.'s leg, under the elastic of the garter. He twisted his wrist and the garter broke. The cash fell in a clump. It landed in one of her bra cups.

Darrell Grant said, "Pick it up."

As she bent over, he said, "Those are some tits you got."

"Please let me go."

He propped the steak knife behind his right ear, like a pencil. Then he reached around Monique Sr. and slapped a hand on each breast. "I would estimate," he said, "these are about three times bigger than my ex-wife's."

Monique Sr. said, "Shit. Now I know who you are."

She threw an elbow that caught Darrell Grant flush in the right temple. No pain registered in the lifeless blue eyes. He locked both arms around the dancer's rib cage and squeezed. He gave a grunt that started low in the throat, then rose to a musical hum.

Monique Sr., who'd taken eight years of piano, recognized the note as a high C-sharp. She was equally startled by the man's strength, and watched herself go pale in the mirror. The walls pulsed as the man's eerie humming filled her head. Within moments she passed out.

When she regained consciousness, Monique Sr. heard Darrell Grant say: "Wake up, Little Dorothy." She felt the man's kneecaps bouncing her bottom and realized that he still held her on his lap. She opened her eyes and saw, in the mirror, that he'd cut off her G-string.

She said, "You want a screw, get it over with."

Darrell squirmed beneath her. "I'd like to, but I sorta lost momentum."

"Then let me go. I was due in the cage ten minutes ago."

"Just hold up," he said. "Maybe if I squeeze them titties again."

"Nope," said Monique Sr. "You're done for the night. I can feel it."

"Shut up!"

"It's not your fault, sweetheart. It's the drugs."

Darrell Grant fumbled one-handed at his fly. There was no point. "Look what you did," he whined.

"Wasn't me."

He traced the point of the blade along her bikini lines. "How about a tattoo down there? Be the first on your block."

Monique Sr. said, "Please don't cut on me again." A dancer with scars didn't get much work—not at the good clubs, anyway.

When Darrell stung her with the knife, she promised to do whatever he wanted. "Thatta girlie," he said.

The door opened and Erin came in. It took a few seconds to absorb the scene: Her ex-husband sitting in the makeup chair, Monique Sr. trembling on his lap, the glint of steel against her tanned belly.

Darrell Grant giggled. "This is perfect. Shut the damn door and pull up a seat."

Erin could see he was wrecked. She regretted leaving the pistol at home.

He said, "I'm gonna give this lady the ride of her life, and you're gonna watch."

"Hot damn," said Erin. She sat down and winked at Monique Sr., who was not reassured. She raised her hand to show Erin the blood.

Darrell Grant said, "We're gonna give you a peep show."

"Anytime you're ready," Erin said, crossing her legs.

Darrell's tipsy smile disappeared and his lips pursed in childlike concentration. He commanded Monique Sr. to touch him. She said she was. He told her to *grab* him, then.

"I am," she said.

"I don't feel a damn thing."

"That makes two of us," Monique Sr. said.

Erin folded her arms. "I'm waiting, Mr. Sex Machine."

Darrell Grant squinted and strained and bared his teeth.

Erin said, "Maybe you need a laxative."

Monique Sr. caught herself laughing. Darrell's muscles—legs, arms, neck—went limp in defeat. "Goddamn you," he said to Erin.

"Fine. Now let Monique go, and we'll discuss the problem like grown-ups."

"Not until you take me to Angie."

Erin said, "You better talk to the judge." She couldn't resist: the exact line he'd used on her so many, many times.

He touched the knife to Monique Sr.'s neck. Teardrops and runny mascara streaked the dancer's cheeks. Erin knew it was important to keep her ex-husband confused and off guard. Any sign of weakness would embolden him.

She said, "Monique, I apologize. Darrell makes a shitty first impression."

"He cut my goddamn hand!" the dancer cried, displaying the wound again. "It's not funny, Erin. Give him what he wants."

"I want my daughter," Darrell Grant snarled.

"Well," said Erin, "I don't have her anymore."

Darrell took the news poorly. He shoved Monique Sr. to the floor and lunged wildly at Erin. The swiftness of his fury caught her by surprise. She tried to raise her legs to push him away, but he was already on top. The chair collapsed, and they went down simultaneously. Darrell Grant dug his knees into Erin's chest. He screamed and cursed until he was breathless. She lost track of how many times he called her a dirty rotten cunt.

She was worried about the knife: where was it? Darrell's arms hung at his side. Pinned flat on the floor, Erin couldn't see her ex-husband's hands, couldn't raise her head to try.

Darrell Grant, panting: "I want Angie back tonight."

"You're crushing me," Erin said.

Monique Sr. must have gotten out, because the door was ajar and the dressing room flooded with dance music from the lounge: something brassy by Gloria Estefan. Not an ideal tune to die by, Erin thought.

"Who's got her?" Darrell said.

Erin, wheezing: "I'll take you there."

His right arm came up with the rusty steak knife. He held it by the tip of the blade, between his thumb and forefinger.

Darrell Grant, weepy, slurring: "I lost my baby girl."

"That's not true," Erin said.

"All because of you."

"Darrell, it's not too late."

He turned the knife in his fingers, closed his palm around the handle. "Don't you understand? I escaped from jail. That means I got no future to speak of."

Erin said, "Everyone fucks up occasionally."

"My plan was me and Angie hittin' the road. Not anymore. Is that a fair statement?"

One of his eyelids had closed. Erin prayed that it would affect his accuracy with the knife. "If you kill me," she said, "you'll never see her again."

"And if I don't kill you," he said, "I'll hate myself for not tryin'."

Erin had always believed that her ex-husband was incapable of homicide, except by accident. Now, watching Darrell Grant fondle the cheap cutlery, she realized she might've misjudged him. What if he stabbed her? Erin thought, ludicrously, of how disappointed her mother would be. When one's only daughter is hacked to death wearing a sequined bra top and a G-string—well, there's really no way to explain it to one's friends at the orchid club.

"Darrell," Erin began.

"Shut your eyes. I can't manage if you're lookin' at me."

But Erin wouldn't close her eyes. She scorched him with a glare. "I won't let you do this to Angela."

"Hush up," he cried. "Who's got the knife, huh?"

"I *won't* let you."

"Shut your goddamn green eyes!"

"Why?" Erin said. "They remind you of somebody?"

"Oh, Lord Christ." He raised the knife with both hands.

Erin said, "Put it down, Darrell." A breathless whisper.

"No way."

"Darrell, please. For Angie's sake."

"I said, shut your eyes."

"Drop the fucking knife!" A man's voice at the door. Erin felt Darrell Grant go rigid. He cocked his head, waiting. He did not drop the fucking knife.

"Junior," said the voice, Shad's voice. "I'm counting to three."

Erin watched her ex-husband mouthing to himself: One Mississippi, two Mississippi . . . and then a branch snapped. That's what it sounded like.

Darrell flew off Erin as if launched by a spring. A plangent wailing now accompanied the melodies of Gloria Estefan. Erin sat up, covering her breasts with her hands. There was Shad with his tire iron, Mr. Orly clutching a can of Dr. Pepper, and Darrell Grant screaming.

Darrell—his arm hanging crooked and splintered at the elbow, a blond spike of a bone poking through the gray skin, dripping darkness down the front of his jeans.

Shad said, "Junior, you count too slow." He whipped off the beret and bowed his shiny dome in Darrell Grant's direction. "You remember carving this punkin? I'll bet you do."

"Take him outside," Orly muttered, and disappeared down the hall.

Erin got to her feet, wobbling. The faces in the mirror were a blur. She pointed at the reflection that most closely resembled her ex-husband. "Darrell," she said. "I knew you couldn't do it." Then: "God, I don't feel so good."

Shad caught her in one arm as she sagged. The whimpering Darrell Grant somehow lurched to his feet and stumbled from the dressing room. Shad placed Erin on a small divan and tucked a musty pillow under her head.

"I'll be right back," he told her. "Junior forgot his knife."

Shad searched the property but he couldn't find Darrell. He stalked next door and checked the fried-chicken joint, and then the restrooms of the video arcade down the street. When he returned to the Tickled Pink, the Pontiac was gone. The asshole had escaped again.

Erin was surprisingly calm. She borrowed Orly's phone and dialed the Martin County Sheriff's Office to report the sighting of her fugitive ex-husband. She described his gruesome injury, and hinted that Darrell might soon surface at a local emergency room. The cop on the other end was no Al García. He took the information haltingly, and asked numerous vague questions. Erin had to spell her name three times because he kept asking her if it was "Aaron—like the baseball player."

When she got off the phone, Orly said, "We got a policy against husbands and boyfriends at this club."

"Darrell is neither," Erin said, "and I didn't invite him."

"He crazy enough to come back?"

"That's hard to say, Mr. Orly. The police are after him."

"Lovely. Maybe we'll have a shootout in the pasta pit."

Shad said, "The boy's in no shape to fight. I busted his ulna to smithereens."

Orly frowned. "His what?"

Erin announced that she was going home to take a hot shower. Shad got the .38 Special and followed in his car. There was no sign of a lurking green Pontiac. He parked by Erin's apartment until the lights went out. Then he circled the complex four times and drove back to the club. Orly was waiting at the front bar.

"Those fucking Lings," he fumed, "they're trying to steal Urbana. A thousand bucks they offered her!"

Shad said nothing. He had a feeling there was more.

Orly, dropping his voice: "Plus they ratted me to the Health Department."

"You mean Beverage."

"No, Health." Orly unfolded a yellow paper and smoothed it violently with the heels of his hands. He pushed it down the bar toward Shad. "Read it," he said.

The complaint charged Orly with using "contaminated food products in a manner that poses a direct and compelling threat to the public safety." Shad assumed it referred to the topless pasta wrestling.

Orly said, "It's a damn lie."

"I know," Shad said. "The stuff is always fresh. I check the packaging dates myself."

"That's exactly what I told the little creep."

"And?"

"He claims he got a sample of bad vermicelli from the wrestling pit—I forgot when, last Tuesday or something. It says right there on the paper. He put it in a jar and hauled it to some goddamn lab in Miami."

Three types of nasty-sounding bacteria—*Escherichia coli, Shigella dysenteriae* and *Staphylococcus*—were listed on the health inspector's complaint. "This is bullshit," Shad said. "We been set up."

"Keep reading," Orly told him.

"Hey, what's this about orifices?"

The report stated: "During the so-called wrestling matches, several male customers were observed attempting to insert said contaminated food product into the mouths and other body orifices of the female performers."

Shad pushed the paper back at Orly. "It doesn't happen every night. Guys get drunk, you know how it goes."

Orly turned away from the bar. "They make it sound so disgusting. Bottom line, it's just fucking noodles."

The two men sat wordlessly. Sabrina was on the main stage, Monique Jr. was in the cage and a new girl named Suzette was dancing tables in the front row. Suzette's claim to fame was a cameo in a recent George Michael video. Orly said she had played a nun in bicycle pants.

Every song Kevin put on was by Prince or Madonna or Marky Mark; the severity of Shad's headache made him wonder if the music had caused his brain to swell. He removed the beret and balanced a bag of ice cubes on his twitching scalp.

"Where's Urbana?" he asked.

Orly said she went to the Flesh Farm to negotiate with the Lings. "So much for loyalty." He paused. "They got a wind machine over there? Because Urbana won't dance near a wind machine."

"That's right," Shad said.

"What'm I saying? A grand is a grand."

Shad told him not to worry. "She won't do friction. Not for a million bucks."

"You ever think," said Orly, "that maybe they don't want her for friction?"

Shad signaled the bartender to bring the boss a fresh Dr. Pepper. Orly continued: "The Ling brothers aren't stupid. They know a liability potential when they see one. With those tits, she could kill a man easy." He tongued the rim of the soda can. "Here's my theory: They're getting out of friction dancing and aiming upscale. They're trying to buy some class, you know? Be respectable like us."

"Respectable," Shad said. Mr. Orly could be very amusing at times. Shad adjusted the ice bag to fit the contour of his skull. "You sure it was them who ratted?"

"Who else. They're still pissed about the snake dancer, what's-her-name."

Kevin approached the bar and buoyantly asked for a Perrier. His expression darkened when he felt Shad's glare. Quickly the disc jockey backed away. Shad lunged for him, but missed. Kevin scurried back to the sound booth.

Orly was saying: "That damn health inspector, he went through the whole joint. I mean brick by brick."

"Yeah?"

"The thing is, I panicked slightly. I dumped your cottage cheese in the toilet."

Shad shut his eyes. "Damn," he said.

"I had to," said Orly. "The guy was relentless. He finds that god-damn scorpion and then what? Already he's threatening to shut us down."

"So you flushed it."

"Get yourself another one. Send me the bill."

Shad was downhearted. "I'm fucking jinxed. That's all."

Orly motioned for the bouncer to follow him outside. Shad couldn't have been more pleased. The traffic noise was a Brahms lullaby compared to the mindless shit that Kevin was blasting on the sound system.

In the parking lot, Orly selected a Volvo sedan and centered himself heavily on the hood. "So—what do we do about these Lings? I'm open to ideas."

Shad said, "My brain hurts."

"You're the only one I can trust."

"I ain't no arsonist, Mr. Orly. I can't light a fuckin' barbecue."

"Well, then, let's you and me think."

A charcoal Acura pulled in and parked near the front awning. Urbana Sprawl got out. She was dressed for a Palm Beach cancer ball. Orly and Shad had never seen her in such sumptuous clothes.

"So, how'd it go?" Orly's voice was tight.

The dancer said, "I'm here, right? So let it drop."

Shad glanced at Orly. "I told you."

With a squeak, Orly slid his butt off the hood. "Wait a minute, girl. You turned down a thousand dollars to stay here and work for me?"

"Don't be a dick," Urbana said, irritably.

Shad squeezed her hand. "You don't have to talk about it."

"He wanted to play 'windshield wiper' with my boobs."

"Who?" Orly said.

"Ling. He tried to pull down my straps and—"

"Which Ling?" asked Shad.

"The little one. I broke two nails on his face." Urbana displayed her damaged manicure. "I wouldn't work for those bastards in a zillion years." She slipped between Orly and Shad and hurried into the club.

Orly said, "One of us should've got the door."

Shad gazed down the street, toward the distant winking neon of the Flesh Farm. "Mr. Orly," he said, "which Ling is the little one?"

"Does it matter now?"

"Nope. It truly doesn't."

The *Princess Pia* began attracting fish the day it settled in seventy-nine feet of water off Fort Lauderdale beach. Dive-boat captains such as Abe Cochran scouted the junked freighter regularly, particularly on those mornings when they were low on fuel and energy, and didn't wish to travel far from port. Where in the Atlantic they took their customers depended on the customers themselves. Well-traveled scuba divers wouldn't settle for exploring such an obvious tourist scam as a newly sunken banana boat. Tourists, however, were suckers for it. They were delighted merely to be blowing bubbles, and vastly enthralled by any fleeting glimpse of marine life. Many of them didn't know a queen angelfish from a sturgeon, leaving Captain Abe Cochran free to embellish the underwater sights.

On the morning of October sixth, Kate Esposito and her boyfriend climbed aboard Abe Cochran's thirty-five-foot charter boat, the *Alimony III*. They were joined by four young travel agents who were visiting Fort Lauderdale for a convention. Abe Cochran recognized the group for what it was, and set a true course for the wreck of the *Princess Pia*. The seas were calm, and the anchor held on the first drop. The travel agents were badly hung over, so Abe Cochran handed out snorkels and instructed them to swim close to the stern, where he could keep an eye on them. This left Kate Esposito and her boyfriend to dive the freighter alone.

Kate had learned to scuba dive as a teenager in a YWCA swimming pool in Boston, but her lifelong dream was to visit the tropics. She was greatly anticipating her first moray eel; her boyfriend had purchased an inexpensive underwater camera for the occasion.

As they tumbled backward off Abe Cochran's boat, Kate Esposito noticed that the water was murkier than she expected. "Gin-clear" is what the tourist brochures had advertised, but Kate could barely see ten feet in front of her face. Her disappointment ebbed as she approached the wreck of the *Princess Pia*, which lay unbroken on its starboard side. To Kate, it seemed as awesome and eerie as the *Titanic*. Together she and her boyfriend swam the length of the bare freighter. Clouds of small aqua-striped fish swam in and out of the dynamite gashes, and once a pair of leopard rays winged gracefully out of the wheelhouse. Each sighting brought bubbles of excitement from Kate and her boyfriend, who attempted to snap pictures of every sea creature they encountered.

Kate was the better diver, and it was she who decided to investigate the interior of the hull. She knew, from documentaries on the Discovery Channel, that moray eels preferred dark and remote crevices; perhaps one had taken up residence inside the scuttled *Princess Pia*. Kate tapped on her boyfriend's tank and signaled her intentions. He waved lamely and handed her the camera. Through the dive mask, Kate's eyes flickered in annoyance. Alone she swam through an open hatch cover on the aft deck. Her boyfriend watched the orange flippers disappear into the ship. He checked his wristwatch: ten minutes, then he was going after her.

Milky shafts of pale light broke the darkness of the cargo hold. Kate Esposito moved slowly, feeling her way. The surface of the metal was smooth and unencrusted because the wreck was so new. Seaweed hung in cinnamon tendrils from the braces, and schools of small fish were abundant, shards of glitter in the fuzzy penumbra. As Kate worked her way deeper into the hold, the water felt cooler and heavier against her legs. A saucer-shaped object shone against the freighter's dull iron skin. Kate reached for the shining disc, knowing that it couldn't be anything precious or valuable, but still not expecting a wire-spoked hubcap. Laughing into her regulator, she let the hubcap fall from her hands.

A long gray form took shape in front of her. Swimming closer, Kate Esposito discerned sharp angles of chrome and glass—a car, chained to the spine of the hull! Not a clunker, either, but a late-model American sedan.

Very weird, Kate thought. On a fender panel, she located a plastic nameplate: Lincoln Continental. Why would someone sink a brand new Lincoln? Maybe it was a gag, she thought, a publicity stunt by one of the radio stations. With one finger, she wrote her first name in the algae film growing on the puckered vinyl roof. Then she snapped a picture of it for her boyfriend.

Except for a cracked driver's window, the Continental was in remarkably good shape. Even the bumper sticker was intact: HAVE YOU HUGGED YOUR LAWYER TODAY?

Kate Esposito saw that the trunk of the car was slightly ajar: *Now there's an ideal place for a moray eel.* From a mesh dive-bag she retrieved a handful of frozen pilchards, which Abe Cochran had given her to feed the marine life, such as it was. Kate picked up one of the stiff minnows and dangled it gingerly above the crack of the Lincoln's trunk. No sinewy green eel emerged to gobble it. After a minute or so, the pilchard came apart in her fingers. Kate got another one and tried again, wiggling the dead fish as enticement. Nothing moved for it.

No one home, Kate thought. With the toe of a flipper she nudged the lid of the car trunk. It opened in slow motion.

Kate Esposito's boyfriend was trying to catch a baby sea turtle when Kate rifled out of the freighter's hatch and kicked frenetically for the surface. Kate's boyfriend followed the trail of bubbles to Abe Cochran's boat, where Kate had crawled up on the teak dive platform. Now she was on all fours, coughing up breakfast. The travel agents, treading water near the bow, warbled excitedly through their snorkels.

Abe Cochran laconically ordered all hands into the boat. Kate's boyfriend yanked off his mask and asked her what she'd seen inside the *Princess Pia*.

"Crabs," she sobbed, "eating a dead lawyer."

It took the Broward sheriff's divers four hours to recover the bodies of Mordecai and his cousin Joyce. Preserving an underwater crime scene proved too much of a challenge, especially when a school of aggressive lemon sharks arrived. The Lincoln Continental was left for another day.

At noon the TV news reported the discovery of two bodies inside the wreck of the *Princess Pia*. Captain Abe Cochran refused to talk with reporters, and emphasized his reluctance by hoisting a scuba tank to bludgeon a Channel 7 cameraman. Kate Esposito's boyfriend was more voluble. In a live dockside interview, he graphically recounted Kate's discovery of the dead lawyer in the new Lincoln. Sgt. Al García, who had a television in his office, immediately phoned a friend at the Broward Medical Examiner's Office and asked permission to sit in on the autopsy. The doctor said sure—there wouldn't be much of a crowd, considering the unpleasantly advanced condition of the deceased.

García, who stopped first at Mordecai's bank, was the last to arrive at the coroner's office in Hollywood. The luckless contingent assigned to the postmortem included two forensic pathologists, three Broward sheriff's detectives and a pair of first-year medical students from the University of Miami. The Florida Bar had declined to send a representative.

Before entering the autopsy room, García stubbed out his cigar and sprinkled the traditional Old Spice cologne inside his disposable surgical mask. The body bag containing Mordecai was the first to be unzipped, and the crabs had been thorough. The skull was practically picked clean, making it easier for pathologists to track the three small-caliber bullet holes. The Broward detectives made notes, and pointed here and there with yellow No. 2 pencils. No one glanced up when the nauseated medical students bolted out the door.

The doctors labored to cut away the dead lawyer's sodden pin-striped suit. García edged up to the table and asked if he could check the pockets. The doctors shrugged and kept cutting.

García held his breath while he pretended to search Mordecai's suit.

One of the Broward detectives grumpily asked what the hell he was looking for.

"This," said Al García. He held up a small key.

Malcolm J. Moldowsky missed the noon news on TV because he was having lunch with two jittery state senators and an overconfident New York bond underwriter. Moldy also missed the six o'clock news; this time he was in the bathroom, grooming himself for an important dinner with the governor. Lately the state of Florida had been pestering operators of phosphate mines about dumping their radioactive sludge into the public groundwater. The phosphate industry regarded as subversive the idea of cleansing its own waste and burying it safely. Malcolm Moldowsky had been hired at a six-figure fee to plead the cause with his old pal, the governor, so that the regulatory climate at the mines might return to normal.

Moldy always dressed by meticulous routine, beginning with his socks. Then came the underwear, shirt, cuff links, necktie, pants and finally the shoes. It was not uncommon for him to spend twenty minutes working a Windsor knot to perfection, and it was at this critical stage that someone knocked on the front door. Moldowsky was irritated, and puzzled, by the interruption; the guard in the lobby was supposed to buzz when a visitor arrived. Moldy strode bare-legged to the door, where he was met by a stocky Cuban with a thick mustache, a damp cigar and a cellular phone under one arm.

"Yes?" Moldowsky made it a demand.

Al García flashed his badge and strolled in. He grinned at the portrait of John Mitchell. "Either you got a great sense of humor," he said to Moldy, "or you're one of the sickest fuckers I ever met."

Moldowsky said, "I didn't catch the name."

García told him.

Moldy felt himself pucker. "And you're with?"

"Metro homicide."

"Is there trouble in the building?"

"I'm sure there is," García said, "but that's not why I'm here. How about putting on some pants?"

Malcolm J. Moldowsky nodded coldly, disappeared into the bedroom and robotically finished dressing. He came out brushing the lint from his wool-blend jacket. His mind swarmed with a hundred possibilities, none of them good. He had gambled too recklessly, leaning on the county commissioner; putting the heat on Sgt. Al García had backfired.

Moldowsky said, "I'm meeting the governor for dinner, so I'm in a bit of a hurry."

"Me, too," said García. "I'm going bowling with Ivana Trump."

The detective's mocking stare was too much. Moldy found a chair. He told himself to shut up, be careful, pay attention!

García said, "You know a lawyer named Mordecai?"

"No, I don't."

"He got murdered. Hey, I know what you're thinking and you might be right. Maybe it was a public service. Maybe we should give the killer a medal. A dead lawyer is a dead lawyer, right?"

Moldowsky said nothing. His throat felt like he'd been swallowing razor blades.

"Without going into gory details," García said, "here's the scenario. In the dead lawyer's pocket they find a key to a safe-deposit box up in Lauderdale. And in the safe box they find a Rolodex card with your name and phone number—"

"That's impossible," said Moldowsky, thinking: *You sneaky prick.* "Sergeant, I never met this man."

"I think you're lying, Malcolm, but that's for another day. Don't you want to hear what else they found in the bank box?"

"It doesn't concern me." Moldy didn't recognize his own voice.

"They found a Kodak slide." Al García paused to measure Moldowsky's reaction, a flurry of blinks. García said, "The picture was taken at a nude dance club. Features a certain well-known congressman."

Moldowsky stoically pretended to know nothing about it. He was afraid to look in the wall mirror; he suspected that his upper lip was moist and curling.

García took out a notebook and uncapped a Bic pen. "This dead lawyer, you sure he didn't try to blackmail you? He and a woman named Joyce Mizner."

Moldy stood up and shot his cuffs. "Sergeant, I'm running very late. Come by the office tomorrow."

The detective, fishing merrily, cast out a name that Erin had picked up from the congressman: "You know a guy named Erb Crandall?"

"Of course," Moldowsky said. His facial muscles were cramping, from trying to appear calm.

"Where do you know him from?" the detective asked.

"From politics. We can talk about this tomorrow."

"You bet." García slapped the notebook shut and crammed it crookedly into his coat. He took out a piece of paper and ran his finger down a column of numbers. Then he picked up his cellular phone and dialed.

The telephone on Malcolm Moldowsky's desk began to ring. He stared at it rigidly, hatefully.

Al García said, "Answer it."

Moldy didn't move. "I'm not fond of games."

The phone kept ringing. "It's for you," García said.

"What's your point?"

García turned the cellular off. Moldowsky's phone fell silent. García smiled; he felt like Columbo. "You got a non-pub number," he said.

"Of course I do," said Moldy. "But you're a police officer. All you need to do is call Southern Bell."

"That's not how I got it." García showed the paper to Moldowsky. It was a copy of the itemized bill from the Holiday Inn in Missoula, where the killers had stayed after they dumped the late Jerry Killian into the Clark Fork River.

García said, "Somebody in Room 212 called here that night. Talked for quite a while."

"I recall no such conversation." Moldy's cheeks were on fire. He had assumed the Jamaicans had dialed on a credit card, not direct from the room. *Direct!*

"Maybe you want to contact your lawyer," García said.

Moldowsky laughed harshly and said don't be ridiculous.

"Your choice," said the detective. "One more question, *chico*. Where can I find David Dilbeck tonight?"

Moldowsky said he had no idea.

"Really? I'm told he doesn't wipe his ass without your permission."

Moldy's composure finally shattered. He bellowed and stomped around the apartment and pounded on the credenza and vowed that Al García would be writing parking tickets for the rest of his miserable career.

"So," García said, "you're a man of some influence."

"Goddamn right."

"And I've insulted you?"

"Worse than that, Sergeant."

"Then please accept my sincere apology." García rose. "I'll find the congressman on my own." He straightened Moldowsky's necktie and told him he looked like a million bucks. "But that cologne of yours could gag a maggot," he said. "Personally, I go for the domestic stuff."

The moment the detective was gone, Malcolm Moldowsky lurched to the desk and seized the phone—the tool of all his genius, the instrument of his betrayal. He was comforted by its feel, the familiar way it fit in his palm, but he was uncertain of his next play. Whom could he call to fix this terrible trouble? Who would have the power to cover it up?

Nobody, Moldy decided gravely. The lawyer's body had been found, and so had the dreaded photograph from the Eager Beaver. The bank box had been opened, emptied, then opened again and salted with evidence—the Rolodex card was a cute touch. At least this prick García had a sense of irony. . . .

Moldowsky's gaze fell on the portrait of the great one, John Newton Mitchell—the hooded eyes, the jowly arrogant smirk. What would *he* do, the canny old toad? *Stonewall the bastards.* Naturally. Admit nothing, deny everything. It would have worked, too. Watergate would have dried up and blown away like a chicken turd, if only . . . if only Nixon, that paranoid gnome, had listened.

Sweet Jesus, thought Moldowsky. I've got to find David before that goddamn Cuban does.

He dialed the congressman's private line. It rang twice before the machine picked up. Moldy left a curt message but gave no instructions, as it would only confuse David Dilbeck. Next Moldy tried to locate Erb Crandall in Atlantic City, but none of the big hotels showed him on the register. Either Erb was staying in a dive, or lying about his destination.

Moldowsky felt a cold, crushing weight on his heart. He hung up the telephone and groped for his car keys.

When was Dilbeck meeting the stripper? Was tonight the night?

28

Erin stopped at the club with a present for Monique Sr. It was a sheer silk blouse from Neiman's.

"Sorry about the other night," Erin said. "Darrell is Darrell. It's a hopeless situation."

Monique Sr. liked the blouse. She buttoned it over a Day-Glo dance bra. "Oh, Erin, it's beautiful."

"That's not for work. That's for somebody special."

"Special? I wish." She twirled in front of the mirror, first one way, then another. "Guess who's ringside at the pit? Garrick Utley."

Erin said, "You can't wrestle. Not with your hand cut up."

"I'm wearing pink evening gloves till it's healed. Mr. Orly says I look like Mamie Van Doren." Monique Sr. told Erin about Urbana Sprawl's dispiriting encounter with the Ling brothers.

Erin said, "Pitiful. I always heard they were gropers."

There was more unsettling gossip from the dressing room. Once more, Orly surreptitiously had lowered the thermostat to sixty-eight degrees, to promote nipple erections on stage. Also, the multi-wigged Sabrina had been offered three thousand dollars to make a porn film on South Beach.

"She's gonna do it," Monique Sr. said.

"Where is she?"

"The cage." Monique Sr. took off the blouse and put it on a hanger. "You're too dressed," she said to Erin. "I'll go out and tell her you're here."

Sabrina was her usual sweet-tempered self. She felt a kinship with Erin because both of them had smallish breasts and felonious ex-husbands.

Erin said, "Tell me about this so-called movie."

"They said I've got to screw two guys in a hot tub and that's all."

"Why are you doing this?"

Sabrina seemed puzzled by the question. "They're paying me," she said.

"You need money, I'll give it to you."

The dancer's eyes widened in amusement. "Three grand? Come on."

"Whatever you want."

"Erin, you don't understand. I can't take any more of this wrestling shit. The pasta is just as gross as the creamed corn."

"But once you do porn—"

"Hey, you don't know what it's like up there. Drunks trying to cram cold niblets up your crack—Jesus, you ought to try it some time." It was one of the few times Erin had seen Sabrina angry.

"I'll talk to Orly. We'll put a stop to it."

"Look, the movie can't be worse than wrestling."

"You ever seen one?"

Sabrina admitted that she hadn't.

"Well, I have," Erin said. "When I worked at the FBI, they seized a truckload of tapes at the airport. The agents had a private screening one night in the basement."

Sabrina's curiosity was earnest. "What's it like? Are they really so bad?"

"You know what a cum shot is?"

Sabrina said she did not. Erin explained.

"Yukky." Sabrina reddened. "The director didn't tell me."

"I'll bet he didn't."

"Let me think about this."

"Take your time," Erin said.

Sabrina freshened her lipstick and returned to the lounge. Urbana Sprawl came to the dressing room and showed Erin her broken fingernails. She said, "Men are the scum of the earth."

"As a general rule," Erin agreed.

"I think you like that Cuban cop."

"He's solidly married."

"Another heartbreaker."

"His wife's taking care of my daughter," Erin said. "She's terrific, too."

"And here you sit on a Saturday night."

"Oh, I've got big plans," Erin said. "Tonight I dance for the congressman."

"Mercy," said Urbana. "Just answer me why."

Erin yawned and stretched her arms over her head. "Because it's my civic duty."

Rita patiently cleansed her brother's wound.

"I can't do much with this fracture," she declared.

"Don't even try."

"What's the goo on your shirt?"

"Mozzarella," Darrell Grant said. "Don't ask."

Rita created a splint for his broken left arm. She used an Ace bandage, hurricane tape and Alberto Alonso's nine-iron. The blade of the golf club stuck out the same end as Darrell Grant's fingers.

"All set," Rita told him, biting off the last piece of tape. "Now get a move on before Alberto comes home."

Darrell's skin was the color of oatmeal, and his breathing was rapid. "I could use some morphine," he said.

"We don't have no morphine. How's about Nuprin?"

"Lord Christ."

"They say it's better than Tylenols."

"Rita, I swear to God—"

"All right, how's about this? I got some special pills for Lupa. The vet gave me a bottle for when she had the puppies."

Darrell Grant looked hopeful. "Dog morphine?"

"Yeah, I guess."

She found the bottle and tried to decipher the name of the drug. Neither she nor her brother had heard of it.

"It says two capsules every six hours."

"That's if you're a fucking poodle," Darrell said. "Gimme four and a cold Busch."

Afterward he vomited for twenty-five minutes. Rita kept daubing his chin and telling him to hurry—Alberto was on the way home from the nuclear plant. Darrell said he was in no shape to travel. Rita assisted him down the front steps and showed him where to hide, in the crawl space under the mobile home.

"Where'd you park the Pontiac?" she asked. "In case Mrs. Gomez puts her glasses on."

"Down behind the Circle K." Darrell Grant shimmied beneath the doublewide. He dragged the splinted arm like a chunk of lumber; the blade of the nine-iron made a groove in the dirt.

Rita said, "I'll bring a blanket."

"What about the damn wolves?"

"Don't you worry. They den on the lee side, strictly."

"Rita, I can't stay down here!"

A car rolled into the driveway. Rita put her fingers to her lips, then she was gone.

Darrell Grant heard Alberto Alonso's voice, the crunch of gravel under his work boots, the screen door slamming. . . .

Trapped! Darrell thought. He turned his head slowly, left then right, to assess conditions in the bunker. He wondered about the chances of Rita's trailer falling off the foundation and crushing him like a bug. Unlikely, he decided; the thing was practically brand-new, replacing the one that Rita and Alberto had lost to the hurricane. Darrell Grant pressed his good arm against the aluminum—it seemed as sturdy as a mobile home could be. Yet he felt edgy in his underground refuge. The air was as cool as a tomb and smelled sharply of rodents. Still, it was better than spending another night in a dumpster behind the Pizza Hut.

The pain in his mangled arm was piercing and unremittant; chills wracked his other limbs. His whole life, Rita always told him how smart and handsome and fortunate he was. "You can do anything you want in this world," she'd say. "You got the looks and the vocabulary." In retrospect, Darrell Grant realized that marrying Erin had been the high point, the main window of opportunity. If ever he was going to turn things around, she was his big chance. Hell, he'd struggled to please her, too. He'd tried the conventional life: sobriety, monogamy, a day job, the whole ball of wax. It simply wasn't meant to be. He was chronically ill-suited for the responsibilities that come with lawful behavior. Erin didn't even try to understand. When the marriage broke up, Rita was disappointed. Darrell explained: "I need a girl that's more of a short-range thinker. Like myself."

Now, in the short range, Darrell Grant focused on a pair of problems: stopping the flaming agony in his arm, and snatching Angie away from his ex-wife.

After supper, Rita came out and peeked under the trailer. She was ready for an outing with the wolf-dogs—catcher's mask, logger's mitts, the frayed housedress. Darrell noticed that she'd added plastic shin guards to the uniform.

"I brought some fried chicken," Rita said. "Extra crispy."

She placed a cold drumstick in his mouth. Darrell tore off a huge bite and spit the bone. He said, "Is it Mrs. Gomez that's got the cancer?"

"No, her husband. He passed in August."

"I bet she's still got his pills."

"Darrell, no!"

"In the bathroom cabinet, I'll bet." He lifted his head. "Rita, I'm damn near crazy from the pain. Please?"

"You already stole the poor woman's car."

"But her husband's croaked, right? So what's the sense of letting good medicine go to waste. Tell me, Rita."

"I dunno what all to look for."

"Demerol, Dilaudids, codeine—shit, bring me everything with the old man's name on it."

"But then you gotta go," Rita persisted, "before the damn cops come by again."

"That's a promise," said Darrell Grant.

There was something else he needed, but he couldn't ask his sister because she'd never agree. Never in a month of Sundays.

But that's all right, Darrell thought, because I know where it is. I know exactly where Alberto keeps it—the same place as every other macho meathead in Miami.

In the glove box of his car. Fully loaded.

Canceling the dinner engagement was easy. In fact, a less distracted Malcolm J. Moldowsky would have noticed the edge of relief in the governor's voice. Stomach problems? he'd said. That's too bad, Malcolm. Give me a ring when you're feeling better. When he hung up, the governor had turned to an aide and said: "Let's pray it's a tumor."

As he drove toward the towers of Turnberry Isle, Moldowsky's mind was preoccupied with thoughts contrived to stave off panic. The cop had nothing, really, but a Kodak slide and a motel bill.

The phone call from Missoula could be explained. Moldy would claim he had houseguests that night. Lots of long-distance calls in and out. It wouldn't be difficult to find someone who would say (for a price): *Yes, come to think of it, so-and-so's boyfriend's foster uncle called from Montana. Drunk as a skunk, yakking his fool head off . . . what was his name again?*

The photograph from the tittie bar was something else. Clearly, that goddamn García knew the story behind it. Malcolm Moldowsky gripped the steering wheel ferociously, zigzagging through the traffic. A ghastly scene played over and over in his head . . .

The congressman, wearing only cowboy boots and boxer shorts, downcast and bleary on the bow of the yacht.

The Cuban cop, puffing maliciously on his cigar, circling like a starved panther, waving the Kodak slide, firing brutal questions faster than David Lane Dilbeck could possibly invent credible answers.

Dilbeck—tremulous, wilting, caving in. Yes, Sergeant, that's me in the picture. Me with the champagne bottle. Please understand, I'm not well. I need help controlling my animal urges. Ask the lady, go ahead. I never meant to harm a soul . . .

Moldy drove faster. For consolation he clutched at the fact that Dilbeck had no knowledge of what had happened to the blackmailers, Killian and the lawyer. The congressman didn't know what drastic steps had been taken to shield him from scandal. This prick García could interrogate him all day long and come up empty. There were many crimes to which a badgered David Dilbeck might legitimately confess, but murder wasn't one of them.

Traffic came to a stop at the Golden Glades cloverleaf, where a truck hauling limerock had jackknifed on a ramp. Moldowsky cursed, snarled, raked his polished fingernails on the dashboard. He couldn't understand García's interest in a drowned fisherman and a murdered lawyer. The cases belonged in Broward County, not Dade. What did he want? What was he after? The way the crazy bastard had come at him, with no pretense of respect or civility. Taunting him, fucking with him—like it was personal.

The cars inched along in maddening spurts. As therapy, Moldowsky jammed both fists on the horn. In the station wagon ahead of him, a frizzy-haired young woman flipped him the finger. The man on the passenger side held a MAC-10 out the window as a hint for Moldy to be patient and shut the fuck up.

For diversion Moldowsky tried the radio, and found a call-in program where the guest happened to be Eloy Flickman, Dilbeck's Republican opponent in the congressional race. Moldy was soothed by what he heard. Flickman now was advocating mandatory tubal ligations for all single mothers applying for food stamps. To another caller, Flickman submitted that Cuba's nascent tourist industry was luring too many European visitors away from Miami, and that only a direct nuclear strike on Havana would remove the burgeoning economic threat. Moldy thought: Wonderful! The man's a certifiable loon. Dilbeck's a lock to win reelection, as long as nothing breaks loose in the headlines.

The traffic jam slowly started to unclog. Malcolm Moldowsky switched to a classical music station, and tried to relax. Tonight's mission was uncomplicated: remove the congressman from the Rojos' yacht, and far away from all naked women.

If the detective got there first, well . . . Maybe a bribe was in order. Maybe that's all García wanted.

Moldy hoped so; it would make life so much easier.

When darkness fell, Darrell Grant snatched the gun from Alberto's car and crawled back under the mobile home. Later Rita showed up with three prescription bottles belonging to the late Rogelio Gomez. Darrell Grant poured the pills into the palm of his good hand, and ate three of everything. An hour later, the whole world was a blur, but Darrell felt marvelous. The pain in his arm was gone, along with much of his short-term memory. Rita had to remind him where he'd hidden the stolen Pontiac.

Once he located the turnpike, Darrell Grant drove northbound at a geriatric pace. His vision and reflexes were abominable. Rita's splint proved sturdy but cumbersome: the nine-iron got in the way of Darrell's driving. He had to hang it out the window of the car, as if permanently signaling for a left turn. Since it was Dade County, no one paid the slightest attention.

The trip to Fort Lauderdale took ninety minutes. Darrell Grant spent most of it in the draft of a slow-moving Pentecostal church bus. Miraculously, he spotted the Commercial Boulevard exit in time to steer off. He stopped at a fast-food restaurant next door to the Tickled Pink, and parked obliviously in the drive-through lane. Rousted by a surly assistant manager, Darrell Grant found a new spot. This one offered a clear view of Orly's strip joint; Erin's shitheap Fairlane was parked near the front awning between a Porsche and a Cadillac.

Like she was somebody special, Darrell thought.

He broke out laughing. Everything seemed hilarious tonight; the sight of a dead opossum on the highway had made him giggle all the way from Okeechobee Road to Miramar. These were absolutely top-notch drugs. "God bless you, Señor Gomez!" he said, saluting the heavens with his nine-iron.

Before long, a limousine appeared at Orly's nightclub. Darrell Grant thought his eyes were playing tricks.

The driver, a black man wearing a cap, got out of the limo and opened one of the doors. In the Pontiac, Darrell leaned forward and tried to squint the blur from his eyes. He was hoping to catch sight of a celebrity. Rock stars were known to hang out at nudie bars; Darrell had seen a video once on MTV.

But it was his ex-wife who walked out of the club toward the limo. She wore blue jeans, a baggy white T-shirt and sandals. She carried a shoulder bag and a shoebox. It looked like she was heading home early. She was alone, too. No trace of Angela.

Darrell Grant was astounded when she got into the limousine.

"The cunt," he said, turning the key in the Pontiac. Who the fuck does she think she is? Who?

Then he started to laugh again.

When the limousine pulled out of the club, the Pontiac was close behind.

29

Shad went to Sears and purchased two jumbo outdoor garbage buckets with clip-on lids. Then he drove to a snake farm near the Tamiami Airport, west of Miami. The man who owned the snake farm called himself Jungle Juan. He told Shad that most of his reptile stock had been wiped out by the hurricane. His insurance company still hadn't paid off.

"They say I padded the claim," complained Jungle Juan, "but I had papers on every damn snake. Certified papers!"

"Like they do for dogs," Shad said.

"Exactamente."

"And they all got killed in the storm?"

"Hard to say." Jungle Juan thoughtfully fingered his diamond ear stud. "They was mostly just gone from sight. I'll assume some escapes, I'll assume some mortalities."

Shad tried to strike a hopeful note. He said, "Snakes are tough customers."

"Some are, some ain't. One old diamondback, the wind picked him up and snapped him like a bullwhip. I seen this myself."

Shad said, "But the rats and mice made out okay."

"By and large, yessir. How many you need?"

"A hundred ought to do it. Rats only."

Jungle Juan said, "Now, these ain't white. These are semi-wild Norways."

"Perfect."

The cage was eight feet long and four feet high. It was fashioned of plywood and chicken wire. Inside was an undulating mass of vermin, two and three deep. Anticipating food, the rats swarmed noisily toward the cage door when Jungle Juan approached. Deftly he barehanded the squealing animals, and dropped them one by one into the jumbo garbage pails.

Shad watched impassively. He had no particular aversion to rodents. "Looks like you got a surplus," he remarked.

Jungle Juan snorted. "Rats up the ass, and no snakes to eat 'em. There's your hundred." He slapped the lids on the garbage cans and said, "Thank God there's a shipment of boas due Monday. I expect they'll be hungry."

Shad said, "We had a dancer that tried a boa."

"How big?"

"The snake? Seven feet."

Jungle Juan said, "Your ball pythons are better for entertainment purposes. They don't bite so damn much."

Shad asked how much he owed. Jungle Juan said fifty bucks.

"Man, that's cheap." Shad handed him the cash.

"Hurricane discount," Jungle Juan explained. "I gotta move these buggers before they fuck me into Chapter 11. Every day they's a dozen new litters and what happens is, I swear, they start to consume one another."

He and Shad carried the garbage buckets out to Shad's car. The sound of many rat paws could be heard, scratching feverishly against the heavy plastic. As they loaded the animals into the backseat, Jungle Juan inquired about the dancer with the boa constrictor. Shad told him that she'd taken ill and gone home to Texas.

"What about the snake?" asked Jungle Juan, shrewdly.

"I got him in a stockroom at the club."

"Healthy?"

"A little farsighted, but otherwise okay."

"Well, I could sure use him," Jungle Juan said, "if you ever wanted to sell."

"Not just yet," said Shad.

When he returned to the club, Mr. Orly asked to see the rats. Shad let him peek in one of the pails.

"Goddamn," said Orly, crinkling his face.

"We all set?"

"Yep," Orly said. "I just wish I could be there to see it. Those fucking Lings." He laughed venomously. "I'd love to get the whole thing on video!"

Shad asked about Erin. Orly said she'd left to meet that goddamn horny no-good congressman.

"Where?" Shad asked.

"I'm assuming the boat. Who cares?"

Shad called Al García's office and left a message. Then he went into the stockroom and emerged with a large dirty pillowcase, knotted at the neck. Orly wished him good luck.

"You come right back," he told the bouncer. "It's gonna get busy as hell around here."

"How long since she took off?"

"Erin? Half hour, tops." Orly studied him warily. "Don't you worry about her. You just get your ass back here, okay?"

Shad circled the Flesh Farm until he spotted the health inspector's car, a gray Dodge Aries with yellow state plates. Monique Jr. had been recruited to make the phone call, because no man could resist her helpless little-girl voice. *The rats, they're everywhere!* she'd exclaimed. *They're biting me, they're biting me!* The health department had kept its promise to send someone right over. The inspectors, Shad knew, trampled each other for such an assignment.

Shad parked the car, threw a ladder against the side of the building and hauled the jumbo garbage pails to the roof. The air-conditioning vents rose like squat chimneys at each end of the building. Shad pried off the rusty grids and poured the rats into the duct system. The little guys seemed grateful to be free.

The Lings were hunkered in the office, dodging the health inspector. They had ordered one of the table dancers to get him drunk and compromised. Then they would talk.

Shad barged in and caught the two brothers by surprise.

"What's in the bag?" asked the one wearing a black tuxedo and a Yankees cap. Shad knew him as the Flesh Farm's floor manager. He sat on a torn Naugahyde sofa that was the color of ox blood. Behind the desk was the other Ling, who wore a gray pullover and two ropey gold chains on his neck. He, too, inquired about the contents of the pillowcase.

"Stand up," Shad said.

Both Lings displayed the identical annoying mannerism of laughing through their teeth, hissing on the inhale. Shad took out the .38 Special and shot three ragged holes in a family portrait on the wall. One of the bullets sensationally disfigured the likeness of the Lings' paternal grandmother; the brothers seemed horrified.

"Bingo," Shad said. "Who's next?"

The Lings stood up quickly. Shad arranged them back-to-back in the center of the floor.

One of them said, "You gone shoot us?"

"Nope," Shad answered, "I'm gonna measure you. Take off the damn cap."

He quickly determined that the tuxedoed Ling was at least two inches taller than the gold-chained Ling. "You're the one," Shad said to the shorter brother, "who grabbed my friend's tits."

The smaller Ling frowned in vexation. Urbana's fingernail tracks were plainly visible on one cheek. Somebody knocked on the door, and Shad concealed the gun in his belt.

A frantic voice of indistinct gender: "Mr. Ling, come quick! Come now!" A woman's scream cut through the dance music. The brothers glanced at one another in alarm. Shad ordered the one in the tuxedo to go check on the trouble.

The larger Ling said, "Maybe we should call police."

"Try an exterminator," Shad advised.

With both hands the larger brother fitted the Yankees cap tightly on his head, the visor practically touching his nose. Wordlessly he slipped out of the office. Shad locked the door and shoved the smaller Ling into a swivel chair.

"This no business of yours," the brother protested. "It's that boss you got. Mister Hotshit Mafia Man."

Shad twisted Ling's wrist to check the time on the phony Rolex. It was getting late.

Ling pulled his arm away. "Fat Tony, my ass," he said, spitting unintentionally. "Orly must think we stupid, huh? They got Mafia in Japan, too. Plenty fucking Mafia!"

Shad untied the knot in the pillowcase. He felt serene and contented—a rare moment of moral clarity.

Ling said, "I didn't grab nobody's titties."

Shad opened the pillowcase and angled it toward the overhead light, so he could see down into the corners. "I feel good about this," he said, to no one.

Ling noticed the sinuated movement in the bottom of Shad's sack. He could see the shape of heavy, muscular coils shifting against the fabric.

"You better not!" he shouted.

Shad commanded Ling to stand up and drop his jeans. Ling refused. Shad drew the pistol and poked the barrel in the man's navel. The brother set his jaw and said, "I rather be shot dead. Make it quick, too."

Shad thought: What an actor, this guy.

Ling regarded the pillowcase anxiously. "You sick man," he said to Shad.

"Really? You're the ones cut poor Bubba to pieces."

The brother scowled in confusion. "Bubba?"

Shad clubbed him in the temple with the butt of the .38. Ling fell briefly unconscious. He awoke naked, hot and discomfited. Shad had hung him from the office door, securing his wrists to the coat hook.

The smaller Ling cursed and writhed, his heels and elbows banging against the wood. From the hallway outside came the sounds of mounting chaos. Stretched on the Naugahyde sofa, Shad tended to the liberated boa constrictor; before leaving town, Lorelei had neglected to remove the tape from the snake's mouth.

"What you doing?" Ling demanded.

Shad said, "This old boy's half-starved." He piled the reptile on the floor, beneath the dangling and helpless Ling. As the tan-and-brown mass unraveled itself, the brother's upper lip curled in fear. The boa, being naturally arboreal, searched for something to climb. In the absence of a tree, it chose Ling's bare leg. The more vigorously the brother kicked, the tighter the snake drew its coils.

"You know what?" said Shad. "Your schlong looks just like a hamster."

After a short contemplation, Ling issued a series of high-pitched screams. The boa's tongue feathered against his quaking skin. He cried: "It's gone bite my wee-wee!"

Shad thought it was very funny. "Your what? Is that what it's called in Japan?"

"Get it off me, goddammit."

The snake continued its ominous ascent.

"You were very rude," Shad said, "to grab my friend's boobs the other night."

"I'm s-s-sorry. I couldn't help it." Ling had lapsed into a pathetic whine. "Some girls don't mind," he said.

"Oh, I doubt that seriously." Shad wondered how long the coat hook would hold fast under the brother's weight.

Ling struggled to make himself motionless. Fighting, he feared, would agitate the creature. "Please," he whispered morosely, "get it off me. I'll do anything you want."

Shad yawned. He removed his beret and brushed the lint off the crown. The boa's tongue flicked in and out. It had drawn a vague bead on Ling's shriveling organ.

"Oh-oh," said Shad. The poor thing *was* starved.

Ling went slack on the door. He let out an involuntary whimper. "It's gone eat me," he asserted. The boa's clouded eyes followed every tremble and sway of Ling's luckless member.

Shad said, "You act like an animal, you get treated like one. Remember that."

"I s-s-said I sorry."

Shad smirked bitterly. "Sorry is the word for it."

The snake's head rose in a fluid arc, as if levitated by hydraulics. Its creamy neck banded to muscle in the shape of an S.

"Get ready," Shad warned.

"Oh my God!"

"Don't be such a pussy. It ain't even poisonous."

"But my wee-wee!"

The boa's strike was too rapid for the human eye. Ling felt the needle sting of teeth before his mind registered the image of the snake's open jaws, lashing. He passed out mid-scream.

When the brother regained consciousness, he found himself face down on the moldy shag carpet. There was no sign of Shad or the farsighted boa constrictor. When Ling rolled over, the effort ignited a burst of pain between his legs. He allowed one hand to explore the jeopardized zone. The brother sighed gratefully: he was punctured but intact, and fully attached.

In exhausted relief, Ling closed his eyes. "Sick man," he said. "Very sick man."

A faint noise in the ceiling caught his attention. He opened his eyes just in time to see a fat brown rat jump from the air-conditioning vent. It landed, with a perturbed squeak, squarely on Ling's sad and astonished face.

Some of the Flesh Farm's customers were so drunk that the infestation didn't bother them. The performers and waitresses, however, reacted more intelligently: they fled. All friction dancing ceased. The larger Ling armed his two bouncers with aluminum softball bats and directed a violent but ineffective counterattack. The rodents proved quick-footed and elusive. As if by destiny, one vaulted from the Michelob display to befoul the health inspector's whiskey sour.

Shad watched from a bar stool. He thought things went pretty well. As sabotage, it wasn't exceptionally clever, but Mr. Orly couldn't expect miracles on short notice. Orly, after all, had wanted to torch the place! A four-alarm blaze might have been more satisfying, visually, but it wouldn't have put the Ling brothers out of business. They'd have simply rebuilt with the insurance money, and probably upgraded—new marquees, new decor, a new sound system. Orly didn't like that prospect one bit, and endorsed the impromptu rat plague as an alternative. Rodent publicity would be fatal to the Flesh Farm.

The TV crews beat the police by five minutes. Onstage, a beautiful nude Brazilian was on her knees, hammering at a lump of lifeless fur. The weapon was a standard high-heeled shoe. With each blow, the dancer's breasts swung back and forth in tandem, like church bells. Shad wondered how the TV people would edit the tape to make it presentable for the eleven o'clock news.

He went to the parking lot to watch the squad cars arrive. He stopped counting at nine. A busload of orphans could plunge off a bridge and you wouldn't see so many cops. Shad smiled cynically. Nothing brought out the cavalry like strippers in distress.

One of the dancers, a petite brunette, recognized Shad in the gathering crowd. She said, "You work down the street."

"Until tonight."

"I auditioned there about two months ago. When it was the Eager Beaver."

Shad said he remembered, although he didn't. The dancer put on a long pink sweatshirt to cover her diaphanous stage costume. Shad found her extremely attractive. He had come to adore women in clothes.

The brunette noticed the pillowcase. "Whatcha got there?"

"A boa constrictor," Shad said. "Want it?"

"For what?"

"For your act."

The brunette said no thanks. One snake dancer in town was plenty.

"But Lorelei's gone," Shad told her. "It's wide-open territory."

"I don't know. I'm not crazy about snakes."

"Who the hell is?" He handed her the boa in the pillowcase. "Think about it," he said. "Work up a routine."

He returned to the Tickled Pink and told Orly that the rats were a huge hit. Orly said he figured as much; the place was filling with customers spooked from the Flesh Farm. Orly wanted to know if Urbana's honor had been avenged, and Shad told him the story of the smaller Ling. Orly laughed so hard that he blew cream soda out of his nose.

"Those fuckers," he gurgled, "are finished!"

"Congratulations," Shad said, turning away.

Orly told him to go check on table four. "It's a bunch of coked-up roofers. One of 'em brought a goddam dildo."

Shad said, "I need to go see about Erin."

"Like hell. You're on the floor tonight."

"No, Mr. Orly. I've pretty much had it." He jumped the bar, punched open the cash register and removed sixty-four dollars. "Yesterday's pay," said Shad, fanning the cash. "What I did tonight, that's for free." He found the Camus paperback and wedged it into his waistband.

Orly said, "Hell, don't quit on me."

"It's time."

"The fuck does that mean? *It's time.*" Orly blocked Shad's path. "You want a raise? Is this your way of hitting me up?"

Shad gripped him by the soft meat of the shoulders. "I'm suffocating," he said, "in this world."

"Get serious," said Orly, pulling free. "Wall-to-wall pussy, and you're suffocating? 'Scuze me if I don't break down and cry."

"It's not your fault, Mr. Orly. I seen too much."

Orly suggested a vacation. He told Shad to take a week off, fly to the islands, get laid repeatedly. Shad shook his head. "A week won't do it," he said.

"Then make it ten days."

"You don't understand, Mr. Orly. I gotta get out completely. I've lost my sense of wonderment."

"Oh, for Chrissake," Orly said. He led Shad to a quiet corner, away from the dance floor. "When you were a little boy, what'd you want to be when you grew up? I mean, was your life plan to break heads in a nudie joint?"

Shad said, "I wanted to play for the Forty-niners."

"Right! And what happened?"

"I got fucking busted in the ninth grade."

Orly rolled his eyes. "Point is, almost nobody gets where they want in this life. Everybody's dream takes a beating. Me, I wanted to be an obstetrician." He waved a pudgy pale hand at the strobe-lit scene behind him. "This is as close as I got. You follow? It's called facing reality."

Shad was sidetracked by the laughable notion of Mr. Orly aspiring to a medical career. It was one of the most spectacular lies he'd heard in a long time.

"There's different kinds of reality," he told Orly. "I want the mystery back in mine."

"Fuck mystery. Let's talk loyalty. When I hired you, hell, you still had eyebrows. That's how long ago."

Shad was unmoved by the sentimentality. He could not recall a single Christmas bonus.

Orly said, "Like it or not, this is God's plan for you. This is what you're cut out for—"

"You should've been a preacher," Shad said, "on TV."

"If it's the scorpion thing, I said I was sorry. Bottom line, I freaked when the inspector showed up."

Shad said it was no big deal.

"Then what the fuck else can I say?"

"Just *adios*," said Shad.

Orly's chest sagged in defeat. He shook Shad's enormous hand and said, "I suppose you got prospects."

"Nope, but I got some interesting ideas." Shad said goodbye. Orly watched, dejectedly, as the huge pearly orb floated above the crowd, toward the door.

Urbana Sprawl hopped off a table and intercepted Shad with a tender hug. "My hero," she purred.

"That's me, babe." Shad took the red beret from his pocket and arranged it at a sly angle on Urbana's head. "Is Erin at the yacht?" he asked.

"Dancing her pretty heart out."

"What the hell's she up to?" Shad was forced to holler over a rap number that Kevin had sadistically cranked to ninety decibels.

Urbana, shouting in his ear: "I think she's out to do some damage!"

The music seemed to affect Shad's focus and equilibrium; each bass beat fell like a sledge on his brainpan. He wondered how many bullets would be required to take out the wall speakers.

"Onward and upward," he said to Urbana Sprawl, and elbowed his way out of the lounge.

The penthouse condominium of Malcolm J. Moldowsky was twenty minutes by automobile from the two-bedroom tract house owned by Jesse James Braden and his wife. It might as well have been a whole other universe, as far as Al García was concerned.

The murder of Jesse James Braden was precipitated by two connected events. At exactly 5:10 p.m. on the sixth of October, Jesse James Braden spilled a shaker of Bloody Marys on the freshly laundered upholstery of his wife's Toyota Camry. That was the first event. At exactly 5:11 p.m., Jesse James Braden laughed uproariously at what he'd done. That was the second event.

At exactly 5:12 p.m., the wife of Jesse James Braden dragged him from the Toyota and shot him fatally in the genitals.

Neighbors were divided on the question of whether Mrs. Braden had been excessive in her reaction. Witnesses agreed that Jesse had been a prodigious sinner and often conducted himself in a manner that invited homicide. The shooting itself was not so much at issue as Mrs. Braden's selection of anatomical targets. The men in the crowd, sober and otherwise, felt that the mere spilling of an alcoholic beverage—and subsequent insensitive laughter—failed to justify three bullets through the penis. The women of the neighborhood, however, asserted that the decedent got exactly what he deserved—a just punishment for years of piggish whoring, drunken violence and general bad behavior. Jesse James Braden, they said, did not respect his wife or her personal belongings.

Into this boisterous debate waded Al García at precisely 6:47 p.m. He didn't want to be there; he wanted to be setting an ambush for a genuine United States congressman—flashing the badge, barking out the Miranda, scaring the piss out of the bastard. He had a gut feeling that the guy would fall apart, start blabbering. García had been looking forward to the moment.

Instead, the detective stood on a front lawn no different from a million other front lawns, except that the man who had mowed it was lying agape in the bromeliads, with his pecker shot off. The paramedics said Jesse James Braden bled out in three minutes flat. It's like a fire hose, they said, the way it leaks.

García hoped to finish the interviews in an hour, since the witnesses concurred on every detail except the precise final utterance of Jesse

James Braden—a brief but vituperative tirade. His wife, now safely handcuffed, insisted on showing García the tomato-juice stains on the seat of her car. She demanded that the police photographer get a picture, so that the judge could see what that worthless Jesse had done. When Al García inquired about the murder weapon, Mrs. Braden led him indoors to the kitchen. She had placed the pistol in the refrigerator with her dead husband's booze.

The detective's work proceeded smoothly until Jesse's grief-stricken brother arrived at the crime scene and opened fire with a 16-gauge shotgun. Francis Scott Braden missed Jesse's wife by twenty feet, but he grazed a patrolman and blew the rear window out of Al García's unmarked Caprice. The chaotic interruption meant two hours of extra paperwork for García, who again was reminded how much he hated domestic homicides. It wasn't detective work—it was purely janitorial.

García didn't receive Shad's message until he was back in the car, rolling on the interstate, the air whipping through the busted window, scattering his police papers. He drove the Caprice as fast as it would go, cursing the Saturday night traffic because he was missing the big show: Erin, dancing up a storm.

30

Erin fixed a drink from the mini-bar in the back of the limousine. She wondered about the dream she'd had the night before: making love to a man in an orchard of coconut palms. The man looked vaguely like Al García. In the dream it was daytime, the lemon sun arcing high and scorching. The man was nude but Erin wore a black dress, cut high to the neck. She remembered getting on top, telling the man to hush now, relax. She remembered her knees stinging on the rough bed of dry fronds. In the dream there was music, too; Linda Ronstadt, singing "Carmelita." It was magical. Erin couldn't remember coming, but she did recall rolling over, gently pulling the man along as if he weighed no more than a child. He lay his head on her breasts and closed his eyes, and mysteriously he no longer resembled Al García. Now it was some-one new, a stranger, but Erin didn't push him away. She let him rest. In the dream, she was still aroused. A sea breeze whisked through the orchard, and the porcelain sky filled with bright tropical birds— macaws, cockatoos, parrots, cardinals and flamingos. Erin remembered kissing the man's forehead to wake him, so he could see the flaming colors dip and scatter overhead. The man stirred and murmured in Spanish, but didn't open his eyes. In the dream, the radiant migration seemed to last all morning. Finally Erin spotted her daughter running barefoot, in and out of the mop-topped trees. Angela was wide-eyed and intent, laughing as she followed the kaleidoscopic train of birds. Erin slipped from beneath the sleeping stranger and ran through the palm orchard after her daughter. In the dream, the bald trunks of the palms stooped and swayed malevolently to obstruct her path. Angie's laughter grew unfamiliar and distant. Erin remembered stopping, breathless, and turning her face to the sun—the sky was empty, the birds had vanished. She had awakened in a hot sweat.

Now, in the limousine, the Beefeater's provided no insight to the dream's meaning. It did, however, fortify Erin for an evening with David Dilbeck. She was impelled by the certainty that the congressman would escape implication in Jerry Killian's murder, that he was out of Al García's reach. The idea of the arrogant old drooler going scot-free was unacceptable, so Erin had made up her mind to destroy him. Dilbeck wouldn't be harmed, crippled or killed—just destroyed. It seemed the least she could do, and it had to be done alone. Women's work.

She finished the martini and began dressing for the congressman. She hooked on a lace bra top and a matching G-string, the one with the red seahorses. Her shoes, too, were candy-apple red. A wine-colored minidress completed the package. Around her neck she hung two long strands of imitation pearls. As Erin dressed, she noticed the Haitian driver, Pierre, watching her in the rearview mirror. Erin stuck her tongue at him.

"I'm sorry," he said, and looked away instantly.

Erin scooted forward to one of the jump seats. She put a hand on the driver's shoulder. "You speak English?"

"At times," he said.

Erin poured him a cola from the mini-bar. Pierre accepted it graciously.

"Is there a phone in this car?" she asked.

The driver nodded at a cellular receiver under the dashboard. Erin turned on the vanity light and opened her purse. She wrote something on a piece of paper and handed it to Pierre. Without reading it, he placed the note in his breast pocket.

"That's a phone number," she told him. "Things may get strange tonight. Say, at eleven sharp."

Pierre said, "It will not be the first time."

"I'll understand if you can't help me," Erin told him. "But I need to know now, before I get started."

"You overestimate my sense of loyalty."

"A job is a job," Erin said. "I wouldn't want to jeopardize your situation."

The guard booth of Turnberry Isle came into view. Pierre flashed the headlights and coasted toward the gate. Without turning, he said to Erin, "But a phone call could come from anywhere, couldn't it?"

She smiled. "You're a decent guy, Pierre."

"Oui," he said, touching the brim of his cap.

Congressman David Lane Dilbeck glistened with excitement, and a light application of petroleum jelly. He put on the Garth Brooks getup, shined his boots, dabbed on some designer-cowboy cologne, tweezered the stray hairs out of his nose. . . .

The dancer had phoned that morning with an intriguing request. A bit frightening, really. Not all men would've agreed to it.

But Dilbeck instantly consented because he felt an incipient carnal connection with the woman. Something was sparking between them, a promise of lust. The first time, she'd acted so tough, all business—hands off, buster, and so forth. But as the night had worn on, Dilbeck had detected a softening of attitude, traces of affection. The signs were subtle, to be sure; she had, after all, mortared his hand with one of her spiked heels.

Yet even that made sense later, when he took the dancer's phone call. Perhaps pain was a necessary ingredient of her love. The prospect excited Dilbeck; he felt adventuresome and bold. The congressman had frequently heard of such wild women. Now was his chance to tame one and possess her.

He arrived at Turnberry shortly after dusk. He brought, in addition to the item Erin requested, two magnums of Korbel champagne, three dozen red roses, a gold bracelet and a shopping bag of assorted compact discs: Smithereens, Pearl Jam, Toad the Wet Sprocket, Men II Boyz, REM, Wilson Phillips. Dilbeck had no inkling about the nature of the music, nor did he care. He had dispatched an eager young assistant to load up at Peaches, in the hopes that one or more of the selections might prove to be a dancing favorite of Erin's. If crass gift-giving failed, he would endeavor to dazzle her with gossip from inside the Washington Beltway.

That first night on the yacht, it had seemed to Dilbeck that Erin was stubbornly unimpressed by his title. Most of the women who slept with him did so mainly because he was a member of the House of Representatives, and therefore he qualified (marginally) as a power fuck. Erin, however, treated him as just another horny rich guy. She displayed no interest in his position or his grossly embellished achievements, and resisted every conversation that might have led to Washington name-dropping. The relationship could not blossom, Dilbeck decided, until the woman was properly enlightened about his importance. In anticipation, he'd been polishing some of his most trusty cocktail-party yarns. Also, for purposes of documentation, he brought photographs.

Erin came aboard the *Sweetheart Deal* at about eight-fifteen. Entering the salon, she again felt claustrophobic, incarcerated. "Where's Frick and Frack?" she asked.

"Who?"

"The guards."

"Grand Bahama," the congressman said, "with the Rojos." The sight of the minidress caused another mild spasm beneath the scar of his double-bypass.

Erin complimented Dilbeck's country-western outfit. "Dwight Yoakam?" she guessed.

"Garth Brooks, actually."

"Well, it certainly flatters you." Erin was pleased at how sincere she sounded. The man looked absurd. And what was that peculiar sheen to his skin?

Dilbeck handed her the gifts. He said, "I brought some pictures, as well."

"Of what?" She wasn't in the mood for porn.

"Pictures of me," said the congressman, "on the job."

"Really?" said Erin, swallowing a yawn.

She thanked him politely for the roses and the bracelet, but Dilbeck thought she wore the expression of one who had received such things before, in the course of commerce. She picked through the stack of CDs and rejected all but the Smithereens. As before, she'd brought her own songs for dancing. In honor of Jerry Killian, she again put on ZZ Top.

The congressman said, with an air of masculine accomplishment: "It took some doing, but I found what you were looking for."

Erin squeezed his arm. "Sweetie, I knew you would."

Her touch made him shiver pleasantly. For a moment, Dilbeck regarded the arm-squeeze as significant, a preliminary to full body contact. Then he realized that Erin was only using him as a brace, to steady her ascent to the captain's table. In a flash she was out of the minidress. The pearls remained.

"What's the hurry?" Dilbeck said. "I thought we might chat for a while."

Erin started dancing. Off came the red bra.

"Jesus," murmured the congressman.

"Sit back, cowboy," Erin told him. "Enjoy."

Malcolm J. Moldowsky approached the docks casually, as if out for an evening stroll. He removed his necktie to look more like a yachtsman.

Twice he walked past the *Sweetheart Deal*. There was no sign of the Cuban detective. Moldy boarded quietly. He heard thumping from inside: drums, heavy guitar licks. The congressman's tastes leaned toward crooners, so Moldowsky knew that David Dilbeck wasn't alone. The show had begun: Erin Grant was there.

Moldy congratulated himself for beating García to the yacht. He put his ear to the door, but heard no human noises mixed with the rock music. He took it as an encouraging sign; silence was always preferable to the sounds of a struggle.

He had his hand on the doorknob when a shadow passed across the deck. Malcolm Moldowsky wheeled to see a man balanced on the transom, backlit by the dock lights. The man rocked from one leg to the other, in time to the muffled backbeat.

"What do you want?" Moldowsky said.

The man hopped down and stepped toward him. "I want my daughter," he said.

Moldowsky smiled with forced patience; the man was too young to be the dancer's father. Moldy said, "There's been some mistake. Your daughter's not here."

"Then I might as well shoot you," the man said.

At the sight of the pistol, Moldowsky raised his hands high. The intruder seemed crazed and displaced. The knees of his jeans were filthy, and his oily blond hair was matted to one side. The eyes were foggy and moist. A golf club was strapped imposingly to a crudely bandaged arm. Moldy figured the man was a hurricane victim, made homeless and insane. They were still out there, addled wanderers, dredging for pieces of scattered lives.

"She's not here," Moldowsky said, "your little girl."

Darrell Grant aimed the pistol and squinted one eye. "Say goodnight, Shorty."

Moldowsky let out a gasp and covered his face. Expecting to die, his blackening thoughts turned egotistically to the aftermath. Slain on a yacht with a drunken congressman and a stripper—that's the headline! What photo would they choose to accompany the story? A studio portrait, Moldy hoped, not crime-scene gore. And how would he be described in the press coverage—political consultant? Power broker? Fixer? Jesus, and the quotes. There'd be no shortage of grief-stricken testimonials, all fulsomely insincere. Moldy assumed he would soil himself, dying. What a laugh the cruel bastards would get from *that*. The dapper Malcolm Moldowsky, pissing in his Perry Ellis.

In bitter dread, he waited for the flat crack of the gunshot. Nothing happened.

The problem was Darrell Grant's unfamiliarity with firearms. He didn't like guns, never carried one, never even fired one. Now, steadying himself on the deck of the yacht, he couldn't find the damn trigger. His finger probed intently but was obstructed by a disc of hard plastic. Darrell Grant held the pistol in the light and scrutinized the impenetrable device.

"Fuck me," he said.

It was a lock. Darrell couldn't believe the rotten luck. That goofy Alberto had to be one of the few citizens in all Dade County with the brains to buy a trigger lock. The advertised purpose of such devices was to prevent dirtbag thieves like Darrell Grant from using a stolen handgun against the innocent citizenry. Darrell, however, suspected that Alberto Alonso harbored other concerns, such as Rita shooting him in his sleep.

In any event, the locked pistol was about as lethal as a doorstop. Darrell Grant hurled it over the wheelhouse, into the Intracoastal Waterway. "Un-fucking-believable," he said, with a dry giggle.

Malcolm Moldowsky peeked through his fingers when he heard the splash. The gun was gone. Why? Moldy didn't care. The action confirmed his assessment that the intruder was deranged.

"Out of my way," Darrell Grant said. He gestured with the blade of the golf club, which protruded from the makeshift splint.

Moldowsky feigned concern. "You really banged up that arm."

"Gee, I hadn't noticed." Darrell Grant hoisted the jerry-rigged limb and poked Malcolm Moldowsky in the belly. "Double compound fracture," Darrell said, "but you know what? I had hangnails hurt worse."

"Let me drive you to a doctor."

Darrell Grant lowered his voice and spoke very slowly, as if giving street directions to a foreign tourist: "Get . . . the . . . fuck . . . out . . . of . . . my . . . way. *Por favor?*"

Moldy flattened himself against the cabin door. ZZ Top pounded up and down the bumps of his spine. "I can't let you in," he said to the stranger. It was imperative that the public, lunatics included, remain unaware of the congressman's runaway debauchery.

"But my daughter," Darrell said, thickly.

"I told you, she's not here. You've made a mistake."

Darrell's face broke into a crooked smile. "Hey, I followed her mother, OK? All the way from the tittie bar. And I saw her walk on this boat not fifteen minutes ago. Now some asshole midget's gonna tell me I made a mistake?"

Beautiful, thought Moldowsky. The stripper's ex-husband. Tonight of all nights.

He said, "Let's go up to the restaurant. I should buy you a drink."

"A drink?" Darrell Grant threw back his head and yowled at the stars. "Man, I don't need a drink. I'm full a drugs, OK? I mean *tanked*. Best fucking drugs known to mankind!"

"Fine," Moldowsky said, tensing.

"These pills are so damn good," Darrell said, "I came out here searching for pain. Understand? I'm here to go one-on-one with pain, because I *cannot* be hurt. It ain't humanly possible. I had a railroad spike, I'd give it to you this very minute—"

"Settle down," Moldy said.

"—and I'd make you hammer that fucking railroad spike straight into my skull, say about here—" Darrell Grant touched the center of his forehead, "—and you know what? I wouldn't feel a damn thing, that's the quality of narcotics I'm talkin' about."

"Please," Moldowsky said, "keep your voice down."

"I never killed a midget before."

"Let's discuss this."

"No, sir, you just move your tiny little ass outta the way. I'm here to fetch my daughter."

"For the last time," Moldy said, "she's not on this boat."

Darrell Grant grabbed him by the sleeve. "You're right about one thing, Shorty. It's the last fucking time." He hurled Malcolm Moldowsky to the deck and stepped on his chest.

Moldy wriggled impotently but did not scream. Ludicrously, he still believed it was possible to avoid a public scene. It wouldn't do to attract a nosy crowd to the Rojos' yacht—not with David Dilbeck inside, doing God knows what to a naked dancer. Fearing a repeat of the Eager Beaver debacle, Moldowsky sought to placate the intruder with promises.

"If you let me up," he told the crazed ex-husband, "I can help you find your girl."

"Weeee-heeeee!" exclaimed Darrell Grant.

"I've got," Moldy panted, "all kinds of connections."

The first blow was not a punch but a chip shot. Moldy felt his nose explode. Through the mush he saw the ex-husband, poised in a one-armed backswing. This time the blade of the club caught Malcolm Moldowsky flush in the throat. Madly he gulped for a breath.

"Fore!" Darrell said.

Moldowsky shut his eyes. This was worse than being shot; the newspapers would have a field day.

He clawed uselessly at the madman's legs. The next two swings dislocated Moldy's lower jaw. His cheeks filled with warm blood, spit and broken orthodonture. Even if he'd decided to cry for help, he couldn't. His face was a divot.

God, he thought, what a sorry way to die.

Is it a nine-iron or a wedge? Those fuckers in the press would make a point to find out. Oh, definitely.

The congressman offered Erin a job as his executive secretary in Washington.

"What would I do?" she asked, twirling her pearls.

"Keep my spirits up," said David Dilbeck. "Forty-five grand a year, plus major medical." He cradled the champagne bottle like a doll.

Looking down from the captain's table, Erin said, "You're so cute." She tapped a foot on his shoulder, teasing. Dilbeck tried to kiss it. Erin reminded herself to stay alert; the dirty old geezer was halfway gone.

He said, "Is it time for the jungle toy?"

"Not just yet. You like this song?"

"Yes, ma'am." The congressman's head lolled, and the cowboy hat fell to the floor. He picked it up and replaced it.

Erin said, "It's called 'Whipping Post.'"

Dilbeck perked up. "Is that right?"

"By the Allman Brothers."

"Well, I've been such a naughty boy," he said, "I believe I could use a whipping."

Erin continued dancing. Apparently there would be no sexual catatonics tonight; Davey was fully conscious, primed for action.

He said, "Wouldn't you care to whip me? I'm a bad, bad boy."

"It's just a song, sweetie."

"But I love you so much."

"Of course you do."

"Here, let me prove it." He shoved the champagne bottle into the ice bucket, and began fumbling with the buttons of his jeans.

Erin spun away, shaking her ass to the bluesy rhythm. She thought: Off we go!

The congressman said, "Look here."

She turned back, smiling the 500-watt smile. "It's adorable," she said.

He stood up, wobbly, and wiggled the limp thing in his hand. "Please touch it," he said.

"I'm a dancer, sweetie, not a urologist." Erin kicked him lightly in the sternum, and he sagged back into the canvas chair.

He said, "God, I've had too much to drink. Did I give you your money?"

"You sure did."

"And did I show you my pictures?"

"Put your little friend away," she said.

"Then you'll look at my pictures?"

Erin said sure. She needed a break, anyway. While David Dilbeck tucked himself in, she stepped off the table and put on her dress. She turned down the stereo, poured a ginger ale over ice and pulled up a chair. She made sure her purse was within arm's reach.

Dilbeck opened a photo album across his lap. He tapped at an eight-by-ten picture of himself with a corpulent white-haired man. "Know who that is?"

"Tip O'Neill," said Erin.

Dilbeck was astounded. "You *are* something special."

"Former Speaker of the House."

"Right!"

"So what do I win," Erin said, "a dinette set?"

Beaming, the congressman said, "Tip and I are very close."

"I can see that. It looks like you're scratching his balls."

Dilbeck flushed. "Please! We were at a prayer breakfast."

Erin reached over and flipped the page. The next photograph had been taken outside the White House: Dilbeck with an arm around General Colin Powell. The general wore an expression that suggested recent taxidermy.

"This was during the Gulf War," said Dilbeck, matter-of-factly. "Colin and the President invited certain members of Congress for a briefing. Classified, of course."

Erin asked if they'd given out balloons. Dilbeck nearly lost his temper. "Darling," he said, "you should have some respect." His tone had turned chilly.

"I'm sorry, Davey."

Rapidly he flipped through the album, jabbing at significant memories. "See here: Bill Bradley, Chris Dodd . . . and there's Al D'Amato—we were on a fact-finder together in Riyadh. This one is me and Newt Gingrich—remind me to tell you my Gingrich story."

Erin said, "I hope that's just cheese dip on his tie."

"You listen," Dilbeck said, lecturing with a champagne slur, "these are important goddamn people. *I'm* an important person." He slapped the album shut and raised it with both hands, as if it were a holy tablet. "These are the men who run this nation," he said, "the men who control the fate of the world!"

Erin tried not to laugh. The poor schlub truly believed himself to be a pillar of state.

The congressman said, "It's difficult to describe the raw power. It's intoxifying, darling. Completely addictive. If you came with me to Washington, you'd feel it immediately. You would also understand its seductions."

Erin said she didn't mean to poke fun. Dilbeck laid the album on the table, and placed a hand upon it. Again he said, "These are important men."

"Chuck Norris?"

"That was a charity benefit in Georgetown—"

"Come on, Davey—"

"For polio or something."

"I know, but—"

"Look, Erin, it's a matter of appreciating who I am. It's a matter of respect."

"Davey, you know whose picture I'd really like to see? Malcolm Moldowsky. Is he in your album?"

Dilbeck's jaw tightened. "No, he's not." Then, suspiciously: "Do you know Moldy?" Was it possible? Had the little ratfucker been holding out on him? Hurriedly Dilbeck reframed the question: *"How* do you know Moldy?"

"By reputation only," Erin said with a wink.

The congressman, more perplexed than ever, cursed in a shaky drunken voice: "Stop, goddammit! Stop making fun and show some goddamn respect."

"Respect?" Erin smiled. "Aren't you the same gentleman who had sex with my laundry lint?"

"Let's change the subject."

She took him by the wrists and guided his slack hands to her breasts. Dilbeck seemed wary and apprehensive, as if anticipating an electric shock.

Erin wouldn't let him pull away. She said, "Thrilling, huh? Two pleasant handfuls of fat."

"Jesus—"

"That's your basic human breast, Davey. Ninety-eight percent fat, with a cherry on top. What's the big attraction?"

He yanked away, clenching his fists to his gut.

"Thousands of dollars," Erin said, "just for a peek and a jiggle. It baffles me, sweetie."

"That's enough." The congressman was gray, despondent. "You're killing me. You're killing the whole evening. Is that the plan?"

Erin said, "I'm curious, that's all." She told herself to settle down, hold her temper.

Dilbeck was saying, "I struggle with fleshly temptations. All men do."

"You have a wife, Davey."

He lunged for the champagne bucket. "Congratulations," he snapped. "The night is officially ruined."

Erin put on her favorite Van Morrison tape. She stripped off the dress, got on the captain's table and began to dance again—this time, slowly. Soon David Dilbeck and his afflicted moans faded from her consciousness. The songs washed over her soul. She felt euphoric and energized. Every move was perfect—every kick, every fluid turn, every thrust of the hip. She took the pearls in her teeth and closed her eyes, imagining moonlight.

Outside on the deck, something made a sharp noise. Erin blocked it out of her mind. She was far away, dancing on a sugary beach in the islands. Above the dune was a palm orchard, and the only sound was a soft chorus of wild birds.

· · ·

Darrell Grant couldn't recall the last time he'd seen his ex-wife without clothes. He was pretty sure it had been in the bathroom—she, washing her hair in the shower; he, covertly looting the medicine cabinet for Darvons. Long fucking time ago, Darrell thought. He'd forgotten what a nice body she had. A little puny up top but, God, what great legs! Swaying in the doorway of the cabin, crutching with the nine-iron, he felt an intriguing tingle in his groin. Amazing, really, considering the high-octane pharmaceuticals he'd ingested. The male plumbing was truly an engineering marvel.

Inside the yacht was an old man wearing stiff new jeans, a striped shirt and a black ten-gallon hat. He looked shitfaced or sick, possibly both. Darrell Grant walked into the salon and sat next to the old cowboy. With his unbroken arm, he waved mischievously at his former spouse, up on the table. Darrell felt himself hardening. He leaned forward and said, "Hey, you're pretty damn good. Let's have a look at that sweet little pussy!"

The sight of her ex-husband hit Erin like a blast of frigid air. She thought Shad had run Darrell off for good, but here he was, fucking things up again. Amazing. His presence greatly enhanced the potential for fiasco. Erin kept dancing and stared straight through him while she weighed her next move.

Darrell Grant felt a leafy hand at his shoulder. It was the old cowboy, pulling himself up in the chair. He put his lips to Darrell's ear and said, "You know who I am?"

The man's breath made Darrell grimace. "Ever heard of Listerine?"

"I'm in love with this lady," the congressman confided.

"You poor old fuck."

"And my boots, they're full of Vaseline."

"I loved her once, too," said Darrell Grant, "but all she did was cut me down."

Dilbeck looked sympathetic. Darrell said, "Call it a basic clash of philosophies. She can be hell on your self-esteem."

"A hard one," the congressman agreed, "but still I'm swept away."

He said there was plenty of club soda in the liquor cabinet, in case Darrell Grant wanted to work on those bloodstains in his shirt. Darrell said no thanks. His shattered bones had begun to throb; whaling on the well-dressed midget hadn't helped. Darrell feared that the late Señor Gomez's painkillers were finally wearing off. He tapped out a half dozen more, tossed them into his cheeks and guzzled lukewarm champagne until his eyes watered.

The congressman said, "I've got some Extra-Strength Tylenols."

"Lord Christ."

The Van Morrison tape ended. Erin kept going. She started singing "Carmelita," to herself. The song was almost too slow for table dancing.

Darrell Grant attempted to hook her ankles with the nine-iron. "Where's Angie?" he demanded. Erin eluded him.

Dilbeck said, "Let her finish. This is so beautiful."

"Yeah, it's a fucking ballet." Darrell Grant grubbed in his pockets. "Hey, beautiful, this is for you!"

He lurched halfway out of the chair, and slipped something under the elastic of Erin's lace garter. It was a nickel. Erin stopped singing and dancing. She removed the coin and held it in the palm of one hand. The two men waited to see what she would do next.

Erin was smiling in a private way as she stepped off the table, still smiling as she got dressed.

The congressman said, "I suppose we're done for the night."

Darrell pounded the nine-iron sharply on the table. "Erin, I want my daughter. No more goddamn games."

"It's over," she said, adjusting the pearls.

"Fuck the courts," Darrell declared. "Angie and me are headed to Arizona. Retirement Capital of North America!"

Erin opened her handbag and dropped the nickel inside. Then she took out the .32.

"Let's go for a drive," she said.

Darrell Grant cursed under his breath. The congressman felt a subtle contraction in his chest.

Some Saturday night, Erin thought. Me and the two men in my life. Aren't I a lucky girl.

31

Predictably, Shad was detained at the guard booth outside Turnberry Isle. The security men remembered his earlier visit with the monkey creature on his neck; tonight they said his name appeared on no guest lists. Shad averted an unpleasant argument by producing coupons for free rum drinks and nude pasta wrestling at Orly's club; the security men couldn't have been more appreciative. Sgt. Al García arrived as they were waving Shad through the gate. The detective flashed his badge and coasted into the compound. He parked next to Shad, and the two men hurried together to the *Sweetheart Deal.*

The first thing they noticed was the blood on the deck. In the salon, García inspected the empty champagne bottles, the congressman's photo album, and a pile of compact discs, still in their wrappings. Shad thumbed through a stack of cassettes left on the stereo cabinet.

"These are hers," he said.

They searched the staterooms and found no bodies, no other signs of violence. Erin and the congressman were gone.

"Mierda," said Al García. He went out to the deck and examined the brownish splatters. Apparently the victim had been dragged, then lifted off the deck. García felt a shudder of nausea; it wasn't the sight of the blood, but the thought of whose it might be. Shad was on the dangerous edge of cold rage. He gripped the rail and stared hauntedly into the tea-colored water. His pinkish skull glistened with perspiration, and he hissed ominously when he inhaled.

García said, "Don't assume too much."

A rumble came from Shad. "Yeah. What's a little blood."

The detective stepped across to the dock. On his knees: "There's more here. Know what that means?"

"He didn't dump her over the side. So what?"

A fifty-three-foot Hatteras convertible was moored next to the Rojos' yacht. García wanted to check it out. Shad located a flashlight on the bridge of the *Sweetheart Deal*. They boarded the fishing boat together and found more freckles of blood in the cockpit, near the fighting chairs. There was also the smudge of a partial footprint: the rounded heel of a man's boot.

Morosely, Shad said, "That's our boy."

"Maybe, maybe not." Al García pointed at the fishbox. "You want me to do the honors?"

"If you don't mind." Shad looked away.

The detective unfastened the latches and threw open the lid.

Buoyant with relief, he said: "Surprise, surprise!"

Shad turned to see. "Who the hell is that?"

"One of the most powerful men in Florida."

"Not anymore."

"No," Al García said. "He be deceased."

Malcolm J. Moldowsky had fit easily into the fishbox, which he shared with three glassy-eyed bonitos. The aroma of the dead fish failed to overpower Moldy's imported cologne.

"I don't get it," Shad said.

"The bonitos probably are shark bait for tomorrow," García speculated. "Mr. Moldowsky is a late addition to the buffet."

Shad leaned in for a closer look. "This is the famous Melvin Moldowsky?"

"Malcolm," García said, "in the past tense."

"Nice threads."

"Feel better now?"

"About a million percent," said Shad. "Who did it?"

García shook his head. "Maybe Dilbeck went batshit."

"Don't say that."

They were worried about Erin. Whoever had bludgeoned Moldowsky owned a monstrous temper. Shad frowned at the mutilated corpse. "I guess you gotta call somebody."

"Not right this minute." Al García closed the fishbox. "He'll keep."

They returned to the *Sweetheart Deal* and searched the salon more carefully. Based on the volume of champagne consumed, García calculated that the congressman was too drunk to drive. "He's got the limo," Shad said. "The girls saw it at the club."

"So the question," said the detective, "is where are they now."

The clue was in the head, where Erin had written in lipstick on the narrow mirror: BELLE GLADE. Shad growled profanely while García fished a gold bracelet from the toilet. Watching the jewelry drip, he said, "She's got a temper, doesn't she? A simple 'no thanks' would've done the trick."

As they hustled to the cars, Shad asked García to radio ahead for help. García told him he'd been watching too much TV. "First off, that's Palm Beach County, which is way out of my territory. Second, what do I tell 'em, *chico?*" Facetiously he rehearsed the phone call: "See, guys, there's this stripper who's been abducted by this congressman who's taking her to fucking Belle Glade, of all places, in a goddamn stretch Cadillac. Yes, I said 'congressman.' Yes, Belle Glade. Why? Well, we ain't too sure. But we'd appreciate six or seven marked units, if you can spare 'em. . . ."

"Fuck it," Shad muttered.

"As much as cops love strippers, they hate politicians," García said. "They hear it's Dilbeck, they'll all be oh-six. Off duty and unavailable."

"So we're the whole damn cavalry."

"Mind if I drive?"

"Sure," Shad said, "you're the one with the siren."

Darrell Grant had never ridden in a limousine. He was enjoying it so thoroughly that the circumstances seemed irrelevant. He accepted the fact that his former wife was holding him at gunpoint.

Darrell said to Dilbeck: "This your car?"

The congressman nodded. "It's made available for my use."

"What do you do? What's your gig?"

"I'm a member of the House of Representatives."

"Which means . . . ?"

"I represent the people of South Florida in Congress. And yourself?"

"I steal wheelchairs," Darrell Grant replied.

Dilbeck glanced plaintively toward Erin, who sat on the bench seat across from the two men. The congressman's roses lay next to her. She held the gun steady in her right hand.

"Darrell and I were married for a time. What else can I say?" Erin felt an inexplicable calm, heightened by the cool soft ride.

Dilbeck asked Darrell Grant what happened to his arm. He said Erin's motherfucking boyfriend broke it with a motherfucking crowbar. Then: "Hey, driver, does the TV work?"

In a wounded tone, Dilbeck whispered to Erin: "What boyfriend?"

Erin iced him with a glare. Pathetic, she thought, both of them. She nonchalantly reached under her minidress to unfasten the G-string and the scalloped dance top. She stuffed them in the shoulder bag. Still holding the gun, she gymnastically attempted to put on a plain cotton bra and white panties. It was a crucial detail; Erin didn't want to be found dressed as a stripper. As she changed underclothes, the congressman watched inquisitively.

With an oily trace of a smile: "Why the white?"

"For you, baby," she said.

Darrell Grant braced his sloshing head against the window. They were on the interstate, racing away from the downtown skyline. The snaky scroll of lines on the pavement, the stream of headlights made him woozy. "I'm seriously loaded," he remarked.

Erin said to the congressman: "My ex-husband has a drug problem, in case you were curious."

"I wish you'd put the gun away," Dilbeck told her.

"You're not listening, are you?"

Darrell Grant, sleepily: "I never saw you dance before. That was damn good."

"Aw, shucks," Erin said.

"Sorry about that business with the nickel."

"I'd almost forgotten," she said, "your scathing wit."

Darrell Grant basked in the limousine's spaciousness. "I could get used to this," he said, stretching his legs. "Climate-controlled comfort. Yessir!"

David Dilbeck, speaking as if Darrell couldn't hear him: "That fracture looks bad, Erin. He should see a doctor."

"Rita's the one who done up my arm," Darrell said, hoisting it in pride. "My big sister."

"She cares about you," Erin told him. "She's the only one left."

"No, Angie cares for me. Angie loves her daddy."

"She finds you entertaining," said Erin. "There's a difference."

"She loves me!"

Erin dropped the subject. Maybe Darrell was right. She didn't want to think about it now.

The congressman said, "How much longer till we get there? I have to relieve myself."

Erin ignored him. Her ex-husband said, "I killed a guy tonight."

"Really?"

"On the boat back there."

"Any particular reason?"

"I'm trying to remember."

Erin assumed that he had hallucinated the incident. Darrell Grant said, "It didn't feel the way I thought it would. Killing a guy."

"You fell for the hype," Erin said, "as usual." She wondered what to do with him. He was screwing up her plans for the congressman.

"I'm serious about Angie," he said.

"You kidding? You're headed for prison, Darrell."

"Nope, Arizona. Wheelchair Capital of North America!"

"Crazy bastard."

"And I'm taking our daughter."

"I'll shoot you first," Erin warned.

David Dilbeck abruptly began sobbing and groping for the door handle. He settled down when Erin jammed the .32 into the hollow of his cheek.

Darrell Grant said, "Since when do you carry a piece? Jesus, I hate guns."

"My prostate is acting up," the congressman announced.

"Quit whining," Erin snapped. "Both of you."

Darrell scratched his shin with the head of the nine-iron. "At least tell us where the hell we're headed. Hey, driver, you speakee American?"

Pierre gave no reaction.

"I'll tell you where we're going," Erin said. "We're going to see our congressman in action."

By early October, the sugar cane near Lake Okeechobee is green, bushy and ten feet tall. The bottomland is the flattest part of Florida; from a passing car, the fields seem to reach and define all horizons. Within a month, nearly two thousand Caribbean migrants arrive to start the cutting, and the mills run twenty-four hours a day. In early October, though, machines do much of the harvesting. An improbable crablike contraption called a cutter-windrower downs the cane and piles it in rows. More machines then retrieve the harvest for transportation to the company mills, where the sugar is made.

Congressman David Lane Dilbeck didn't give much thought to the science or mechanics of cane farming. It was enough that the Rojos were

nice people, well-bred and so generous. The mountainous campaign
donations were important, of course, but Dilbeck would have traded his
congressional vote for just the occasional use of that gorgeous yacht. He
also valued the social company of young Christopher, who shared his
tastes in bawdy entertainment and never failed to pick up the tab. For
David Dilbeck, the attention of wealthy, powerful people was a flattering fringe benefit of the job.

The congressman saw no injustice in the price supports that had
made multimillionaires of the Rojos. The grain, dairy and tobacco
interests had soaked taxpayers for years by melodramatically invoking
the plight of the "family farmer." Why not sugar, too? Similarly, Dilbeck lost no sleep over the damage done to the agricultural economies
of impoverished Caribbean nations, virtually shut out of the rigged U.S.
sugar market. Nor did the congressman agonize over the far-reaching
impact of cane growers flushing billions of gallons of waste into the
Everglades. Dilbeck didn't understand what all the fuss was about. In
truth, he didn't much care for the Everglades; it was torpid, swampy,
crawling with bugs. Once, campaigning at a Miccosukee village, the
congressman consented to an airboat ride because Erb Crandall saw it
as a sensational photo opportunity. The airboat ran out of fuel on the
Shark River, and Dilbeck spent two wretched hours picking blood-
swollen mosquitoes out of his ears.

"And I've seen prettier water," he told Erin, "in a pig trough."

She was giving him a hard time about whoring for the Rojos. "Where
do you think our drinking water comes from?" She pointed through the
window of the limousine. "Out there, Davey. And your pals are pissing
fertilizer into it."

Darrell Grant was bored silly. He repeatedly sought to engage
Pierre in conversation, with no success. The highway narrowed to two
unlit lanes that Darrell recognized as U.S. 27. Blackness engulfed the
limousine; the only trace of the city was a fuzzy sulfurous glow, far to
the east. Darrell couldn't figure out where Erin was taking them, or why.
The geezer in the cowboy getup remained a riddle. Was this a rich new
boyfriend? The idea of Erin as a gold digger engaged him—like mother,
like daughter? Anything was possible.

Darrell struggled to hatch a plan, but the drugs interfered with his
concentration. What he really wanted to do was sleep for about six
months.

It was half-past ten when they arrived in Belle Glade ("Her Soil Is

Her Future," proclaimed a welcome sign). Pierre turned off the main highway and drove slowly through an empty migrant camp. David Dilbeck was alarmed by what he saw. He told Pierre to step on the gas before desperadoes swarmed from the slum and trashed the limo. "It's a leaser," he explained to Erin.

"Don't tell me you've never been out here."

"What's your point," the congressman groused. The warm embrace of the Korbel had dissipated into a staggering migraine.

Pierre got back on the highway and drove until the town gave way to more green cane fields. Erin asked him to pull over.

"He doesn't understand English," Dilbeck said, impatiently.

"Is that so?"

Pierre steered off the pavement and stopped on the shoulder of the road. He left the engine running.

"Out we go," Erin said, brightly. "And, Davey, don't forget our jungle toy."

Dilbeck peered into the night suspiciously.

Before harvest, sugar cane is burned to consume the leafy tops, which are useless, and to drive the animals from the fields. In the heart of the season, smoke roils off the stalks in prodigious columns that sometimes block out the sky. Tonight, though, was crystalline—washed with constellations that one never saw in the city. A waning yellow moon hung low.

Pierre got out and opened the back door of the limo. The congressman emerged first, holding a slender brown package. He was followed by Darrell Grant, unsteadily; the protruding nine-iron dinged noisily off a rear fender panel. The last to emerge from the car was Erin, stepping gingerly in her heels. Pierre gave her a small flashlight to go with the pistol.

Darrell Grant complained of a gassy stomach. "Let me stay here and crash."

"Sure. In the trunk." Erin motioned with the gun. "Pierre, prepare Mr. Grant's *boudoir*."

The Haitian driver obliged. He popped the trunk and moved the spare tire, making room.

"The trunk?" Darrell Grant slapped the congressman on the back. "Didn't I tell you she's fucking murder on the ego?"

David Dilbeck looked worried. "Erin, I've got a heart condition."

"Who doesn't? Darrell, get in the damn trunk." She shined the flashlight in his eyes.

"You gonna shoot me?" He gave a dopey laugh. "Somehow I don't think so."

Erin told him to lie down and take a nap.

Darrell Grant, slouching against the fender of the limousine: "One thing I been dying to ask: How do you do it? I mean shakin' your poon at strangers." He jabbed the congressman contemptuously with the golf club. "Sick old fucks like him, I don't see how you do it."

"The music takes over. That's all."

"You mean it's an act? I ain't so sure about that."

"Men are easily dazzled."

An urgent moan from David Dilbeck: "I have to pee."

Erin waved the flashlight toward the cane rows. "So pee," she said. Dilbeck waddled off, clawing at the buttons of his jeans.

Darrell Grant snorted drunkenly. "I never thought of you as a stripper. It's actually funny as hell."

Erin said, "You emptied the savings account. I had a lawyer to pay."

"Plus you figured out the hustle at these nudie joints, am I right? You mess their hair, play with their necktie, tell 'em how good they smell."

"Maybe that's why they call it a tease."

"God, you're a cold one."

The congressman could be heard irrigating the sugar cane. From over his shoulder, he called: "I truly *do* love her!"

"Pity-ful," Darrell said.

Erin smiled. "I rest my case."

"Know what I think? I think you get off on it."

"Darrell, you're just *full* of theories tonight." Was this a sermon, she wondered, from a wheelchair thief? "Get in the trunk," she told him, "you like the damn car so much."

He ignored her. "I ain't givin' up on Angie. Just so you know: I'll track the both of you to hell and back." He brushed past her and headed into the cane fields.

"Darrell, stop." She raised the .32 in one hand, the flashlight in the other.

Her ex-husband turned. The beam of light caught him grinning. "You won't kill me. Not the father of your only child!"

Erin was considering it. She pictured him hacking up Angie's dolls, and her gun arm stiffened. "You told the judge I was an unfit mother. Is that what you believe?"

"It was lawyer talk, for Chrissakes. You always take shit so personally." Beseechingly he spread his arms, the shaft of the nine-iron glinting. "Hell, you were a good mother. Same as I was a good daddy. It was lawyers talkin', that's all."

At that moment Erin knew she wouldn't fire. She didn't need to; the sorry bastard was already finished. Broke, strung out, maimed, running from the law—Darrell Grant was history. Killing him would be redundant.

"Come back," she told him. "I've got plans for you."

"You mean 'plans' as in jail? No thanks, cutie pie." He gave a cocky wave and resumed his getaway.

Erin remembered what Shad advised her about the gun: when in doubt, shoot at something, *anything*.

She fired twice at the ground near Darrell Grant's boots. The crack of the shots was absorbed by the thickets of high cane. She heard her ex-husband yell the word *cunt*. When she aimed the flashlight where he'd been standing, he was gone, crashing like a deer through the crops. She panned the beam in a slow circle until it landed on the congressman, nervously buttoning his fly. He waded from the tall grass and asked, "Are you all right?"

The gun felt hot in Erin's fist. She thought, Goddamn that Darrell. Maybe he'll step on a rattler.

She wheeled on David Dilbeck. "Take off your clothes," she told him.

"I knew it. You're going to make me dance."

Erin said, "You wish."

After cane is cut and stacked, a machine scoops the stalks, thins the excess vegetation and dumps the load into a field wagon. When the wagons become full, a mechanical belt feeds the cane into long steel-mesh trailers attached to truck cabs. Each bin holds twenty tons and dumps from the side. The trailers are parked at intervals along the farm roads bordering the Okeechobee sugar fields.

At first Darrell Grant thought he had come upon the fence of a medium-security prison, a nightmare of ironies. Weaving closer, pawing at the darkness as if it were fog, he saw that the mesh edifice actually was the side of a long truck rig. Using a jumbo tire as a foothold, Darrell began to climb.

The cane trailer offered dual enticements: it looked like a safe place to hide from a homicidal ex-spouse and also a fine place to nap. It was important for Darrell to lie down soon, before he fell. The cancer pills had blown his circuit breakers; he accepted the likelihood that he'd guessed wrong on the dosages, seriously misjudged his tolerance. Oh well.

After scaling the mesh, he flopped into the damp sheaths of smoky cane and burrowed like a worm; he felt clever, invisible and safe. Had he been sober, he might have anticipated the destination of the truck and the disposition of its contents.

Once loaded at the fields, the trailers are driven to the mill and emptied on conveyors. The first stage of processing is the shredding of the cane, which is accomplished by many rows of gleaming, turbine-driven knives. The fiber then is mashed beneath five hundred tons of pressure. In this way the essential liquids are removed. Evaporators convert the purified cane juice into a syrup, which is heated carefully until it forms a mixture of sweet molasses and crystals. Separation is achieved using a high-speed centrifuge.

Usually it takes half a ton of cane to produce a hundred pounds of raw sugar. However, both weight and purity can be markedly affected by the introduction of foreign substances, such as human body parts.

Darrell Grant had medicated himself too heavily and concealed himself too well. He was deep in a junkie nod at dawn, when the cane trailer in which he'd hidden began rolling toward the sugar mill. Darrell did not awaken, at least not in a meaningful way. No cries, shrieks or moans halted the sugar-milling process; rather, it was the nine-iron strapped to Darrell Grant's arm that jammed the turbine-driven blades and brought the boys from Quality Control scurrying toward the shredders.

The mill shut down for three hours while local police collected and bagged the remains. The Palm Beach Sheriff later issued a press release saying that a vagrant had died in a freak milling accident at Rojo Farms. Authorities appealed to the public for help in identifying the victim, who was described as a white male, early 30s, with blond hair. No composite sketch of the man was provided, as the shredder left precious little for the police artist to work from. The press release said that the victim wore jeans and boots, and was possibly a golf enthusiast. The

Sweetheart Sugar Corporation was reported to be cooperating fully in the case.

At the mill, a memo went up assuring employees that the unfortunate mishap had not compromised the superb quality of the company's product. In private, however, workers anxiously wondered exactly how much of the dead vagrant had ended up in the day's tonnage. The consensus was that one drop of blood, one lousy pubic hair, one microscopic sliver of a wart was too much.

Distasteful rumors spread wildly, and many workers stopped putting sugar in their coffee and tea. Rojo Farms, like most cane processors, maintained a long-standing rule against the use of artificial sweeteners by employees on company property. Violation was regarded as an act of disloyalty—the agribusiness equivalent of a Chrysler salesman buying himself a Toyota. However, within days after Darrell Grant's gruesome death, a clandestine network of body carriers began smuggling packets of Sweet 'n Low into the Rojo company cafeteria. An internal investigation failed to identify the culprits or shut down the pipeline. To avoid the publicity of a labor confrontation, mill management quietly dropped the matter and rescinded its sugar-only policy. The Rojos themselves were never told.

Shad punched the dashboard, hard.

"Enough!" said Al García. "Christ, have a smoke."

"Some fucking heroes we are."

García was doing ninety-four on the interstate. Shad's slick dome whimsically reflected the blue strobe of the dashboard light. The highway wind howled through the shotgun-shattered window. Shad spit scornfully into the night.

"Easy," García said. "Hey, I gave up on being a hero a long time ago. Sometimes the best you can do is set things in motion." The detective puffed expansively on a fresh cigar. "That's why I put my card in the dead lawyer's bank box. I had a hunch it would motivate Mr. Moldowsky toward foolish behavior."

Shad said, "This ain't a game. You said yourself."

"Still, there's plays to be made. We made ours."

"And look what happened. Erin gets snatched."

"Don't underestimate the lady." The detective lowered the window and tapped out an inch of dead ash. "You notice anything odd about the writing on that mirror? Besides it was lipstick?"

Shad hunched sullenly. He occupied himself with devising a suitable fate for the congressman. He thought in terms of muriatic acid and gaping facial wounds.

"Here's what jumped out at me," García went on. "The words on the mirror weren't printed in block letters, they were done in cursive. The style was beautiful, no? So tell me, *chico*, who writes perfect longhand when they got a gun to their head and they're about to be kidnapped? Nobody, that's who."

Shad's naked eyebrows crinkled in concentration. In the shadows, his silky pink orb suggested the head of a 250-pound newborn. "You're saying she planned it all?"

García said, "It's possible, yeah."

"No way did she whack that guy in the fishbox."

"I agree." The detective's expression was obscured by a swirling shroud of blue smoke. "Still, she had a game plan."

Shad remembered what Urbana Sprawl had said: that Erin was out to do some damage.

"In these situations," the detective said, "I ask myself who's holding the high cards? And it's definitely Erin, not Dilbeck. Here's this arrogant old fart who thinks he's God's gift to pussy, but all he wants in the whole wide world is the love of this one gorgeous dancer. I mean, he'd be in heaven if this girl just *smiled* in the general direction of his dick. You follow?"

Shad plucked a cigar from Al García's shirt pocket. He tore off the wrapper with his teeth.

García chuckled. "All that champagne, I'll bet old Davey couldn't get it up with a block-and-tackle tonight. And Erin, she's got thirty I.Q. points on him, easy."

Shad said, "Men get crazy over her. I seen it before."

"Dilbeck's not your typical rapist, he's too full of himself."

"He don't need to be typical," said Shad, biting the nub off the stogie. "He just needs the idea to take hold."

García said nothing for several miles. The traffic thinned as they headed west.

Shad mumbled, "Belle Glade, shit. *Where* in Belle Glade?" He turned toward García. "I suppose you got some ideas."

"What I said before, about setting things in motion—see, people have this concept of justice. They talk about 'the system,' meaning cops, judges, juries and prisons. If only the system worked, they say, there wouldn't be a crime problem! The streets would be safe, the bad guys would be locked up for life!"

Shad gave a desolate laugh. He pulled the lighter from the dented dash and fired up the cigar. He said, "Look at Erin's crazy fucker of an ex-husband. That's how terrific the system works."

"Exactly," García said, chopping the air with his hand. "Darrell Grant was a snitch for the cops. Good guys putting bad guys on the payroll, in the name of almighty justice. Your average taxpayer can't understand. See, 'the system' is a game and that's all. Guy like Moldowsky, I can't touch him. Same goes for the congressman. So what I do then, I try and set things in motion. Make the shit fly and see where it sticks."

"Because you got no case," Shad said.

"None whatsoever. But it doesn't mean there can't be justice."

"Man, you're a dreamer."

"Maybe so," said Al García, "but I'm sure Moldowsky arranged the murders of Jerry Killian and that sleazoid lawyer and the lawyer's cousin. And I'm also sure I couldn't put the case together in a trillion years." He arched a shaggy black eyebrow. "But this much I also know: Tonight I open a stinking fishbox and find Mr. Malcolm J. Moldowsky permanently expired. Fate, irony, call it whatever. Least now I got something to tell my boy."

"Your boy?" Shad said.

"He's the one that found the body in the river."

Shad grunted somberly.

"Least I can tell him it's over," said García. "For once the bad guy got what he deserved."

Shad said, "I ain't ready to celebrate. I want to see Erin alive." He took a loud, noxious drag on the cigar. "You better hope you didn't set the wrong damn thing in motion."

"Yeah," the detective said quietly. "There's always that chance."

Shad settled in for the ride. He felt better, kicking around the possibility that Erin was on top of the situation.

"Just promise me one thing," he said to Al García. "Promise you ain't got another human head in the Igloo." He jerked a thumb toward the trunk of the Caprice.

García grinned. "The night is young," he said.

The congressman stripped to his boxer shorts and cowboy boots. Erin's flashlight played up and down his gelatinous physique. She was mildly embarrassed for him, but the feeling passed quickly.

"What now?" Dilbeck said, swatting at the bugs.

"Time for you-know-what."

"Ah." His tone changed. Excitedly he unwrapped the brown package. He held the machete with both hands, the blade flat across his palms, to show Erin. "Willie Rojo loaned it to me. It hangs on the wall of his private study."

"Very tasteful," she said.

The congressman ran a finger along the squared-off blade. With a coy smile: "I think I understand what you're after."

"Doubtful," Erin muttered.

"You're into games," Dilbeck said, hopefully.

"Oh, please."

"Role playing—"

"No, sweetie."

"You're the master, I'm the slave!"

Erin thought: The creep is really getting turned on.

Dilbeck said, "So how does it work, your little game?"

"Here's how it works: I want you to cut some sugar."

He chuckled anxiously. "But I don't know how."

"Oh, give it a try," Erin said. "For me."

"I'd feel much better if you put the gun away."

"Soon," she said. "That's a promise."

With the flashlight she directed the congressman to a row of maturing cane. He stepped forward and swung the machete sidearm. The stalks shook but didn't fall.

Erin said, "You do better with a champagne bottle."

David Dilbeck snorted. "Just watch," he said, and began whaling. Each blow brought a high-pitched grunt that reminded Erin of Monica Seles, the tennis star. The congressman's reaping technique needed improvement, too; the cane wasn't being cut so much as pulverized. Erin kept the flashlight aimed at the crop row, so Dilbeck could see what he was hacking. She didn't want him to harvest his own toes by accident.

After less than a minute, the congressman stopped. His face was flushed, his chest heaved and the blotched flab of his belly was sprinkled with sweat. The boxer shorts had slipped below his waist, exposing the crack of his marbled buttocks. He was panting like a toothless old lion.

Erin said, "Sweetie, don't quit yet. You're giving new meaning to the term 'public servant.' "

Dilbeck bent at the waist, sucking to catch his breath. Momentarily he said, "You've still got your dress on."

"I certainly do."

"Fine, fine." He wiped his palms on his underwear. "How much more till we can play?"

"I was thinking at least a ton."

"Very funny—"

"A migrant," Erin said, "cuts eight tons a day."

"Eight tons," the congressman murmured. That's what Chris Rojo had told him, too. It seemed absolutely impossible.

"One cutter, all by himself," said Erin. "I read up on cane farming so we could have a meaningful discussion." She kicked off her high heels. "I figured you knew all there was to know about sugar, considering the Rojos own your ass."

"That's a damn lie." Dilbeck stiffened.

Erin put the flashlight on him—he was pissed, all right. It wasn't easy to look indignant in boxer shorts. She said, "Guess what the Rojos pay their cutters."

"I couldn't care less," the congressman snapped. "It's better than starving to death in the *barrios* of Kingston."

"So that's it—a humanitarian enterprise!" Erin dabbed an imaginary tear. "Please forgive me, Congressman, I misunderstood. Here I assumed your pals were just greedy businessmen, taking advantage of poor desperate souls. Now I find out they're saints!" She motioned with the gun. "Keep cutting, sweetheart. And by the way, Jamaica doesn't have *barrios*. They're called slums. You're getting your Third World cultures mixed up again."

Reinvigorated by anger, Dilbeck went at the sugar cane like a dervish. Between grunts: "Who are you to lecture me!"

"Merely a constituent," Erin said. She reminded him that his drinking buddy, young Señor Rojo, had given her a thousand dollars for one of her shoes. "But I guess he can afford it," she remarked, "considering what he pays the migrants."

The congressman paused in his cutting: "That's a very simplistic view, young lady. Very simplistic."

"Davey, when does your committee vote on the sugar subsidies? I wonder what the Rojos would do if you didn't show up."

Dilbeck couldn't understand how an evening that had started with such promise had deteriorated to this: a stripper with a pistol, in the middle of fucking nowhere—and him, up to his sweaty aching balls in sugar cane. Ruefully he concluded that wild cowboy sex was no longer on the agenda; more harrowing scenarios began to streel through his imagination. All this talk of slave labor, the Rojos, the House committee vote . . . why would a woman speak of such things?

He swung at the cane until his arm was numb. He dropped to his knees, braced himself upright with the machete.

"Good work," said Erin. "Only nineteen hundred pounds to go." She wondered what her mother, the cruising opportunist, might make of this scene. David Dilbeck was the sort that Mom would view as a matrimonial prize—wealthy, prominent and presentable, when properly attired.

He said, "What is it you really want?"

Erin crouched beside him. "You remember a man named Jerry Killian."

Dilbeck nodded guardedly. "He's the one who tried to blackmail me. That's when I spoke to the judge about, uh, 'reconsidering' your custody case."

"And what happened, Davey?"

"Judge said no deal. Got on his high horse."

"And what about Killian?"

"Was he a boyfriend of yours?" The congressman spoke hesitantly. "I don't know what happened. Malcolm said it was taken care of. We never heard from the man again."

"That's because he was murdered."

Dilbeck fell forward to his hands and knees. "My God," he said. "Is that true? It can't be."

"Oh, it's true." Erin stood up. "All because of you, because of the Rojos,"—waving the handgun—"because of all this sugar out here." She watched him struggle to a sitting position. "A man's dead, Davey, all because you're a crook."

The congressman looked ashen and haggard. He told Erin to get the damn light out of his eyes. "Nineteen years," he said, hoarsely. "Nineteen years I've served in Washington, D.C. Don't you dare belittle me."

Erin said, "A man is dead."

"Go look up my record, young lady. I've voted for every civil rights bill that's come through Congress. The vital issues of our time—Social Security, equal-opportunity housing, lower cable TV rates—go look up my votes. And farmers, yes, you're damn right. I support the family farmer and I'm not ashamed to say so!"

Erin sighed inwardly. Dilbeck was parroting a boilerplate campaign speech.

"—and who singlehandedly blocked the last congressional pay raise? Me! I cast the deciding vote. You don't think that took courage?"

Hastily Erin moved to derail the monologue. She said, "I phoned your office once myself."

Dilbeck paused. "In Washington? Why?"

"To ask about Jerry Killian. You were busy."

The congressman said, "If I'd known—"

"What did the Rojos do for you? Parties, girls, boat rides—what else? Las Vegas? The occasional vacation to the islands?" Erin circled him. "I think you're a man who can't say no to anything that's free."

Dilbeck dragged a forearm across his brow. "My father," he said with well-practiced reverence, "was an ordinary working man with ordinary dreams. Know what he did for a living? He pumped septic tanks!"

Erin said, "We could sure use him now." She walked back to the limousine to double-check a detail with Pierre. She returned carrying a martini in a plastic glass.

"Bless you," the congressman said, slurping like a hound.

She unzipped the minidress, tugged it down to her heels and kicked it away. A pleasant confusion returned to David Dilbeck's face; sunken eyes flickering with hope. In a simple white bra the dancer looked virginal, scrumptious. The congressman felt a familiar tremor of lust. The woman was an angel in the night.

"You are diabolical," he murmured. "I truly love you."

"Do you have," she asked, "the foggiest clue what's happening here?"

Dilbeck shook his head placidly. "It's all in the hands of the Lord."

"Oh brother."

He discarded the empty glass and said, "I'm a deacon in the church!"

"Yeah, and I'm the singing nun. Stand up, Davey."

Raising himself proved to be a long-term project, the congressman top-heavy with exhaustion. Using the machete as a crutch, he eventually levered himself erect, arms slack, while Erin made a final inspection with the flashlight. Sprouting from the silly boots were knobby blue-veined legs, still slick with Vaseline. The light moved up his body: red and wrinkled knees, the droopy boxers, the pendulous gray belly, the engorged surgical scar, the expectant patrician face and the silvery hair, now a ragged thatch garnished with flecks of jet muck and diced cane.

Erin said, "You are a sight."

She guessed the time as between eleven and eleven-thirty. Now or never, she thought. She threw the flashlight as far as she could into the tall cane, where it landed without a sound. Then she did the same with the gun.

I must be nuts.

Dilbeck said, "Well, well."

In the yellow moonglow, Erin could see his widening smile.

"So I was right about you," he said.

I must be crazy.
"David," she said, "do you want to talk, or dance?"
"Friction?"
I must be totally insane.
"Whatever you like, sweetheart." Somewhere in the night, Jackson Browne began to sing.
Where the hell are they?

Seventeen minutes away, on a two-lane road skirting the Loxahatchee wildlife preserve, three cars sped northwest toward the town of Belle Glade. Each of the cars was a slate-gray, late-model Ford. Each was driven by a clean-cut man in a dark suit. There were six in all—two in each sedan—and an attractive dark-haired woman with a young girl. The men all carried guns in shoulder holsters under their suit jackets. The little girl held two Barbie dolls, one blonde and one brunette. The woman sat next to the small girl in the back of the third sedan. She told the girl not to worry, everything was going to be all right.

Angela Grant said she wasn't worried one bit.

Sgt. Al García was stuck behind a slow-moving station wagon that was plastered with upbeat religious slogans. The driver either failed to see the flashing blue light in the mirror, or was unfamiliar with its purpose. García wondered why people with JESUS stickers on their bumper always drove twenty miles per hour under the speed limit. If God was *my* co-pilot, he thought, I'd be doing a hundred and twenty.

Shad was sucking the cigar and telling sad tales of lost opportunity—the roach in the yogurt, the scorpion in the cottage cheese. "It was all worked out," he lamented. "It was fucking golden."

García said, "That sounds a lot like fraud."

"Shit. You got a soft spot for insurance companies?"

García mashed the accelerator and passed the Christian station wagon on the shoulder. A few minutes later, the unmarked Caprice rolled into the modest commercial district of Belle Glade. The detective turned off the dashboard light and slowed down, scouting for the congressman's limousine. He expected it to stand out dramatically.

Shad continued to describe the art of concealing an adult cockroach in a refrigerated dairy product. The secret, he confided to García, was a good pair of tweezers.

The detective, ever eager for insight to the criminal mind, asked: "What about the roach itself? Anything special?"

"The fresher the better," Shad advised.

Just then, a convoy of three gray Fords whipped past in the opposite direction. "So that's the deal!" said García, digging the Caprice into a grinding U-turn. Smart girl, he thought. Gotta give her credit.

Shad said, "Who the hell are they?" For purchase, he planted both hands on the dashboard. "Lemme ask something," he said, cigar bobbing with the bumps. "Suppose you were an ex-con and you happened to be packin' a piece right now."

Al García said, "I believe I'd toss it."

"Yeah?" Shad rolled down the window. "Close your eyes," he told the detective.

Erin said, "Relax, sweetie."

"How can I?"

She pressed lightly against him, swaying, dreaming that she was with someone else. She tried to remember the last time she'd been held by a man, in a way that meant something.

"Now I get it," the congressman said. "You're trying to kill me. You're trying to give me a damn heart attack."

Erin said, "Don't be ridiculous. I could give you a heart attack anytime I choose."

Damp arms enfolded her waist. One hand still gripped the machete.

"Careful," Erin whispered.

David Dilbeck said, "We could go away together in a few weeks. We could take the yacht."

"Sounds interesting."

"I could make you happy," he said. "After the election, you could come with me to Washington."

"I don't think so, sweetheart."

Dilbeck, playing sugar daddy: "You'd like it there. The shopping is phenomenal."

Erin resisted the urge to bite. "Tell me about that night at the club," she said, "the night you attacked the young man."

The congressman said, uneasily, "I remember so little of it." He tightened his hold. "I was overcome, dazed, powerless—normally I'm not a violent person. I think that's obvious."

"You frightened me," Erin said. The seconds ticked away so slowly. Gazing into the rows of cane, she thought of Darrell Grant, wondered if he was planning a counterstrike. What would he do if he saw the congressman molesting her? Applaud, probably.

Dilbeck said, "Malcolm tells me the young fellow is just fine, the one who got hurt with the bottle."

"You didn't even send a fruit basket."

"How could I?" The congressman stopped dancing and took her by the elbows. "You still don't understand, do you? The position I hold is significant and sensitive and powerful. It's an election year, darling."

"You nearly killed a man," Erin said.

"Look, I do not wish to be remembered in the same snickering breath with Wilbur Mills and Gary Hart and the rest. Can't you appreciate my situation?" He hugged her fiercely to his sticky chest. "It's an unforgiving world we live in, angel."

How right you are, she thought. "Davey, please don't put your hands in my panties." The blade of the machete was cool against her thigh.

He said, "Well . . . I'm waiting for the friction."

"This is it."

"No, dear, this is slow dancing."

"Sorry," said Erin, maintaining the sway.

"I didn't come all this way for a dry hump."

"Davey, you're so romantic."

"Don't be like this!" Again Dilbeck's arms locked around her. Clumsily he began to grind his pelvis against her belly. "There! What about that?" he demanded.

"Stop it," Erin said, inaudibly. The moist hairs of Dilbeck's chest felt like moss against her cheek. In a way, she was grateful for the darkness, so she wouldn't have to see every awful detail, if things went wrong.

"I'm tired of this game," the congressman declared. Abruptly he embarked on his own convulsive rendition of an erotic dance—jerking, jumping, his greased flab slapping against Erin's body. She felt the bra peel up, the plastic pearls indent her breasts. With both hands she held her panties in place, thinking: So much for being in control.

David Dilbeck's haphazard thrusting lifted Erin's toes off the ground. Beating on his shoulders proved futile, so she tried a scream.

The congressman displayed no alarm; rather, her panic seemed to please him. "Finally," he said, "you're beginning to understand." He grabbed the pearl necklaces and began to twist them into a noose. Gradually they came tight on Erin's throat.

She screamed again—not her best effort—and again until it hurt. Finally the strands snapped and the pearls scattered down her breasts, falling into the cane like tiny hailstones.

33

While waiting, Pierre leaned against the door of the Cadillac limousine. He plugged his fingers in his ears because, at the young woman's instruction, the stereo was full blast. The song was something about lawyers in love. Pierre didn't understand, suspected he never would.

When he spotted the oncoming cars, he reached into the limo and shut off the music. Gravel dust swirled as three gray sedans braked to a stop in a triangle. The headlights sliced up the night, moths whirling like confetti in the hot white beams.

Pierre slapped his hands on his head, crumpling the chauffeur's cap. He counted six men in dark suits, like pallbearers. They drew guns as they emerged from the sedans. The tallest one, who had neat sandy hair and tortoiseshell glasses, approached Pierre and asked if he was the man who called.

"M-pa konprann," Pierre said, repeating it twice in a chatter intended to convey incomprehension. It worked temporarily.

The armed strangers held a short huddle in which it was determined that none of them spoke Creole. The sandy-haired man took Pierre firmly by the collar. "Where is she?" he asked, formidably. "You know who I mean."

His hands still fastened to the cap, Pierre pointed urgently with an elbow. At that moment a scream broke the stillness, followed by more. The sandy-haired man and three others disappeared into the cane rows. Pierre was impressed by how fast they could run, dressed as they were for a funeral.

The congressman frictioned himself into a trance. His eyelids drooped half-staff, and the sallow folds of his throat quivered when he moaned.

Yet his grip on Erin was cast-iron. He pushed her deeper into the fields, the stalks leaning and shaking with the surge. Erin fought to keep her footing, because she certainly didn't want to go down. Dilbeck was a large man; once he got on top, there would be little to do but grit her teeth, close her eyes, ride with the music . . .

She attempted another scream, but only a faint cry came out. She was suffocating on the man's acrid heat, his foul panting, the rankness of his sweat. A stubby but determined stiffness poked at her from his boxer shorts.

"Baa-aaby," he whimpered for the hundredth time.

Erin attempted a death grab for the congressman's testicles. Not knowing there was only one, she came up empty-handed. Dilbeck tightened his hug and toppled slowly, like a rotted oak, taking Erin with him. Falling, she reflected on what a bad idea the machete had been—clever, sure, but not terribly smart. Because now she stood a fair chance of being speared by the damn thing when they hit the ground.

Fortunately it was the congressman who landed first, Erin bouncing on top. The impact roused Dilbeck from his reverie. He began smooching the crown of her head, murmuring about how sexy she smelled. The white bra remained bunched above her breasts, her cheek flattened against his ribs. She no longer heard the music from the limousine. Maybe the cane was too deep; maybe it had swallowed her screams as well.

Then she thought: Will they ever find me out here?

Suddenly, brutally, the congressman bucked her off. She landed hard on her neck and shoulders. The damp muck gave her a chill. Dilbeck crawled on top, awkwardly, subdued her with dead weight. Erin felt the blade of the machete sliding flat up her hip, sawing the elastic of her panties.

Fumbling at himself with the other hand, Dilbeck was saying: "Now *this* is true love."

Erin turned and pressed her lips softly to his chest.

"Oh, that's it," he said.

Then her tongue, teasing—

"Heaven," said the congressman.

—exploring, until she tasted the tracks of the scar—

"Circles," he said. "Do circles."

—biting down with all her strength, tearing at him like a cat until he pushed away, keening, groping feebly at the ragged wet hole in his chest . . .

Erin got up spitting blood, meat and hair. "True love," she said, wiping her mouth violently. "So how was it?"

Incredulous, Dilbeck struggled to his feet. "You little b-b-bitch."

"Fair enough." Erin covered herself with her arms. "You owe me a new pair of undies," she said.

In the violet darkness, amid the broken matted cane, the congressman somehow relocated Willie Rojo's machete.

"Oh, don't be ridiculous," Erin told him.

Dilbeck's breath came in hydraulic gasps. With both hands he raised the blade. "You tried to chew my heart out," he said, coiling for the swing.

Erin turned and dashed barefoot through the fields. She imagined Dilbeck suddenly imbued with Olympian swiftness, crashing the cane in his boots; imagined spiders, worms, moccasins, vermin writhing underfoot; imagined Darrell hiding in the tall grass, awaiting revenge. But she ran on, imagining a cool deep pool in which she would dive, wash herself clean, then vanish like an otter. She imagined Angela, waiting with her dolls on the shore, and ran harder.

Straight into the arms of a familiar sandy-haired man.

Special Agent Thomas Cleary.

The congressman said: "I can explain."

The three men ordered him to drop the weapon and raise his hands. They had already identified themselves, definitively, as FBI. David Dilbeck was positively relieved.

"Do you know who I am?" he asked, blinking into the sharp cones of light. He tossed the machete away; it landed upright, twanging in the black marl. "Gentlemen, please," he said, "I can explain."

The FBI trained its agents in many tasks, but memorizing the faces of all 535 members of Congress was not one of them. Moreover, Dilbeck's closest friends and colleagues might not have recognized him in baggy boxer shorts and boots; radish-eyed, shirtless, semi-erect, his trademark silver mane dirty and spiked. An agent's flashlight lingered on the congressman's grisly bite wound, scabbing in the scraggly opossum fur of his chest. Standing nearly nude in a farm field, Dilbeck looked nothing like the distinguished fellow on his campaign billboards. To the agents, he looked very much like a common degenerate, captured mid-rape.

"Thank God you're here," the congressman said warmly. He thought he was being rescued. Wasn't that the FBI's job?

An agent informed him of his right to remain silent.

"Jesus, Mary and Joseph," Dilbeck hissed. "Don't you know who I am?" He told them, repeating it vehemently as they put him in handcuffs.

The FBI men remained polite, firm and unflappable, even when Dilbeck addressed them as junior Nazi brownshirts.

"Sir, is this yours?" One of the agents had come upon the black cowboy hat. He propped it on Dilbeck's head.

"That's backward," the congressman groused.

"Naw," said the agent. "It looks good. Who are you s'posed to be—George Strait? Dwight Yoakam?"

"Nobody!" Dilbeck barked. "For God's sake!"

The FBI men bandaged his bleeding wound, gave him four aspirins for the pain and locked him in one of the sedans. Squinting out the window, Dilbeck was engulfed in bewilderment. The gathering commotion revealed more FBI agents, his driver Pierre, a dark-haired woman, a small girl in pajamas being hoisted on the shoulders of an enormous bald Cro-Magnon. At one point a gruff-looking Cuban lowered his face to the glass and grinned, blue smoke seeping from between his teeth.

It's a goddamn circus! the congressman thought.

He ached for a telephone so he could call Moldy. Straighten out this whole damn mess.

Al García kissed his wife and said, "Fancy meeting you here."

"They came for Angie," Donna explained. "I wouldn't let them take her alone—Al, what's going on?"

García knew that his wife had busted the agents' balls, phoning downtown to verify the IDs. Boy, they hated that. He asked Donna about Andy and Lynne.

"They're at your mother's, and don't change the subject. Tell me what's happening out here."

"Chaos, near as I can tell." García introduced his wife to Shad, who'd been galloping through the cane rows with Angela whooping on his shoulders.

"Where's Momma?" the girl wanted to know.

"She'll be here soon," García said, hoping it was true. The Feebs, as usual, were saying nothing. They eyeballed his sergeant's badge the same as they'd eyeballed the shot-up Caprice, with minimal curiosity and zero tolerance.

Shad remarked on their snotty attitude. "Why'd she call *them?*" He kept his voice low. "The hell they got that you don't?"

"Jurisdiction," García said. His feelings weren't hurt too badly; by calling the FBI, Erin had saved him a ton of paperwork.

Shad lowered Angie to the ground so that she could retrieve her dolls. He strolled to one of the gray sedans and scrutinized the face at the window: a disheveled old lech in a backward rodeo hat. David Dilbeck wore the agitated look of a stray dog being hauled to the pound.

"Pervie," Shad muttered. He remembered the asshole from that night at Orly's club.

"Have some respect." It was García, standing next to him. "The man is a United States congressman!"

"Un-fucking-believable," said Shad. Maybe it was time to get a voter's card.

They stood together in the sugar cane. Agent Cleary wrapped Erin in his suit jacket. He looked anxious and a little embarrassed. It rattled him, seeing her this way.

"Where's Angie?" Erin asked. "Didn't you bring her?"

Cleary nodded, wiped the condensation from the lenses of his eyeglasses. "I'm not sure why. I'm not sure what we've got here."

"A kidnapping, more or less." Erin gave an abridged account of the evening. She was tempted to tell all she knew about the congressman, starting with the Eager Beaver, but there was no point. Cleary was a linear thinker, not a dreamy conspiracist. He wanted overt acts and provable crimes.

In a tight voice he said, "So you're a dancer."

"Until tonight," said Erin. "Lawyers are expensive, Tom. I told you before, Darrell was running me in circles. By the way, he's out here somewhere—" sweeping an arm toward the fields "—my darling ex-husband."

At the mention of Darrell Grant, the agent's expression darkened. Erin knew that Cleary felt rotten about not helping with the Darrell problem on the night she'd come to his house. Rules were rules. Now here they were, out in the sugar fields.

Cleary said, blankly, "Seems you've had quite a time."

His well-ordered brain was downshifting, trying to find traction in the mayhem. He struggled briefly with the image of his wholesome ex-secretary dancing naked on tables. Then out came the notebook, and the questions: Did Mr. Dilbeck rape you? "No." Did he assault you? "Yes." Did he attempt penetration? "Sort of." Did he have a weapon? "Yep." Did he threaten you? "Definitely." Did he expose himself? "Tried."

The agent scribbled and ruminated simultaneously. "I'm still not entirely comfortable with our authority here." Scribble, scribble. "He didn't take you across the state line, so technically we've got a gray area." More scribbling. "On the other hand, he did use a weapon so that's a possibility."

Erin impatiently snatched the ballpoint pen. "Tom, the man is a congressman. That's your damn jurisdiction."

"Yes," said Cleary. No getting around it.

"You look pale," she said, "or maybe it's the moonlight."

The pallor was genuine. Tom Cleary had become nauseated, anticipating the fallout—the daily inquiries from Justice, the not-so-subtle pressure for investigatory details, the maddeningly accurate media leaks. It was a field agent's nightmare, a sex case against a prominent politician. Cleary envisioned paperwork as high as the Washington Monument, and the turning point of a once-promising career. "I need the whole story," he told Erin dourly, "if you expect us to prosecute."

Laughing, she touched his arm. "Tom, I definitely don't expect you to prosecute."

"Then what?" Anger came to his voice. "This isn't a lark, Erin. We're talking about a member of the House of Representatives."

"The sleazy old shit tried to boink me."

When Cleary closed the notebook, Erin returned the pen. She said, "The man is sick."

"You want your name all over the newspapers?"

"Not particularly," she conceded. Not before the final custody hearing.

"Then we're stuck, aren't we?"

She told him to quit thinking like an FBI man, think like a guy who's running for office. Cleary puffed his cheeks and pretended to gag.

Erin said, "You don't have to arrest him, Tom. Just explain the facts of life."

They talked for a few more minutes, then started back toward the cars. "I've still got loads of questions," Cleary complained.

"There's a guy you need to talk to. A detective." She took the agent's hand, leading him between the cane rows. "Hasn't Angie gotten tall?"

"She's beautiful," Cleary said. "Has her mom's pretty green eyes." Moments later, quietly: "Did the bastard hurt you?"

"No, Tom, I'm fine."

The roadside scene was like a drug raid: the sweep of lights, the bustle of armed men, the broken gargle of police radios. Cleary had pulled out all the stops. Erin was touched, and told him so. She didn't recognize the other agents, but made a point of thanking each one. They were unfailingly courteous, and tried not to be obvious when peeking at her breasts beneath the loose-fitting jacket.

When Angela spotted Erin, she thrust her dolls at Shad and ran, darting through the legs of the FBI men. Erin scooped her up, tweaked her chin and kissed the tip of her nose. Angela, giggling, did the same to her mother.

Sgt. Al García watched, a relaxed spectator on the hood of the Caprice. He was out of cigars so he'd resorted to bubble gum. Donna was retrieving two beers from the mini-bar in David Dilbeck's limousine. Erin walked up, bouncing Angela in her arms. The detective said she certainly had a flair for the dramatic.

"Now don't be mad," Erin said.

"Who the hell's mad?"

"Al, I didn't want to get you in trouble. Shad, either."

"Whatever," García said, chiding. "I'm just grateful for the invitation. This is more fun than Wrestlemania." He pointed at the doughy figure hunched in the government sedan. "So that's your guy. Congressman Romeo."

Dilbeck rapped his cuffed wrists against the glass, beckoning Erin. She waved airily over one shoulder.

"Will you speak to Agent Cleary?" she asked García.

"A genuine FBI man! I would be greatly honored." García offered Angela a stick of grape-flavored gum.

Erin said, "I think there's a way to pull this off."

"I think you're absolutely right."

Shad lumbered to the car, holding the Barbie dolls like two sticks of dynamite. "You owe me," he said to Erin, who couldn't help but laugh.

He took her aside and told her about finding Malcolm Moldowsky dead in the fishbox. Erin was stunned. In a whisper she recounted

Darrell Grant's mad narco-escapade. Shad generously offered to hunt him down and beat him into puppy chow. Erin said no thanks, she and Angie were out of danger for now.

"We're taking a vacation, starting tonight."

"You deserve it," Shad said, thinking how much he would miss her.

David Lane Dilbeck, believing himself a master of supple oratory, assumed that he could talk his way out of the trouble. To bolster his credibility, he audaciously scoffed at the suggestion that he call a lawyer. So the FBI agents perched him on the bumper of the car and gathered in a tribal semi-circle to listen. Cleary allowed Al García to join them.

The detective was tickled by the spectacle—the moon, the crickets, the rustling cane fields. "All we need is a campfire," he whispered to Cleary, "and some marshmallows."

Dilbeck told quite a story. The agents took notes by penlight. García pitied their secretaries.

When the congressman was finished, Cleary said: "Let's get this straight: You are the victim here, not the perpetrator."

"Absolutely, yes, abducted at gunpoint."

"Hmmm," Cleary said. Al García thought the moment called for a stronger response, something along the lines of hooting and derision.

David Dilbeck said, "She's been after me for weeks."

"So you're alone on the yacht," said Cleary, "working on a campaign speech, when all of a sudden this crazed woman breaks in and attempts to seduce you?"

"Forcefully," Dilbeck added, "and when I rebuffed her, she became enraged."

"And for this attempted seduction she wore a nine-dollar cotton bra from Kmart?"

"No, she wore red. Lace cups. P-p-paisley G-string! Later she changed all into white, when we were in the car."

Agent Cleary realigned his glasses. "So we're to believe that Ms. Grant kidnapped you for sexual purposes. Is that a fair summary?"

"She was infatuated," said the congressman. "Certainly you've heard of such sad cases."

García piped in: "Politicians have groupies, too? I thought it was just rock stars and homicide cops."

Cleary, keeping order: "Mr. Dilbeck, explain the injury to your chest."

"She bit me," he said, "like a wild animal!"

The agent asked Dilbeck who might verify that he was being stalked by a nude dancer. "One person," he replied. "His name is Malcolm J. Moldowsky. He'll confirm every detail."

"Unlikely," said García.

"What do you mean?" the congressman bleated.

García turned to Cleary. "May I tell him? Please?"

"Yeah, go ahead."

"Tell me what?" Dilbeck demanded.

"Your friend Malcolm," said the detective, "he sleeps with the fishies."

The congressman slumped sideways off the bumper. The agents dutifully rushed forward to pick him up out of the dirt.

Cleary sighed, frowning at Al García. "Was that really necessary?"

The two men sat alone in the Caprice. García balanced a bottle of beer on one knee. He jangled the gold bracelet in the congressman's face.

"You lose this?"

Dilbeck turned away coldly. He said, "I've changed my mind about contacting a lawyer."

"Too late." García popped his gum. It didn't taste too bad with Beck's dark. He coiled the bracelet in the palm of his hand. "You're cooked," he told Dilbeck.

"Now listen—"

"Just shut up," suggested the detective, "and try to comprehend what's happened here. The FBI gets an anonymous call about a kidnapping in progress. The alleged suspect is a U.S. congressman. The alleged victim is a former employee of the Bureau. You with me?"

"Erin worked for them?"

"Ain't it a hoot. Anyhow, the agents arrive to find the suspect—that's you—stripped to his skivvies and armed with a machete. You're chasing the alleged victim across farmland belonging to Joaquin and Wilberto Rojo. Subsequent investigation will reveal that the weapon used in the assault also belongs to this prominent and influential family. Congressman, I want you to imagine all this on the front page of the *Miami Herald.*"

Dilbeck rocked sideways, tugging absently on his lower lip. Al García wondered if he was lapsing into autism.

"Now if I'm you," the detective said, "I'm trying to guess how my version of the story is going to play with the Rojos and also the voting public—namely, that I was kidnapped by a nympho stripper. Remember there's no gun, no evidence, not a single witness to back you up. Even your driver says the lady is telling the truth."

"Impossible," Dilbeck said, thickly. "He speaks no English."

García smiled. "Your driver is a modest guy. He's got a degree in hotel management from FIU. Didn't he tell you?"

The congressman stopped rocking. He wrapped both arms around his head, as if bracing for incoming mortars. "There was another man on the yacht," he said, a dry rasp. "Durrell something."

"You mean Mr. Darrell Grant, currently a fugitive on several violent felonies." García spoke from behind a fat purple bubble. "I were you, I wouldn't count on a junkie for my alibi."

"But what about this!" David Dilbeck slapped at his bandaged chest. "I've been viciously attacked—any damn fool can see." He clawed at the tape and gauze until the bloody crater was exposed. "Look!" he said. "My goddamn nipple is gone! I mean *gone.*"

Al García said, "I hate to be negative, *chico*, but that's your basic defensive bite wound. Man's got a woman pinned, what else can she do?"

The congressman gathered up the mangled bandage and, half-wittedly, attempted to replace it.

"Prosecutors love bite wounds," García elaborated. "One time we had a victim chomp some guy's pecker half off. That's how we caught him, too—turned up in the E.R. at Jackson, said it was a freak gardening accident. Anyhow, we got forensics to match the punctures in the guy's schlong with the bite pattern of the victim's teeth. The jury was out maybe thirty seconds."

Bereft, Dilbeck stared at his mutilation as if branded. "What will happen now? The campaign and all."

García said, "It was up to me, I'd throw your fat ass in jail. Lucky for you, it ain't." He took the empty beer bottle and slid from the car. Erin Grant got in. She crossed her legs and adjusted Agent Cleary's suit jacket to make sure her breasts weren't showing; she wanted Dilbeck undistracted.

"David," she said, "what a mess you're in."

The congressman pulled back like a scalded snail, huddling against the opposite door. His voice cracked with reproach: "You even called me 'sweetie.'"

"Maybe I call everyone 'sweetie.'"

He shouted: "I don't love you anymore!"

"Oh yes you do."

After a few moments of silence, Dilbeck offered a squirmy apology for his coarse behavior. He inquired whether Erin intended to press charges.

"That's Plan B," she said.

"And Plan A?"

"You go home tonight," she told him, "and have yourself a heart attack."

The congressman sneered. "That's not the slightest bit funny."

"A mild one," Erin proposed, "requiring weeks of bed rest, bland dieting and seclusion."

"In other words, tank the election."

"Davey, I'm trying to cut you a break. Now if you'd prefer Plan B, that's fine. Have you ever been on 'Hard Copy'?"

The last of Dilbeck's hope drained away. "A heart attack, for God's sake. Is there more?"

"Sweetie, of course there's more." Erin reached up and turned the congressman's cowboy hat, so it wasn't backward on his head.

Breakfast, predawn. A truckstop on old Route 441, jammed with semis, dump trucks, dairy tankers, pickups, flatbeds hauling farm equipment. The place smelled like a diesel fart.

Shad, Donna García and her detective husband sat three abreast in the front of the unmarked Caprice. Donna nursed a black coffee, Shad inhaled his seventh glazed donut and Al García attacked spicy pork sausages with the hope of scouring multiple layers of grape, beer and stale cigar from his palate.

"Disney World," the detective mused, munching steadfastly.

"I think it's sweet," said his wife, "though I'm not sure about the driver."

Shad said don't worry, the driver's cool.

Pierre was gassing up the limousine at the high-test pump. He felt the weight of the gold bracelet in the left pocket of his trousers; a gift for your wife, the cop had said. Very strange, Pierre thought. The whole evening.

Angela was curled asleep in the jump seat. Erin had changed into her jeans, T-shirt and sandals; her hair was tied in a ponytail. She stood at the door of the limo and chatted with Cleary, the FBI man, finishing his notes. He looked haggard, rumpled, eager to leave. It pleased García to see another lawman labor in that familiar hollow-eyed condition, particularly a Feeb.

Donna asked, "Where are the others?"

"They escorted the congressman home," her husband said. "He wasn't feeling so great."

Shad interrupted his donutfest to complain that Dilbeck was getting off easy. "I vote for jail," he said, "or a bullet in the brain. That's what the sonofabitch deserves."

García disagreed good-naturedly. "For politicians, some fates are worse than death. Erin came up with a beaut, no?"

Donna said that Angela was excited about the Disney World trip. "Her favorite ride is the teacups. She says it's fun to get dizzy." Donna paused. "On the way here, she asked about her father."

García said that Darrell Grant remained at large in the cane. "He'll come out when they burn the fields. Him and the rest of the critters."

Shad, his cheeks stuffed bulbously: "Any luck, he'll sleep through the goddamn fire."

Donna told him to stop, don't take another bite. She lifted a half-crescent of donut from his hand. "This is so gross," she said. "A darn bug!"

Shad snatched it away, flipped on the dome light and examined the find. His hopeful expression faded.

"It's awful damn small," he observed, doubtfully. He extracted the culprit from a dry crumb of donut—a centipede with a shiny, cocoa-colored carapace. It drew into a protective ball at Shad's touch.

"Long shot," García remarked. "You'll need a jury of total suckers."

"Yeah?" Shad placed the bug on the tip of his pinkie and held it near the light bulb.

"It was me," said García, "I'd wait for another jumbo cockroach."

Donna, annoyed: "What in the world are you talking about?"

"Dreams," said Shad. "Nothing important." He flicked the centipede out the window and inserted the remainder of the donut in his glaze-crusted lips.

Agent Cleary had trundled his notes to a pay phone, where he was deeply absorbed in official conversation. Pierre backed the Cadillac away from the gas pumps. Erin Grant stuck her head out the window and gave a high-spirited wave. Shad and Donna waved back; Al García pantomimed operatic applause.

"Great smile," he said, as the limo drove away.

"She looks sixteen," said Shad, "I swear."

García eased the Caprice up to the gas pumps to top off the tank before the long drive home. He had one leg out the door when the car shuddered violently. He heard the tinkle of taillights breaking, and said, "Aw, shit."

A tractor-trailer had crunched the rear of the unmarked police car. The driver stood sheepishly over García's crimped bumper. Damage to the Caprice was minor, but the detective was not consoled: another lengthy accident report would be required, in triplicate. Witnesses interviewed. Tedious diagrams sketched. Polaroids snapped for the insurance company and Risk Management. Hours of useless department bullshit .

"Congratulations," he told the trucker. "You just hit a cop."

"Sorry." The man was a wiry redhead with twitchy Dexedrine eyes. "I never saw you guys."

"That was my guess, too," García said. He popped the trunk of the Caprice to search for the proper goddamn forms. Donna and Shad got out to see what had happened.

After circling the rig, Shad said, "Hey, Al. Guess what."

"What?" García was bent over, rummaging fiercely.

"My neck hurts," said Shad.

Pad in hand, García slammed the trunk lid. He said, "You don't *have* a fucking neck."

The bouncer gave a crafty wink, nodded slightly toward the trailer. "No kidding, man, I'm in serious pain."

Donna stood on tiptoes to scout the injury. "Show me where it hurts."

"Everywhere," Shad said, with a theatrical grimace.

Gingerly Donna rubbed the taut slopes between his skull and shoulders. She said, "Come back to the car. You'd better sit down."

"Yeah," Shad agreed, "I'm pretty damn traumatized."

The worried truck driver excused himself, creeping off to improve his blood readings with black coffee. Al García walked back to the tractor-rig for a close look. Soon Donna heard him laughing, although she couldn't imagine why; hearty laughter that boomed raw and care-free. Other truckers began to stare, irritated by the disruption of their early-morning routine. García sounded daffy and stoned.

Donna found him holding the trailer, his fingers hooked in the steel mesh. He was shaking hysterically. The bin was full of sugar cane. A blue-and-white sign bolted to the side said: ROJO FARMS.

Donna said, "Now I get it."

"Well, go ahead," said her husband, wheezing. "Call Mr. Shad an ambulance."

"Really, Al."

"Sweet justice," the detective said. He wiped his eyes, tried to compose himself, act like a grown-up. Then he felt the laughter rising again like a grand tide. It was one fine moment.

EPILOGUE

Three weeks before the election, DAVID LANE DILBECK was reported to have suffered a minor heart attack while reading in bed. Although missing the remainder of the campaign, he pulled fifty-two percent of the vote and easily won reelection to the House of Representatives. The following day, he stunned political supporters by resigning his seat, citing chronic health problems. The congressman's chiropractor, cardiologist and urologist issued an unusual joint statement endorsing his decision to retire.

Dilbeck's opponent, ELOY FLICKMAN, gave up politics and became a right-wing radio commentator in South Florida. Within months he was leading the daytime Arbitrons, touting himself as "the weight-watcher's Rush Limbaugh." One day after signing a contract with the Liberty Radio Network, Flickman was accidentally killed while picketing an abortion clinic during a live remote broadcast. The driver of the death car lost control when one of her seven children got his sneakers tangled in the steering wheel.

In January, the agricultural committee formerly chaired by Congressman Dilbeck approved a bill renewing multimillion-dollar subsidies for U.S. sugar growers. The measure passed the House 271–150 after a brief floor debate. Speaking eloquently in its favor was REP. BO TOOLEY, the Republican from northern Alabama, who had never before sailed on a yacht as long or luxurious as the *Sweetheart Deal,* and was delighted that its short-wave radio picked up all his favorite Bible stations.

Shortly after its mysterious rat infestation, the FLESH FARM was shut down for multiple health-code violations. Two weeks later, the building burned to the ground. The LING brothers claimed that the blaze started when a dancer's trained snake became entwined in the electric wiring. Indicted later for insurance fraud, the Lings fled to western Canada and opened a chain of massage parlors with a hockey motif.

The remains of DARRELL GRANT were identified from a single fingertip. Three days later, the SWEETHEART SUGAR CORPORATION discreetly notified wholesalers that it was recalling all granulated sugar milled between October 6th and October 9th, due to "possible rodent contamination during processing."

After interviewing PAUL GUBER and other clients, the Florida Bar issued a harsh public reprimand of ATTORNEY JONATHAN PETER MORDECAI, for "gross ethical misconduct." The effect of the discipline was minimal, since Mordecai was dead and no longer practicing law. Paul Guber quit his brokerage firm and entered rabbinical college in Chicago. He never spoke of his brief engagement to the late JOYCE MIZNER, or of his ill-fated bachelor party at the EAGER BEAVER lounge.

ERB CRANDALL did not return to Florida. Instead he settled in Atlantic City, accepting a job as the top political aide to a popular but recklessly overextended city councilman. The following summer, after collecting a large cash bribe on behalf of his boss, Crandall was accosted by three muggers demanding the paper bag he was carrying. His dead body—the shredded sack clutched loyally in one fist—was found by German tourists beneath the legendary boardwalk. The city council promptly named a street in Crandall's memory.

The group of orthopedic surgeons who owned the TICKLED PINK sold the nightclub to a group of dentists, who chose a saucy new name (Bare Essentials II) and bold new management (Johnny "Three Toes" Spladiano). Mr. Spladiano's first three business decisions were to fire ORLY, add valet parking, and enlarge the wrestling pit. Considering himself more fortunate than his predecessor, Orly closed out a modest IRA account and moved to Pensacola, where he and his wife opened a topless oyster bar called Eat Me Raw.

URBANA SPRAWL continued to dance at Bare Essentials II until the day Mr. Spladiano replaced creamed corn with sardines in the wrestling arena. She is now pre-med at Emory University in Atlanta. SABRINA left dancing and worked briefly in adult films before landing the role of Lucette, the perky Parisian spokesmodel for Thigh Diver exercise equipment. The two Moniques also retired from nude dancing, each marrying one of her customers. MONIQUE JR., whose real name was Loretta Brickman, wed a seventy-four-year-old wholesale diamond broker who had outlived three previous wives. MONIQUE SR., whose actual name was Frances Cabrera, married a middle-aged pottery instructor who was, in her adoring eyes, a dead ringer for Keith Richards.

The man known as SHAD, whose real name was Gerard L. Shaddick, sued Rojo Farms, Rojo Trucking and the Sweetheart Sugar Corporation for injuries allegedly sustained when the loaded cane trailer rear-ended Sgt. Al García's police car. In the lawsuit, Shad complained of neck pain, migraines, blurred vision, vertigo, sexual dysfunction and chronic anxiety. The case was settled out of court for $2.3 million dollars. Shortly afterward, Shad purchased a split-level condominium in Telluride, Colorado, and became engaged to his physical therapist, a recent emigrant from Norway.

RITA GRANT also sued Rojo Farms, seeking $5 million compensation for the accidental mulching of her brother, Darrell. The lawsuit was swiftly abandoned when Rita was forced to flee Dade County with Lupa, her beloved wolf hybrid. Animal-control officers had ordered her to surrender the animal after it jumped a nine-foot wall at the Metrozoo and brought down a full-grown African springbok.

The murder of MALCOLM J. MOLDOWSKY remains unsolved. In the days following his death, news stories described the crime scene in gruesome detail, revealing that the murder weapon was a nine-iron made by MacGregor. A local columnist characterized Moldy as a ruthless and shady political fixer who had finally crossed the wrong person. Moldy's eulogist, Congressman Bo Tooley, angrily denounced the story as a "damnable lie"—a quote lovingly borrowed from Moldowsky's Watergate idol, John Mitchell. The funeral was brief and sparsely attended. From his sickbed, David Dilbeck sent profound regrets.

CHRISTOPHER ROJO was arrested during a late-night disturbance at the Kennedy compound in Palm Beach. Witnesses claimed that he attempted to demonstrate his oil-wrestling prowess upon Maria Shriver, Daryl Hannah and other female guests. Threatened with the loss of several trust funds, Christopher voluntarily entered a facility for treatment of drug and alcohol abuse. There he met his future wife, a copy editor at *Vanity Fair*.

The elder ROJOS remain prominent in Florida's sugar industry, while secretly optioning vast tracts of cane acreage for future development as condominiums and golf resorts. A few days before Congress voted new price supports for sugar growers, Wilberto and Joaquin Rojo announced the funding of two full scholarships at Georgia State University. The student recipients were KATHERINE and AUDREY KILLIAN, whose father had recently perished in a rafting accident in Montana.

PIERRE ST. BAPTISTE resigned from Gold Coach Limousines to become catering manager of a new Sheraton in Key West. In the evenings he teaches English to the children of Haitian exiles.

A Broward County judge awarded ERIN GRANT permanent custody of her daughter, ANGELA. They moved to Orlando, where Erin took a night dancing job as Cinderella's eldest stepsister in Disney World's famous Main Street Parade. During the day she works as a data-entry specialist for the local office of the FBI. Her application to the academy at Quantico is currently under review.

A NOTE ON THE TYPE

This book was set in a digitized version of Janson. The hot-metal version of Janson was a recutting made direct from type cast from matrices long thought to have been made by the Dutchman Anton Janson, who was a practicing type founder in Leipzig during the years 1668–1687. However, it has been conclusively demonstrated that these types are actually the work of Nicholas Kis (1650–1702), a Hungarian, who most probably learned his trade from the master Dutch type founder Dirk Voskens. The type is an excellent example of the influential and sturdy Dutch types that prevailed in England up to the time William Caslon (1692–1766) developed his own in-comparable designs from them.

Composed by ComCom, a division of Haddon Craftsmen,
Allentown, Pennsylvania
Printed and bound by Arcata Graphics/Martinsburg,
Martinsburg, West Virginia
Designed by Virginia Tan